BRUNSWICK
GARDENS

By Anne Perry
Published by Fawcett Books

Featuring Thomas and Charlotte Pitt

The Cater Street Hangman
Callander Square
Paragon Walk
Resurrection Row
Bluegate Fields
Rutland Place
Death in the Devil's Acre
Cardington Crescent
Silence in Hanover Close
Bethlehem Road
Highgate Rise
Belgrave Square
Farriers' Lane
The Hyde Park Headsman
Traitors Gate
Pentecost Alley
Ashworth Hall
Brunswick Gardens

Featuring William Monk

The Face of a Stranger
A Dangerous Mourning
Defend and Betray
A Sudden, Fearful Death
The Sins of the Wolf
Cain His Brother
Weighed in the Balance
The Silent Cry

BRUNSWICK GARDENS

Anne Perry

FAWCETT COLUMBINE

The Ballantine Publishing Group • New York

A Fawcett Columbine Book
Published by The Ballantine Publishing Group

Copyright © 1998 by Anne Perry

All rights reserved under International and Pan-American Copyright Conventions. Published in the United States by The Ballantine Publishing Group, a division of Random House, Inc., New York, and simultaneously in Canada by Random House of Canada Limited, Toronto.

http://www.randomhouse.com

Library of Congress Cataloging-in-Publication Data

Perry, Anne.
Brunswick gardens / Anne Perry.—1st ed.
p.   cm
ISBN 0-449-90845-3 (hardcover)
1. Pitt, Charlotte (Fictitious character)—Fiction.   2. Pitt, Thomas (Fictitious character)—Fiction.   3. Women detectives—England—London—Fiction.
4. Police spouses—England—London—Fiction.   5. Police—England—London—Fiction.   I. Title.
PR6066.E693B78   1998

823'.914—dc21   97-38441
                                                                        CIP

Designed by Jie Yang

Manufactured in the United States of America

First Edition: April 1998

10 9 8 7 6 5 4 3 2 1

To Marie Coolman in Friendship

BRUNSWICK
GARDENS

CHAPTER
ONE

Pitt knocked on the assistant commissioner's door and waited. It must be sensitive, and urgent, or Cornwallis would not have sent for him by telephone. Since his promotion to command of the Bow Street station Pitt had not involved himself in cases personally unless they threatened to be embarrassing to someone of importance, or else politically dangerous, such as the murder in Ashworth Hall five months earlier, in October 1890. It had ruined the attempt at some reconciliation of the Irish Problem—although with the scandal of the divorce of Katie O'Shea, citing Charles Stewart Parnell, the leader of the Irish majority in Parliament, the whole situation was on the brink of disaster anyway.

Cornwallis opened the door himself. He was not as tall as Pitt, but lean and supple, moving easily, as if the physical strength and grace he had needed at sea were still part of his nature. So was the briefness of speech, the assumption of obedience and a certain simplicity of thought learned by one long used to the ruthlessness of the elements but unaccustomed to the devious minds of politicians and the duplicity of public manners. He was learning, but he still relied on Pitt. He looked unhappy now, his face, with its long nose and wide mouth, was set in lines of apprehension.

"Come in, Pitt." He stood aside, holding the door back. "Sorry to require you to come so quickly, but there is a very nasty situation in Brunswick Gardens. At least, there looks to be." He was frowning as he closed the door and walked back to his desk. It was a pleasant room, very different from the way it had been during his predecessor's tenure. Now there were some nautical instruments on the surfaces, a sea chart of the English Channel on the far wall, and among the necessary books on law and police procedure, there were also an anthology of poetry, a novel by Jane Austen, and the Bible.

Pitt waited until Cornwallis had sat down, then did so himself. His jacket hung awkwardly because his pockets were full. Promotion had not made him conspicuously tidier.

"Yes sir?" he said enquiringly.

Cornwallis leaned back, the light shining on his head. His complete baldness became him. It was hard to imagine him differently. He never fidgeted, but when he was most concerned he put his fingers together in a steeple and held them still. He did so now.

"A young woman has met with a violent death in the home of a most respected clergyman, highly esteemed for his learned publications and very possibly in line for a bishopric: the vicar of St. Michael's, the Reverend Ramsay Parmenter." He took a deep breath, watching Pitt's face. "A doctor who lives a few doors away was sent for, and on seeing the body he telephoned for the police. They came immediately, and in turn telephoned me."

Pitt did not interrupt.

"It appears that it may be murder and Parmenter himself may have some involvement in it." Cornwallis did not add anything as to his own feelings, but his fears were clear in the very slight pinching around his mouth and the hurt in his eyes. He regarded leadership, both moral and political, as a duty, a trust which could not be broken without terrible consequences. All his adult life so far had been spent at sea, where the captain's word was absolute. The entire ship survived or sank on his skill and his judgment. He must be right; his orders were obeyed. To fail to do so was mutiny, punishable by death. He himself had learned to obey, and in due time he had risen to occupy that lonely pinnacle. He knew both its burdens and its privileges.

"I see," Pitt said slowly. "Who was she, this young woman?"

"Miss Unity Bellwood," Cornwallis replied. "A scholar of ancient languages. She was assisting Reverend Parmenter in research for a book he is writing."

"What makes the doctor and the local police suspect murder?" Pitt asked.

Cornwallis winced and his lips pulled very slightly thinner. "Miss Bellwood was heard to cry out 'No, no, Reverend!' immediately before she fell, and the moment afterwards Mrs. Parmenter came out of the withdrawing room and found her lying at the bottom of the stairs. When she went to her she was already dead. Apparently she had broken her neck in the fall."

"Who heard her cry out?"

"Several people," Cornwallis answered bleakly. "I am afraid there is no doubt. I wish there were. It is an extremely ugly situation. Some sort of domestic tragedy, I imagine, but because of the Parmenters' position it will become a scandal of considerable proportion if it is not handled very quickly—and with tact."

"Thank you," Pitt said dryly. "And the local police do not wish to keep the case?" It was a rhetorical question, asked without hope. Of course they did not. And in all probability they would not be permitted to, even had they chosen to do so. It promised to be a highly embarrassing matter for everyone concerned.

Cornwallis did not bother to answer. "Number seventeen, Brunswick Gardens," he said laconically. "I'm sorry, Pitt." He seemed about to add something more, then changed his mind, as if he did not know how to word it.

Pitt rose to his feet. "What is the name of the local man in charge?"

"Corbett."

"Then I shall go and relieve Inspector Corbett of his embarrassment," Pitt said without pleasure. "Good morning, sir."

Cornwallis smiled at him until he reached the door, then turned back to his papers again.

Pitt telephoned the Bow Street station and gave orders that Sergeant Tellman was to meet him in Brunswick Gardens, on no account to go in ahead of him, and then took a hansom himself.

It was nearly half past eleven when he alighted in bright, chill sunshine opposite the open space and bare-leafed trees near the church. It was a short walk to number seventeen, and he saw even at twenty yards' distance an air of difference about it. The curtains were already drawn, and there was a peculiar silence surrounding it, as if no housemaids were busy airing rooms, opening windows or scurrying in and out of the areaway, receiving deliveries.

Tellman was waiting on the pavement opposite, looking as dour as usual, his lantern-jawed face suspicious, gray eyes narrow.

"What's happened here then?" he said grimly. "Been robbed of the family silver, have they?"

Tersely, Pitt told him what he knew, and added a warning as to the extreme tact needed.

Tellman had a sour view of wealth, privilege and established authority in general if it depended upon birth; and unless it was proved otherwise, he assumed it did. He said nothing, but his expression was eloquent.

Pitt pulled the bell at the front door and the door was opened immediately by a police constable looking profoundly unhappy. He saw that Pitt's hair was rather too long, his pockets bulging, and his cravat lopsided, and drew in his breath to deny him entrance. He barely noticed Tellman, standing well behind.

"Superintendent Pitt," Pitt announced himself. "And Sergeant Tellman. Mr. Cornwallis asked us to come. Is Inspector Corbett here?"

The constable's face flooded with relief. "Yes sir, Mr. Pitt. Come in, sir. Mr. Corbett's in the 'all. This way."

Pitt waited for Tellman and then closed the door. He and

Tellman followed the constable across the outer vestibule into the ornate hall. The floor was a mosaic in a design of black lines and whirls on white, which Pitt thought had a distinctly Italian air. The staircase was steep and black, set against the wall on three sides and built of ebonized wood. One of the walls was tiled in deep marine blue. There was a large potted palm in a black tub directly beneath the newel post at the top. Two round white columns supported a gallery, and the main article of furniture was an exquisite Turkish screen. It was all very modern and at any other time would have been most impressive.

Now the eye was taken with the group of figures at the bottom of the stairs: a young and unhappy doctor putting his instruments back into his case; a second young man standing stiffly, his body tense, as if he wanted to take some action but did not know what. The third was a man a generation older with thinning hair and a grave and anxious expression. The fourth, and last, figure was more than half covered by a blanket, and all Pitt could see of her was the curve of her shoulders and hips as she lay sprawled on the floor.

The older man turned as he heard Pitt's step.

"Mr. Pitt," the constable said to this man, his face eager, as if he were bearing good news. "And Sergeant Tellman. The commissioner sent them, sir."

Corbett shared his constable's relief and made no pretense about it.

"Oh! Good morning, sir," he responded. "Dr. Greene here has just finished. Nothing to do for the poor lady, of course. And this is Mr. Mallory Parmenter, the Reverend Parmenter's son."

"How do you do, Mr. Parmenter," Pitt replied, and nodded to the doctor. He looked around at the hallway, then up the stairs. They were steep and uncarpeted. Anyone pushed from the top and falling all the way likely would be injured severely. It did not surprise him that in this instance such a fall should have proved fatal. He moved closer and bent down to look at the body of the young woman, holding back the blanket. She was on her side, her face half turned away from him. He could see she had been extremely handsome in a willful and sensuous fashion. Her features were strong, brows level and her mouth full-lipped. He could easily believe that she had been intelligent, but he saw little gentleness in her.

"Died from the fall," Corbett said almost under his breath. "About an hour and a half ago." He pulled a watch out of his waist-coat pocket. "The hall clock struck ten just after. I expect you'll be speaking to everyone yourself, but I can tell you what we know, if you like?"

"Yes," Pitt accepted, still looking at the body. "Yes, please." He noticed her feet. She wore indoor slippers rather than boots, and both of them had come half off in the fall. Carefully he examined the hem of her skirt, all the way around, to see if the stitching had come undone and she could have caught her heel in it and tripped. But it was perfect. On the sole of one of the slippers was a curious dark stain. "What's that?" he asked.

Corbett looked at it. "Don't know, sir." He bent down and touched it experimentally with one finger, then held it to his nose. "Chemical," he said. "It's dry on the sole, but there's still quite a sharp odor, so it's not been there long." He stood up and turned to Mallory Parmenter. "Did Miss Bellwood go out this morning, do you know, sir?"

"I don't know," Mallory answered quickly. He looked very pale and kept his hands from shaking by knotting them together. "I was studying . . . in the conservatory." He shrugged apologetically, as if that needed some explanation. "Quietest place in the house some-times. And very pleasant. No fire lit in the morning room then, and the maid's busy, so it was also the warmest. I suppose Unity could have gone out, but I don't know why. Father would know."

"Where is Reverend Parmenter?" Pitt enquired.

Mallory looked at him. He was a good-looking young man with smooth, dark hair and regular features which might easily appear either charming or sulky depending upon his expression.

"My father is upstairs in his study," he replied. "He is naturally deeply distressed by what has happened and preferred to be alone, at least for a while. If you need any assistance I shall be happy to offer it."

"Thank you, sir," Corbett acknowledged, "but I don't think we need to detain you any longer. I'm sure you would like to be with your family." It was a dismissal, politely phrased.

Mallory hesitated, looking at Pitt. He was obviously unwilling to leave, as if something he should have prevented might happen in his absence. He looked down at the still figure on the floor. "Can't you cover her up again . . . or something?" he said helplessly.

"When the superintendent's seen everything he needs to, we'll take her away to the mortuary, sir," Corbett answered him. "But you leave us to get on with it."

"Yes . . . yes, I suppose so," Mallory conceded. He swiveled on his heel and walked across the exquisite floor and disappeared through an ornately carved doorway.

Corbett turned to Pitt. "Sorry, Mr. Pitt. It seems like a very ugly business. You'll want to speak to the witnesses for yourself. That'll be Mrs. Parmenter and the maid and the valet."

"Yes." Pitt took a last look at Unity Bellwood, fixing in his mind's eye the way she lay, her face, the thick honey-fair hair, the strong hands, limp now but long-fingered, well cared for. An interesting woman. But he would probably not need to learn a great deal about her, as he had to in most cases. This one seemed regrettably clear, merely tragic, and perhaps difficult to prove before a court. He turned to Tellman, standing a couple of yards behind him. "You had better go and speak to the rest of the staff. See where everybody was and if they saw or heard anything. And see if you can discover what that substance is on her shoe. And be discreet. Very little is certain so far."

"Yes sir," Tellman replied with an expression of disgust. He walked away, shoulders stiff, a little bounce in his step as if he were spoiling for a fight. He was a difficult man, but he was observant, patient and never backed away from any conclusion, no matter how he might dislike it.

Pitt turned back to Corbett. "I had better see Mrs. Parmenter."

"She's in the withdrawing room, sir. It's over that way." Corbett pointed across the hall and under the white pillars to another highly ornate doorway.

"Thank you." Pitt walked across, his footsteps on the tiny marble pieces sounding loud in the silence of the house. He knocked on the door, and it was opened immediately by a maid.

Inside was a beautiful room, decorated in a very modern style again, with much Chinese and Japanese art, a silk screen covered in embroidered peacock tails dominating the farther corner—even the wallpaper had a muted bamboo design on it. But at the moment all Pitt's attention was taken by the woman who lay on the black-lacquered chaise longue. It was difficult to tell her height, but she was slender, of medium coloring, and her features were handsome and most unusual. Her enormous eyes were wide set, her cheekbones high and her nose unexpectedly strong. She gave the air that in normal circumstances she would smile easily and laugh at the slightest chance. Now she was very grave and kept her composure only with difficulty.

"I beg your pardon for disturbing you, Mrs. Parmenter," Pitt apologized, closing the door behind him. "I am Superintendent Pitt, from Bow Street. Assistant Commissioner Cornwallis has asked me to conduct the investigation into the death of Miss Bellwood." He did not offer any explanation. It seemed like an admission that they were prepared to conceal something, or to prejudge the depth and the out-come of the tragedy.

"Of course," she said with the ghost of a smile. "I understand, Superintendent." She turned a little to face him but did not move from her reclining position. The maid waited discreetly in the corner, perhaps in case her mistress should need further restorative or assistance.

"I imagine you need me to tell you what I know?" Vita Parmenter continued, her voice dropping a little.

Pitt sat down, more to save her staring up at him than for his own comfort. "If you please."

She had obviously prepared herself, and her mind seemed very clear; there was only the slightest trembling in her hands. She kept her amazing eyes steadily upon his.

"My husband had taken his breakfast early, as he frequently does when he is working. I imagine Unity—Miss Bellwood—had also. I did not see her at the table, but that was not remarkable. The rest of us ate as usual. I do not think we discussed anything of interest."

"The rest of us?" he questioned.

"My son, Mallory," she explained. "My daughters, Clarice and Tryphena, and the curate who is staying with us at present."

"I see. Please go on."

"Mallory went into the conservatory to read and study. He finds it an agreeable place, quiet and warm, and no one interrupts him. The maids do not go in there, and the gardener has little to do at this time of year." She was watching him carefully. She had very clear gray eyes, with dark lashes and high, delicate brows. "Clarice went upstairs. She did not say why. Tryphena came in here to play the pianoforte. I don't know where the curate went. I was in here also, as was Lizzie, the downstairs maid. I was arranging flowers. When I had finished them I started towards the hall and was almost at the doorway when I heard Unity cry out ..." She stopped, her face pinched and white.

"Did you hear what she said, Mrs. Parmenter?" he asked gravely.

She swallowed. He saw her throat jerk.

"Yes," she whispered. "She said, 'No, no!' And something else, and then she screamed and there was a sort of thumping ... and silence." She stared at him, and her face reflected her horror as if she were still hearing it in her head, replaying again and again.

"And the something else?" he asked, although Cornwallis had

already told him what the servants had said. He did not expect her to answer, but he had to give her the opportunity.

She showed the loyalty he had expected.

"I . . . I . . ." Her eyes dropped. "I am not certain."

He did not push her. "And what did you see when you entered the hall, Mrs. Parmenter?" he continued.

This time there was no hesitation. "I saw Unity lying at the bottom of the stairs."

"Was there anyone on the landing above?"

She said nothing, avoiding his eyes again.

"Mrs. Parmenter?"

"I saw a man's shoulder and back as he went behind the jardiniere and flowers into the passage."

"Do you know who it was?"

She was very pale, but this time she did not flinch; she met his eyes squarely. "I cannot be sure enough to say, and I will not guess, Superintendent."

"What was he wearing, Mrs. Parmenter? What did you see, exactly?"

She hesitated, thinking hard. Her unhappiness was profound.

"A dark jacket," she said at last. "Coattails . . . I think."

"Is there any man in the house whom that description would not fit? Do you recall height, build, anything else?"

"No," she whispered. "No, I don't. It was only momentary. He was moving very quickly."

"I see. Thank you, Mrs. Parmenter," he said gravely. "Can you tell me something about Miss Bellwood? What kind of a young woman was she? Why should anyone wish her harm?"

She looked down with a fractional smile. "Mr. Pitt, that is very hard to answer. I . . . I dislike to speak ill of someone who has just met with a tragic death, in my house, and so young."

"Naturally," he agreed, leaning forward a little. The room was very comfortable, the warmth of the fire filling it. "Everyone does. I regret having to ask you, but I expect you understand that I must know the truth, and if indeed she was pushed, then it is going to be painful—and inevitably ugly. I am sorry, but there is no choice."

"Yes . . . yes, of course." She sniffed. "I apologize for being so foolish. One keeps hoping . . . it is not very sensible. You want to understand how such a thing could have happened and why." She remained still for some moments, perhaps searching for words to explain.

The rest of the house was in complete stillness. There was not even a clock audible anywhere. No servants' footsteps sounded across the hall beyond the door. The maid in the corner seemed like part of the elaborate decoration.

"Unity was very clever," Vita began at last. "In a scholastic sort of way. She was a brilliant student of languages. Greek and Aramaic seemed as natural to her as English is to you or me. That was how she helped my husband. He is a theologian, you see, quite outstanding in his field, but his ability with translation is only moderate. He knows fully the meaning of a work, if it is religious, but she could grasp the words, the flavor, the poetic instinct. But she also knew quite a lot of secular history." She frowned. "I suppose that happens if you study a language? You find yourself learning rather a lot about the people who spoke it . . . through their writings, and so on."

"I should imagine so," Pitt agreed. He was quite well read in English literature, but he had no knowledge of the classics. Sir Arthur Desmond, who had owned the estate on which Pitt had grown up, had been good enough to educate Pitt, the gamekeeper's son, along with his own son, now Sir Matthew Desmond. But his learning had leaned toward the sciences rather than Latin or Greek, and certainly Aramaic had not entered his thoughts. The King James translation of the Bible was more than adequate to meet all religious enquiry. Pitt concealed his impatience with difficulty. Nothing Vita had said so far seemed in any way relevant. And yet it must be very difficult for her to bring herself to the point. He should not be critical of the cost to her of this honesty.

"The Reverend Parmenter was writing a theological book?" he prompted.

"Yes," she said quietly. "Yes, he has already written two, and a great number of papers which have been highly acclaimed. But this was to be of a much deeper nature than before, and possibly more controversial." She looked at him closely to make sure he understood. "That is why he needed Unity's skills in the translation of sources for the work."

"Was she interested in the subject?" He must be patient with her. This meandering might be the only way she could bring herself to tell the one bitter truth which mattered.

Vita smiled. "Oh, not the theological side of it, Superintendent. Not in the slightest. Unity is . . . was . . . very modern in her beliefs. She did not believe in God at all. In fact, she was a great admirer of the work of Mr. Charles Darwin." A look of deep distaste flickered across her eyes and mouth. "Are you familiar with it? Of course you are. At least you have to be aware of what he propounds on the origins of mankind. There was never a more dangerous and daring idea put forward by anyone since . . . I don't know what!" She was concentrating fiercely, turning her body on the chaise longue until she faced him more fully, regardless of the discomfort it must have caused her. "If we are all descended from apes and the Bible is not true at all and there is no God, then why on earth should we go to church or keep any of the Commandments?"

"Because the Commandments are based upon virtue and the best social and moral order we know," he replied. "Whether they originate with God or with the long-fought-for and refined ideas of men. Whether the Bible is right, or Mr. Darwin is right, I don't know. There may even be some way in which they may both be. If not, I hope profoundly that it is the Bible. Mr. Darwin leaves us with little more than the belief in progress and human morality steadily ascending."

"Don't you believe it will?" she said seriously. "Unity believed it very strongly. She thought we were progressing all the time. Our ideas are getting nobler and freer with every generation. We are becoming more just, more tolerant and altogether more enlightened."

"Certainly our inventions are improving every decade," he agreed, measuring his words. "And our scientific knowledge increases almost every year. But I am not at all sure that our kindness does, or our courage, or our sense of responsibility towards each other, and they are far truer marks of civilization."

She looked at him with surprise and confusion in the shadows of her eyes.

"Unity believed we are far more enlightened than we used to be. We have thrown off the oppression of the past, the ignorance and the superstition. I heard her say so a number of times. And also that we are far more responsible for the care of the poor, less selfish and unjust than ever before."

A flash of memory came to him from the schoolroom thirty years ago. "One of the pharaohs of ancient Egypt used to boast that in his reign no one was hungry or homeless."

"Oh . . . I don't think Unity knew that," she said with surprise—and what could have been a flash of satisfaction.

Perhaps she was at last approaching the truths which mattered.

"How did your husband feel about her views, Mrs. Parmenter?"

Her face tightened again. She looked down, away from him. "He found them abhorrent. I cannot deny they quarreled rather often. If I do not tell you, then others will. It was impossible for the rest of us to be unaware of it."

He could imagine it very easily: the expression of opinions around the meal table, the stiff silences, the innuendo, the laying down of law, and then the contradictions. There was little as fundamental to people as their beliefs in the order of things—not the metaphysics, but their own place in the universe, their value and purpose.

"And they quarreled this morning?" he prompted.

"Yes." She looked at him with sadness and apprehension. "I don't know what about precisely. My maid could probably tell you. She heard them as well, and so did my husband's valet. I only heard the raised voices." She looked as if she were about to add something, then changed her mind or could not find the words for it.

"Could the quarrel have become violent?" he said gravely.

"I suppose so." Her voice was little more than a whisper. "Although I find it difficult to believe. My husband is not—" She stopped.

"Could Miss Bellwood have left the study in a temper and then lost her balance, perhaps stumbled and fallen backwards, by accident?" he suggested.

She remained silent.

"Is that possible, Mrs. Parmenter?"

She raised her eyes to meet his. She bit her lip. "If I say yes, Superintendent, my maid will only contradict me. Please don't press me to speak any further of my husband. It is terribly . . . distressing. I don't know what to think or feel. I seem to be in a whirlpool of confusion . . . and darkness . . . an awful darkness."

"I'm sorry." He felt compelled to apologize, and it was sincere. His pity for her was immense, as was his admiration for her composure and her dedication to truth, even at such personal cost. "Of course, I shall ask your maid."

She smiled uncertainly. "Thank you," she murmured.

There was nothing more to enquire of her, and he would not stretch out the interview. She must greatly prefer to be alone or with her family. He excused himself and went to find the maid in question.

Miss Braithwaite proved to be a woman in her middle fifties, tidy and sensible in manner, but at present profoundly shaken. Her face was pale and she had trouble catching her breath.

She was perched on the edge of one of the chairs in the housekeeper's sitting room, sipping a steaming cup of tea. The fire burned briskly in the small, thoroughly polished iron grate and there was a little-worn rug on the floor and most agreeable pictures on the walls, and several photographs on the side table.

"Yes," she admitted unhappily after Pitt had assured her that her mistress had given her full permission to speak freely and that her first duty was to the truth. "I did hear their voices raised. I really couldn't help it. Very loud, they were."

"Did you hear what they were saying?" he asked her.

"Well . . . yes, I heard . . ." she replied slowly. "But if you were to ask me what it was, I couldn't repeat it." She saw his expression. "Not that it was vulgar," she amended quickly. "Reverend Parmenter would never use bad language—it just would not be him, if you know what I mean. A complete gentleman in every way, he is." She gulped. "But like anyone else, he can get angry, especially when he's defending his principles." She said it with considerable admiration. Obviously they were beliefs which she shared. "I just didn't understand it," she explained. "I know Miss Bellwood, rest her soul, didn't believe in God and wasn't averse to saying so. In fact, took pleasure in it—" She stopped abruptly, a tide of color washing up her face. "Oh, God forgive me, I shouldn't speak ill of the dead. She'll know different now, poor soul."

"The argument was a religious one?" he deduced.

"Theological, I should say," she corrected him, ignoring her tea but still holding the cup. "About what certain passages meant. Wasn't often they could agree. She believed in the ideas of that Mr. Darwin, and a lot of other things about freedom which I would call indulgence. At least that was what she was always saying." Her lips tightened. "I did wonder sometimes if she said it for devilment, just to get Mr. Parmenter all riled up."

"What makes you think that?" he asked.

"Look in her face." She shook her head. "Like a child, pushing you so far to see what you'll do." She took a deep breath and let it out in a sigh. "Not that it matters now, poor creature."

"Where did this argument take place?"

"In Mr. Parmenter's study, where they were working, same as always . . . or nearly always. Once or twice she'd work downstairs in the library."

"Did you see or hear her leave?"

She looked away. "Yes . . ."

"And Mr. Parmenter?"

Her voice dropped. "Yes, I think so. Followed her out into the corridor and up to the landing, to judge from the voices."

"Where were you?"

"In Mrs. Parmenter's bedroom."

"Where is that in relation to the study and the landing?"

"Other side of the corridor from the study, one door along, further away from the stairs."

"Was the door open or closed?"

"Bedroom door was open. I was hanging clothes up in the cupboard and putting away linen. I went in with my hands full, never bothered to close it. Mr. Parmenter's study door was closed. That was why I only heard part of what they were saying, even when they shouted at each other." She looked at him unhappily.

"But when Miss Bellwood opened the study door to come out, you might have heard what she said then," he pressed her.

"Yes . . ." she acknowledged reluctantly.

"What was it?"

He heard footsteps in the passage, light and rapid, a click of heels, but they did not stop.

The color rose in Braithwaite's cheeks again, and she was obviously uncomfortable. Modesty and loyalty fought with her sense of duty to the truth—and perhaps fear of the law.

"Miss Braithwaite," he said gently, "I have to know. This cannot be concealed. A woman is dead. Perhaps she was a foolish woman, mistaken, unpleasant, or even worse, but that does not take from her the right to an honest enquiry into her death and the nearest to the truth of it that we can come. Please tell me what you heard."

She looked extremely unhappy, but she did not resist any further.

"He said she was an arrogant and stupid woman, for all her supposed brains, that she was too obsessed by her ideas of freedom to see that what she was actually talking about was chaos, disorder and destruction," she said. "He said she was like a dangerous child, playing with the fire of ideas, and one day she was going to burn down the house, and everyone would perish with her."

"Did Miss Bellwood reply?"

"She shouted that he was an arbitrary old man." She closed her eyes. The words obviously embarrassed her. "And he was too intellectually limited and emotionally crippled to be able to look with honesty at reality." She hurried the words to get them out as quickly as she could. "That's what she said, and wicked, ungrateful it was." She stared at Pitt challengingly. "Where would she be, I'd like to know, if it wasn't for gentlemen of importance, like Mr. Parmenter, giving her a chance to work for them?"

"I don't know. Was there anything else?" he prompted.

Her lips tightened.

"I do realize you hate repeating her words, Miss Braithwaite, and that it is far from your own opinion."

She shot him a look of gratitude. "Well, she said he was a spiritual coward trading in superstition and fairy stories because he had not the courage to face the truth," she said bitterly.

"It sounds like a very unpleasant quarrel indeed," he observed with a leaden feeling inside. "And you heard him follow Miss Bellwood out onto the landing?"

"I think so. I was trying not to hear. It . . . it wasn't meant for anyone else, sir. I bent over and started putting the linen in the drawers. And I wouldn't hear their feet, because the corridor and the landing's carpeted. Next thing I heard was her giving a little cry, and then a sort of thump, and then her calling out."

"What words did she call out?"

"I . . . I don't know as I'm not sure now," she equivocated, but the lie was naked in her face. She concentrated on her tea, setting the cup down carefully on the table near her.

"What did she say, Miss Braithwaite? I am sure you can remember if you try."

She did not reply.

"Do you not wish to help the police discover the truth of what happened?" he persisted.

"Well, yes, of course . . . but . . ."

"But what you heard is so damning to someone that you would rather protect him than repeat it."

She was thoroughly alarmed.

"No . . . I . . . you're puttin' me in the wrong, sir, and I've done nothing."

"What did you hear, Miss Braithwaite?" he said gently. "It is very wrong indeed to lie to the police or to conceal evidence. It makes you a part of whatever happened."

She looked horrified and her voice was sharp with fear. "I've no part in it!"

"What did you hear, Miss Braithwaite?" he repeated.

"She said, 'No . . . no, Reverend!' " she whispered.

"Thank you. And what did you do?"

"Me?" She was surprised. "Nothing. Their quarrels is none of my business. I finished with the linen and started tidying the room. Then I heard Mr. Stander call out that there was something terribly wrong, and of course I went to see what it was, like we all did." She met his eyes unhappily. Her voice dropped. "And there was Miss Bellwood lying on the floor in the hall."

"Where was the Reverend Parmenter?"

She was sitting very still, her knees close together, her hands folded.

"I don't know. The study door was closed, so I suppose he was in there."

"You didn't pass him in the corridor?"

"No sir."

"Did you see anyone else?"

"No . . . no, I don't think so."

"Thank you. You have been most helpful." He wished she could have told him something different, something that would make murder less likely, but he had pressed her hard, and she had told him the truth as she knew it.

He went upstairs and spoke to Stander, Parmenter's valet, who said very much the same. He had been brushing a suit in the dressing room and had caught only the occasional word, but he had heard Unity Bellwood cry out and then say 'No, no, Reverend!' as nearly as he could remember, and then Mrs. Parmenter call for help. He was extremely reluctant to admit it, but he knew Miss Braithwaite had heard the same, and he did not equivocate.

Pitt could no longer put off speaking to Ramsay Parmenter himself and asking him for his own account of what had happened. He dreaded it. If Parmenter denied his involvement then there would have to be a further investigation. Step by step, Pitt would have to draw from the family each miserable piece, until Parmenter was cornered and desperate, dragged down by weight of detail, fighting against the inevitable.

If he confessed it would be quicker, but still a wretched and destructive affair, the sort of thing that, in spite of himself, he pitied, regardless how sordid or absurd.

He knocked on the study door.

"Come in." The voice was gracious, the diction perfect. He should have expected it. This was a man used to preaching in church. He was apparently on the brink of becoming a bishop.

Pitt opened the door and went inside. The room was oak-paneled and very formal. The left wall was lined with bookcases; to the right was a large oak desk. The windows ahead stretched almost from floor to ceiling and were curtained in heavy velvet which did not quite match the wine color of the Indian carpet on the floor.

Ramsay Parmenter was standing beside the fireplace. He looked older than Pitt had expected, considerably older than Vita. His hair was receding from his brow and was gray at the temples. He had regular features and must have been handsome enough in his youth, in a quiet way. It was a careful face, that of a thinker and a student. Now he looked harassed and deeply unhappy.

Pitt introduced himself and explained why he was there.

"Yes ... yes, of course." Ramsay came forward and offered his hand. It was an odd gesture from a man who had just been implicated in murder. It was as if he did not realize it. "Come in, Mr. Pitt." He pointed to one of the large leather chairs, although he himself remained standing with his back to the fire.

Pitt sat down, simply to convey that he intended to remain until the conversation was concluded.

"Will you please tell me what happened between yourself and Miss Bellwood this morning, sir?" he asked. He wished the man would sit down, but perhaps he was too tense to remain in one position. He was shifting his weight from foot to foot, even though he did not actually move from the spot on which he stood.

"Yes . . . yes," Ramsay answered. "We quarreled, as I am afraid we did rather frequently." His mouth tightened. "Miss Bellwood was a very fine scholar of ancient languages, but her theological opinions were unsound, and she insisted upon airing them, even though she was well aware that everyone in the house found them offensive . . . except perhaps my younger daughter. I am afraid Tryphena is rather willful and likes to feel she is independent in her thought . . . whereas in fact she is rather easily led by someone of Miss Bellwood's power of conviction."

"That must have been distressing for you," Pitt observed, watching Ramsay's face.

"It was most displeasing," Ramsay agreed, but there was no increase of emotion in him. If he were angry he concealed it perfectly. Perhaps it had happened for so long he was used to it now.

"You quarreled," Pitt prompted.

Ramsay shrugged. He was obviously unhappy, but there was no sign of anxiety in him, still less of actual fear. "Yes, rather fiercely. I am afraid I said some things to her which I now regret . . . in light of the fact that we no longer have the opportunity to find any resolution between us." He bit his lip. "It is a very . . . very . . . unfortunate thing, Mr. Pitt, to find you have spoken in anger your last words to someone . . . the last words they will hear in their life . . . before entering the . . . hereafter."

It was a strange speech for a man of religion. It was obviously without heat, even without certainty. He was searching for words and casting aside what to Pitt would have been the obvious ones. There was no mention of God or of judgment. Perhaps he was more deeply shocked than he pretended. If he had indeed killed her, as Braithwaite seemed to believe, then he should be in a state of inner numbness.

And yet all Pitt could see in his face was confusion and doubt. Was it conceivable he had blocked the horror of it out of his mind and did not actually remember?

"Miss Bellwood left this room in considerable anger," Pitt said aloud. "She was heard shouting at you, or at least speaking very loudly and offensively."

"Yes . . . yes, indeed," Ramsay agreed. "I am afraid I spoke to her equally offensively."

"From where, Reverend Parmenter?"

He opened his eyes wide. "From where?" he repeated. "From . . . from here. From this room. I . . . I went to the doorway, I followed her that far . . . then . . . then I realized the futility of it." His hands clenched. "I was so angry I was afraid I would say things I might later regret. I—I returned to my desk and continued to work, or tried to."

"You did not go after Miss Bellwood onto the landing?" Pitt kept the disbelief out of his voice with difficulty.

"No." Ramsay sounded surprised. "No. I told you, I was afraid the quarrel would become irreparable if I continued it. I was very angry with her." His face pinched with remembered irritation. "She was a remarkably arrogant and objectionable young woman at times." He shifted his weight again and moved a little farther from the fire. "But she was an excellent scholar, in her way, even though areas of her understanding were limited and biased by her own very eccentric beliefs." He looked at Pitt directly. "Rather more of emotion than of the intellect, I fear. But then she was a woman, and young. It would be unfair to expect more of her. Like all of us, she was limited by her nature."

Pitt regarded him carefully, studying his features to try to understand the emotions which prompted such a mixed and peculiar speech. That he had disliked Unity Bellwood was apparent, but it seemed he was trying to be both honest and as charitable as that dislike allowed him. And yet there was no discernible sense of tragedy in him, as if he had not grasped the reality of her death. Even the maid and the valet appeared to have more appreciation of the shadow of murder over them. Did Parmenter really feel that the reasons for her scholastic inabilities could possibly matter now? Or was this his way—at least temporarily—of escaping the horror of what it seemed he had done? Pitt had seen people retreat into trivialities to escape the overwhelming before. Women sometimes compulsively occupied themselves with food or housework in times of bereavement, as if the exactness of placement of a picture on a wall were of permanent importance. Silver must be polished like mirrors, ironing make fabric as smooth as glass. Perhaps the attending to irrelevancies in reasoning was Parmenter's way of keeping his mind from the truth.

"Where were you when you heard Mrs. Parmenter call out for help and that something dreadful had happened?" Pitt asked.

"What?" Ramsay looked surprised. "Oh. I did not hear her. Braithwaite came and told me there had been an accident, and I went to see what it was, naturally, and if I could help. As you know, help was impossible." He looked at Pitt without wavering.

"You did not follow Miss Bellwood out and continue your quarrel on the landing?" Pitt asked, although he knew what the answer would be.

Ramsay's rather sparse eyebrows rose. "No. I already told you, Superintendent, I did not leave the room."

"What do you believe happened to Miss Bellwood, Reverend Parmenter?"

"I don't know," Ramsay said a little more sharply. "The only thing I can suppose is that she somehow slipped . . . overbalanced . . . or something. I am not really sure why it needs a policeman from Bow

Street to look into the affair. Our local people are perfectly adequate, or even the doctor, for that matter."

"There is nothing to trip over on the stairs. No carpets or stair rails to come loose," Pitt pointed out, still watching Ramsay's face. "And Stander and Miss Braithwaite both heard Miss Bellwood call out 'No, no, Reverend' just before she fell. And Mrs. Parmenter saw someone leaving the landing and heading in this direction."

Ramsay stared at him and slowly horror filled his face, etching the lines around his nose and mouth deeper. "You must have misunderstood!" he protested, but his skin was very white and he seemed to have difficulty forming his words, as if his lips and tongue would not obey him. "That is preposterous! What you are suggesting is that . . . I pushed her!" He gulped and swallowed. "I assure you, Mr. Pitt, I found her most irritating, an arrogant and insensitive young woman whose moral standards were highly questionable, but I most certainly did not push her." He drew in his breath. "Indeed, I did not touch her at all, nor did I leave this room after our . . . difference." He spoke vehemently, his voice rather loud. His eyes did not waver in the slightest from meeting Pitt's, but he was afraid. It was in the beads of sweat on his skin, the brightness of his eyes, the way his body was held rigid.

Pitt rose to his feet. "Thank you for your time, Reverend Parmenter. I shall speak to the rest of the household."

"You . . . you must find out what happened!" Ramsay protested, taking a step forward and then stopping abruptly. "I did not touch her!"

Pitt excused himself and went back downstairs to look for Mallory Parmenter. When Braithwaite and Stander realized that everything rested upon their word, they might both retract their statements, and Pitt would be left with nothing, except a death and an accusation he could not prove. In a way that would be perhaps the most unsatisfactory outcome of all.

He crossed the spectacular hallway, the body of Unity Bellwood

now removed, and found Mallory Parmenter in the library. He was staring out of the window at the spring rain now beating against the glass, but he swung around as soon as he heard the door opening. His face was full of question.

Pitt closed the door behind him. "I am sorry to disturb you, Mr. Parmenter, but I am sure you will appreciate that I need to ask further questions."

"I suppose so," Mallory said reluctantly. "I don't know what I can tell. I have no knowledge of my own as to what happened. I was in the conservatory all the time. I didn't see Miss Bellwood at all after breakfast. I assume she went upstairs to the study to work with my father, but I don't know that or what happened after."

"Apparently they quarreled, so Reverend Parmenter says, and according to the maid and the valet, who both heard them."

"That doesn't surprise me," Mallory replied, looking down at his hands. "They quarreled rather often. Miss Bellwood was very opinionated and had not sufficient tact or sense of people's feelings to refrain from expressing her beliefs, which were contentious, to put it at its best."

"You did not care for her," Pitt observed.

Mallory looked up sharply, his brown eyes wide. "I found her opinions offensive," he corrected himself. "I had no personal ill will against her." It seemed to matter to him that Pitt believed this.

"You live at home, Mr. Parmenter?"

"Temporarily. I am shortly to go to Rome, to take up a position in a seminary there. I am studying for the priesthood." He said it with some satisfaction, but he was watching Pitt's face.

Pitt was floundering. "Rome?"

"Yes. I do not share my father's beliefs either . . . or lack of beliefs. I do not mean to disturb your sensibilities, but I am afraid I find the Church of England to have lost its way somewhat. It seems not so much a faith as a social order. It has taken me a great deal of thought and prayer, but I am sure of my conviction that the Reformation was

a profound mistake. I have returned to the Church of Rome. Naturally my father is not pleased."

Pitt could think of nothing to say which did not sound foolish. He could hardly imagine Ramsay Parmenter's feelings when his son had broken such news to him. The history of the schism between the two churches—the centuries of blood, persecution, proscription and even martyrdom—was part of the fabric of the nation. Only a few months before—the past October, to be exact—he had closely observed Irish politics, rooted in passionate hatred between the two religions. Protestantism was immeasurably more profoundly and intensely critical, whether one agreed with those ethics or not.

"I see," he said grimly. "It is hardly surprising you found Miss Bellwood's atheism offensive."

"I was sorry for her." Again Mallory corrected him. "It is a very sad thing for a human being to be so lost as to believe there is no God. It destroys the foundation of morality."

He was lying. It was in the sharpness of his voice, the quick bright anger in his eyes, the speed with which he had replied. Whatever he had felt for Unity Bellwood, it was not pity. Either he wished Pitt to think it was or he needed to believe it himself. Perhaps he did not think a candidate for the priesthood should feel personal anger or resentment, especially towards someone who was dead. Pitt did not want to argue about the foundation of morality, although a rebuttal rose to his tongue. The number of men and women whose morality was founded in love of man rather than love of God was legion. But there was something closed in Mallory Parmenter's face which made the idea of reasoning on the subject pointless. It was a conviction of the heart rather than the mind.

"Are you saying, as kindly as possible, that Miss Bellwood's morality was questionable?" Pitt asked mildly.

Mallory was taken aback. He had not expected to have to reply. Now he did not know what to say.

"I . . . I don't know in any immediate sense, of course," he denied

it. "It is only the way she spoke. I am afraid she advocated a great many things which most of us would find self-indulgent and irresponsible. The poor woman is dead. I should greatly prefer not to discuss it." His tone was final, ending the matter.

"Did she air these views in this house?" Pitt asked. "I mean, did you feel she was influencing members of your family or your staff in an adverse way?"

Mallory's eyes widened in surprise. Apparently this was something that had not occurred to him. "No, not that I am aware. It was simply—" He stopped. "I prefer not to speculate, Superintendent. Miss Bellwood met her death in this house, and it appears more and more as if you are not satisfied it was accidental. I have no idea what happened, or why, and I cannot be of material assistance to you. I'm sorry."

Pitt accepted the dismissal for the present. There was nothing to be gained from forcing the issue now. He thanked Mallory and went to look for Tryphena Parmenter, who seemed to be the one most profoundly distressed by Unity Bellwood's death. He learned that she had gone upstairs to her bedroom, and he sent a maid to ask if she would come down to see him.

He waited in the morning room. Someone had now lit an excellent fire there, and already the chill was off the room. The rain beating against the windows was quite an agreeable sound, making him feel isolated in warmth and safety. The room was also furnished in highly fashionable taste, with a considerable Arabic influence, but softened to blend with the English climate and materials for building. The result was more to Pitt's taste than he would have expected. The onion dome shapes stenciled on the walls and echoed in the curtains did not seem alien, nor did the geometrically patterned tiles in green and white around the fireplace.

The door opened and Tryphena came in, her head high, eyes red-rimmed. She was a slender, handsome woman with thick, fair hair, excellent skin, and a very slight space between her front teeth that was revealed when she opened her mouth to speak.

"You are here to find out what happened to poor Unity and see that some justice is done her!" It was more a challenge than a question. Her lips trembled and she controlled herself with difficulty, but her overriding emotion at the moment was anger. Grief would probably follow soon.

"I am going to try to, Miss Parmenter," he answered, turning to face her. "Do you know anything that can be of help in that?"

"Mrs. Whickham," she corrected, her mouth tightening a little. "I am a widow." The expression with which she said the last word was unreadable. "I didn't see it, if that's what you mean." She came forward, the light falling bright on her hair as she passed under the chandelier. She looked very English in this exotic room. "I don't know what I could tell you, except that Unity was one of the bravest, most heroic people in the world," she went on, her voice charged with emotion. "At whatever the cost, she should be avenged. She, of all the victims of violence and oppression, deserves justice. It's ironic, isn't it, that one who fought for freedom so fiercely and honestly should be stabbed in the back?" She gave a sharp little shudder, and her face was very white. "How tragic! But I wouldn't expect you to understand that."

Pitt was startled. He had not been prepared for this reaction.

"She fell down the stairs, Mrs. Whickham . . ." he began.

She looked at him witheringly. "I know that! I meant it in a higher sense. She was betrayed. She was killed by those she trusted. Are you always so literal?"

His instinct was to argue with her, but he knew it would defeat his purpose.

"You seem very certain it was deliberate, Mrs. Whickham," he said almost casually. "Do you know what happened?"

She gulped air. "She didn't fall; she was pushed."

"How do you know?"

"I heard her cry out, 'No, no, Reverend!' My mother was in the doorway. She'd actually have seen him except for the edge of the screen. As it was she saw a man leaving the landing and going back along the corridor. Why would any innocent person leave instead of going instantly to try to help her?" Her eyes were bright, challenging him to argue.

"You said it was someone she trusted," he reminded her. "Who might she have expected to attack her, Mrs. Whickham?"

"The Establishment, the vested interests in masculine power and the restrictions of freedom of thought and emotion and imagination," she replied defiantly.

"I see . . ."

"No, you don't!" she contradicted him. "You have absolutely no idea!"

He put his hands in his pockets. "No, perhaps you are right. If I were fighting for those things, and were a woman rather than a man, I would expect a high official in the church to be the very bastion of entrenched privilege and the keeping of ideas exactly as they are. It is where I would expect my opposition, even my enemies."

The color rushed up her face. She started to speak and then stopped.

"Whom did she consider her enemies?" he pressed.

She regained her composure with an effort, her shoulders rigid, her hands stiff. The argument concentrated her mind, and it was easier than grief. "Not anyone in this house," she responded. "One does not expect such violence behind the face of friendship, not if you are utterly honest yourself and you approach everyone thoroughly openly and without fear or deceit."

"You had a very high opinion of Miss Bellwood," he observed. "Would you mind telling me something more about her, so that I can try to understand what must have happened?"

She softened a little, her face reflecting an obvious vulnerability and even a dawning awareness of being alone in a new and terrible sense. "She believed in progress towards more freedom for everyone," she said proudly. "All kinds of people, but especially those who have been oppressed for centuries, forced into roles they did not want and denied the opportunity to learn and to grow, to use the talents they possessed and could have refined into great art."

She frowned. "Do you know, Superintendent, how many women who composed music or painted pictures were obliged to publish or show their work only if they used their father's or their brother's names?" Her voice rose and she almost choked on her outrage. Her hands were clenched into fists at her sides, elbows bent a little. "Can you imagine anything worse than creating great art, the realization of your ideas, the visible mark of your soul's dreams, and having to pretend it was someone else's just to conform to an oppressor's vanity? It . . . it is unspeakable! It is a tyranny beyond any kind of forgiveness!"

He could not argue with her. Put into those words, it was monstrous.

"She was fighting for artistic freedom?" he asked.

"Oh, a great deal more than that!" she said hotly. "She was fighting for freedom of all kinds: the right of people to be themselves, not to have to conform to other people's old-fashioned ideas of what they ought to be. Do you know what it is like to be alone in your fight, really alone? To have to pretend you don't understand things in order to pander to the vanity of stupid people, just because they are born a different gender from yourself?" Her face tightened with impatience. "No, of course you don't! You're a man, part of the Establishment. You take power as your birthright. Nobody questions you or tells you you haven't the nature or the intelligence to achieve anything—or even to make your own judgments and decide your own fate!" She looked at him with wide, round blue eyes glowing with contempt. Her slender shoulders were still locked rigid, and her hands were clenched at her sides.

"My father was a gamekeeper and my mother did the laundry," he replied, looking straight back at her. "I know quite a lot about birthrights and different people's places in society. I also know what it is like to be cold and hungry. Do you, Mrs. Whickham?"

She flushed a deep pink.

"I . . . I'm . . . not talking about . . . that," she said, stumbling on her words. "I'm talking about intellectual freedom. It's a . . . far bigger thing."

"It's only a bigger thing if you are warm and safe and have food in your stomach," he responded with just as much feeling as she. "There are lots of battles which are worth fighting, not only Miss Bellwood's belief in equality of intellectual opportunity and recognition."

"Well . . ." Honesty struggled with grief and anger within her. Honesty won, but only just. "Well, yes, I suppose so. I didn't mean there weren't. You asked me about Unity. She challenged the rigid ideas of society, and of the church, and she upset the hypocrites and the cowards who don't have the spiritual honor or the bravery to dare to think for themselves."

"Does that include your father?"

She lifted her chin. "Yes . . . yes, it does." She dared him to disapprove her devastating candor. "If you need the truth, then he's a moral coward and an intellectual bully. Like most academic men, he's terrified of new ideas or anything that challenges what he was taught. Unity was full of new perceptions that he was too limited to understand, and he wouldn't try. Anyway, he hasn't the imagination. He knew she was surpassing him, so he tried to overpower her, shout her down, intimidate her. I'm speaking metaphorically, or course. You do understand that?"

"I heard that this morning it was fairly literal," he pointed out.

Her eyes suddenly filled with tears and she blinked hard, trying to dispel them, and failed. They slid down her cheeks. She looked like an angry and frightened child.

Pitt found she stirred his sympathies at the same time as she exasperated him.

"I am sure such people as Miss Bellwood are very rare," he said with more humor, and gratitude for that fact, than she was aware.

"Unique," she agreed urgently. "You must seek justice, Superintendent . . . no matter what that is or who stands in the way. You must, for honor's sake! You mustn't be afraid of anyone. Unity wasn't. And she deserves that of her avenger. You mustn't let privilege or superstition deter you, or . . . or even pity for who else is affected." Her voice was husky with the power of her feeling. "If people can be dismissed simply because they are dead, if we don't owe them anything because they are powerless to demand it from us, then we are worth nothing." She slashed her hand in the air. "All civilization is worth nothing! The past is meaningless, and the future will forget us just the same. Only we shall have deserved it. Can you fulfill your role in history, Superintendent Pitt?" she demanded. "Are you equal to it?"

"I have every intention of trying, Mrs. Whickham, because that is my job, whether I like the results or not," he replied, keeping his expression perfectly straight. Her words were pretentious enough, but behind them she was not unlike his almost-nine-year-old daughter, Jemima. She fed on just such unself-conscious extremes. And her feelings were very easily hurt if she thought anyone was laughing at her.

Tryphena studied him. "I am glad. It is what must be. I . . . I only wish my father were not so . . . implacable, so domineering." She shrugged. "But I suppose weak people are very often stubborn because they don't know what else to cling to."

There was no courteous answer he could make to that, and he let it pass.

"Thank you. I'm sorry to have had to ask you these things," he said formally. "I appreciate your frankness, Mrs. Whickham. Now, would you be kind enough to ask your sister if she would come and see me, either here or in some other room in which she would prefer to talk."

"I'm sure she'll come here," she replied. "Although I don't suppose she can tell you anything. She didn't know Unity as well as I did. And she'll defend Papa. She's loyal to people." Again the flicker of contempt crossed her face. "She cannot see that ideas are more important. Principles must govern us or they are not principles. If we can bend them to suit us, then they are worth nothing! 'I could not love thee, dear, so much, loved I not honour more!' Richard Lovelace, you know?" She raised her eyebrows. "No, I don't suppose you do. Never mind, it is true. I'll get Clarice for you." And without waiting for his answer she turned and went out, leaving the door wide open behind her.

It was more than ten minutes before Clarice Parmenter came in. He heard her quick footsteps moving across the tiles of the hall before he saw her. She was of similar height and build to her sister, but her hair was dark and she was not as pretty. Her mouth was wider and her nose was fractionally crooked, giving her face a lopsided air, perhaps unconsciously humorous.

She came in and closed the door behind her.

"I can't help," she said without preamble. "Except to say that the whole thing is ridiculous. It must have been an accident. She tripped over something and fell."

"Over what?" he asked.

"I don't know!" She waved her hands impatiently. They were very fine hands, slender and expressive. "But you don't push people downstairs because they don't believe in God! That's absurd! Well . . . of course you don't, if you are a Christian yourself." She shrugged and made a face. "Actually you burn them at the stake, don't you." She did not laugh, she was too near hysteria to dare, but there was a wild flash of humor in her eyes. "We haven't got any stakes here, but it would be very infra dig to heave someone down the stairs. Execution for blasphemy has to be done with all the proper ceremony or it doesn't count."

He was startled. She was not like anything he could possibly have foreseen. Perhaps she cared more than he had been led to believe. "Were you very fond of Miss Bellwood?" he asked.

"Me?" She was surprised. Her very gray eyes widened. "Not in the slightest. Oh . . . I see. You think I am emotionally overwrought, because I made remarks about burning atheists? Yes, I probably am. It isn't every day that someone dies in this house and we have the police supposing it was murder. That is why you're here, isn't it? Doesn't it upset most people a bit? I thought you would be used to people weeping and fainting." It was almost a question. She waited for a moment to give him time to answer.

"I am used to people being very shocked," he agreed. "Not many people actually faint." He moved back, inviting her to be seated.

"That's convenient." She perched on the edge of the chair opposite the fire. "I don't suppose fainting people are much use to you." She shook her head a little. "I'm sorry. That has nothing to do with anything, has it? I didn't like Unity particularly, but I do care very much about my father. I really don't believe he would have pushed her, no matter how much she annoyed him, at least not intentionally. They may have struggled. Could she have pushed him and slipped?" She looked up at him hopefully. "Perhaps if he stepped aside or tried to push her away? That's possible, isn't it? That would be an accident. And anyone can have an accident."

He sat down opposite her. "That is not what he said, Miss Parmenter. He said he did not leave his study at all. And your mother's maid and the valet both heard Miss Bellwood call out 'No, no, Reverend!' So did your sister."

She said nothing. Her face reflected her misery and confusion, and equally her complete refusal to believe her father responsible for anything more than mischance.

"Would he have been involved in an accident like that and then lied rather than own to it?" Pitt asked, hoping she would say yes. It would answer all the evidence and still not be murder.

She thought about it for several seconds, then lifted her chin and met his eyes squarely. "Yes. Yes, he would."

He could tell that she was lying. It was precisely what Tryphena had said. She was putting her personal feelings for her father before truth. And he thought he might well have done the same thing were he ever to be in a similar dilemma.

"Thank you, Miss Parmenter," he acknowledged. "I am sorry I have had to trouble you. I believe there is also a curate living in the house, is that so?"

She tensed slightly. "Yes. Do you want to see him? I don't sup-pose he can help either, but you have to go through the motions, don't you? I'll fetch him." She stood up and went to the door, and then turned as he rose also. "What are you going to do, Super-intendent? You can't arrest my father, can you, without proof or a confession?"

"No, I can't."

"And you don't have either, do you." That was a challenge, a statement she desperately wanted to be true.

"Not so far."

"Good! I'll get the curate for you." She went out with quick, light steps, and Pitt was left alone to turn over in his mind the peculiar situation in which he found himself. It seemed, from Tryphena's evi-dence, and that of the maid and the valet, as if Unity Bellwood had quarreled violently with Ramsay Parmenter, and after being highly abusive, stormed out of the room in temper. He had followed her, continuing the quarrel, and there had been some sort of struggle at the top of the stairs. She had called out, and then had fallen with such impetus she had pitched right to the bottom and broken her neck. It was absurd to enter into a physical struggle over issues of the-ories of God and the origin of man. It was the last way on earth to prove either argument true. Any bodily conflict between a middle-aged clergyman and a young female scholar was unseemly and held elements of farce. Clarice, the one person who disbelieved it, was cer-tainly right.

And yet it seemed undeniably what had happened.

He did not hold any hope that the young curate would be any use whatever. He would probably support Ramsay Parmenter, out of pro-fessional and religious loyalty, and disclaim any knowledge of the whole matter.

The door opened and a startlingly handsome man came in. He was slender, almost Pitt's height, dark haired with fine aquiline fea-tures and a mouth of humor and sensitivity. He was wearing a clerical collar.

"Hello, Thomas," he said quietly, closing the door behind him.

Pitt was so stunned for a moment he could not find speech. The man was Dominic Corde, the widower of Pitt's wife's sister, who had been murdered nearly ten years before, when Charlotte and Pitt had first met. If Dominic had not remarried, then presumably they were still brothers-in-law.

Dominic walked over to the chair by the fireplace and sat down. He looked noticeably older than when Pitt had last seen him. He must be at least forty now. There were fine lines around his brow and around his eyes. The furrows from nose to mouth were deeper, and there were a few gray hairs at his temples. The brashness and the smoothness of youth were gone. Pitt thought, with some reluctance, that it became him. He had not entirely forgotten that when he and Charlotte had met, Charlotte had been in love with Dominic.

"I can't believe it," Dominic said gravely, watching Pitt. "Ramsay Parmenter is a serious and compassionate man dedicated to learning and a life in the church. Unity Bellwood could be enough to try the patience of a saint, at times, but it is outside reality to imagine that Reverend Parmenter would deliberately have pushed her downstairs. There has to be some other explanation."

"Accident?" Pitt asked, finding his tongue at last but still standing. "How well do you know him?" What he meant, what was racing through his head, was: What on earth are you doing here in this house, taking holy orders? You, of all people! You who were married to Sarah and seduced maids and at the very least flirted inexcusably with other young women.

Dominic almost smiled, but the smile died on his lips before it was real.

"Ramsay Parmenter helped me when I was close to despair," he said earnestly. "His strength and patience, his calm belief and endless kindness, brought me back from the brink of self-destruction and set me on the best path possible. For the first time I can remember, I am looking towards a future with purpose and use to others. Ramsay Parmenter taught me that—and by example, not word."

He looked up at Pitt.

"I know it is your job to learn what happened here this morning, and you are honor-bound to do that, wherever it leads you. But you want the truth, and that will not include Ramsay Parmenter indulging in violence against another person, even Unity, no matter how far she provoked him." He leaned forward a little, his face creased with urgency. "Think about it, Thomas! If you are a rational man and are trying to persuade someone of the reality and the purpose and the beauty of God, the very last thing you would do is attack them. It makes no conceivable sense."

"Religious emotion very seldom makes sense," Pitt reminded him, sitting in the opposite chair. "Didn't you have to study that before you were allowed to wear that collar?"

Dominic flushed very slightly. "Yes, of course I did. But this is 1891, not the sixteenth century. We are in an age of reason, and Ramsay Parmenter is one of the most reasonable men I have ever known. When you have spoken with him more, you will know that, too. I cannot tell you anything about what happened. I was in my bedroom reading, preparing to go out and visit parishioners."

"Did you hear Miss Bellwood call out?"

"No. My door was closed, and my room is in the other wing of the house."

"Mrs. Whickham seems to believe her father could be guilty. And both the maid and the valet heard Unity call out his name," Pitt pointed out.

Dominic sighed. "Tryphena will be much distressed at Unity's death," he said sadly. "They were very fond of each other. She admired Unity enormously. In fact, I think she adopted quite a few of Unity's beliefs." He took a deep breath. "The servants I cannot explain. I can only say that they must be mistaken. I don't know how." He was obviously confused by their evidence. He searched for something to explain it away and found nothing. He looked deeply unhappy.

Pitt could understand torn loyalties, the sense of shock at sudden death. It left most people physically shaken, emotionally raw, and mentally lacking the ability to think with their normal ease or to follow reason.

"I am not going to arrest him," he said aloud. "There is insufficient evidence for that. But I must pursue it. There is too much to indicate murder for me to walk away."

"Murder!" Dominic was ashen. He stared across at Pitt with eyes almost black. "That's . . ." He dropped his head into his hands. "Oh, God . . . not again!"

For a moment both of them remembered Sarah, and the other dead women in Cater Street, and the fear and the suspicion, the crumbling of relationships and the pain.

"I'm sorry," Pitt said, barely above a whisper. "There is no choice."

Dominic did not speak.

The coals settled in the fire.

CHAPTER
TWO

After Pitt left, Dominic Corde was acutely aware of the distress which at least to some extent had been masked during the presence of strangers. Unity's body had been removed. The police had seen everything they needed to and notes had been taken of the scene. Now the house was unnaturally quiet. The curtains and blinds were closed in decent respect for death, and to signify to all passersby and potential callers that this was now a house of mourning.

No one had wanted to continue with normal pursuits until the last formalities were completed. It looked callous—or worse, as if they might be afraid of something. Now they stood in the hall, self-conscious and unhappy.

Clarice was the first to speak.

"Isn't it absurd? So much has happened and yet everything looks the same. Before this, I had a dozen things to do. Now every one of them seems rather pointless."

"Nothing is the same!" Tryphena said angrily. "Unity has been murdered in our house by a member of our family. Nothing is ever going to be the same again. Of course everything you were going to do is pointless! How could it have meaning?"

"We don't really know what happened . . ." Mallory began tentatively, shifting his weight from one foot to the other. "I think we should not rush into saying things . . ."

Tryphena glared at him, her eyes red-rimmed, the tears standing out in them.

"If you don't know, it is because you refuse to look at it. And if you start preaching to me I shall scream. If you come up with your usual platitudes about the mysteries of God and abiding God's will for us, I swear I'll throw something at you, and it will be the heaviest and sharpest thing I can find." She was struggling for breath. "Unity had more courage and honesty than all the rest of you put together. Nobody can ever replace her!" She turned on her heel and ran across the mosaic floor and up the stairs, her heels loud on the wood.

"You might," Clarice murmured, presumably referring to Tryphena's replacing Unity. "I think you'd do it rather well. You've got just the same sort of wild ideas and you never listen to anyone else or look where you're going. In fact, you'd be perfect."

"Really, Clarice!" Mallory said impatiently. "That is uncalled for. She is distraught."

"She's always distraught about something," Clarice muttered. "She lives her life being distraught. She was beside herself when her marriage with Spencer was arranged. Then when she decided he was a bully and a bore, she was even more beside herself. And she still wasn't satisfied when he died."

"For heaven's sake, Clarice!" Mallory was aghast. "Have you no decency?"

Clarice ignored him.

"Aren't you distressed?" Dominic asked her quietly.

She looked at him, and the anger melted out of her face. "Yes, of course I am," she admitted. "And I didn't even like her." She looked at her father, who was standing near the newel post. He was still very pale, but he seemed to have regained at least some of his composure. He was usually a man of great calm, and reason always prevailed over emotion, self-indulgence, or any kind of indiscipline. So far he had avoided meeting anyone's eyes. Naturally he was aware of what Stander and Braithwaite had told the police, and he must be wondering what the rest of his family made of the extraordinary charge. Now he could no longer put off some kind of communication.

"I don't think there is anything new to be said." His voice was husky, thin, totally lacking its usual timbre, his face white. "I don't know what happened to Miss Bellwood. I sincerely trust that no one else in the house does either. We had best continue with our duties as far as possible in the circumstances, and bear ourselves with dignity. I shall be upstairs in my study." And without waiting for any reply, he turned and left them, walking with measured and rather heavy tread.

Dominic watched him with a mixture of sadness and guilt because he knew of no way to help him. His admiration for Ramsay Parmenter was profound, and it had never been long absent from his mind. Ramsay had found him at a time of acute distress—*despair* would not be too strong a word for it. It was Ramsay's patience and strength he had leaned on, and which had helped him eventually to find his own. Now, when Ramsay needed someone to believe in him and to offer a hand to lift and sustain him, Dominic could think of nothing to say or do.

"I suppose I might as well continue my studies, too," Mallory remarked miserably. "I don't even know what time it is. I don't know why the maid muffled the clock. It's not as if a member of the family were dead." He shook his head and walked away.

Clarice left without explanation, going to the side door to the garden and closing it behind her, leaving Vita and Dominic alone.

"Did I do the right thing?" Vita asked softly, her voice little more than a whisper as she looked up at him. She was an extraordinary woman, not beautiful in an accepted way—her eyes were too large, her mouth too wide, her whole face a little short. And yet the longer one looked at her, the more beautiful she became, until the classic features of other women seemed too thin, too elongated, possessed of a uniformity which became tedious. "Should I have told that policeman nothing?"

He wanted to comfort her. She was in a most appalling situation, a dilemma no one should have to face. With the faith he had found in these last years, how could he advocate lying, even to protect a husband? The greatest loyalty of all must be to the right. That was never a question. The difficulty was in knowing what was the right, which of all the ways was the least evil. For that, one needed to be able to see the outcome, and too often it was impossible.

"Did you hear her cry out?" he asked.

"Of course I did." She looked at him with clear, steady eyes. "Do you imagine I would say such a thing if I had not? I did not mean it was not true, I meant should I have kept silent?"

"I know that," he answered quickly. "I thought your knowing it was the truth would tell you that you must speak it . . . I think . . ." Would he have said it had he been in her place, had he been the one to hear the cry? Would gratitude and loyalty have held his tongue? What then? What if murder was provable in some other way, and then another person was blamed? Even if that did not happen, should murder go unknown, unpunished? "No, of course you had to speak," he said with confidence. "I am just so terribly sorry that burden had to fall on you. I cannot imagine the courage it must have taken you, or how deeply you must be hurt now."

She reached out and laid her fingertips on his arm.

"Thank you, Dominic," she said softly. "You have no idea how you have comforted me. I am afraid we have terrible times ahead of us. I don't know how we are going to bear it, except by supporting one another." She stopped and gazed at him for a moment with her pain completely undisguised. "I don't think we are going to persuade Tryphena . . . do you? I am afraid she is very angry and very hurt. She regarded Unity in quite a different light from the way the rest of us did. Her loyalties are very . . . torn."

He would have liked to disagree with her, but a lie would be of no comfort; it might only make her feel more alone in her distress.

"Not yet," he said quietly. "But she has barely had time to think or to realize that the rest of her family is going to need her."

"We are, aren't we, Dominic?" Her voice was tense, husky with fear as she realized more and more sharply what must happen. "This policeman is not going to go away. He is going to persist until he has the truth. And then he is going to act upon it."

That was the one thing Dominic knew without any doubt at all. "Yes. He has little choice."

She looked wistful, a half smile on her lips. "What miserable luck! We might have had someone foolish, or more easily impressed by the church, or diverted by difficulties, or afraid to say something uncomfortable and unpopular. And it will be unpopular. I have no doubt influence will be exerted—by Bishop Underhill, if no one else. I think it is largely on his recommendation that Ramsay may become a bishop himself." She sighed almost silently. "Sometimes it is very hard to know what is right, what is best for the future. It is not always what seems best now. The world's judgments can be very harsh."

"Sometimes," he agreed. "But they can be kind as well."

Again the smile hovered about her lips, and then it vanished.

"You are going to tell me I shall find out who my true friends are?" A shadow of humor crossed her mouth. "When the scandal comes, newspapers are writing dreadful things about us and hardly anyone comes to call anymore?" She lifted one shoulder in a characteristically graceful gesture, but one of denial. "Please don't. I really don't think I wish to know. There are bound to be most unpleasant surprises, people I cared for and trusted, and believed that they cared for me." She was looking away from him, across the extraordinary hall, her voice very low. "We shall discover cowardice in places we least thought, and prejudice, and all sorts of ugly things. I would far rather not know. I would prefer to look at smiling faces and not see behind them to the weakness or the fear or the spite." She turned back to face him. "Dominic, I'm terribly afraid . . ."

"Of course you are." He wished to touch her, but it would have been unseemly. It was the most instinctive way to offer comfort when there were no words that could help, but it was not a way available to him, not even with her, nor with any parishioner. He must find the words. "We all are. There is nothing to do but face each day with the best courage we can and love one another."

She smiled. "Of course. Thank God you are here. We shall need you desperately. Ramsay will need you." She lowered her voice still further, and there was a fragile edge to it. "How can this have happened? I know Unity was an exceedingly difficult young woman, but we have had difficult people here before." She searched his eyes. "Heaven knows, we have had some curates who would drive a saint to desperation. Young Havergood was such an enthusiast, always shouting and waving his arms around." She moved her hands delicately in imitation of the remembered curate. "I can't count how many things he broke, including my best Lalique vase, which my cousin gave me as a wedding present. And there was Gorridge, who was always sucking his teeth and making bad jokes." She smiled at Dominic. "Ramsay was so good with them. Even Sherringham, who would keep on repeating things and remembered everything you ever said to him, but slightly wrong, just enough to ruin the meaning completely."

Dominic was about to say something, but she moved towards the conservatory door and led the way in. The damp smell of leaves was very pleasant, almost invigorating. The conservatory was all glassed arches and white wood above the palms and lilies.

"What was so different about Unity?" Vita went on, walking along the brick path between the beds. Twenty feet away, the chair where Mallory had been studying was empty, but his books and papers were still there, piled on a white-painted, cast-iron table. She was moving very slowly now, looking down at the ground. "Ramsay has changed, you know," she went on. "He is not the man he used to be. You couldn't know that, of course. It is as if there is a dark shadow over him, something that eats away at the confidence and the belief he had before. He used to be . . . so positive. Once he was full of fire. The very quality of his voice would make people listen. That's all changed."

He knew what she was referring to: the secular doubts that had afflicted many people since the popularity of Charles Darwin's theories on the origin of mankind, an ascent from lower forms of life rather than a unique descent from a divine Father in Heaven. He had heard the doubts in Ramsay's voice, the lack of passion in his belief and in his reiteration of it for parishioners. But Unity Bellwood was not responsible for that. She was certainly not the only person to believe in Darwinism, or the only atheist Ramsay had encountered. The world was full of them and always had been. The essence of faith was courage and trust, without knowledge.

Vita stopped. There was a dark stain of something across the pathway, at least four feet wide and in a spreading, irregular pattern. She wrinkled her nose at the faint, sharp smell which still came from it.

"I wish that gardener's boy would be more careful. Bostwick really shouldn't let him in here. He keeps forgetting to put the tops on things."

Dominic bent down and touched the stain with his finger. It was dry. The brick must have absorbed it. It was brown, like the mark on Unity's shoe. The conclusion was inescapable. But why had Mallory lied about having seen her?

"What is it?" Vita said.

He stood up. "I've no idea. But it's dry, if you want to walk over. It must have gone into the brick very quickly."

She picked up her skirts anyway, and stepped over the stain lightly. He followed her into the open central area amid the palms and vines. She gazed past winter lilies, oblivious of their delicate scent, her face pale and set.

"I suppose it was the unbearable frustration," she said quietly. "She went on and on, didn't she?" She bit her lip, and there was acute sadness in her eyes and in the angle of her head. "She never knew when to allow a little kindness to moderate her tongue. It is all very well to preach what you believe to be the truth, but when it shatters the foundations of someone else's world, it isn't very clever. It doesn't help; it only destroys." She reached out and touched one of the lilies. "There are people who cannot cope with losing so much. They cannot simply rebuild. Ramsay's whole life has been the church. Ever since he was a young man, it is all he has lived for, worked for, sacrificed his time and his means for. He could have been outstanding in university life, you know."

Dominic was not sure if that was true. He had an uncomfortable feeling that Ramsay's scholarship was limited. He had thought it brilliant when he had first known Ramsay, but gradually over the last three or four months, as Unity Bellwood had worked with Ramsay, Dominic had overheard remarks, discussions and arguments which he had been unable to forget. He had tried not to be aware that she was quicker than Ramsay to see a possibility, an alternative meaning to a passage. She could grasp an idea she did not like, instead of refusing to consider it. She could make leaps of the imagination and connect unlikely concepts and then visualize the new. Ramsay was left angry and confused, failing to understand.

It had not happened often, but enough for Dominic now to think, painfully against his will, that academic jealousy might have been at the root of some of Ramsay's dislike of Unity. Had her intellect, its speed and agility, frightened him, made him feel old, inadequate to fight for the beliefs he cared about and to which he had given so much?

Dominic's own mind was confused, uncertain what to think. Violence was so unlike the man he knew. Ramsay was all reason, words, civilized thought. In all the time Dominic had known Ramsay, the older man's kindness and his patience had never failed. Was it a veneer beneath which there was emotion only barely controlled? It was hard to believe it, yet circumstance forced it into Dominic's mind.

"Do you really believe he meant to push her?" he asked aloud.

She looked at him. "Oh, Dominic, I wish I could say no. I'd give anything to be back in yesterday again, with none of this having happened. But I heard her, too. I couldn't help it. I was just coming into the hall. She cried out 'No! No, Reverend!' And the moment after that, she fell." She stopped, her breathing rapid and shallow, her face white. "What else can I believe?" she said desperately, staring at him with horror.

It was as if someone had closed a door on hope, an iron door without a handle. Until this moment some part of him had believed there was a mistake, a hysteria prompting ill-judged words. But Vita would never have confirmed such a thing. She had no love for Unity, no divided loyalties, and no one had questioned or pressured or confused her. He tried to think of an argument, but there was nothing that did not sound foolish.

Vita was looking at him with frightened eyes. "As the policeman said, there is nothing up there to trip over."

He knew that was true. He had gone up and down those stairs hundreds of times.

"It is something I would much rather not face," she went on softly. "But if I run away, it will only make it worse in the end. My father—you would have liked my father, I think—he was a truly great man. He always used to teach me that lies get more dangerous every day. Every time you feed them by another lie, they grow bigger, until in the end they become bigger than you are, and consume you." She looked down at last, and away from him. "And dearly as I love Ramsay, I must honor my own beliefs as well. Does that sound selfish and disloyal?"

"Not at all," he said quickly. She looked very fragile in the dappled light through the leaves. She was a smaller woman than she at first appeared. The strength of her personality sometimes made one forget. "Not at all," he repeated with greater conviction. "No one has the right to expect you to lie about such a thing in order to protect him. We must do what we can to contain the damage, but that does not include denying either the law of the land or God's law." He was afraid he sounded pompous. He would have said the same words to a parishioner without a moment's hesitation, but with someone he knew well, saw every day, it was different. And she was in every way senior to him; that she was older in years did not matter, but she was so much senior in the life of the church.

He was startled by her reaction. She swung around and gazed at him with wide eyes, bright, almost as if he had offered her some real and tangible comfort.

"Thank you," she said sincerely. "You don't know how much you have strengthened me with your conviction of what is right and true. I don't feel as if I am alone, and that is the most important thing. I can bear anything if I do not have to do it alone."

"Of course you are not alone!" he assured her. In spite of the chill of shock inside him, and a strange tiredness, as if he had been up all night, with her words a kind of ease spread through him, an unraveling of long-knotted muscles. He would never have wished such a tragedy upon anyone, least of all upon the family who had given him so much, but to have the strength and the compassion to be of help to them was the core of the faith he believed and upon which he built his calling. "I shall be here all the time."

She smiled. "Thank you. Now I think I must compose my thoughts for a while . . ."

"Of course," he agreed quickly. "You would prefer to be alone." And without waiting for her response, he turned and went back along the brick path to the hall. He was crossing towards the library when Mallory came out. As soon as he saw Dominic his face shadowed.

"What have you been doing in the conservatory?" he said sharply. "What did you want?"

"I wasn't looking for you," Dominic replied guardedly.

"I would have thought you'd be seeing what you could do to help Father. After this, he's barely going to be able to carry on with his pastoral care. Isn't that what your duty is supposed to be?" The criticism was sharp and brittle in his voice.

"My first care is in this house," Dominic replied. "As yours is. I was speaking to Mrs. Parmenter, trying to reassure her that we would all support one another during this time . . ."

"Support one another?" Mallory's dark eyebrows rose, filling his face with sarcasm. "Isn't that rather absurd, considering that the highly objectionable young woman who was assisting my father has just met a violent death in this house? One of my sisters is all but implying that my father is responsible, and the other is as busy defending him and making irresponsible remarks she imagines are amusing. We have the police on the doorstep, and no doubt it will all only get worse." The dislike sharpened still further in his voice. "The best you can do is take the pastoral care off Father's shoulders so he doesn't have to leave the house. Then at least you will give us a little privacy to deal with our shock and grief, and those people Father is responsible for will have someone to minister to them."

Dominic felt his temper rising. All the differences of opinion he had had with Mallory over the months he had been in the Parmenters' home welled up in his memory, and the suppressed anger flashed to the surface. He was too raw with shock to control it.

"Perhaps if you were to set aside your studies for Rome for a few days and comfort your mother, reassure her of your loyalty, then I would not need to," he snapped back. "And I should feel free to perform my usual duties. As it was, you went off to read more books, which may be very enlightening, but it is hardly helpful!"

Mallory's face flushed pink. "I don't know what you found to say to her that could possibly help and still be even remotely true. Unity was a Godless woman who insisted on parading her immoral and blasphemous views in our house. My father was wrong to employ her in the first place. He should have investigated what kind of woman she was before he took her on." He drew breath. A maid scurried across the back of the hall and disappeared along the passage to the side door.

"A little time and effort, a few enquiries," Mallory went on, "and he could have known what she was like. Whatever her academic abilities, they were overwhelmed by her radical moral and political views. Look what she has done to Tryphena! That alone should be enough to condemn her." His lips tightened and his chin came up a little, showing the clenched muscles of his throat. "I know you have very liberal views in your church, allowing people to do more or less as they please, but perhaps now you can see the folly of that. We cannot help but be influenced by the wrong ideas around us. Mr. Darwin is accountable for more misery in the world than all the poverty and disease imaginable."

"Because he raised doubt?" Dominic said incredulously. "Does he make you doubt, Mallory?"

"Of course not!" And indeed there was no doubt in his eyes. They blazed with certainty. "But then I am of a faith which does not equivocate and hedge and trim its creed to suit the climate of the day. Father was not so fortunate. He had already committed himself, his life, his time and all his energy. He could not go back upon it, sacrifice it all."

"That's a piece of sophistry," Dominic said angrily. "If a faith is true, it ought to be able to withstand all the arguments thrown at it, and if it is not, how much you have invested in it is irrelevant. No human being can make God one thing or another."

"Perhaps you should go upstairs and comfort Father with that thought?" Mallory suggested. "You seem to have taken it upon yourself to lead the family, although I cannot imagine who asked you."

"Your mother. But if you had been there, no doubt she would have asked you," Dominic rejoined. "I did not know you disliked Unity so much. You always seemed very civil to her."

Mallory's eyebrows rose. "What did you expect, that I should be rude to her under my father's roof? She knew perfectly well what I thought of her views."

Dominic could recall several highly uncomfortable confrontations between Mallory and Unity Bellwood. They had centered mainly upon two subjects: her mockery of his absolute belief in the

Roman Catholic Church and its teachings; and a far subtler taunting of the celibacy his choice would place upon him. It had been delicately done. Had Dominic himself known Unity less well, had he been Mallory's age instead of a widower of over forty with a more than passing acquaintance with women, he might not even have known her deeper meaning under the banter. The suggestions were slight; the remarks had double meanings. He might not have understood her looks or her laughter, the hesitations close to him, and then the smile. Mallory himself was never entirely certain. He knew he amused her, and that it was a joke he did not share. It was not surprising he did not mourn her now.

"You think I was too mealymouthed to tell her," Mallory went on accusingly. "Let me assure you, I know what I believe, and I will permit no one to speak the blasphemy she did and not challenge them." He spoke firmly, pleased with himself. "She was utterly misguided, and the standards of morality she espoused were appalling. But I would greatly have preferred to persuade her of her error than see any harm come to her. As I imagine anyone would." He took a deep breath. "This is a very tragic day for all of us. I hope we shall survive it without greater loss." For a moment he looked very directly at Dominic. "I cannot offer my father any comfort. He needs faith now, and I disagree with him too profoundly to be of any service to him." In spite of his height, he looked very young, like a child who has outgrown his strength. The expression in his face was sad and confused beneath the anger. "We have been too far apart in the ways which matter most. You seem to have a belief rooted in something more than words and a way to earn your living in a respectable fashion. I have been racking my mind since I have been able to concentrate at all, but I can think of nothing to say to him. There are too many years of difference between us."

"Is this not the time to forget the differences?" Dominic suggested.

Mallory's body tightened up. "No," he said quickly, without even thinking about it. "For God's sake, Dominic! If Tryphena is right, it is possible he has just cold-bloodedly pushed a woman down the stairs to her death!" His voice rose close to panic. "What can anyone in his family say to him? He needs spiritual counsel! If he has done something terrible, he must come to some kind of terms with it and then search his soul for repentance. I can't ask him! He's my father!" He looked helpless, but his unhappiness focused on Dominic, so there was nothing Dominic could say that would help.

"You don't have Confession in your faith—you don't have Absolution!" Mallory went on with pent-up rage twisting his mouth. "You threw out all that when Henry VIII had to have his divorce to go after Anne Boleyn. You have nothing left for the times of worst trial, the dark of the night when only the blessed sacraments of the true church can save you!" He stood with his chin high, his shoulders squared. One might have thought he was facing an actual physical fight.

"If he did kill her, and any part of him meant to," Dominic replied, struggling in his own mind between refusal to believe such a thing and the incredible meaning of Vita's words, "then it will take more than anyone else's comfort or counsel for him to work through this towards any kind of peace with himself." He waved his hand sharply, dismissing the idea. "You cannot simply say 'I forgive you' and it all disappears. You have to see the difference between what you are and what you ought to be, and understand it! You must—" He stopped. Mallory was ready for a long theological argument about the true church and its mysteries, and the heresy of the Reformation. He had already drawn in his breath to begin. It was easier than talking about the realities which faced them.

"This is not the time," Dominic said firmly. "I'll go and see him when I've thought about it a little more."

Mallory shot him a disbelieving look and walked away.

Dominic turned and nearly bumped into Clarice. Her hair was coming undone, and actually it would have looked rather becoming were her eyes not pink and her skin so pale.

"He used not to be so pompous," she said grimly. "Now he

reminds me of the stuffed carp in the morning room. It always looks so surprised, like a vicar who has accidentally backed into one of the organ stops."

"Clarice . . . really!" Dominic wanted to laugh, and he knew it was entirely inappropriate. She herself still looked profoundly upset.

"Not you, too!" She pushed her hand through her hair and made it worse. "Tryphena is locked in her room, which I suppose is reasonable. She really cared for Unity, heaven help her. Although I suppose it is a good thing she did. Everyone should have at least one person to mourn for them when they die, don't you think?" Her eyes were full of pity, her voice hushed. "How terrible to die and have no one to weep, no one to feel as if they have lost something irreplaceable! I couldn't replace Unity, but then neither would I try. I think she was pretty odious. She was always mocking Mal. I know he asks for it, but he's too easy a target to be worthy of anyone who's worth anything themselves."

She was talking quickly, nervously, her hands twisting together. Dominic knew without asking that she too was afraid that her father might be guilty.

They were standing in the hall, by now far nearer the door to the morning room. He was aware that Vita must still be in the conservatory.

"I'm going up to see Father." Clarice made as if to move away and go towards the stairs. "Mal may think he wants a long theological conversation. I don't. If it were me, I should simply want to know that somebody loved me, whether I had lost my temper and pushed that miserable woman down the stairs or not." She said it defiantly, challenging him to disagree.

"So should I," he answered. "At least at first. And I think I would want someone to consider the possibility that I was innocent, and perhaps to listen to me if I needed to talk."

"You can't imagine pushing her down the stairs, can you?" She looked at him curiously. Her eyes were earnest, but there was the characteristic flicker of laughter there, far beneath the hurt, as if she were picturing it in some part of her mind, and the absurdity of it.

"Actually, I can imagine it only too easily," he confessed.

"Can you?" She was surprised, and he thought there was a hint of satisfaction also. Was it because she would rather it were he than her father? The thought chilled him. He was suddenly aware of being an outsider, the one person in the house who was not a member of the family. It was a shock that it should be Clarice of all of them who reminded him of it. She had seemed the warmest, the one who had the fewest barriers between herself and the world.

"I imagine we all could, if we were hurt," he said a little coolly. "Mallory certainly expressed plain enough satisfaction that she was gone."

"Mal?" Her eyebrows rose. "I thought he rather liked her, underneath all the arguments."

"Liked her?" Dominic was amazed.

"Yes." She turned and started towards the foot of the stairs. "He hung that Rossetti picture back in the library for her. He hates it. He hid it away in the morning room where none of the family ever go."

"Are you sure he doesn't like it?"

"Yes, of course I am. It is far too sensuous, almost provocative." She shrugged. "She liked it, but then she would."

"So do I. I think Rossetti's subject is lovely."

"She is, but Mal thinks she is wanton."

"Then why did he hang it back in the library?"

"Because Unity asked him to!" she said with a lift of impatience at his slowness. "He also went for her to pick up a parcel of books from the station . . . three times in the last two weeks. He was in the middle of studying, and it was pouring with rain. Why?" Her voice rose. "Because she asked him to! And he stopped wearing that green jacket he is so fond of . . . because she objected to it. So I am not entirely sure that he disliked her as much as you think."

He cast his mind back to the incidents she was referring to, and in each case she was right. The more he thought about it, the less did Mallory's behavior seem in character. He hated the rain. He spoke often of how he looked forward to the warmer, drier climate of Rome; it was an incidental blessing of his vocation. Dominic had never known him to run errands for anyone else. Even his mother met with a polite refusal when she asked him to go to the apothecary. He was studying; it took precedence over everything. Dominic knew nothing about the green jacket. He seldom noticed what men wore—though always what women did. But the Rossetti picture was different. That was unforgettable.

How curious. So Mallory had done Unity a number of favors in spite of his apparent contempt for her. Dominic did not have to look far for an explanation that was believable. Unity had been a remarkably attractive woman. It had been far more than a beauty of face or coloring, it was a vitality, an intelligence, a constant awareness of the joy and the challenge of life. He still remembered it himself with pain. But he had not realized it had touched Mallory.

"Perhaps you are right," he said aloud. "I didn't know about that."

"He was probably trying to convert her," Clarice remarked dryly. "He could have beaten Father soundly if he won her for the Church of Rome after all the time she's spent translating learned documents for the Church of England."

"They were the same at the period of time they are dealing with," he pointed out.

"I know that!" she said tartly, although it was obvious she had forgotten. "That's why they need all these different translations. One for each sect, don't you know," she added, and with that she went up the stairs quickly and without looking back at him.

No one bothered with luncheon. Ramsay remained upstairs in his study. Vita wrote letters, Tryphena mourned in private, and Clarice went down to the music room and played the Dead March from "Saul" on the piano.

It would be nice to think the tragedy would be left as an unsolved mystery, something about which the truth could never be known. But Dominic recalled his past acquaintance with Pitt too vividly to nurse that illusion. Pitt had gone for now, but he would be investigating evidence, details, possibly things no one else had thought of. He would examine the body. He would see the mark on the shoes, and sooner or later, the mark on the conservatory floor. He would know about Unity's going in to see Mallory. He would question and argue and reason until he knew why.

He would be very cautious, but he would probe into every detail of life in Brunswick Gardens. He would unearth any quarrel between Ramsay and Unity; he would uncover their personal weaknesses, all the little sins that might have nothing whatever to do with Unity's death but were painful and so very much better hidden.

Dominic was alone in the library. He closed his eyes and could have been back in Cater Street ten years before, feeling the prickle of fear in the air around him. He remembered with a flush of embarrassment that Charlotte had been in love with him then. He really had not known it until it was almost too late. Pitt knew it. Dominic had seen it in his eyes. The shadow of dislike was still there.

Cater Street seemed like a world away. Hundreds of things had happened to him since then, good things and bad. But for the moment he could have been there, ten years younger, more arrogant, more frightened. He could be married to Sarah; they could all be afraid of the "Hangman," who had killed again and again in the neighborhood. They could be looking at each other, wondering, suspecting, discussing things about frailties and deceits they would so much rather not know but could not forget.

Pitt had persistently uncovered everything until he knew the answer. He would do that now. And as before, Dominic was afraid, both of what that answer would be and of what the process of finding it would uncover about himself and those things in the past he would rather forget. It was easier here, in the Parmenter house, because they saw him as he wished to see himself: young in his calling, making occasional mistakes, but dedicated and whole of heart. Only Ramsay knew what had gone before.

Without making a conscious decision to do it, Dominic found himself going to the far end of the hall and through the door into the servants' quarters. Since Ramsay was in his study, and hardly in a position or a frame of mind to do it, perhaps it fell to Dominic to reassure the servants, offer them whatever comfort and reminder of duty they needed. Mallory did not seem inclined to, and he already knew the feelings in the house over his conversion to "Popery," as they called it, even though they had known him since childhood. Some of the more devout among them even regarded it as a betrayal. Perhaps that very fact made it cut the deeper.

The first person he encountered was the butler, a portly, usually comfortable man of middle years who managed the household with avuncular pleasantries masking an excellent discipline. However, today he looked deeply disturbed as he sat in the pantry checking and rechecking his cellar stocks, having counted the same things three times over and still unable to remember what he was doing.

"Good morning, Mr. Corde," he said with relief at being interrupted. He stood up. "What can I do for you, sir?"

"Good morning, Emsley," Dominic replied, closing the door behind him. "I came to see how everyone is after this morning's events . . ."

Emsley shook his head. "I just don't understand it, sir. I know what they're saying, but I can't see how it's possible. I've served in this house for thirty years, since before Mr. Mallory was born, and I just don't believe it, no matter what Stander and Braithwaite say they heard."

"Sit down," Dominic invited, and sat on the other chair to make Emsley comfortable.

"The sergeant came in here, sir," Emsley continued, accepting gratefully. "Asked a lot of questions that seemed pointless. None of us know anything." His lips tightened.

"None of you were near the stairs?" Dominic did not know what answer he hoped for. The whole thing was a nightmare from which there seemed no waking.

"No sir," Emsley said grimly. "I was in Mrs. Henderson's room going over some accounts with her. We needed more linen. Funny how it all goes at once. At least a dozen sheets. Best Irish linen, too. Still, they don't wear forever, I suppose."

"And Cook?" Dominic prompted, trying not to sound as he knew the police must have.

"In the kitchen." Emsley shook his head. "All the kitchen staff were, or in the scullery. James was cleaning the knives. Lizzie was laying the fire in the withdrawing room; Rose was in the laundry room. She'd just turned the mattresses and changed the beds and taken the linen down. Margery was polishing the brasses, so she'd got them in the main pantry on the table, and Nellie was dusting in the dining room."

It was ridiculous to think of one of the maids' having pushed Unity down the stairs. But then it was absurd to think of Ramsay's doing it, either.

"Are you sure?" he said, then, seeing the look of vulnerability on the butler's face, wished he could think of some way of explaining himself. "No one could have seen or heard anything and be afraid to say so?"

"The police sergeant asked that, too," Emsley said unhappily. "No, Mr. Corde. I know how fast a maid should be able to polish brasses. I'd know if she'd left her job. And Mrs. Henderson'd know if Rose wasn't where she said, or Nellie."

"How about the between maid, what's her name, Gwen?"

"She was telling off the bootboy," Emsley said with the shadow of a smile which vanished again instantly. "They were well heard by the kitchen staff. None of us knows what happened. I only wish we did." He shook his head. "There's got to be some explanation better than the one they've come up with. I've known Reverend Parmenter since before he married, sir. That Miss Bellwood was a mistake, I don't mind saying. I didn't care for it when she came here. I don't think young women have any place in serious thought about religion."

He looked at Dominic very gravely. "Don't misunderstand me, Mr. Corde, I think women can be as religious as any man, in some ways more so. They have a simplicity and a purity about them, the best of them do. But they aren't built for studying the deep things, and it only ends in trouble when they do. But then Reverend Parmenter wanted to be fair. A very fair man he always was, and open to reason, maybe a bit too open, poor man." He regarded Dominic anxiously, his eyes dark and troubled. "Can you help him, sir? This is a very terrible thing, and I swear I don't know which way to turn."

Dominic was every bit as confused. But it was his task to offer comfort, not to seek it. "I agree with you, Emsley." He made an effort to smile. "There must be some other explanation." He rose to his feet before Emsley could press him as to what it might be. "How is Mrs. Henderson?"

"Oh, very distressed, sir. We all are. Not that anyone liked poor Miss Bellwood so much. She could be very difficult. Unsettled people with her ideas."

"Did she?"

"Oh yes, sir. Made mock of our prayers . . . ever so polite, never open, but let slip little remarks that made people worry." His face pinched with distress. "Found Nellie in tears once. Her grandmother had just passed over, and Miss Bellwood was making remarks about Mr. Darwin's notions. Poor Nellie was convinced her grandmother wasn't going to heaven after all."

"I didn't know about that," Dominic said quickly. He should have. If someone was bereaved right there under the same roof, how was he so blind he had not seen it and offered her some assurance himself? If he was not good for that, what purpose had he? "No one told me!"

"No, of course not, sir," Emsley said calmly. "Wouldn't want to trouble you with our worries. Mrs. Henderson gave her a talking-to. Good Christian woman, Mrs. Henderson, none of these silly modern fancies. Nellie was all right after that. Just avoided Miss Bellwood, and we had no more nonsense."

"I see. I still wish I had known." Dominic excused himself and went to speak to the rest of the staff individually. He spent some time with Nellie, trying to make up for his earlier shortcoming. He realized within a few moments that his effort had been unnecessary. Whatever Mrs. Henderson had said had been more than sufficient. Nellie harbored no uncertainties as to the nature and existence of God, or that, given time, He could ultimately forgive even Unity Bellwood her sins, which Nellie had no doubt were many.

"Were they?" Dominic asked innocently. "Perhaps I did not know her as well as I thought."

"Yer'd want ter think well of 'er, sir," Nellie replied with a nod. "It's yer job. But it in't mine. I see'd 'er plain. Got some terrible ideas, she 'as. Leastways, she 'ad. She'll know better now, poor soul. But gave poor Mr. Mallory a terrible 'ard time, she did. Used ter make fun of 'im summink awful." She shook her head. "I could never make out why 'e took it. Mus' be summink ter do wiv 'is religion, I s'pose." For her that explained everything. It was foreign, and no one should be expected to understand it.

He left Nellie and continued on his course, but none of the servants was able to help, except in the most negative sense. At the time which mattered, and was fixed very clearly at five minutes to ten, they were all accounted for and nowhere near the stairhead. The only two upstairs at all were Miss Braithwaite and the valet, Stander, and they would have had to pass Ramsay's study door to reach the landing.

Was it possible that Ramsay really had pushed her? Had her constant erosion of his confidence, his belief in his faith and its root in reality, been wearing him down over the weeks and months to the point at which suddenly he had lost control and lashed out at his tormentor, at the voice which had robbed him of all the old certainties, the very meaning of all his work? Had he so lost touch with the realities of faith, the human spirit, the living emotion, that his despair had robbed him of all sense?

Dominic came into the hall again from the kitchen and the servants' dining room. It was so familiar, for all its exotic design, so very functional with its umbrella stand, reminding one of the English climate and the practicalities of walking in the rain. The tall clock normally chimed the quarter hours, the daily needs of punctuality. Of course it was muffled now, with death in the house. The side table held the salver for calling cards. The hat stand stood in the corner, next to the settles where carriage rugs were sometimes kept. The mirror, for last-minute adjustments to the appearance, reflected the light. The window pole for the footman to close the upper sash, the bell rope, the telephone machine discreetly in the corner, all seemed so anchored in sanity. Even the potted palm was an ordinary one, a little overgrown, perhaps, but just like those common enough in thousands of houses. The screen and the floor he barely noticed, he had seen them so often.

He walked slowly up the stairs, one hand on the black wooden banister.

It was like Cater Street all over again. He found himself thinking of people and wondering if they could be feeling something utterly different from what they said, from the facade they presented. Even as his feet climbed from step to step, suspicions took shape in his imagination. Mallory's behavior towards Unity did seem inconsistent. He remembered small cruelties she had displayed towards him. He should have hated her for it, or at least despised her. And yet it seemed he had gone out of his path to do her favors. Was that his way of battling against his own emotions, of trying to be the person he believed he should?

Vita must have loathed her at times, too. She could not have failed to see how Unity undermined the confidence and the happiness of both her husband and her son.

But Vita and Tryphena were the two members of the family who could not possibly have pushed her. They were both downstairs at the time. Lizzie swore to that. Not that Tryphena would have harmed Unity in any way. She was the only person in the house who truly grieved for her.

It was Tryphena whom Dominic now intended to speak with. No one else seemed to offer her any understanding. They were fairly naturally consumed in their own fears.

Unity had quarreled with Clarice several times, but it was over ideas, nothing violent or touching on the personal emotions or needs that mattered. It had all been on the surface of the intellect . . . at least that was how it had appeared. Perhaps that too was an illusion?

He knocked on Tryphena's door.

"Who is it?" she asked sharply.

"Dominic," he replied.

There was a moment's silence, then the door opened. She looked disheveled, her fair hair falling out of its pins. Her eyes were red-rimmed, and she made little effort to conceal the fact that she had been weeping.

"If you've come to try to persuade me to alter my view of Father, or to try to defend him, you are on a fool's errand." She lifted her chin a little higher. "My friend is dead, a person I admired more than anyone else I've ever known. She was a bright light of honesty and courage in a society that is black with hypocrisy and oppression, and I am not going to allow her to be snuffed out and no one raise a voice to protest." She glared at him as if he were already guilty.

"I came to see how you were," he said quietly.

"Oh." She tried to smile. "I'm sorry." She pulled open the door to the small sitting room she shared with Clarice. "Just don't preach at me." She led the way in and invited him to sit down. "I really couldn't stomach a sermon now. I know you mean well, but it would be insupportable."

"I should not like to be so insensitive," he said honestly, but with the shadow of a smile in return. He knew something of her dislike for what she regarded as the tedium and the condescension of the church. He had never met Spencer Whickham—Tryphena's marriage and widowhood predated his acquaintance with the family—but he had heard about him from Clarice and seen the pain he had caused reflected in Tryphena now in a dozen different ways. Without having the slightest idea of it, the man had apparently been a natural bully. It was hardly surprising Tryphena had such a fierce admiration for Unity, who had both the will and the weapons to fight back where she saw masculine domination and what she saw as injustice.

"Can I say anything to help you?" he asked gently. "Even that there was much in Unity that I admired?"

She stared at him, her brows puckered, mastering her tears with difficulty. "Was there?"

"Certainly."

"I feel so alone!" There was anger and pain behind her words. "Everyone else is horrified, of course, and frightened, but it is for themselves." She jerked her hands angrily. They were small-boned and delicate, like her mother's. This gesture was full of contempt. "They are all terrified there is going to be a scandal because Father did something appalling. Of course there will be! Unless they all get together and hush it up. That's exactly what could happen, isn't it, Dominic?" That was a question, but she rushed on without waiting for an answer. Her shoulders were stiff; he could see the strain on the fabric of her dress. It was floral. She had not yet thought to change to black.

"That's what they're all doing right now," she went on. "They sent that important policeman from Bow Street, which is miles from here, just so they could keep it quiet." She nodded her head. "You watch. Any time now the bishop will arrive full of false sorrow and bending all his mind on how he can deal with it discreetly, pretend it was an accident, and everyone will heave a great sigh of relief. Unity will be forgotten in their desire to save themselves embarrassment." She spat the last word. "For all their cant about God and truth and love, they'll save their own faces and do whatever is expedient." She moved her hand again sharply. The tears spilled over her cheeks. "I am the only one who really cared about her, who loved the person she was."

He did not interrupt her. She needed to say it and not be argued with. And in truth, he was horribly afraid she might be at least partly right. Certainly she was the only person who grieved for Unity rather than for the situation. He would not offend her, nor demean himself, by trying to say otherwise.

She gulped.

"You didn't know what it was like for her!" It was an accusation, and she stared at him challengingly, her blue eyes bright and hard through the tears. "You don't know how hard she had to fight to be allowed to learn, to be accepted, or what courage it took. It's all so easy for you. You're a man, and no one tells you you are not meant to have any intelligence." She sniffed fiercely. "People don't conspire silently to keep you out, looks and nods, unspoken agreements. You simply have no conception." She was thoroughly angry now through her misery. "Unity made trouble," she went on. "She showed you some of your own prejudices, the fear and oppression you exercise without even knowing it." Her hands clenched. "You are so convinced you are righteous sometimes I could hit you! In your heart you are all glad she's gone, because she asked questions and made you feel uncomfortable. She'd have forced you to look at yourselves, and you wouldn't like what you'd see—because you'd see hypocrites. God! I've never felt so alone!"

"I'm sorry," he said with as much sincerity as he could. He thought she was wildly wrong; she seemed to have caught Unity's passions as if they were a contagion. But her feeling was real, of that he had no doubt at all, and it was that he addressed. "I can see that you do mourn her more honestly than the rest of us. Perhaps you will be able to carry on her ideas and beliefs?"

"Me?" She looked startled, but then not entirely displeased. "I'm not fit to. I haven't any education except to sew and paint and to manage a household." Her face twisted with disgust. "Given a good housekeeper and a good cook, of course. Clarice was the one who studied . . . theology, of all the useless pursuits for a girl. I think she only did it to please Father and to show she was cleverer than Mallory."

"Didn't you learn French at school?"

"I had a French governess for a while. Yes, of course I speak French. But that's no use, for heaven's sake! Nothing ancient or theological is written in French." She still dismissed it.

"Wouldn't any branch of learning do just as well in which to succeed and make the same point about women?"

Her eyes blazed. "Is that what I am supposed to do? Are you now going to tell me Unity's death is all part of God's plan, which we are meant to accept but not to understand? Will it all be explained to me when I get to heaven?"

"No, I wasn't," he said tartly. "You don't want to hear it, and I don't think it's true anyway. I think Unity's dying was a very human plan, and nothing whatever to do with God."

"I thought God was all-powerful," she said derisively. "Which means that all this"—she flung out her arm—"is His fault."

"You mean like a puppet master, pulling everybody's strings?" he enquired.

"I suppose so . . ."

"Why?"

She frowned at him. "What?"

"Why?" he repeated. "Why would He bother? It sounds like a very pointless exercise to me, and hideously lonely."

"I don't know why!" She was exasperated with him. Her voice rose high and sharp. "You're the curate, not me. You're the one who believes in God. Ask Him! Doesn't He answer you?" She was angry, but there was a ring of triumph in her now. "Perhaps you aren't speaking loudly enough?"

"That depends on how far away God is," Clarice retorted, coming in through the door. "I could hear you halfway down the stairs."

"What are you suggesting?" Tryphena asked her sister angrily. She resented the intrusion. "That God lives halfway down the stairs?"

"Hardly," Clarice replied, her mouth twitching. "If He did, He could have stopped Unity from reaching the bottom, and she'd only have sprained her ankle instead of breaking her neck."

"Oh, for God's sake!" Tryphena shouted, and turned on her heel and stormed out of the door at the farther side of the room, slamming the door so hard the pictures on the wall shook.

"I shouldn't have said that," Clarice observed contritely. "I never know when to hold my tongue. I'm sorry."

Dominic did not know what to say. He had thought he was used to Clarice's irresponsible notion of humor, but he found he was not. Part of him wanted to laugh, as a release from grief and anxiety, but he knew it was utterly inappropriate—in fact, quite shocking. He was guilty for not disapproving more than he did.

"It was very wrong of you, Clarice," he said sharply. "Most thoughtless. Poor Tryphena is grieving for a friend, not just shocked and afraid like the rest of us."

Clarice winced, and the misery was plain in her face. She turned away from him.

"Yes, I know. I wish I could say I had liked Unity, but I didn't. I'm terrified of what will happen to Father, and it makes me say things without thinking." She took a deep breath. "No, it doesn't. I did that anyway . . . and I am thinking. That's just the way my mind is." There was defiance in her now. She turned back and looked at him very directly. "I wonder if we are all meant to wear black for dinner? I suppose I had better. But I'm not wearing it for a year," she added. "A week is good manners, a year is hypocrisy. I refuse to be a hypocrite. I'd better go and see if Braithwaite can find me something." She shrugged and turned to walk away.

Dinner was extremely difficult. Ramsay remained in his room, and whether he ate what was taken up for him or not, no one in the dining room knew. They sat around the long mahogany table in near silence. The servants brought the various courses and removed plates hardly touched. Vita tried to begin some trivial conversation, but no one assisted her.

"Cook will be insulted," Tryphena observed, watching the dishes being taken away. "She thinks eating is the answer to any problem."

"Well, not eating doesn't help, except an upset stomach," Clarice pointed out. "And other unmentionables. Being weak doesn't make you any use. Nor does staying awake all night."

"No one has stayed awake all night," Mallory said patiently. "It only happened this morning. But if we do, it will be because we are too distressed and worried to sleep. God knows what is going to happen now."

"Of course," Clarice muttered.

"Of course what?" Mallory stared at her. "What do you know? What are you talking about? Did you hear something?"

"Of course God knows," she explained with her mouth full of bread. "Isn't He supposed to know everything?"

"Please!" Vita interrupted sharply. "Let us keep our ideas of God out of the dinner table conversation. I would have thought that subject had caused sufficient trouble for us all to be more than willing to leave it alone indefinitely."

"I don't know why we bother to try to talk at all." Tryphena looked from one to the other of them. "We none of us know what to say, and we are all lost in our own thoughts anyway. We aren't going to say anything we mean."

"Because it is the civilized thing to do," Vita replied firmly.

"Something very dreadful has happened, but we are going to carry on with our lives with the courage and dignity we desire. And Tryphena, my dear, if you admire Unity as much as you seem to, you know she would be the last person to wish us to give in to our emotions. She had no time for self-indulgence."

"Unless it was her own," Clarice said under her breath. Dominic heard, but he hoped no one else had. He reached out sideways with one foot and kicked her sharply under the table.

She gasped as the toe of his shoe caught her ankle, but she knew better than to make any sound.

"Of course," Dominic said aloud, "I shall be making the usual calls on parishioners tomorrow. Are there any errands I can do for anyone?"

"Thank you," Vita accepted. "I am sure there are several things. Perhaps if you go near the haberdasher's you could get some black ribbon."

"Yes, of course. How much?"

"I think a dozen yards, thank you."

He tried to think of something else normal to say, but nothing came to mind. It all sounded stilted and callous. He was aware of Tryphena looking at him with loathing, and Mallory studiously avoiding saying anything at all. It seemed he and Vita must carry on the conversation to prevent the silence from becoming unbearable.

"I shall write the appropriate letters tomorrow," Vita went on, looking across the table at him, her eyes wide. "I shall ask Ramsay, of course, but I think as things are he may consider it more suitable for you to find out what the formalities are."

"We all know what the formalities are, Mother!" Mallory jerked his head up. "We were practically born in the church. We know church rituals—breakfast, luncheon and dinner!"

"Not with the church, Mallory," she corrected. "With Superintendent Pitt."

Mallory flushed dull red and said nothing, bending to concentrate on his food, although he ate hardly any of it.

This time the silence was beyond rescue. Vita looked across at Dominic, but with resignation.

When he could decently escape, and knowing he could put it off no longer, Dominic left the dining room and went up to Ramsay's study. If he hesitated he would lose his nerve. Surely if he had the calling he imagined, no situation should be beyond his ability to face it with honesty and a degree of kindness.

He knocked.

The answer was immediate. "Come in."

Now he was committed. He opened the door.

Ramsay was sitting at his desk. He seemed almost relieved to recognize Dominic. Perhaps he had feared an encounter with one of his own family more.

"Come in, Dominic." He waved towards one of the other chairs and marked the book he was reading with a loose piece of paper, then closed it. "It's been a truly terrible day. How are you?"

Dominic sat down. It was difficult to begin. Ramsay was behaving as if there had been a simple domestic accident and Tryphena's accusations were no more than the product of grief.

"I admit, I feel very distressed," Dominic said frankly.

"Of course you do," Ramsay agreed, frowning and fiddling with a pencil that lay between his hands on the desk. "Death is always a shock, especially of one so young and whom we all are accustomed to seeing daily. She was a very trying person, at times, but no one would have wished this upon her. I grieve that it happened so soon after I had quarreled with her." He met Dominic's gaze quite steadily. "It leaves me with a feeling of guilt because one cannot repair it. Foolish, I know." His lips tightened. "My reason tells me not to feel such things, but the sadness remains." He sighed. "I am afraid Tryphena is going to take it very badly. She had a great fondness for her. I did not approve of it, but there was nothing I could do." He looked tired, as if he had been struggling for a long time and saw no end in sight, certainly no victory.

"Yes, she is." Dominic nodded. "And she is very angry."

"A common part of grief. It will pass." Ramsay spoke with certainty, but of a flat, comfortless kind. There was no lift of hope in it for better times.

"I'm so sorry," Dominic said impulsively. "I wish I could say something that would make sense of it, but all I can do is repeat what you said to me in my worst despair." It still touched him deeply. "Take each day at a time, cling onto the faith of your own worth and build on it, no matter how slowly or how little each step. You cannot go backward. Have the courage to go forward well. At the end of each day, praise yourself for that, and then let go . . . rest, and hope. Never let go of hope."

Ramsay smiled bleakly, but his eyes were gentle. "Did I say that to you?"

"Yes . . . and I believed you, and it saved me." Dominic remembered it only too vividly. It had been four years before. In some ways it was as sharp as yesterday, in others a world away, another life where he had changed from being one man to being another, totally different, with new dreams and new thoughts. He longed to be able to help Ramsay as Ramsay had helped him, to give back the gift now that it was so badly needed. He searched Ramsay's face and saw no answering spark.

"I had a different sort of faith then," Ramsay said, looking beyond Dominic as if he were talking to himself. "I have done a great deal of studying in the years since it became so spoken about I could no longer avoid it." He shook his head a little. "At first, thirty years ago, when it was published, it was just the scientific theory of one man. Then gradually one began to realize how many other people accepted it. Now science seems to be everywhere, the origin and the answers to everything. There is no mystery left, only facts we don't yet know. Above all, there is no one left to hope in beyond ourselves, nothing greater, wiser, or above all kinder." He looked for an instant like a lost child who suddenly knows the full meaning of being alone.

Dominic felt it like a physical pain.

"I can admire the certainty all these old bishops and saints seem to have had," Ramsay went on. "I can't share it anymore, Dominic." He sat oddly still for the emotions which must have been raging inside him. "The hurricane of Mr. Darwin's sanity has blown it away like so much paper. His reasoning haunts my mind. During the day I look at all these books." He waved his arm at them. "I read Saint Paul, Saint Augustine, Saint Thomas Aquinas, and every theologian and apologist since. I can even go back to the original Aramaic or Greek, and for a little while I am fine. Then at night the cold voice of Charles Darwin comes back, and the darkness engulfs all the candles I've lit during the day. I swear I would give anything I possess for him not to have been born!"

"If he hadn't said these things, someone else would have," Dominic pointed out as gently as he could. "It was a theory ripe for its time. And there is a thread of truth in it. Any farmer or gardener would tell you that. Old species die out, new ones are created, by accident, or purpose. That does not mean there is no God . . . only that He uses means that can be explained by science . . . at least in part. Why should God be unreasonable?"

Ramsay leaned back in his chair and closed his eyes. "I can see that you are trying very hard, Dominic, and I am grateful to you for it. But if the Bible is not true, we have no foundation, only dreams, wishes, stories that are beautiful, but eventually just fairy stories. We must go on preaching them, because the majority of people believe them—and more importantly than that, they need them." He opened his eyes again. "But it is a hollow comfort, Dominic, and I find no joy in it. Maybe that is why I hated Unity Bellwood, because at least in that she was right, even if she was wrong in everything else, and utterly, devastatingly wrong in her morality."

Dominic felt as if he had swallowed ice. There was a bitterness in

Ramsay he had never seen unmasked before, a depth of confusion which was more than mere tiredness or the shock of death and accusation, a fear far older and more familiar than anything this day had brought. It was the loss of inner belief, the core of hope that lies deeper than reason. For the first time he was touched by the possibility that Ramsay really could have killed Unity. It no longer seemed beyond the realm of the thinkable that she had assaulted his faith one time too many, and his loss had escaped his control and he had lashed out, she had slipped, overbalanced, and the next moment she had pitched down the stairs to lie dead at the bottom. It was a hideous mischance. They could have quarreled a hundred times and even physically struck each other without any serious injury done. Perhaps in the innocence of his intent Ramsay had not realized that it was at the very least a manslaughter—and the end of his career.

But it was still a far cry from murder.

How could Dominic begin to help? What could he say to reach Ramsay's despair?

"You taught me that faith is a thing of the spirit, of trust, not knowledge," he began.

"It was what I believed at the time," Ramsay retorted with a dry laugh. He looked very directly at Dominic. "Now I am terrified, and all the faith on earth is not going to help. That wretched policeman seems to think that Unity was pushed, and that is murder." He leaned forward earnestly. "I did not push her, Dominic. I never left the room until after she was dead. I cannot imagine any of the servants did . . ."

"They didn't," Dominic agreed. "They were all accounted for and in sight of someone else, or performing duties they could prove."

Ramsay stared at him. "Then it could only be one of my family . . . or you. And both thoughts are dreadful. Faith may be gone, a dream from which I have awoken, but kindness is real, help to another person in their distress will always be precious and good and lasting. You are my one real success, Dominic. When I think I have failed, I remember you, and I know I have not."

Dominic was hideously uncomfortable. He had wanted to speak honestly to Ramsay, to brush aside the usual politeness and trivialities with which real emotion was hidden, and now that it had happened he did not know how to face it. Such naked hunger for comfort embarrassed him; it was personal, a debt between them. Ramsay had given his hand and pulled Dominic out of the morass of his despair, a morass of his own making. Now Ramsay needed the same help, needed to know he had succeeded, that Dominic was what he wished him to be. And he was afraid Dominic had killed Unity Bellwood.

And he would know why!

"And Mallory is my son," Ramsay went on. "How can I bear to believe it was he?"

Should Dominic remind him it was his name, or to be exact his title, that she cried out . . . not "Dominic," not "Mallory." The words came to his lips, and then he could not say them. It was futile. He had not killed her. If Ramsay had not, it left only Mallory . . . or the impossible . . . Clarice! No one else could have.

"There must be something they have not thought of," he said miserably. "If . . . if there is anything I can do to help, please allow me to. Any duties . . ."

"Thank you," Ramsay said quickly. "I think perhaps in the circumstances it is right for you to make the funeral arrangements. You might begin that tomorrow. I imagine it will be very quiet. She had no family, I understand."

"No . . . no, I believe not . . ." It was ridiculous. They were sitting in a quiet study with its books and papers and the fire flickering in the hearth, making civilized remarks about the details for the funeral of a woman they each believed the other might have killed.

Except that Dominic found himself believing more and more wretchedly that Ramsay simply refused to recognize what had happened. He was still in a state of shock, with death, with the physical reality of it, and with the spiritual reality of what he had done.

Tomorrow it might be very different. He might wake to the knowledge and the fear of all the terrible consequences which would follow.

Dominic knew the suspicion, the close, crushing terrors which would haunt the house until the truth was known. He had seen it all before, lived through it, the relationships that crumble, the old wounds recalled, the ugly thoughts that would not be dismissed, the trust eaten away day by day.

It was hard to remember that there had also been new friendships gained, honor and kindness where he had not looked to find it. At the moment there was only the breaking apart.

Ramsay was giving instructions for the conduct of the funeral, and Dominic had not heard a word of it.

CHAPTER THREE

Charlotte Pitt was relaxing in the parlor with her feet up on the sewing stool, the fire pleasantly warm and a most enthralling novel in her hands, when she heard the front door open and close. She put down the book with something close to reluctance, even though she was pleased to hear Pitt return. She had been right in the middle of a dramatic scene between two lovers.

Jemima raced downstairs in her nightgown calling out "Papa! Papa!"

Charlotte smiled and went to the door. Daniel, retaining his masculine dignity, was coming down slowly, grinning.

"You are early," Charlotte observed as Pitt kissed her, then turned his attention temporarily to the children. Jemima was telling him excitedly about a lesson she had learned on Queen Elizabeth and the Spanish Armada. Daniel, at the same time, was trying to explain about steam engines and a wonderful train he wanted to see, and better still, to ride on. He had even learned the fare, and his face was bright with hope.

It was nearly an hour before Pitt was alone with Charlotte and could tell her the extraordinary news of the events in Brunswick Gardens.

"Do you really think the Reverend Parmenter lost his temper completely and pushed her down the stairs?" she asked with surprise. "Can it be proved?"

"I don't know." He stretched out further, balancing his feet on the fender. It was his favorite position. His slippers were scorched every winter. She was always buying new ones.

"Could she have fallen?" she asked. "People do fall downstairs . . . sometimes."

"They don't shout out 'No, no!' and someone's name if they slip," he pointed out. "And there was nothing there to trip over. The stairs are black wood, no carpet or stair rods to be loose."

"One could trip over a skirt, if the hem were down . . ." she said thoughtfully. "Was it?"

"No. I looked at that. It was perfect."

"Or even one's own feet," she went on. "Were the shoes all right? Nothing loose or broken, no wobbly heels or loose laces? I've tripped over my own feet before now."

"No wobbly heels or laces at all," he said with a slight smile. "Only a dark stain, which Tellman says comes from something spilled in the conservatory, and that means Mallory Parmenter lied about having seen her this morning."

"Perhaps he was out of the conservatory for some reason for those few moments?" she suggested. "She went in, but she missed seeing him."

"No, he wasn't, or he would have trodden in the same thing when he went out," he reasoned. "And he hadn't. Tellman checked for that, too."

"Does that mean anything?" she asked.

"Probably not, except that he was frightened and told a stupid lie. He didn't know she called out."

"Could she have called out 'No, no,' to one person and called the Reverend to help her?" she said quickly. "I mean 'No, no!' and then his name to call him to come to her?"

He sat up a little, his attention sharpening. "Possibly . . . just possibly. I shall at least hold it in mind. He admits quarreling with her very badly, but he swears he did not leave the study."

"Why would Mallory want to kill her? The same reason?"

"No . . . he's very dedicated to his calling, at least he appears so, but he has no doubts." He stared into the fire, watching as the coals settled. He would have to put more on in a few minutes. "It seems from the little I know so far as if Parmenter was very troubled in his faith, and it was Unity Bellwood's intellectual challenge to religion which angered him. Mallory seems to have no such conflict."

"Well, who else is there?"

He pursed his lips and stared back at her; she could not read the expression in his eyes. They were bright and gray, and very clear.

"Who is there?" she repeated, a shiver of apprehension running through her.

"One of the daughters who disliked Unity, but not a great deal, so far as I know . . . and the curate."

She dismissed the daughter. She knew him well enough to be certain it was the curate who was on his mind.

"Go on!"

He hesitated for a moment, as if unsure how to tell her. He drew in his breath and let it out slowly. "The curate is Dominic Corde . . ."

For just an instant, gone again before it was there, she thought he was making a bad joke, then she knew he was serious. There was a furrow between his brows that was only there when something troubled him and he did not understand it.

"Dominic! Our Dominic?" she said.

"I had never thought of him as 'ours,' but I suppose you could say so," he agreed. "He has taken the cloth . . . can you imagine it?"

"Dominic has?" It did not seem possible. With a wave of memory so sharp it was as if it had carried her physically back ten years, she recalled being in her parents' home in Cater Street, her mother's exasperation because she would not behave appropriately and encourage suitable young men. She could not imagine loving anyone but Dominic then. She had cared for Sarah, of course, but been painfully jealous of her as well. Then Sarah had been killed, and the whole world had been thrown into turmoil. Dominic had shown his weaknesses. In the space of a week he had fallen from an idol of gold to one of clay. Disillusion had been bitter indeed, mixed as it was with grief and fear.

In the end she had learned to love Pitt, not as a dream or an ideal but as a real man, human, exasperating at times, fallible, challenging, but with a courage and honesty Dominic had never had. And for Dominic she had learned a friendship rooted in tolerance and a certain kindness. But Dominic giving his life to religion! That was beyond her power to imagine.

"Dominic is a curate in Reverend Parmenter's house?" Her voice rose, her disbelief still sharp.

"Yes," he replied, watching her carefully, searching her face. "Dominic is the other person who could conceivably have killed Unity Bellwood."

"He couldn't!" she said instantly.

A shadow crossed his eyes. "Probably not," he agreed. "But someone did."

She sat silently, trying to think of another explanation, something that would make sense of the little she knew, that would not sound silly and defensive when she said it, but nothing came. Pitt leaned forward and put more coal on the fire. Eventually, after twenty minutes with no sound but the ticking of the clock, the flames and settling of coal in the fire, and the wind splattering rain in gusts onto the window, she spoke about something else. Her sister Emily was on the Grand Tour, and her letters from Italy were full of anecdotes and descriptions. She told him about the latest, written from Naples and including vivid descriptions of the bay, of Vesuvius, and of her trip to Herculaneum.

At eleven o'clock the following morning, when courteous enquiry had assured her that Pitt would be busy pursuing the medical evidence and reporting to Cornwallis, Charlotte alighted from a hansom in Brunswick Gardens and pulled the bell at number seventeen. She could not help but notice the drawn blinds and the discreet crepe on the door, and that they had gone so far as to put straw on the roadway to muffle the horses' hooves, even though Unity had not been a member of the family.

When a somber butler answered she smiled at him.

"Good morning, ma'am. May I be of any assistance?" he enquired.

"Good morning." She produced her card and offered it to him. "I am sorry to trouble you at such an unfortunate time, but I believe there is a Mr. Dominic Corde staying here? He is my brother-in-law. I have not seen him for some years, but I should like to offer him my congratulations on his recent ordination." She did not mention Unity's death specifically. Possibly it had not been in the newspapers, and even if it had, a household such as this might disapprove strongly of ladies who read of such things. Ignorance was a far better approach.

"Certainly, ma'am. If you care to come in I shall see if Mr. Corde is at home." He led her through the vestibule and across a most extraordinary hallway she would have liked to look at more carefully. He left her in a morning room only slightly less exotic. He took her rain-spotted hat and cloak and departed, presumably to ask the curate if indeed he had a sister-in-law, and if so did he wish to see her.

It was less than ten minutes before the door opened and she swung around to see Dominic, older, definitely touched with a little gray, and handsomer than she had remembered. Maturity suited him; whatever pain he had experienced had refined the callowness from him. The old arrogance had been replaced by something wiser. And yet it still seemed absurd to see a clergyman's high, white collar around his neck.

Suddenly her voice dried in her throat.

"Charlotte!" He came forward with a rueful smile. "I suppose Thomas told you about the tragedy here?"

"Actually, I came to congratulate you on your calling and your ordination," she said with slightly stiff politeness, and not a great deal of truth.

His smile widened, and now there was humor in it. "You were never a good liar."

"Yes, I was!" she said instantly. "Well . . . not bad."

"You were terrible!" He looked her up and down. "There is no need to ask how you are, you are obviously very well indeed. How is Emily . . . and your mother?"

"In excellent health, thank you. Mama has married again." This was perhaps not the moment to mention that it was to a man seventeen years her junior, an actor, and a Jew.

"I am glad, it sounds wonderful." He was obviously envisioning someone older than Caroline, probably a widower, solid and respectable—in fact, as unlike Joshua Fielding as possible.

Charlotte's resolve vanished. "He's an actor." She blushed. "He's a great deal younger than Mama, and extremely attractive." She was very satisfied with the amazement on his face.

"What?"

"Joshua Fielding," she elaborated, watching him with pleasure. "He's one of the best actors on the London stage at the moment."

He relaxed, his shoulders easing, the familiar smile curving his lips. "For a moment I believed you."

"So you should," she approved. "It is the precise truth, except that I omitted that Grandmama has never forgiven her, because he is Jewish and because she will not live under the same roof with them. She made such a fuss refusing to, that when Mama ignored her she had no choice but to leave. She lives with Emily and Jack now, and she doesn't like it much because she has hardly anything to complain about, other than that she has no one to talk to. Actually, Emily and Jack are on holiday in Italy at the moment."

"Jack?" he asked, looking at her with curiosity in his eyes, and something that for an instant was close to amusement.

"After George's death, Emily married again, too. He is a member of Parliament," she explained. "He wasn't when she married him, but he is now."

"Is it really so long since we last met?" His voice rose in surprise, but there was pleasure in his face and a happiness to see her. "You make it sound as if it were decades. Are you still the same?"

"Oh, definitely. But you are not!" She looked pointedly at the white collar.

He touched it a trifle self-consciously. "No. No, a lot has happened to me since then." He did not elaborate, and for a minute there was a sudden uncomfortable silence, before the door opened and a most striking woman came in. She had very large, wide-set eyes and unusual features combining humor and strength. She was quite small in build, and extremely elegant. She wore dark colors, very plain, as if intending to create a sober effect, and yet the bodice was so beautifully cut it was anything but sober. Far from appearing like mourning, the gown enhanced the clarity of her skin and accentuated the grace of her figure.

Dominic turned as he heard her.

"Mrs. Parmenter, may I present my sister-in-law, Mrs. Pitt. Charlotte, Mrs. Parmenter."

"How do you do, Mrs. Pitt," Vita said politely, her eyes going quickly to Charlotte's dark brown skirt, assessing neither her income nor her social rank, as other women might, but her skin, her eyes and lips, her very handsome shoulders and bosom. Her smile was cool.

"How do you do, Mrs. Parmenter," Charlotte replied with a smile, as if she had not noticed. "I came to congratulate Dominic on his vocation. It is most excellent news. I know my mother and sister will be happy for him, too."

"You must have lost touch for some time," Vita observed, not quite critically but with a very slight arch of her perfect eyebrows.

"I am afraid we had. I am delighted for the opportunity to meet again, although I offer my sympathies on the news which has made it possible. I am deeply sorry."

"I am amazed you know of it already," Vita said with surprise. The very slightest smile curved her generous mouth. "You must read the very earliest editions of the newspapers."

Charlotte put on an air of surprise. "Is it in the newspapers already? I did not know that. But then I have not seen them." She left the suggestion unspoken that she did not do such things.

Vita was temporarily thrown off balance. "Then how did you know of our tragedy? It is hardly common discussion."

"Superintendent Pitt told me because of the family connection. He is my husband."

"Oh!" For a moment it seemed as if Vita were going to laugh. Her voice strayed dangerously near hysteria. "Oh . . . I see. That explains everything." She did not expand on what she meant by that, but a curious expression filled her eyes and then was gone. "It was kind of you to call," she added quietly. "I imagine you have much to learn since the last time you met. We are naturally not entertaining at present, but if you would care to take luncheon with us, you would be most welcome."

Dominic shot her a glance of appreciation, and she smiled in answer.

"Thank you," Charlotte accepted before she might change her mind.

Vita nodded to her, then turned to Dominic. "You will not forget to collect the black ribbon for us this afternoon, will you?" She touched his arm briefly with her fingers.

"No, of course not," he said quickly, meeting her eyes.

"Thank you," she murmured. "Now, if you will excuse me."

When she had gone Dominic gestured to Charlotte to sit down, and he sat opposite her.

"Poor Vita," he said with feeling, his face reflecting both his sympathy and the warmth of his admiration. "This is terrible for her. But I expect you know that as well as I do." He bit his lip, his eyes full of regret. "We have both experienced the same horror and the fear that grows worse every day. The thing about this is that we all know it must have been someone in the house, and it seems to have been Reverend Parmenter himself. I expect Thomas told you?"

"A little," she conceded. She wanted to offer some kind of comfort, but they both knew there was none. She also wanted to warn him, but again, they had both already lived through all the dangers, the obvious ones of saying and doing something ill-judged, of telling less than the truth to cover the small acts of stupidity or meanness which one would so much rather others did not know of. And there were always some. And the less-obvious traps, the desire to be honest and to tell something one believed to be true, to find when it was too late that one had known only half the truth, and the rest of it altered everything. It was too easy to judge and too hard to teach oneself to forget. One saw far more than one wished to see of the weaknesses and the vulnerabilities of other people's lives.

She leaned a little forward. "Dominic, be terribly careful," she said impulsively. "Don't do—" She stopped, smiling at herself. "I was going to say 'Don't do anything quickly,' but that's nonsense. Then I was going to say 'Don't try to solve it yourself,' and 'Don't try to rescue anyone.' I think I had better not say anything at all. Just do what you think right."

He smiled back at her, for the first time since she had seen him again allowing himself to relax.

But luncheon was agonizingly tense. The food was excellent. Course after course was served, beginning with soup, followed by perfectly cooked fish, then meat and vegetables, and no one did justice to any of it. Ramsay Parmenter had decided to eat with his family and their guest. He presided at the table, offering a stiffly worded grace before they began. Charlotte could not help thinking he sounded as if he were addressing a public meeting of town councillors, not a loving God who must know him infinitely better even than he knew himself.

Everyone echoed the "Amen" and began to eat.

"Had we better get some thick veiling as well as ribbons?" Clarice asked with her soup spoon halfway to her mouth. "I am sure Dominic wouldn't mind fetching it from the haberdasher, would you?" She looked across at him.

"Not at all," he agreed quickly.

"Don't bother for me," Tryphena said grimly. "I shall not be going anywhere that requires a hat."

"You'll require a hat for the garden if it rains," Clarice pointed out. "And knowing England in spring, that is even more certain than death or taxes."

"You are not dead, and you have no money, so you don't pay taxes!" Tryphena snapped.

"Precisely," Clarice agreed. "And I am rained on regularly." She looked at Dominic. "Do you know what to get?"

"No. But I thought I would ask Mrs. Pitt to come with me, and I am sure she will know."

"Please don't trouble yourself." Vita looked across at Charlotte with a smile. "We did not mean to impose upon you like that."

Charlotte smiled back at her. "It would be a pleasure to help. And I should be delighted to have the opportunity to talk to Dominic and hear his news."

"It is not very far to the haberdasher," Tryphena said dryly, bending to her soup again. The light shone on her fair hair, making a halo of it. "Half an hour at the most."

"Dominic is going to make the arrangements for Unity's funeral," Vita explained. "In the circumstances it seems more appropriate." Her face pinched a little, but she did not add anything further.

"Funeral!" Tryphena jerked her head up. "I suppose you mean something in church, something pompous and self-important, with everyone wearing mourning to make a parade of the grief they don't feel. That's what you want the black for. You are all hypocrites! If you couldn't care about her and appreciate her when she was alive, what good is it to sit in solemn rows like crows on a fence pretending you do now?"

"That will do, Tryphena!" Vita said sternly. "We already know your feelings and we do not require to hear them again, certainly not at the table."

Tryphena looked from her mother to Ramsay at the head. "Do you imagine your God believes you?" she demanded, her voice hard-edged and brittle. "He must be a fool if He's taken in by your poses. I'm not! Nor is anyone who knows you." She swiveled to face Mallory. "Why do you all treat your God as if He's an idiot? You use stilted language and go on explaining yourselves over and over, as if He didn't understand you the first time. You speak to Him the same way you speak to old ladies who are deaf and a bit senile."

Clarice bit her lip and covered her mouth with her napkin. She made sounds as if she had something stuck in her throat.

"Tryphena, either hold your tongue or leave the table!" Vita said sharply. She did not even glance at Ramsay; presumably she had given up hope that he would step in to defend himself or his beliefs.

"So do you," Clarice said challengingly, lowering her napkin again.

"I don't talk to God at all!" Tryphena swung back to stare at her sister angrily. "It's ridiculous. It would be like talking to Alice in Wonderland or the Cheshire cat."

"You might get a better audience from the March Hare or the Mad Hatter," Clarice suggested. "They would be mad enough to listen to you repeat yourself over and over on social finances, free love, artistic liberty and general license for everyone to do as they please and hope someone else will pick up the bits."

"Clarice!" Vita said sharply, her eyes hard, her body stiff. "You are not helping! If you cannot say something appropriate to the occasion, please say nothing at all."

"Clarice never says anything appropriate on any occasion," Tryphena said with a sneer, bitter and full of hurt.

Charlotte knew what Tryphena was doing. For some reason Unity Bellwood's death had wounded her more than she could contain, and her anger was against everyone else who did not share her loneliness and loss, or whose fear she could not see. Charlotte looked up at

Ramsay Parmenter, sitting at the head of the table, nominally presiding, but in effect doing nothing.

She turned to Vita and saw a shadow of an old tiredness cross her features, and she wondered how many times before Vita had had to make the decisions, mark where the boundaries of behavior should be, when she had expected it of him. Perhaps that was the ultimate loneliness, not the bereavement of death but the isolation of failure to share in life, to find yourself linked to the shell of your dreams when the substance has gone.

"Well, fortunately the church will pick up our shortcomings and say all the appropriate things." Mallory passed his soup plate to the maid who was collecting the dishes. "At least as far as it goes."

"It goes far enough," Dominic responded for the first time. "The rest is up to God."

Mallory turned to him sharply. "Who gave us the sacraments of Confession and Absolution for our salvation, and Extreme Unction to fit us to accept His grace and be saved in the end, in spite of our frailties and sins." His long, slender fingers were lying on the white linen of the tablecloth, stiff and held still with an effort.

"That's totally immoral!" Tryphena said with disgust. "You are saying that in the end all it comes down to is magic. Say the right words and the spell will remove guilt. That is really and truly wicked!" She stared around at them each in turn. "How can any of you believe that? It's monstrous! This is an age of reason and science. Even the Renaissance had more enlightenment than this . . ."

"Not the Inquisition," Clarice pointed out, her dark brows lifted. "They burned anyone whose belief differed from theirs."

"Not anyone," Ramsay corrected pedantically. "Only those who had been baptized Christian and then reverted to heresy."

"What difference does that make?" Tryphena's voice rose in disbelief. "Are you saying that makes it all right?"

"I am correcting a misstatement," he replied. "All we can do is the best we know, according to our faith and our understanding, and leave the rest. We shall have a funeral for Unity and observe the formalities of the Church of England. God will know that we have done what we believe right for her and will accord her His due mercy and forgiveness."

"Forgiveness!" Now Tryphena's voice was an octave higher and shrill with emotion. "It isn't Unity who needs forgiving. It's whoever killed her! How can you sit there and talk about forgiving as if she were the one in the wrong? It's preposterous!" She pushed her chair back roughly, almost upsetting it, and stood up. "I can't stay and listen to this. It's a madhouse." She swept out of the room without looking back, leaving the door swinging on its hinges and only just missing the footman coming in with the next course.

"I'm sorry," Vita murmured, looking apologetically at Charlotte. "I am afraid she is very upset indeed. She and Unity were very close. I do hope you will excuse her."

"Of course." Charlotte made the only reply possible. She had endured enough family life to have sat through many such scenes. She blushed slightly now to remember a few she had created herself, more than one centered on her infatuation with Dominic. "I have suffered bereavement, and I know how very shaken you can be."

Vita flashed her a bright, shallow smile. "Thank you. You are very generous."

Clarice was looking at Charlotte curiously, but she did not say anything. The rest of the meal was finished with Dominic and Vita making polite remarks and Charlotte joining in in order to keep some semblance of courtesy. Ramsay agreed as was appropriate, and politely asked Charlotte's opinion once or twice. Mallory made no attempt to join in, and Clarice kept a modest and uncharacteristic silence.

In the afternoon Charlotte accompanied Dominic as he had invited her to. They rode in the second-best carriage. It was open, but the weather was dry and breezy, and with a rug over her knees, she was very comfortable. Dominic sat beside her after first giving the coachman his instructions.

"It was very nice of you to come," Dominic began ruefully as they set off. "I wish we had not had to meet again in these circumstances. Luncheon was dreadful. We are all so raw, it seems the slightest touch and we lose control."

"I know," she said softly. "I do remember . . ."

"Yes, of course you do." He smiled quickly. "I'm sorry."

"So much has happened since we last met . . ."

"You don't look very different." He swiveled to face her as he said so, regarding her carefully. "Your hair is just the same." There was admiration in his eyes, and she felt a warmth of pleasure which embarrassed her, but she would not have forfeited it.

"Thank you," she accepted. She smiled in spite of herself. "A good few years have gone by, and I would like to think I have become a little wiser. I have two children—"

"Two?" He was surprised. "I remember Jemima."

"I have a son as well, two years younger. His name is Daniel. He's six and a half." She could not entirely keep the pride or the tenderness out of her voice. "But you look different—very. What happened? How did you meet Ramsay Parmenter?"

The humor was reflected in his eyes, but there was hurt in there as well.

"Detecting again?" he asked.

"No." This was not entirely truthful. "Detecting" had become a habit with her, but this time she was thinking primarily about Dominic and how this tragedy would affect him. Also, she could not rid herself of the image of Ramsay Parmenter's face as he sat at the head of his dining room table seemingly adrift in a confusion which all but drowned him. "No," she said again. "You have changed so much, extraordinary things must have happened to you. And I can see that you are very concerned for him, not simply because of how it will affect his family but for his own inner distress. You don't believe he pushed her intentionally, do you." It was a statement, not really a question.

He hesitated a long time before he answered, and when he did it was slowly; he was frowning, and looking not at her but straight ahead of him at the blur of the street and the other traffic.

"It is completely unlike the man I know," he said. "When I first met Ramsay I was at the lowest point I have ever been in my life. Every day seemed a gray desert with nothing beyond the horizon but more of the same pointless struggle." He was nervously chewing his lower lip as if even the memory of that time still disturbed him, the knowledge that it was possible to feel such an utter inability even to hope. It was an abyss whose existence was a fear in itself. The darkness of it was naked in his eyes.

She wanted to ask why, but it would be intrusive, and she had no right to know. She wondered if it had anything to do with Sarah's death, even though it must have been several years after. She wanted to touch him, but that also would be too personal. It was too long since they had known each other so well, and one could not bridge that gap in an instant.

"I despised myself," he went on, still not looking at her, and speaking only loudly enough for her to hear, but not the coachman in front of them.

"For feeling despair?" she said softly. "You shouldn't. It is not a sin. Oh, I know religious teaching says it is, but sometimes one cannot help it. Perhaps self-pity is, but not genuine despair."

"No," he said with a dry laugh. "I didn't despise myself for my misery; I was miserable because I despised myself. And I had cause." His hands tightened in his lap. She could see the leather of his gloves shining as it stretched over his knuckles. "I have no intention of telling you how worthless I had become, because I don't wish you to think of me like that, even in the past. But I had sunk into being completely selfish, thinking of no one else, living for the moment and my immediate appetite."

He shook his head fractionally. "That is no life for any creature with the intelligence to think. It is less than human, a waste of life, a denial of the mind, the spirit, the soul, if you like. It is killing by neglect all that makes anyone worth valuing or loving. There is no kindness, no courage, no honor or grace or dignity in it." He glanced at her, then away again. "I despised myself for being almost nothing of what I could have been. I was wasting all my possibilities. You can't truly condemn anyone who had no chances, but you can those who had them and threw them away out of cowardice, laziness or dishonesty."

Excuses came to her mind, but she saw in his face that he would not have found them a kindness, only a failure to comprehend, so she remained silent. They were coming into a street with shops on either side, and they would shortly reach the haberdasher.

"And Ramsay Parmenter helped you?" she prompted.

He straightened his shoulders again, a slight smile touching his lips as if the memory were sweet. "Yes. He had the charity and the strength of faith to see far more in me than I saw in myself." He gave a jerky laugh. "He had the patience to persevere with me, to put up with my mistakes and my self-pity, my endless doubts and fears, and continually help me to the point where I believed in myself as strongly as he did. I can't tell you how many hours and days and weeks that took, but he never gave up."

"You didn't take the cloth to please him, did you?" she asked, then wished the moment after that she had not. It was insulting, and she had not meant to do that. "I'm sorry . . ."

He turned to look at her, and he was smiling fully now. The years had suited him very well. His face was less beautiful in an obvious way, but the lines in it made it subtler, more refined. There was nothing bland or unfinished in him anymore. It was a greater beauty because it had meaning.

"You haven't changed, have you." He shook his head. "Still the same Charlotte, saying what you think the minute you think it."

"I have changed!" she defended herself instantly. "I do it far less often. I can really be both tactful and devious, if it is called for. And I can say nothing and listen very well."

"And not voice your own opinion when you feel passionately about stupidity or injustice or hypocrisy?" he asked with his eyebrows arched. "Or laugh at all the wrong times? Please don't say so. I don't want the world I know to have changed all that much simply because I have taken to the ministry. Some things should stay the same . . . always."

"You are making fun of me, and we are at the haberdasher's," she said cheerfully, a little bubble of warmth inside her. "Would you like me to go in and purchase the ribbon and the veiling?"

"I should be greatly obliged." He pulled several shillings from his pocket and held them out to her. "Thank you."

She returned nearly fifteen minutes later, the footman handed her up, and she gave Dominic the package and the change. The carriage moved forward.

"No," he answered the original question. "I did not join the ministry to please Ramsay. It would have been unworthy of him, or of me, and it certainly would have been of little use to the parishioners I would one day serve."

"I know," she said contritely. "I'm sorry I asked. I was afraid for you because it would be such an easy thing to do. We all feel gratitude an intense weight and want to repay. It is natural, and what better honor than to try to be like him? Haven't we all done right things for wrong reasons at one time or another?"

"Oh, yes!" he agreed. "And wrong things for what we thought were right reasons. But I joined the ministry because I believe in all it teaches, and it is what I want to do with my life. Not out of gratitude to anyone, or as a refuge from the past or from failure, but because I love it. I have faith in its meaning and its purpose." His voice was strong when he said it; there was no hesitation.

"Good," she said quietly. "You had no need to tell me, but I am very glad you did. I am happy for you . . ."

"If you care for me in the slightest, then you should be—" He stopped and blushed hotly. "I . . . I didn't mean . . ."

She laughed outright, even though her own cheeks were a little hot. "I know you didn't! And, yes, of course I care for you. I have long considered you a friend as well as a brother-in-law. I am truly pleased you have found yourself."

He sighed. "Don't be too satisfied. I don't seem to be any help whatever to poor Ramsay. What use is my faith if I can't help another person, the one who gave me so much of what I have?" The frown was back between his brows. "Why am I so empty when it comes to offering him back some of all that he gave me? Why can't I think of the right words? He did it for me!"

"Maybe there are no right words," she replied, searching to say what she meant and yet not distress him, or lose in him the strength or the pity she admired.

The carriage came to a stop as they reached the crossroads. An open landau passed in front of them, a group of fashionable young ladies giggling and pretending not to stare at Dominic. They failed miserably. One of them was twisted around in her seat as they passed. Dominic himself seemed unaware of the stir he had caused. Last time she saw him he would not have been.

"Then there is a right time and a right gesture," he argued urgently. "There is something I could do! He never gave up with me, and believe me, it would have been extremely easy. I was obstinate, argumentative, angry with myself and with him for wanting me to succeed and for believing that I could. It was such hard work! I resented him for making me do it, for making me believe there was a purpose in trying."

"Did you want to be helped?" she asked.

He looked at her. "Are you saying Ramsay does not want to be?"

"I don't know. Do you?"

His eyes widened, very dark.

"You are asking as if I think he murdered Unity."

That was true. "Do you?" she pressed. "Why would he? Was she really so dangerous to his peace of mind? How can one doubter shake a true faith?" She searched his face. "Or is that not what it is about? Was she beautiful in any way, not necessarily conventionally?"

"She was ..." A shadow crossed his eyes. Something in him ceased to be as open as it had, and she felt it immediately, a withdrawing from the intimacy of the moment before. "She was very full of ... vitality, life ..." He was seeking the right words. "It's hard to think of her being dead." He sounded surprised as he said it. "I suppose I don't fully believe it yet. It will take a while ... weeks, perhaps. Part of me expects her to come back tomorrow and give her opinion on all this, tell us what it means and what we should be doing." He smiled fleetingly; there was humor in it, and a touch of bitterness. "She always had opinions."

"And always gave them?" she asked.

"Oh yes!"

She looked at him steadily, trying to read his expression from his profile as he stared down at the leatherwork and the railing at the front of the carriage. She did not know whether he had liked Unity Bellwood or not. One moment there seemed a smoothness in his face, almost a relief she was gone, as though her death had taken some weight from him; then it changed to the sadness, the oppression one would have expected at the closeness of violent death. Once she caught a self-mockery about his mouth, but there was no explanation for it in his words.

"Did you work with her, too?" she asked, meaning had he liked her, but afraid to ask so directly. She had no right to probe his feelings. Their friendship was tenuous, more a thing of length of time than a depth of understanding or trust. They had many shared experiences, grief and terror which they both felt. Looking back on it now, it seemed the same, but at the time they had been very different, very separate, aware then only of aloneness.

"No," he answered, still with his eyes forward, as if he were concerned where they were going. "It was Ramsay's personal scholarship she was involved in. I had nothing to do with that. I expect I shall be posted to a church somewhere else quite soon. As it is for Mallory, my situation here is only temporary."

She had a feeling he was leaving unsaid something far more important than the factual details he spoke about.

"But you must still have seen her at table and in the evenings, times when they did not work," she pointed out. "You must know something of her and of what he felt for her. . . ." She was pressing him, but she was too anxious not to.

"Yes, of course," he agreed, pulling the rug across her where it had slipped away. "As well as one knows anybody whom one . . . with whom one shares no common perception or belief. It all seems such a waste. We shall have to try to make sense of it for the others. I suppose that is my job . . . to make sense of pain and confusion, and people doing things which seem ugly beyond all possible explanation. Are you warm enough?"

"Yes, thank you." Her comfort did not matter in the slightest; she was hardly aware of it.

"It takes a great deal of courage," she said sincerely. For the first time since he had come to Cater Street courting Sarah, over fourteen years ago, she felt an admiration for him which was based on the man he was, not the beauty of his face. This time there was no mirage, no preoccupation with her own dreams or her needs for him to fulfill. She found herself smiling. "If I can help, please allow me."

He swiveled to face her. "Of course." He put his hand on hers in a momentary gesture of warmth. "I wish I knew how. I'm guessing it step by step myself."

The carriage stopped. They had reached the undertaker's establishment, and there were formalities to arrange, times, places, choices to be made. He alighted and offered her his hand.

Isadora Underhill watched as her husband paced the floor of the withdrawing room, back and forth, every so often running his fingers through his thinning hair. She was used to his being preoccupied with anxieties of one sort or another. He was a little older than she, and bishop of a diocese where a great many influential people lived. There was always some sort of crisis which commanded his attention. Many duties were required both of him and of his wife, but when she was not needed she had learned to occupy herself in other pursuits both with people and on her own. She had great pleasure in reading, especially about the lives of men and women in other lands or of other times. During the spring and summer she spent many hours in the garden, doing more of the physical work than her husband thought suitable. But she had entered into a tacit conspiracy with the gardener that he would solemnly take credit for much that was actually her work if the bishop should happen to notice and comment, which was very infrequently. He did not know a hollyhock from a camellia, or have any but the faintest notion of what care went into the beauty which surrounded him.

"Really, it is quite the worst thing which has ever happened!" he said sharply. "I don't think you are appreciating the seriousness of this, Isadora." He stopped pacing and stood staring at her, his brows furrowed, small lines of anger around his mouth.

"I can see that it is very sad," she replied, threading her tapestry needle with a deep rose madder silk. "It is always deeply distressing when a young person dies. And I daresay her scholastic skills will be sorely missed. I understand she was brilliant." She put the skein away among the others.

"For heaven's sake!" he said exasperatedly. "You have not been paying attention at all. That is hardly the point. Really, I think you could at least put your sewing away and listen with all your mind." He waved his hand irritably at the tapestry roses. "That is of no importance. This is quite devastating."

"I don't see why death should devastate you," she replied reasonably. "It is very sad, but regrettably we hear of death very often, and surely that is part of the blessing of having a faith that you—"

"It is not the wretched woman's death which is the problem!" he cut across her, jerking his head in the air. He was wearing a dark suit, gaiters, and a very high white collar. "Of course it is sad, but we deal with death all the time. It is a part of life, and absolutely inevitable. We have all sorts of ways of coping with it, things with which to comfort ourselves and those who mourn. As I said, if you were listening, that is not the point."

She heard the temper sharp in his voice, and behind it a fear more genuine and urgent than she could remember ever perceiving in him before. She pushed the silks towards the box in which she kept them. "Then what is the point?" she asked.

"I told you! She was pushed down the stairs and broke her neck. It now appears quite possible it was Ramsay Parmenter himself who did it."

She was startled and suddenly quite tight and cold inside. She knew Ramsay Parmenter. She had always rather liked him; he was invariably kind, but she had sensed an unhappiness in him which she could not forget or dismiss. Now, in the space of a few words, it became pity.

"No, you did not tell me," she said with acute sorrow. "That is indeed very terrible. What makes anyone think such a thing could have happened? Why? Why should Ramsay Parmenter push anyone downstairs? Was it an accident? Did he overbalance? He doesn't drink, does he?"

The bishop looked thoroughly annoyed.

"No, of course he doesn't drink! Whatever possessed you to say such a thing? For heaven's sake, Isadora, it was I who pushed for him to be given a bishopric. The Archbishop of Canterbury is not going to forget that . . . nor is the Synod."

She was unperturbed by his tone. Any suggestion of impropriety disturbed him, and she was used to it. "Canon Black drank a great deal," she remembered. "No one knew it because he could walk quite steadily even when he was very much the worse for it."

"That was malicious gossip," he denied. "You of all people should know better than to listen to it, let alone repeat it. The poor man had an impediment in his speech."

"I know he did. It is called Napoleon brandy." She did not wish to be gratuitously unkind, but there were times when tact became cowardice and was intolerable. "You would have done him more good not to turn a blind eye to it."

His eyebrows rose. "Leave me to be the judge of my duty, Isadora. Canon Black is in the past. There is nothing to be served by debating that issue again. At the present I have a far graver matter upon which I must make a judgment, and a very great deal will depend upon it. It is an enormous responsibility I have."

She was confused. "What judgment can you make, Reginald? We must support poor Reverend Parmenter and his family, but there is nothing for us to do. Do you think I should call tomorrow, or is it too soon?"

"Certainly it is too soon." He dismissed the idea with a flick of his well-cared-for hand with its large bloodstone ring. She was used to his hands, strong and square, with spatulate fingers, but she had never found them attractive. It was something about which she felt guilty.

"It only happened yesterday," he went on. "I heard about it this morning, half an hour ago. The decision is what I must do. I have insufficient information. I have been going over and over in my mind upon Parmenter's career. What could have unbalanced him to the point where such a thing can even be contemplated?"

She stared at him in disbelief. "What are you saying, Reginald? Are you suggesting there is something uglier than an accident?"

"The police are!" he replied sharply, his sandy eyebrows drawn together. "Therefore I must. I cannot evade reality, no matter how much I might prefer to. If the police bring charges against him, it may even be as dreadful as murder."

She wanted to deny it, but that was foolish. Reginald would never have said it if it were not true. She looked at him as he swung around and started to pace back and forth again, clenching and unclenching his hands. She had never seen him so distressed or so worried; the muscles of his strong, thick body were knotted hard, his jacket stretched over his shoulders.

"Do you think it is possible?" she asked quietly.

He stopped. "Of course it is possible, Isadora. There is sometimes a darkness in people the rest of us have no idea exists." He was angry with her because he had to explain, and yet he would have explained anyway, he always explained everything, and she had long ago stopped telling him she understood.

"Parmenter is a man who never achieved his potential," he went on, wagging his finger. "Think back to when we both met him. He was brilliant. His whole future lay ahead of him. He could have risen to be a bishop then. He had all the talents necessary, the intellectual understanding and the personal ability. He preached superbly." His voice was getting a sharper edge to it with every sentence. "He had tact, intelligence, judgment, dedication, and all the right sort of family background. He married very well. Vita Parmenter would be an asset to any man. And where is he now?" He stared down at her as if he expected her to supply the answer, but he did not wait. "He has lost the . . . the promise he used to have, the . . . the dedication to the purposes of the church. Somewhere he has gone astray, Isadora. I just wonder how far."

She also had noticed a difference in Ramsay Parmenter over the years. But many people changed. Sometimes it was health, sometimes personal unhappiness, sometimes a disillusion or simply a weariness, a lack of hope. It took great courage to maintain all the fire and energy of youth. Still she found herself defending Ramsay. She did not even think to do it, it was instinctive.

"Surely we must assume it was an accident, unless we hear something which makes that impossible? We must be loyal to him . . ."

"We must be loyal to the church!" he corrected her. "Sentiment is all very well, in its place, but this is a time for principle. I have to consider the very real possibility that he may be guilty. We are all frail. We all have temptations and weaknesses, both of the flesh and of the spirit. I have seen far more of the world than you have, my dear. I know more of humanity and its darker aspects than you ever will, thank heaven. It is not what a woman should even be aware of, far less see. But I must be prepared to face the worst." He lifted his chin a little, as if the blow were expected any moment, even in this quiet, comfortable room with the morning sun on a pot of early hyacinths.

She would have been angry were it not for the real fear she heard in the edginess of his voice and saw in the tight tracery of lines around his mouth. She had never known him to be so distressed before. During their thirty years of marriage she had seen him face many difficult decisions, many tragedies where he had to comfort the shocked and grieving and find the right words to say to everyone. She knew he had mediated in difficult internal rivalries between ambitious clerics, breaking bad news, both personal and professional, to many. He had usually found the way. His confidence had appeared to be serene and based upon an inner certainty.

Perhaps it had been more of a facade than she realized, because now he was rattled. There was a thin edge of panic she could not miss, not for Ramsay Parmenter but for himself, because he had lent his name to recommending him.

"Why on earth would he do such a thing?" she asked, trying to comfort him that it could not be true. It seemed wildly at odds with the man she had met a dozen times every year. He was an intelligent and very worthy man. Lately he had seemed drier than usual. She hesitated to use the word *boring*; if she did, she was not sure when she could stop. She might find a great many senior clergy boring. It was a rogue thought she dared not entertain.

He looked at her impatiently. "Well, the obvious reason which springs to mind is that he was conducting himself improperly towards her," he replied.

"You mean he was having an affair with her?" Why did he always put things in such roundabout euphemisms? This obscured meaning, but it did not alter it.

He winced. "I should prefer you were not so blunt, Isadora," he said critically. "But if you must, then yes, it is what I fear. She was a handsome woman, and I have since learned that her reputation in that area is far from admirable. It would have been a great deal better if Parmenter had employed a young man for his translation—as I advised him at the time, if you recall?"

"I do recall," she answered with a frown. "You said it was an excellent thing to give a young woman an opportunity. It was most liberal and a good example of modern tolerance."

"Nonsense! That is what Parmenter said," he contradicted her crossly. "I find your memory a good deal less reliable than it used to be."

She remembered it very precisely. They had been sitting in this very room. Ramsay Parmenter had leaned forward in his chair and described Unity Bellwood's academic achievements and his intention to employ her, on a temporary basis, with the bishop's permission. Reginald had thought about it for a few moments, sitting with his lips pursed, staring into the fire. It had been November and particularly cold. The butler had brought brandy. Reginald had rolled it gently around in the glass; the firelight made it look like amber. Finally he had given his opinion that it was a liberal and advanced thing to do. Learning should be encouraged. The church should set the example in modern tolerance of all peoples, rewarding on merit.

She looked up at him now where he stood frowning, his collar a little high on one side, his shoulders raised in tension. It would not help to argue. He would not believe her anyway.

"The question is," he stated, "how can we limit the damage this will do to the church? How can we prevent the great work of the body of Christian men and women from being impeded by the scandal this may create if it is not handled to the best? Can you see the headlines in the newspapers? 'Prospective bishop murders his mistress'?" He closed his eyes as if in physical pain, his face bleak and very pale.

She could imagine it, but her first thought was for Vita Parmenter and the shock and distress she would feel, indeed must be feeling now. No matter how well Vita knew her husband, or what confidence she had in him, she could not help but be gripped by a terrible fear that he could be accused. Innocent people did sometimes suffer, even die. And Ramsay himself must be in a turmoil of emotions, every one of them painful, whether he was guilty of anything at all or absolutely nothing. It must be a living nightmare for him.

"Perhaps I could persuade him to plead madness," the bishop said aloud. He looked at Isadora. "He certainly must be quite mad. No sane man could embark on an affair with a woman of Unity Bellwood's type, and then lose all touch with morality, his own lifelong beliefs and everything he has been taught, and in hysteria murder her. It would be a totally truthful plea." He nodded, determined to convince her. "One cannot blame madness, one can only pity it. And of course put the person under suitable restraint, naturally." He leaned forward. "He would be cared for in the best and safest institution we can find. He would be treated with the necessary care. It would be the best thing for everyone."

She was dizzy with the speed with which he had moved from a question to a supposition and then to an assumption, and an answer where Ramsay Parmenter was judged and his sentence decided. It had taken less than three minutes. She felt detached from it, as if she were only in a sense present in the room. Part of her was far away, looking on at the quiet dignity of it with its deep wine patterned carpet, its gentle fire, the bishop standing with his hands clenched in front of him, rendering his judgment. He seemed so familiar in his physical presence, and yet a total stranger, a mind and soul she did not know at all.

"You don't know anything about it yet." The words were on her lips before she had considered how he would react to them. "He may not be guilty of anything at all."

"I can hardly wait until he is charged, can I?" he demanded angrily, stepping back and closer to the fire. "I must act to protect the church. Surely you can see that? The damage will be appalling." He stared at her accusingly, as if she were willfully slow-witted. "We have enemies enough in the modern world without this sort of disaster. There are people on every side denying God, setting up citadels of the mind dedicated to reason as if it were a deity, as if it could answer all our desires and aspirations towards righteousness." He poked at the air. "Unity Bellwood was just one apostle of the mind without morality, the indulgence of the basest instincts of the body, as if learning somehow set one free from the rules which govern the rest of us. Parmenter was quite mistaken to imagine he could teach her better things, reform her, convert her, if you like. It was the supreme arrogance, and look how he has paid for it." He started to pace again, striding in decisive steps to the far end of the room, turning and coming back, turning and retracing his way exactly across the carpet. He was wearing marks in the pile of it. "Now I must think what is best for all. I cannot indulge the one at the cost of many. It is a luxury I do not have. This is no time for sentimentality."

"Have you spoken with him?" She was searching for something to delay him. Without realizing it, she had made a decision to fight him.

"Not yet, but of course I shall. First I must think what to say. I cannot go unprepared. It would be dishonest to him, and disastrous."

She felt even more separate from him, almost a stranger. And the most painful thing was that she wanted to be separate, apart from the thoughts he had as much as the action he would take.

"Well, perhaps he will tell you something which will explain it," she argued. "You must not act before that. You would look dreadful to have condemned him and then find he was innocent. How would people view the church then . . . to have abandoned one of your own the moment he was in trouble? What about honor, loyalty, or even compassion?" She said the last word harshly, unable to keep back her anger any longer and, in truth, unwilling to hide it.

He stopped in the middle of the floor, staring at her. He took a deep breath. He looked worried, even frightened.

She wanted to be sorry for him. It was a wretched situation. Whatever he did there was a strong possibility it would be wrong, and it would certainly be perceived as such by many. There were always people only too happy to criticize. They had their own reasons, political reasons. Church politics seethed with rivalry, hurt feelings, ambition, guilt, thwarted hopes. The bishop's miter was in some ways as heavy and uneasy an ornament as a crown. Too much was expected of the wearer, a sanctity, a moral rightness beyond any mortal to achieve.

And yet as she looked at him she did not see a man struggling valiantly to do right in a dreadful dilemma. She saw instead a man seeking the expedient in case he was caught in the wrong, even a man relishing a certain self-importance as he thought of himself as the one person to save the reputation of the church under such pressure. There was even a certain joy of martyrdom in him. Not once had he expressed pity for any one of the Parmenter family, or grief for Unity herself.

"Do you suppose it will be misunderstood?" he asked seriously.

"What?" She did not know what he was talking about. Had he said something she had not heard?

"Do you think that people will misunderstand our reasons?" he said in what he must have supposed was a plainer form.

"Misunderstand what, Reginald?"

"Our counsel to Ramsay Parmenter to plead madness, of course! Where is your attention?" His face was furrowed with anxiety. "You sounded as if you believed they might see it as lack of loyalty or a certain cowardice, as if we had abandoned him."

"Isn't that exactly what you are proposing to do . . . abandon him?"

He flushed red.

"No, of course it isn't! I don't know how you could even think of such a thing!" he responded angrily. "It is simply a matter of putting the church first, and that means not only doing what is right but doing what is perceived to be right. I would have thought after all these years you could have understood that."

Her own ignorance astounded her, not of her lack of sympathy with the argument, but her lack of perception of herself, and of him. How could she have known him so little as not to have seen this in him before? It was a shabbiness which hurt so deeply she could have wept with the loneliness and the disappointment of it.

He was talking to himself, voicing his thoughts aloud. "Perhaps I should speak to Harold Petheridge. He could bring some influence to bear. After all, the government has an interest in this." He started to walk again. "No one wants a scandal, and we should think of the family. This must be fearful for them."

She stared at him, wondering if he thought for a moment about Ramsay Parmenter himself, how frightened he must feel, how torn with doubts, confusion, and perhaps guilt. Could anyone feel more alone than he must? Would Reginald think of going to offer him some kind of spiritual strength, the support of a friend if he were innocent, the courage to stand and fight for his vindication? Or if he were guilty, then the office of a priest to listen to his confusion and his sin, and to help him seek some form of repentance, at least the beginning of the long road back. She had to believe there was a way. The man she knew might have lost his path and committed some fearful error, but he was not a wicked man, not to be abandoned like an object no longer needed. Was not the whole essence of the church's purpose to preach the Gospel to all people and to cry repentance to all who would hear . . . and that was everyone.

"You are going to see Ramsay, aren't you?" she said with sudden urgency.

He was at the far window. "Yes, of course I am," he answered crossly. "I told you that when you asked before. It is vital I speak with him. I need to know a great deal more about this situation, then I can make an informed judgment as to how we should deal with it . . . for the best." He straightened his jacket a little. "I am going upstairs to my study. I need to compose myself. Good night."

She did not answer, and he seemed not to notice. He went out and closed the door with a click.

CHAPTER
FOUR

The morning after Unity Bellwood's death Pitt called at the office of the medical examiner. He did not expect to hear anything helpful, but it was a duty which must not be overlooked. It was another sharp early spring day, and in spite of the unpleasantness of his task, he walked with a lift in his step. So far he had seen nothing on the billboards, and the newspaper headlines were largely to do with Cecil Rhodes's African politics, domestic economics and the perennial Irish Problem.

He went up the steps two at a time and along the corridors almost as if he were unaware of the carbolic and formaldehyde odor. He knocked on the examiner's office door and went in. It was a small room, crowded with books on shelves, on the floor, and in piles on the desk.

"Good morning, Dr. Marshall," he said cheerfully. "Anything for me?"

Marshall, a small, spare man with a graying beard, looked up from the paper he was writing on, the quill poised in his hand.

"Aye, I have, and ye'll not like it," he said with a smile of friendliness but no pleasure. "There are times I think my job is no' fit even for a man on a fine sunny day. But then there are times I'd sooner have it than yours. And this is one o' them."

"What did you find?" Pitt asked with a sinking heart. "Wasn't it the fall that killed her? Don't tell me she was strangled. There were no marks. I looked. Was she struck before she fell?" That was going to make accident impossible, even a quarrel resulting in a struggle and then a fall, which was what he hoped for. Parmenter's lie could still possibly be explained and then concealed. It was only twenty-four hours. Shock could account for much distress and temporary mental aberration. It could be announced in such a way as to make it seem that Parmenter had acknowledged his part almost immediately.

"Oh, aye," Marshall said dryly. "Not a thing wrong with the lassie except bruises, no doubt collected as she banged against the stairs and the banister and the wall as she went down, and of course a broken neck. If everyone were as healthy as she, I'd be out of a profession."

"Then what am I not going to like?" Pitt asked, moving books off the only other chair and sitting sideways on it.

"She was about three months with child," Marshall answered.

Pitt should have guessed it. It was the disaster he should naturally have foreseen. Unity's reputation for radical thought could so easily have included the sexual freedom that was fashionable among certain of the intellectual and artistic elite. Throughout history there had been leaders in thought and creativity who had not considered the usual restrictions of behavior as applying to them. And they had always had their acolytes. No wonder Ramsay Parmenter had found her dangerous.

Had he also found her attractive . . . irresistibly so?

It could as easily have been Mallory—or Dominic Corde. Pitt thought of Dominic as he had first known him: handsome, charming with such ease he barely knew he did it, and availing himself of far too many opportunities, too many willing young women. Had he really changed so much, or was the same weakness only masked by the clerical collar, not eradicated?

He was aware, even as the thoughts came to his mind, that they were motivated by personal feelings as well as reason.

"I don't know," Marshall interrupted.

"I beg your pardon?" Pitt looked at him questioningly.

"I have no idea who the father was," Marshall elaborated. "No way to tell, but nasty, considering the household she was living in."

That was an understatement. Any one of the men would have been ruined by the scandal, possibly all of them if it were unresolved. This was exactly what Cornwallis had hoped to forestall.

"I suppose she would have known she was in that condition?" he said aloud.

Marshal made a slight gesture of doubt. "Probably, but I have met women who've gone to full term and been taken by surprise. But from what you say of this one, I expect she knew. Women usually do."

"I see." Pitt leaned back in his chair and shoved his hands hard into his pockets.

"Blackmail?" Marshall asked, watching him with sympathy. "Or a great love affair? Betrayal of the wife, a woman wronged after thirty years of loyal marriage?"

"No," Pitt said with a smile. "Not this time. I don't think Vita Parmenter would be the sort of woman to allow such a thing to happen or to react with wounded violence if it did. Anyway, she is one of the only two members of the family who could not have pushed Unity. If you had said she was strangled after she fell, then she could have."

"No . . . just the fall," Marshall said definitely, sucking in his breath. "Which still leaves you with several possibilities. Thwarted love—If I can't have you, no one will. Blackmail of any of the men in the house if he were the father of the child and she threatened exposure—or if he feared he was the father." He was looking at Pitt as he spoke. "Jealousy of another man because he was not the father and felt she had betrayed him with somebody else—and was a slut, or worse." He cocked an eyebrow. "Or jealousy of one of the women if the father were the curate. Or even possibly one of them to defend the father of the child from blackmail."

"Thank you," Pitt said sarcastically. "I had thought of most of those for myself."

"Sorry." Marshall smiled bleakly. "As I said, there are times when I think you have a worse job than I do. The people I deal with are at least beyond all mortal pain. And with this particular one, it would have been brief, a few seconds at most."

Pitt had known it, but it was still a certain satisfaction to hear it said aloud. It was one less hurt to think of.

"Thank you," he said, his tone without the cutting edge. "Is there anything else at all? Any evidence that could help? We know the time. We know what happened. I don't suppose anything on the body gives an indication of who pushed her—height, weight, a thread of fabric, the mark of a hand?"

Marshall looked at him witheringly. "I can tell you that the stain we found on her shoe was a substance used for killing pests out of a greenhouse or conservatory."

"Since we found it on the conservatory floor, that doesn't help," Pitt replied. "Except that Mallory said she was not there, and apparently she was. People often lie out of fear, not necessarily guilt."

"Have you thought that more than one of them may be involved?" Marshall suggested helpfully, his eyes wide and steady. "Perhaps the father of her child and someone willing to protect him?"

Pitt glared at him and rose to his feet, unintentionally scraping the chair on the floor. "Thank you for your information, Dr. Marshall. I shall leave you to your own task, before you think of anything more to make mine even worse." And then with a half smile he went to the door.

"Good day!" Marshall called out cheerfully.

Pitt went directly to Cornwallis's office. It was necessary to inform him of Dr. Marshall's finding. He doubted it would alter his instructions regarding the case, but it was necessary for the assistant commissioner to know. If it came to light later, as it almost certainly would, he would appear incompetent if he were not fully aware.

"How long?" he asked, standing beside the window, the patterns of early spring sunlight on the oak floor near his feet.

"About three months," Pitt replied, watching Cornwallis's face and seeing him wince. He knew that for a moment he had hoped her condition had predated her arrival in Brunswick Gardens.

Cornwallis turned back towards Pitt, his face bleak. There was no need to spell out what it meant. Every one of the possibilities was potentially disastrous and certainly tragic.

"This is very bad," he said quietly. "What impression did you form of Parmenter? Is he a man likely to have been tempted by a young woman and then panic?"

Pitt tried to think honestly. He recalled Ramsay's rather ascetic face, the deep grief and confusion in his eyes, the anger he betrayed in flashes when he spoke of Charles Darwin.

"I don't believe so," he answered carefully. "He disliked her, at times intensely, but it seemed for her ideas—" He stopped, remembering Ramsay's remarks about her immorality. But would he have made them if he himself were part of it?

"What?" Cornwallis demanded, his attention sharp.

"He felt she was immoral," Pitt explained. "But he did not say in what way in particular. He might not have meant sexually."

Cornwallis raised his eyebrows in a look of disbelief.

Pitt did not argue. It was a fragile attempt and he knew it. He had understood Ramsay to mean unchastity at the time, not some intellectual dishonesty or selfishness, coldness or cruelty, or any of the other human sins. It was a convention of the language that the word *immorality* usually conveyed only one meaning.

"I don't think he would have mentioned it to me if he were involved," he pointed out. "Especially after she was dead. He would have to know we would discover her condition."

"You think he's innocent?" Cornwallis was puzzled. "Or that this has nothing to do with it?"

"I don't know," Pitt confessed. "If he is guilty, then he is brilliantly subtle in some aspects and uniquely clumsy in others. I don't understand it at all. The physical evidence seems plain enough. Four people heard her cry out 'No, no, Reverend.' "

"Four?" Cornwallis asked. "You said the maid, the valet, and one of the daughters. Who's the fourth?"

"Mrs. Parmenter. She avoided saying so directly, but she must have. She didn't deny it, she was merely evasive about the words, naturally enough."

"I see. Well, keep me informed—" Before he could add anything further there was a knock on the door, and upon Cornwallis's word, a constable put his head in and said that Sir Gerald Smithers from the Prime Minister's office was here and wanted to see Captain Cornwallis urgently. Immediately behind him Smithers appeared, pushing past him and coming into the room with a smile that crossed his face and disappeared without trace. He was a very ordinary working man except for his air of supreme assurance. He was beautifully dressed in a discreet and expensive way.

"Morning, Cornwallis," he said hastily. He glanced at Pitt. "Mr. . . . I'm glad you came here. Most convenient." He closed the door, leaving the constable on the outside. "Miserable business in Brunswick Gardens. Must all work together on it. I'm sure you appreciate that." He glanced at each of them as if it were a question, but did not wait for an answer. "Anything further?" he addressed himself to Cornwallis.

Cornwallis was tense, his body rigid, almost as if he were balancing himself against the pitch and roll of the quarterdeck.

"Yes. Unity Bellwood was three months with child," he replied.

"Oh." Smithers absorbed the shock. "Oh, dear. I suppose something of the sort was to be expected. Very unfortunate. What are you doing to contain the situation?"

"I have only just learned of it," Cornwallis answered with surprise. "I doubt we can keep it concealed. It may well prove to be the motive for the crime."

"I trust it will not come to that." Smithers waved his hand, the sunlight catching small, monogrammed, gold cuff links. "It is our responsibility to see that it does not." He looked at Pitt at last. "Is there any chance that it was simply an accident?"

"She was heard by four people to call out 'No, no, Reverend!'" Pitt pointed out. "And there was nothing to trip over."

"What people?" Smithers demanded. "Are they reliable? Are they to be believed? Could they be mistaken on second thoughts?"

Cornwallis was standing as if to attention, his face bleak. Pitt knew him well enough to be aware the formality was a mask for dislike.

"One is Parmenter's wife," he said before Pitt could reply.

"Oh! Good." Smithers was eminently pleased. "She cannot be forced to testify against him." He rubbed his hands. "The outlook is improving already. What about the others?"

The pattern of sunlight faded on the floor. Outside the noise in the street was steady.

"Two are servants." Pitt answered this time. He saw the satisfaction increase in Smithers's eyes. "And the last is his daughter, who is adamant," he finished.

Smithers's eyebrows rose. "Young woman? A bit hysterical, is she?" He was smiling. "Lightly balanced? In love, perhaps, feeling parental disapproval and reacting with emotionalism?"

His whole body had relaxed.

"I'm sure she can be persuaded to reconsider. Or at worst be discredited, if it should come to that necessity. But I am trusting that you will see it does not." He looked at Pitt meaningfully.

"Then we had better hope for proof of some other solution," Pitt replied, trying to conceal the contempt he felt. "She would make an excellent witness. She is intelligent, articulate and extremely angry. She believes passionately in honesty and justice and is not likely to be persuaded to conceal something she perceives as monstrous. If you are hoping she will perjure herself to defend her father, I think you will be disappointed. She had an extremely high regard for Miss Bellwood."

"Indeed?" Smithers said coldly, his lip curling. He regarded Pitt with distaste. "Well, that sounds unnatural. What normal young woman would choose the hired help, however well educated, over her own father?" He stared at Cornwallis. "I don't think anything more need be said about that! It speaks for itself. Most unpleasant. Do try to keep that out of the matter, for decency's sake and the feelings of the family."

Cornwallis was now thoroughly angry, but he was also confused. He had no idea what Smithers was referring to. His years at sea had taught him much of men and of command, of mental and physical leadership, of courage and in many ways of wisdom. But there were areas of human relationships of which he was completely ignorant, and he knew little of the society of women.

"Yes sir," Pitt said to Smithers, his eyes wide. He had seldom disliked a man so quickly or so much. "Although if it comes to trial, Mrs. Whickham will almost certainly testify, since she heard Miss Bellwood cry out, and any prosecution would find her an excellent witness. Her views on justice and integrity would command respect."

"I beg your pardon?" Smithers was taken aback. "You said 'his daughter.' Who is Mrs. Whickham?"

"His daughter," Pitt replied steadily. "She is widowed."

Smithers was thoroughly angry.

"I understood you to imply she had unbalanced fondness for Miss Bellwood, preferring her to her own family," he accused.

"I said she had a great admiration for Miss Bellwood's fight for educational and political rights for women," Pitt corrected him. "And for justice in general, and would be highly unlikely to perjure herself in order to defend whoever murdered her friend, even if it should prove to be someone in her own family."

Smithers's eyebrows shot up.

"Oh! You mean a 'new woman'! One of those absurd and grossly unfeminine creatures who want women to behave like men, and men to accept it?" He gave a sharp laugh. "Well, if that is so, it is a good thing that you are merely investigating, and not making the final decisions as to what shall be done." He turned to Cornwallis. "If this wretched Parmenter is guilty, it would be the best thing for everyone if it could be proved he had some mental collapse, plead guilty but insane, and have the matter dealt with with discretion and dispatch." His voice was sharp. "Poor man must have been afflicted by madness. He can be taken care of in a suitable institution where he cannot harm anyone. His family need not be told any more than necessary. Justice will be tempered with mercy." He smiled, a baring of the teeth, but he was pleased with the phrase.

Rain spattered against the windows like a shower of tiny stones.

Cornwallis stared at Smithers, his face white. "And if he is not guilty?" he asked, his voice quiet and very low.

"Then someone else is," Smithers retorted simply. "If it is the Roman Catholic son then it hardly matters, and if it is the new young curate, that is unfortunate but not tragic." He swiveled back to Pitt. The rain was streaming down the window now, a typical March storm. "But whatever the answer, it is of the utmost importance that you reach a conclusion with all haste. Ideally I should like ... it would be best ... if you were able to make some statement by tomorrow. Can you do that?"

"Not unless Reverend Parmenter confesses," Pitt replied.

Smithers smiled icily. "Then see if you can bring that about. Point out the advantages to him. It would be greatly in his best interest. I am sure you can persuade him of that." He issued it as a command. "Keep me informed, in case I can be of any assistance."

"Which government department, sir?" Cornwallis asked.

"Oh, this is not official," Smithers said, a flicker of irritation crossing his face. "Just a word of counsel, as it were. I am sure you understand. Good day, gentlemen." And without waiting any further he went back to the door, hesitated a moment, then went out.

"If Parmenter has lost his hold on sanity," Pitt said with bitter sarcasm, "enough to have an affair with a radical 'new woman' in his own home and then murder her by throwing her downstairs, I doubt he will be open to arguments of reason as to why he should quietly submit to being locked up in an asylum, private or public. I don't think I shall be equal to persuading him at all."

"You will not be trying!" Cornwallis rejoined, his back to the window, the gray light draining the color from the room. "The whole idea is monstrous!" He was so angry he was unable to keep still. He was white to the lips. "You cannot protect a faith rooted in honor, and obedience to the laws of justice and integrity, by lying." He paced back and forth. "Compassion is the greatest of all virtues, but it is not a matter of the liberty to move blame or cover sin by deceit. That erodes the very rock on which it all rests. Forgiveness comes after remorse, not before."

Pitt did not interrupt him.

Cornwallis moved jerkily, his shoulders locked, his fists clenched, knuckles shining where the skin was tight. "And he did not even consider the possibility that Parmenter may not be guilty. I admit it is most likely, but it is not certain, and the man denies it."

He swung around and went back towards the window, but still looking at Pitt as he spoke. "Smithers has no right to assume without proof beyond a reasonable doubt. If we deny Parmenter his proper hearing in court, if he wants it, we are guilty of hideous injustice . . . unforgivable, because we are charged with upholding the law, administering it. If we fail, who can anyone hope in?" He stared at Pitt almost challengingly, although it was his own outrage which spoke.

"So I have your instructions to continue the investigation?" Pitt asked.

"Weren't you going to?" Cornwallis was dismayed.

Pitt smiled at him. "Yes, I was, but I was not necessarily going to tell you so . . . if it would have placed you in an invidious position."

"Thank you," Cornwallis acknowledged with the flicker of an answering smile. "But I do not wish to be protected from my responsibility. I am ordering you to do everything you can to discern the truth, and the whole truth, about what happened in Brunswick Gardens. I shall give it to you in writing, if you feel that prudent."

Outside the rain stopped.

"Thank you, but I feel it imprudent," Pitt replied. He wanted to be tactful, but sometimes Cornwallis did not understand the necessities of politics. "A straight line is not always the shortest route between two points," he added.

There was a flicker of understanding in Cornwallis's eyes, but his anger at Smithers was still too hot to permit him to relax. "Take whatever route you judge," he said. "But do it! Do I make myself plain?"

Pitt straightened up a fraction.

"Yes sir. I shall tell you as soon as I have anything definite."

"Do." Cornwallis drew breath as if to ask something, then changed his mind and wished Pitt good day.

There was no more physical evidence to pursue. Pitt could think of no practical way of learning who had been the father of Unity's child, at least until he had a great deal more knowledge about the various members of the household. Dominic he had known in the past, although not in the last six or seven years, when it seemed a great deal had happened to him. In honesty he had to admit it was grossly unjust to judge a man on his past and not include his present.

He should learn something of Mallory Parmenter also. He had little reason to suspect him, except for the mark on Unity's shoe, but that was understandable, if childish and lacking either the dignity or the maturity of judgment he would have expected from a man about to enter the priesthood of any faith.

But first he must look far more deeply into the character of Ramsay Parmenter. If he were indeed as close to mental or emotional imbalance as the murder of Unity suggested, then there must have been some indication of it, if he could understand the signs.

He had spent the latter part of yesterday enquiring where he might find those who had known Ramsay over the years. It was Tellman who had discovered a university friend and fellow student now living in Highbury, towards the outskirts of London, and made an appointment for Pitt to see him.

Pitt took the train to the Islington and Highbury Stations, and then a hansom to the quiet residence of the Reverend Frederick Glover, in Aberdeen Park near St. Saviour's Church.

"How can I assist you, sir?" Glover enquired, leading Pitt into a small, overcrowded study. It was lined on every wall with books, except where tiny windows in deep bays overlooked a garden bright with early flowers and sheltered by trees and moss-laden walls. At any other time Pitt would have asked him about the garden, perhaps learned a few aspects of gardening skill. It was obviously a place tended with love and great joy.

But Ramsay Parmenter's situation precluded all else for the moment.

"I believe you studied at university with Ramsay Parmenter," Pitt said, accepting the invitation to sit in a large, brown leather chair at least half facing the window.

"I did," Glover agreed. "I told your man that yesterday." He looked at Pitt with a mild manner. He was in his late fifties, a tall man grown portly with the years, his hair receding far across the top of his head. His features were pleasant, although his nose was rather too long. In youth he must have been comely enough. His nature had marked his face with kindness but by no means foolishness.

"Why is it you are interested in Ramsay Parmenter?" He did not need to explain his question. He did not discuss people lightly, and he did not break a confidence. It was in his manner and his polite attention, but a certain distance that commanded respect.

There was no useful answer except the truth, or at least some part of it.

"Because there has been a tragedy in the Parmenter house," Pitt replied, crossing his legs and settling comfortably into the chair. "At the moment we do not know exactly what happened. There are accounts which appear to conflict with the physical evidence, and indeed with people's retelling of it."

"A police matter, and of some gravity." Glover nodded. "Or you would not be concerned. Did you not say you were from Bow Street?" His brow wrinkled. "I thought Parmenter lived in Brunswick Gardens."

"He does. The matter is very delicate."

"I think you had better tell me the truth, Superintendent, and I will be of whatever assistance I can." He looked puzzled. "Although what I could tell you I cannot imagine. I have not seen Ramsay Parmenter in years. I have met him briefly at functions, of course, but it must be fifteen or even twenty years since I spoke to him at any length. Precisely what is this about? You may trust my calling to keep in confidence anything we say. It is my duty, as well as my wish."

"I will tell you, Reverend Glover," Pitt replied. "But I would prefer to ask you questions first. They will not be of a private or confidential matter."

Glover locked his hands across his rather ample stomach and leaned his head very slightly to one side, ready to listen.

From the ease with which Glover assumed it, Pitt imagined that it was an attitude he adopted fairly frequently.

"When did you first meet Ramsay Parmenter?" Pitt began.

"In 1853, when we went up to university," Glover replied.

"What manner of young man was he? What kind of student?"

"A quiet man in his personal life, rather intense." Glover retreated into memory, his eyes focused on the past. "We used to tease him because he had little sense of humor. He was extremely ambitious." He smiled. "Personally, I have always thought God must have an excellent appreciation of the humorous and the absurd, or He would not have begotten us as His children or thereafter have loved us. We are so very often ridiculous."

He was watching Pitt quite closely behind his benign and rather casual manner. "Apart from that, I perceive the ability to laugh as a supremely sane and intelligent response to both the trials and the pleasure of life," he continued. "Sometimes it is the foundation and the outward sign of courage. But you did not come here to hear my philosophy. I beg your pardon. Ramsay was an excellent student, even brilliant. Certainly far better than I. He passed all his examinations with high marks, often the best."

"What was he ambitious to achieve?" Pitt asked curiously. He was not quite sure what a young theologian desired. "High office in the church?"

"Ah, that was part of it, without question." Glover nodded. "But also to write the definitive work on some subject or other. That is a kind of immortality, after all. Not, of course, that that is the sort the soul achieves. I admit, this would be a matter of vanity, would it not? I did not mean to imply that Ramsay was vain."

"Wasn't he?"

Glover shrugged, surrendering the point. "Yes, he was. Academically, at least. And he was also a brilliant preacher. He had great fire and enthusiasm in those days, and a very fine voice. His vocabulary was wide and varied, and his knowledge broad enough he seldom repeated himself."

It did not sound like the man Pitt had met. Had Unity Bellwood's death robbed him of that fire, or had it faded before then?

"You expected him to have a brilliant future, an outstanding career in the church?" Pitt asked aloud.

"I think we all did," Glover agreed. There was a shadow of regret in his face, a slight pinching of the lips, something around the eyes.

"But he did not quite fulfill it," Pitt concluded. He could still see a reflection of the gold of daffodils in the corner of his vision, and a ripple of light across the grass.

"Not as I saw it for him then." Glover looked back at him, trying to measure how much more to say. "I expected the . . . the passion to remain, the tremendous sense of conviction. I expected something more personal than learned, and heaven help me, rather dry books."

"What happened to his passion?" Pitt pressed.

Glover sighed, a gentle sound, sad and without blame.

"I am not sure. I can only guess. When I knew him he had fewer doubts than any of the rest of us." He smiled to himself. "I can remember sitting up all night drinking terrible wine and talking fiercely about all manner of things: God and the meaning of life, the fall from Eden, the role of Eve, predestination, grace and works, the justification for the Reformation, all manner of heresies about the nature of the Godhead . . . we picked them all apart. Ramsay was the one who seemed to doubt himself least. His arguments were always so cogent, so perfectly reasoned, that he usually won."

"Did you know him after he left university?" Pitt asked.

"Oh, for a while. I recall his meeting Vita Stourbudge and courting her." His eyes had a faraway look, soft and mildly amused. "We all envied him that. She was so very pretty." He shook his head. "No, *pretty* is the wrong word; she was more than that. She was utterly charming, full of enthusiasm and intelligence. I am sure he loved her, but even had he not, he could hardly have done better for a wife. She supported him in everything. She seemed as dedicated as he was." He gave a little laugh. "And, of course, she was an excellent catch in that her father was a man of both wealth and distinction, and a pillar of the church."

So Vita had not changed. Pitt could see in her now the woman Glover described, except he had not known of her family background, but it did not surprise him.

"Has he written the definitive works on any of the questions you discussed?" he asked. They were all subjects he had never even considered. For him religion had been a matter of behavior based on the true foundations of a faith in a greater being—simply, one he had been taught in childhood—and a moral conduct springing from the ever-deepening understanding of compassion and honor. Perhaps he had that much in common with Cornwallis, in spite of their having come by it so differently.

"Not so far, I think," Glover replied. "His work is highly respected by the Establishment, but for the general reader a little—" He stopped, unable to decide on the word.

Pitt looked beyond him to the daffodils and the sun.

"Abstruse," Glover finished. "Too difficult to understand because of the complexity of the arguments. Not everyone is intellectually equipped to grasp such things."

"But you do?" Pitt brought his attention back with reluctance. It all seemed irrelevant to the issue.

Glover smiled apologetically. "Actually, I don't. I only read half of it. That sort of thing bores me stiff. A live debate was all right, at least when I was young, because I liked to argue. But when the opponent is not there in the flesh—or perhaps 'in the mind' would be more accurate—it has no appeal to me. I admit, Superintendent, I don't care about the obscurities of higher learning. It is my weakness, professionally speaking."

"And Ramsay Parmenter does care?"

"He used to. I don't feel any passion in his work nowadays. There is no point in your asking me. I don't know. It may be that I am lacking the ability to follow him. There are certainly those who do. He is much admired."

"Can you refer me to someone who could tell me more of his present convictions and abilities?"

"If you wish. But you still have not told me why you need to know."

"A young woman died in tragic circumstances in his home. There is much about it which needs explanation."

Glover was obviously startled; he jerked further upright and his hands dropped. "Suicide?" he said sadly, his voice subdued with shock. "Oh, dear. I am so sorry. Of course it does happen, I am afraid. A love affair, I daresay. Was she with child?" He saw from Pitt's face that it was so. He sighed. "How very tragic. Such a waste. I always feel it is so unnecessary. We should have a better way of coping with such things." He took a deep breath. "But what can Ramsay's academic achievements possibly have to do with it? Oh, dear—it was not one of his daughters, was it? I do recall the younger one, Clarice her name is, I think, was to be married to some young man, but at the last moment refused to enter the arrangement. The betrothal never took place. All very unfortunate. I think she expected rather too much of a romantic nature and would not make the necessary compromises with life." He smiled ruefully, his expression not unsympathetic.

"No," Pitt replied, making a note of the incident in his mind. "It was not one of Ramsay's daughters. She was a scholar of ancient languages, assisting him in his work."

Glover still looked puzzled.

"It was not suicide," Pitt enlarged. "At present it seems it could only have been intentional."

Glover was stunned. "You mean murder?" he said hoarsely. "Well, it would not be Ramsay, I assure you, if that is what you are thinking. He has not the passion now, apart from the cruelty, which he never had."

When he recalled his meeting with Ramsay Parmenter, Pitt was not surprised. But he had assumed the cleric's cool demeanor was shock, the self-control expected of a man of his position. It still startled him to have someone else say such a thing. It was a defense, and yet it was also a damnation. When had the passion died, and why? What had killed it?

Glover was watching him. "I am sorry," he said, his face a little crumpled with contrition. "I should not have said that." A self-mockery filled his eyes. "Perhaps I am jealous of his intellectual ability and angry because he did not realize it as I thought he should. I wish I could help you, Superintendent, but I fear I know nothing of use. I am extremely sorry about the young woman's death. May I at least offer you a cup of tea?"

Pitt smiled. "I should rather walk around your garden, and perhaps you can tell me how you grow such magnificent daffodils?"

Glover rose to his feet instantly, almost in a single movement, ignoring the twinge of pain in his back. "With the greatest pleasure," he responded, and he proceeded to explain his method even before they were through the door, waving his hands to illustrate his meaning, his face filled with enthusiasm.

———

Dr. Sixtus Wheatcroft was an entirely different matter. He lived in Shoreditch, five stops away on the train and another short cab ride. His rooms were spacious but without a garden. If anything, he possessed even more books than Glover.

"What can I do for you, sir?" he asked with a touch of impatience. He was obviously in the middle of studying something of great interest to him and he made no secret of having been interrupted.

Pitt responded formally, stating his name and rank. "I am enquiring into the violent death of a Miss Unity Bellwood . . ." And he described the circumstances very briefly.

Wheatcroft clicked his tongue. "Very regrettable. Most unfortunate." He shook his head. "I must visit the Reverend Parmenter and convey my condolences. Distressing thing to have happen in one's home, most particularly to an assistant in one's work, of whatever quality. No doubt he will find someone more suitable quite quickly, but it is bound to be most disturbing. Poor young woman. How does this concern you, Superintendent?" He peered at Pitt over his spectacles. He was still standing and he did not offer a seat.

"We need to know more precisely what happened . . ." Pitt began.

"Is it not plain enough?" Wheatcroft's eyebrows rose over his round, light brown eyes. "Can it take so much observation and deduction?"

"She fell downstairs and broke her neck," Pitt answered. "It appears she was pushed."

Wheatcroft took a moment or two to digest this startling information, then he frowned, his impatience returning.

"Why, for heaven's sake? Why should anyone push a young woman downstairs? And what can I possibly tell you? I am familiar with his scholastic reputation and her political and radical views, which I abominate. She should never have been permitted into serious study of theological matters." His lips tightened, and unconsciously the attitude of his body had altered to be more rigid, as if under his rather ill-fitting jacket, his muscles were knotted. "It is not a fit subject for women. They are constitutionally unsuited to it. It is not an area for emotion but for pure spirit and reason, free from the clouding of the natural feelings and prejudices." He mastered his own emotion with something of an effort. "Still, that is all past now and we cannot alter it. Poor Parmenter. Sometimes we pay heavily for our errors of judgment, and I am sure he intended only to be liberal in his views, but it does not pay."

"Was she not a good scholar?" Pitt asked, wondering if conceivably Ramsay had formed some attachment for her and employed her for personal rather than professional reasons.

Wheatcroft remained standing, as if he had no intention of allowing Pitt to be comfortable enough to forget he was an interruption. He lifted his shoulders very slightly, frowning as he spoke. "I thought I had already explained to you, Superintendent. Women are, by their nature, unsuited to serious intellectual study." He shook his head. "Miss Bellwood was no exception. She had a quick mind and could grasp the mere facts and remember them as well as anyone, but she had no deeper understanding."

He peered at Pitt as if trying to estimate his probable educational level. "It is one thing to translate the words of a passage; it is quite another to be at one with the mind of the writer of that passage, to grasp his fundamental meaning. She was not capable of that, and that is the essence of pure scholarship. The other is mere"—he spread his hands—"is merely technical. Very useful, of course. She might have served an excellent purpose in teaching young people the mechanics of a foreign tongue. That would have been the ideal place for her. But she was willful and headstrong, and would not be guided. She was a rebel in all things, Superintendent. Her personal life was completely without discipline. That in itself should demonstrate the point to you perfectly."

"Why do you suppose the Reverend Parmenter would have employed her, if he was such an excellent scholar himself?" Pitt asked, although he had little hope of a useful answer.

"I have no idea." Wheatcroft was obviously not interested in considering the matter.

"Might it have been a personal reason?" Pitt pursued.

"I cannot think of one," Wheatcroft said impatiently. "Was she the daughter of a relative, perhaps, or a friend or colleague?"

"No."

"No . . . I thought not. She was a different type of person altogether. From a liberal and artistic background." He said the words as if they were a condemnation in themselves. "Really, Superintendent, I don't know what it is you wish to hear from me, but I fear I cannot help you."

"What did you think of the Reverend Parmenter's academic publications, Dr. Wheatcroft?"

He spoke without hesitation.

"Excellent, quite excellent. Outstanding, in fact. He is a man of the most profound and intricate understanding. He has chosen to explore some of the deepest subjects and with exhaustive study." He nodded enthusiastically, his voice rising. "His work is taken most seriously by those few men who value such things in their true worth. His work will live long after him. His contribution is priceless." He fixed Pitt with a grim stare. "You must do all you can to deal with this matter with the utmost dispatch. It is all most unfortunate."

"It appears to be murder, Dr. Wheatcroft," Pitt said with equal severity. "To be right is more important than to be quick."

"One of the servants, I expect," Wheatcroft said irritably. "I am sorry to speak ill of the dead, but in this case, no doubt, to be honest is more important than to be charitable." He mimicked Pitt's tone. "She was a woman who believed self-discipline in matters of the fleshly appetites was neither necessary nor desirable. I am afraid such behavior gathers its own rewards."

"You are as good as your word," Pitt said acidly.

"I beg your pardon?"

"You have decidedly favored honesty above charity."

"Your remark is in poor taste, sir," Wheatcroft said with surprise and annoyance. "I find it offensive. Please be so good as to remember your position here."

Pitt wriggled his shoulders and changed his balance as if uncomfortable. He smiled, baring his teeth. "Thank you for your hospitality, Dr. Wheatcroft. It was remiss of me not to have mentioned it earlier."

Wheatcroft flushed.

"And for your assistance," Pitt went on. "I shall convey your condolences to the Reverend Parmenter next time I have occasion to question him on the matter, although I imagine he might appreciate it if you wrote them yourself. Good day, sir." And before Wheatcroft could retaliate, he turned and went back to the door, and the manservant showed him out.

He walked briskly as he left. He was extremely angry, both with Wheatcroft for his graceless behavior and with himself for allowing it to provoke him into retaliation. Except that he had enjoyed it considerably and hoped Wheatcroft was livid.

He arrived home in Bloomsbury a little before dark, still smoldering. After dinner, when Jemima and Daniel were in bed and he and Charlotte were sitting beside the parlor fire, she asked him the cause of his anger, and he told her about his visits to Glover and then Wheatcroft.

"That's monstrous!" she exploded, letting her knitting fall. "He says all that about her because she is a woman and he doesn't like what he imagines are her morals. And then has the colossal hypocrisy to say that she is incapable of detached reasoning but is governed by her emotions. He is the ultimate bigot!"

She warmed to the battle, pushing the needles into the ball of wool to keep them safe. "If Unity Bellwood had to fight against people like that in order to find any position where she could use her abilities, no wonder she was difficult to get on with now and then. So should I be, if I were patronized, insulted and dismissed in such a way, not for what I actually did but simply because I was not a man."

She drew breath but gave him no chance to interrupt. "What are they afraid of?" she demanded, leaning forward. "It doesn't make any sense. If she is better than they are, or if she is worse, foolish or incompetent, what difference does it make if she is a man or a woman? Isn't the result the same? If she is better, they lose their position and she takes it. If she is incompetent, she loses a piece of work, or spoils it, and is dismissed. Wouldn't exactly the same be true if she were a man?" She waved her hand. "Well, wouldn't it?"

He smiled in spite of himself, not because his anger was ameliorated but at her outburst of righteous indignation. It was so characteristic of her. In that much at least she had not changed a whit since he had first met her ten years before. The spontaneity was exactly the same, the courage to sail almost unthinkingly into battle where she saw injustice. Anyone oppressed instantly had her support.

"Yes!" he said sincerely. "I begin to have some sympathy with Unity Bellwood. If she lost her temper now and again or took pleasure in every error Ramsay Parmenter made, and let him know it, I should find it very understandable. Especially if she really was cleverer than he." He meant it. Standing in Wheatcroft's study, he had been oppressed by an awareness of the impenetrable barrier which must have blocked Unity Bellwood's attempts to be taken seriously as a scholar, based not upon any limitations to her intellect but entirely upon other people's perceptions and fears. It was not surprising she had been consumed with an anger which had prompted her to provoke as much discomfort as she could in those men she found intolerably complacent in their security. And Tryphena's rage at injustice, her belief that Unity had been silenced for her challenge to vested interest, was equally easy to understand.

He looked up and saw Charlotte watching him, and he knew from her face that the same thoughts were in her mind.

"He could have, couldn't he," she said aloud. It was a statement.

"She was so suffocated by injustice, she lashed out—the only way she could, with ideas he couldn't bear, challenging him! And he had not the intellect to argue against her, and they both knew it, so he lost his temper and struck at her physically. Perhaps he did not mean her to fall. It was all over in a few seconds, and he denied it because it seemed almost unreal, a nightmare."

"Yes," he said quietly. "He could."

The following day Pitt visited other people who had known Ramsay Parmenter for some time. In mid-afternoon he called upon Miss Alice Cadwaller. She was well into her eighties, but quicker of wit and observation than either of the previous two people he had spoken to, and certainly far more hospitable than Dr. Wheatcroft. She invited him into her small sitting room and offered him tea on an exquisite bone china service hand-painted with blue harebells. There were sandwiches about the size of one of his fingers, and cakes no more than an inch and a half across.

She was propped up in her chair with a shawl around her shoulders. She held her cup delicately in one hand and regarded him rather as an elderly and weather-beaten thrush might have.

"Well, Superintendent," she said, nodding a little, "what is it you want to hear? I do not care to speak unkindly. I always judge people by what they say of others. One's unkind comments reveal far more of oneself than one realizes."

"Indeed, Miss Cadwaller," he agreed. "But in cases of sudden and violent death, where justice must be served and injustice avoided, it is usually necessary to speak truths one would otherwise prefer to keep to oneself. I would like you to tell me your opinion of Ramsay Parmenter. I believe you have known him for at least twenty years."

"I have, in a manner of speaking," she agreed. "Shall we say I have observed him. It is not the same thing."

"You do not feel you know him?" He took a sip of his tea and a bite of his sandwich, trying to make it last for two.

"He had a public face which he showed to his parishioners," she explained. "If he had a private one or not I do not know."

"How do you know this was not his private face as well?" he asked curiously.

She looked at him with patient amusement. "Because he addressed me as if I were a public meeting, even when we were alone; rather as he addressed God . . . like someone he wished to impress but not to become too closely acquainted with, in case we should trespass upon his privacy or disturb his plans or his ideas."

Pitt kept himself from smiling only with great difficulty. He knew precisely what she meant. He had sensed exactly that same distance in Ramsay. But considering their relationship and the circumstances, he had expected it. For Miss Cadwaller it was different.

"I believe he was of the greatest help to Mr. Corde when he was in distress some few years ago," he observed, wondering how she would respond to the idea.

"That does not surprise me." She nodded. "Mr. Corde has spoken most highly of him. Indeed, his regard and gratitude are most heartening. He is a young man of deep conviction, and I believe he will be of great service to the Lord."

"Do you?" Pitt asked politely. He could not imagine Dominic Corde as a minister. Preaching from the pulpit was one thing. It was almost like acting, which he had always thought Dominic would be good at, in a minor way. He had the eyes, the beautiful profile, the charm, the bearing, and an excellent voice. And he knew how to be the center of attention gracefully; it was in not being the center that he exhibited less grace. Ministering quietly to the needs of people was something very different.

"You find that surprising?" she observed acutely.

"I . . ." He hesitated.

"I can see it in your face, young man." She smiled, not unkindly.

"Yes, I do," he admitted. Should he tell her they were brothers-in-law? It might prejudice her answers. Although looking at her wrinkled face with its bright eyes, perhaps it would have no effect whatever. Then he remembered with distinct discomfort her observation about remarks upon other people reflecting more upon the speaker than the object. "Please explain to me. I can see you have grounds for your belief."

"It concerned Miss Dinmont's brother," she said, taking another sip of her tea.

He waited.

"I am afraid he was not a very good man, but she still felt a great loss when he died. One does. The ties of blood cannot easily be dismissed, no matter how much one might care to. And he was her younger brother. I think she felt a great sense of failure over him."

"And Mr. Corde?"

"I sat with her for some time after the news came of her brother's death," she went on at her own pace. She could not allow some young policeman who needed the attention of a good barber to hurry her in explaining something of importance in principle, if not of any actual use. "She is a good churchgoer. Naturally, Reverend Parmenter came to offer her his comfort. There was to be a funeral, here in this parish."

He nodded and took another sandwich.

"She was very distressed," she continued. "The poor man had no idea what to say or to do when faced with real grief. He read various scriptures which were perfectly appropriate. I daresay he reads them to everyone who has been bereaved. But his heart was not in it. One can tell."

She looked sad, her eyes far away. "I had the profound impression he did not believe the words himself. He spoke of the resurrection of the dead as if it were a railway timetable." She set down her cup. "If the trains run on time it is very convenient, but it is not a miracle of God, it is not a matter for joy and eternal hope. It is very irritating if they do not, but it is not the end of all light and life. One will merely be obliged to wait rather longer. And railway platforms, while not being ideal, are by no means hell, nor oblivion." She looked at him over the top of her teacup. "Although I have at times felt they were akin. But that was when I was younger and the reality of death seemed a great deal further away. And I was in a hurry then."

"And Dominic Corde?" he asked, smiling back at her and taking the last of the cakes.

"Ah . . . that was quite different," she declared. "He came later, I think two days later. He simply sat down next to her, took her hand in his. He did not read, but told her in his own words of the thieves on the crosses on either side of Our Lord, and then of Easter morning, and Mary Magdalene seeing Him in the garden and mistaking Him for the gardener until He spoke her name." There was a sudden misting of tears in her eyes. "I think it was knowing her name that made the difference. Suddenly poor Miss Dinmont realized that God knows each of us by name. Love is a personal thing, Thou and I, not a matter of arguments and teachings. That is the power which transcends all else. In those few moments she was comforted. Mr. Corde understood that. Reverend Parmenter did not."

"I see," he said gently, surprised at himself that he did see, perfectly.

"Would you like some more tea?" she offered.

"Yes, please, Miss Cadwaller, I would," he accepted, holding out his cup and saucer. "I think I understand something now about Reverend Parmenter which I did not before."

"Of course you do," she agreed, lifting up the pot and pouring from it. "The poor man lost his belief, not in what he was doing but why he was doing it. Nothing can replace that. All the reason in the world does not warm the heart, nor comfort grief and failure. The ministry is about loving the unlovable and helping people to bear pain and suffer unexplainable loss without despair. In the end it is about trust. If you can trust God, all else will fall in its place."

He did not argue or even comment. She had summed up in a few words all that he had been struggling to find. He finished his tea, talked a little more of commonplace things, admired her china and the embroidered cloth on the table, then thanked her and took his leave.

By five o'clock he was at the home of Bishop Underhill, trying to clarify in his mind what he could ask him that would teach him anything further about Ramsay Parmenter. Surely as Ramsay's bishop, Underhill would have insights more profound than anyone else? Pitt was afraid he might meet with a rebuff based on the sanctity and privilege of their relationship. He was prepared to be politely refused.

However, when the bishop came into the red and brown library where Pitt had been asked to wait, his air was anything but one of calm and assured denial. He closed the door behind him and faced Pitt with his features creased by acute anxiety, his thinning hair ruffled, his shoulders braced as if expecting an almost physical onslaught.

"You are the policeman in charge of this miserable affair?" he asked Pitt accusingly. "How long do you expect it to take before you can reach an acceptable conclusion? It is all very distressing indeed."

"Yes sir," Pitt agreed, standing almost to attention. After all, he was in the presence of a prince of the church. Underhill was due respect. "Any crime is distressing, and this one peculiarly so," he added. "That is why I have come here, in the hope that you can help me learn exactly what happened."

"Ah!" The bishop nodded, looking slightly more hopeful. "Do sit down, Superintendent. Make yourself comfortable, sir, and let us see what we can accomplish. I am very pleased you have come." He sat down on the red leather chair opposite the brown one on which Pitt had sat, and gave him his earnest attention. "The sooner we can resolve this, the better for everyone."

Pitt had an uncomfortable moment's thought that their ideas of resolution were not the same. He told himself instantly that he was being unjust.

"I am making enquiries as speedily as I can," Pitt assured the bishop. "But beyond the physical facts, which seem indisputable, it immediately becomes far less clear."

"I understand the unfortunate young woman was most difficult in manner and morality, causing ill feeling. She quarreled with Reverend Parmenter and fell down the stairs." He breathed heavily, his mouth closing in a tight line, the muscles of his cheek and jaw tensed. "You have no doubt she was pushed, I presume, or you would not take any further interest in the matter. A simple domestic tragedy does not require your investigation." A flicker of hope lit his eyes.

"There is no indication that she tripped, sir," Pitt replied. "But her cry, apparently accusing Reverend Parmenter, makes it necessary we investigate the incident more thoroughly."

"Cry?" The bishop's voice lifted sharply. "Precisely what did she cry out, Superintendent? Surely that is open to interpretation? Have you found any other evidence whatever to suggest that a man of Reverend Parmenter's reputation and learning would so lose his wits, all his life's work, as to push her? Really, sir, it defies belief."

"She cried out 'No, no, Reverend!' " Pitt replied.

"Could she not have slipped and called for his assistance, as the nearest person to her and the most likely to come to her aid?" the bishop said urgently. "Surely that is a far more likely explanation? I am sure if you put that to the person who heard the cry, they will confirm it to you." He said it almost in the tone of an order—and an assumption that it would be obeyed.

"That is not what they say, sir," Pitt answered, watching his face. "But it is possible she cried 'No, no' to the person who pushed her, and then called out to Mr. Parmenter to help her. But she did not use any words such as *help* or *please*."

"Of course." The bishop leaned forward. "She fell before she could. That is most easily explained. She may even have begun to and been cut off by her fall, poor creature. It seems we have resolved the matter already. Most excellent." He smiled, but there was no warmth in it.

"If it was not Reverend Parmenter who pushed her, then it was someone else," Pitt pointed out. "The servants are all accounted for, as are Mrs. Parmenter ..." He saw the bishop wince. "And Mrs.

Whickham. This leaves Miss Clarice Parmenter, Mr. Mallory Parmenter, and the curate who is lodging there at present, Mr. Dominic Corde."

"Ah, yes . . . Corde." The bishop leaned back in his chair. "Well, it is probably young Mallory Parmenter. Very regrettable, but a lightly balanced young man of emotional instability. You will not be aware of his history, but he has always been of a doubting and argumentative nature. As a youth he quibbled over everything. He could accept nothing without making an issue over it." He drew his mouth tight in an expression of annoyance as memory became sharp. "One moment he was bursting with enthusiasm, the next he was equally full of criticism. Altogether an unsatisfactory young man. His rebellion against his father, his entire family and all its values, is witness of that. I cannot think why he should do something so violent and tragic, but I have never understood such behavior. I can only deplore and regret it." He frowned. "And, of course, pity the victims," he added hastily.

"Miss Bellwood was with child," Pitt said bluntly.

The bishop paled. The satisfaction drained from his face. "How very unfortunate. From some liaison before she was employed, I presume?"

"Since. I am afraid it is very probable the father was one of the three men in the house."

"Only of academic import now." The bishop stretched his neck, easing his collar as if it were tight. "We can never know who it was, and we must assume it was young Parmenter, and that was his reason for . . . killing her. It is the lesser sin, Superintendent, and there is no need to blacken the young woman's reputation by letting it become public now. Let us allow her to rest in peace, poor creature." He swallowed. "It is not a necessity, nor is it our place, to judge her weakness."

"It may be Mallory Parmenter," Pitt agreed, unreasonably angry deep inside himself. He had no right to judge the bishop; he had no idea what young Mallory had been like, or how he had tried his patience. All the same, his dislike was intense. "But it may not," he added. "I cannot act without proof."

The bishop looked agitated. "But what proof can you have?" he demanded. "No one has confessed. The act was not seen, and you have just told me any of three people could have been responsible. What do you propose to do?" His voice was rising. "You cannot leave the matter unsolved! All three men's reputations will be ruined. It would be quite monstrous."

"Can you tell me something further about Mallory Parmenter, something specific, Bishop Underhill?" Pitt asked. "And Dominic Corde, perhaps? Certainly you must know Ramsay Parmenter better than almost anyone else, in some ways."

"Yes . . . of course. Well . . . I'm not sure."

"I beg your pardon?"

A flicker of discomfort crossed the bishop's face. He started to explain himself. "I have known Mallory Parmenter for a long time, naturally. As a boy he was always a little difficult, lurching from one enthusiasm to another, as I have said. Most people grow out of it. He does not seem to have. Could not make up his mind what to do with his life. Indecisive, you see?" He stared at Pitt critically. "Considered going up to Oxford to study, but didn't. Never fell in love. No one would meet his impossibly high criteria. Lived in a world divorced from reality. An idealist. Never came to terms." He hesitated.

"Yes?" Pitt prompted after a moment.

"Unsound," the bishop finished, satisfied with the word. "Yes, unsound. Obvious enough now, I am afraid."

Pitt took that to refer to his conversion to Rome, but did not say so. "And Mr. Corde?" he asked.

"Ah. Yes. A most promising man." Underhill's voice was suddenly filled with satisfaction, a momentary smile on his mouth. "Most promising. Always a joy to see someone discover a true faith and be prepared to sacrifice all to follow it."

"Is it a sacrifice?" Pitt asked innocently, thinking of the despair

Dominic had described and the peace he now saw in Dominic's face and his manner. "I should have thought it the opposite. Surely he has gained far more than anything it could have cost him?"

The bishop flushed angrily. "Of course! You misunderstood me. I was speaking of . . ." He flapped his hand. "It is not something I can describe to you, the years of study, of self-discipline, the financial restrictions of a very minimal income. Gladly undertaken, but of course it is a sacrifice, sir."

"And you believe Dominic Corde is a morally excellent man, above the weakness and temptations of vanity, anger or lust . . ."

The bishop sat forward in the great red chair. "Of course I do! There is no question. I take most unkindly even the suggestion that—" He stopped abruptly, aware of just how far he was committing himself. "Well . . . naturally, I am speaking as I find, Superintendent. I have many reasons to believe . . . there has never been the slightest word . . ."

"And Ramsay Parmenter?" Pitt asked without hope of any answer of meaning, let alone value.

"A man hitherto of unimpeachable reputation," the bishop replied grimly.

"But surely, sir, you know him better than merely by repute?" Pitt insisted.

"Of course I do!" The bishop was unhappy now, and thoroughly annoyed. He shifted his position in his chair. "It is my calling and my vocation, Superintendent. But I know of nothing in his nature or his acts to suggest he was not all he seemed and that he had any weaknesses graver than those that afflict all mankind." He seemed about to add something, then changed his mind. Pitt wondered if he was remembering that it was he who had recommended Ramsay Parmenter's forthcoming promotion.

"Doubts about his vocation, his faith?" he pressed. "Moods of despair?"

The bishop's tone became condescending.

"We all have doubts, Superintendent. It is merely human to do so, a function of the intelligent man."

Pitt had a sense of futility arguing with him. He was prevaricating in order to leave room for himself to appear in the right whatever the outcome.

"Are you saying that the clergy who lead us have no greater faith than the ordinary layman?" Pitt said aloud, looking at the bishop squarely.

"No! No, of course I am not! What I am saying is . . . is that moods of despondency come upon us all. We are all beset by . . . by certain . . . thoughts . . ."

"Has Ramsay Parmenter ever shown temptations towards self-indulgence, or violent loss of temper? Please, Bishop Underhill, we are sorely in need of honesty before a desire to mask the truth with kindness."

The bishop sat silent for so long Pitt thought he was not going to answer at all. He looked wretched, as if tormented by thoughts he found acutely painful. Pitt had the uncharitable thought that it was concern for his own increasingly awkward position that troubled him.

"I must consider the matter further," the bishop said at last. "I am not, at this point, happy to speak on the subject. I am sorry, sir. That is all I can tell you."

Pitt did not press him any further. He thanked him and took his leave. Immediately the bishop went to the telephone, an invention about which he had very ambivalent feelings, and made a call to John Cornwallis's offices.

"Cornwallis? Cornwallis . . . ah, good." He cleared his throat. This was absurd. He should not allow himself to be nervous. "I would greatly appreciate an opportunity to speak privately with you. Better here than in your office, I think. Would you care to come to dinner? Very welcome. Good . . . very good. We dine at eight. We shall look forward to seeing you." He hung up the receiver with a motion of relief. This was all quite appalling. He had better inform his wife. She should in turn inform the cook.

———

Cornwallis arrived a few moments after eight o'clock. Isadora Under-hill knew who he was, but she had never met him before. She had begun the evening extremely annoyed at her husband's thoughtless-ness in inviting a stranger to dine on an evening when she had planned to sit quietly. Every night the previous week there had been some duty or other demanding her attention and her polite interest, most of them exceedingly dull. Tonight she had intended to read. She had a novel which transported her utterly into its passion and depth. She forfeited it with reluctance—and something less than the grace she usually showed.

She also knew perfectly well why Reginald had called the police-man. He was terrified there was going to be a scandal he could not contain and that it was going to reflect on him badly since he had been the one to insist Ramsay Parmenter should be elevated to a bishopric of his own. He wanted to try to persuade this man to deal with the issue discreetly and expeditiously, even if that meant outside the normal rules. It disgusted her, and far more powerfully than that, it was the end of a slow disenchantment which she realized had been happening for years; she simply had not recognized it as such. This was her life, the man whose work she shared, the meaning she had chosen to take for herself. And she no longer admired it.

She chose to dress very simply in a dark blue gown with high, pleated silk sleeves. It became her extraordinarily with her dark hair and its silver streak.

Cornwallis surprised her. She did not know what she had expected—someone like the church dignitaries she already knew so well: habitually polite, confident, a trifle bland. Cornwallis was none of these things. He was obviously uncomfortable, and his manners were exact, as though he had to work at thinking what to say. She was used to a civility which acknowledged her while looking beyond her. He, on the contrary, seemed highly aware of her, and although he was not a large man, she found herself conscious of his physical presence in a way she had not felt before.

"How do you do, Mrs. Underhill." He inclined his head, the light shining on its totally smooth surface. She had never thought she could find baldness appealing, but his was so completely natural she only realized its appeal afterwards—and with surprise.

"How do you do, Mr. Cornwallis," she replied. "I am delighted you were able to come with so little proper invitation. It really is very kind of you."

The color touched his cheeks. He had a powerful nose and wide mouth. He obviously did not know what to say. It seemed against his instinct to gloss over the fact that he had come in answer to the bishop's panic, and yet disastrous to admit it.

She smiled, wishing to assist him. "I know it is a call to arms," she said simply. "It was still generous of you to come. Please sit down and be comfortable."

"Thank you," he accepted, sitting very upright in the chair.

The bishop remained standing by the mantelpiece, no more than a foot from the fender. The evening had turned cold and it was the most advantageous position.

"Very unfortunate," he said abruptly. "Your policeman was here this afternoon . . . late. Not a man sensitive to the issues at stake, I'm afraid. Is it possible to change him for someone a trifle more . . . understanding?"

Isadora felt acutely uncomfortable. This was not a suitable thing to be suggesting.

"Pitt is the best man I have," Cornwallis said quietly. "If the truth can be uncovered, he will do it."

"For heaven's sake!" the bishop retorted crossly. "We need a great deal more than uncovering of the truth! We need tact, diplomacy, compassion . . . discretion! Any fool can lay bare a tragedy and display it to the world . . . and ruin the church's reputation, destroy the faith and work of decades, injure the innocent who trust us to . . ." He stared at Cornwallis with genuine contempt in his eyes.

Isadora felt herself cringe inside. It was acutely embarrassing to hear Cornwallis spoken to with such scorn and have him believe she was associated with the sentiment, but a lifetime's loyalty prevented her from setting herself apart from it.

"I am sure the bishop is stating what he means rather simply," she said, leaning forward a little and feeling the blood hot in her cheeks. "We are all very distressed at Miss Bellwood's death and at the dark emotions it suggests prompted it. We are naturally most anxious that no suspicion be allowed to fall upon those who are innocent, and that even whoever is guilty may be dealt with with as little exposure of private tragedy as possible." She stared at Cornwallis, hoping he would accept her altered explanation.

"We all want to avoid unnecessary pain," Cornwallis replied very stiffly, but his eyes were quite gentle as he looked back at her. She could see no criticism in them, and no answering hostility. Reginald had mentioned that he was a naval man. Perhaps some of his unease was due to spending most of his life at sea and entirely in the company of men. She tried to picture him in uniform, standing on the deck with the great sails billowing above him, altering his balance to the heave and pitch of the waters, the wind in his face. Maybe that was why his stare was so clear and his eyes bright and calm. There was something about the elements, the sheer magnitude of them, which reduced pomposity to a tiny, ridiculous thing. She could not imagine Cornwallis blustering or being evasive, or sheltering behind a lie.

"Then you take my point that we need very great skill in the matter," the bishop was saying, his voice sharp with urgency and, Isadora thought, a note of uncharacteristic fear. She could not remember seeing him so rattled before.

"We need honesty and persistence as well," Cornwallis said firmly. "And Pitt is the best man. It is a very delicate matter. Unity Bellwood was with child, and we may assume it is very likely her murder was connected to that fact."

The bishop winced and looked hastily at Isadora. Cornwallis blushed.

"Don't be absurd!" she said quickly. "You have no need to skirt around such a subject because I am here. I have probably spoken to far more unmarried young women expecting children than you have. More than a few of them were seduced by their betters, but some of them did the seducing."

"I wish you would not speak of such things in those terms," the bishop said disapprovingly. He stepped forward from the fire. He was scorching the backs of his legs. "It is both a sin and a tragedy. To compound it with malice is appalling. If it is . . . was . . . Ramsay Parmenter, then I can only assume that he is mad, and the best thing we can do for everyone is to have him certified so and put into a place of safety where he can harm no one any further." He winced as the hot fabric of his trousers brushed against his leg. "Is it not possible that you can do that, Cornwallis? Exercise a little judicious compassion rather than ruin a whole family for the sake of following every letter of the law. Dragging out the inevitable to make a public spectacle of the very private fall from grace of a most excellent man . . . I mean hitherto excellent, of course," he corrected.

Isadora held her breath. She looked at Cornwallis.

"Murder is not a private fall from grace," Cornwallis said coolly. "The law requires that it be answered publicly, for the sake of everyone concerned."

"Nonsense!" the bishop retorted. "How can it possibly be in Parmenter's interest, or that of his family, let alone that of the church, that this should be dealt with in public? And it is not in the public's interest, above all, that they should witness the decay and descent into madness of one of the leaders of their spiritual well-being."

The butler came in quietly. "Dinner is served, sir," he said with a bow.

The bishop glared at him.

Isadora rose. Her legs were shaking. "Mr. Cornwallis, would you care to come to the dining room?" What could she say to make this dreadful situation better? Did Cornwallis imagine she was part of this hypocrisy? How could she tell him she was not without in the same moment becoming disloyal and exhibiting a greater duplicity. He was a man who would value loyalty. She valued it herself. She had remained silent countless times when she disagreed. On a few occasions she had learned her error or shortsightedness afterwards, and was glad she had not displayed her lack of knowledge.

Cornwallis rose to his feet. "Thank you," he accepted, and the three of them walked rather stiffly through to the very formal dining room in French blue and gold. For once Isadora's taste had prevailed over the bishop's. He had wished for burgundy carpets and curtains with heavy skirts to spread over the floor. This was less heavy, and the long mirror gave it a look of greater space.

When they were seated and the first course served, the bishop took up the point again.

"It is in no one's interest to make this public," he repeated, staring at Cornwallis over the soup. "I am sure you understand that."

"On the contrary," Cornwallis said very levelly. "It is in everyone's interest. Most of all it is in Parmenter's own interest. He maintains he is not guilty. He deserves the right to stand trial and demand of us that we prove it beyond a reasonable doubt."

"Really . . ." The bishop was furious. His face was pink and his eyes hectically bright.

Isadora looked at him and felt overwhelmed with guilt. He did not look like a familiar friend who had temporarily lost his way and made a mistake. He was a stranger—and one she did not particularly like. She should not have felt that. It was inexcusable. Everything in her turned towards Cornwallis, calm and angry, certain of himself and his beliefs.

"That is a piece of sophistry, sir," the bishop accused. "I will not insult you by suggesting the reasons."

"Oh, Reginald!" Isadora said under her breath.

"What would you prefer we do, Bishop Underhill?" Cornwallis stared back at him. "Bundle Parmenter away secretly, without giving him the opportunity to prove his innocence or our necessity to prove his guilt? Leave him in a madhouse for the rest of his life to save our embarrassment?"

The bishop was scarlet. His hand trembled. "You have misquoted me, sir! That suggestion is appalling!"

It was precisely what he had implied, and Isadora knew it. How could she rescue him and maintain any integrity of her own?

"I am sure you are right, Mr. Cornwallis," she said very guardedly without looking up at him. "I think we had not realized the consequences of what we were saying. We are not familiar with the law, and thank heaven nothing like this has ever happened before. Of course, we have had our misfortunes, but they have not included actual crime, only sins before the church." She lifted her eyes to face him at last.

"Of course." He was staring at her intently, and what she saw in his expression was not disgust but shyness, and admiration. It was as if a warmth had unfolded inside her. "It is . . . it is a tragedy we none of us are accustomed . . ." He faltered, not knowing what he wanted to say. "But I cannot step outside the ways of the law. I dare not, because I am not sure enough of what is true to take the judgment upon myself." He laid his soup spoon on his plate. "But I believe I know what is right, at least as far as the necessity to learn the truth. It is extremely probable that Ramsay Parmenter killed Miss Bellwood because she was a forthright and offensive young woman who defied everything in which he believed."

His voice dropped and his face was full of sadness. "He may have been the father of her child, but equally, he may not. If either Mallory Parmenter or Dominic Corde were, then they also had reason to wish her dead. She could have ruined either of them in their chosen vocations. Whether she exercised blackmail over anyone we do not know, but I fear we must learn. I am sorry. I wish it were not so."

"We all do." She smiled ruefully. "But that has never changed anything."

The bishop cleared his throat noisily. "I trust you will keep me apprised of any progress you make on the matter?"

"Anything that affects the well-being of the church I shall tell you immediately," Cornwallis promised, his face without a flicker of warmth. He could have been facing the captain of an enemy ship across an icy sea.

Isadora wondered if he was a religious man. Perhaps the power of the oceans, man's relative helplessness, his dependence upon the light of the stars, the winds and great currents, had instilled in him a deeper kind of knowledge of God, the reliance on the faith that held life in its hands, not the mere convenience or the praise and reputation of fellowmen. How long had it been since Reginald had dealt with issues of life and death, not mere administration?

The conversation was stilted. The servants removed the soup dishes and brought the next course. The bishop made some remark. Cornwallis replied and added a comment.

Isadora should be entertaining, filling in the silences with some innocent observations, but her mind was on far deeper and more urgent issues. Why did Reginald not know Ramsay Parmenter well enough to be aware if he had had an affair with this woman or not? He should know of such a terrible flaw in the faith and the morality, let alone the trespass, of one of his clergy.

Why on earth had he pushed so hard for Parmenter's elevation if he scarcely knew him? Was it simply a matter of having his own man? Had he ever talked with him on anything that truly mattered? On good and evil, on joy, on repentance and understanding of the terrible self-destruction of sin. Did he ever speak of sin at all as a real thing, not a word to roll around the lips from the pulpit? Did he take time to look at selfishness and the misery which produced it, the confusion and the bleakness?

Did he ever do anything except administer, tell other people what to do and how to do it? Did he visit the sick and the poor, the confused and the lost, the angry, the overbearing, the ambitious and the cruel, and face them with a mirror to their weaknesses? Did he nourish with faith the tired and the frightened and the bereaved?

Or did he talk about buildings, music and ceremonies—and how to stop Ramsay Parmenter from causing a scandal? If he could not face the reality of pain, what was all the singing and praying worth?

What was the real man like beneath the vestments? Was it somebody she loved or simply somebody to whom she had become accustomed?

Cornwallis left as soon after the meal was over as was civil. Reginald returned to his study to read, and Isadora went to bed in silence, her thoughts still too loud in her head for her to rest.

And when she closed her eyes, it was Cornwallis's face which at least allowed her to relax, and for a moment the ghost of a smile touched her lips.

CHAPTER
FIVE

At the same time as Pitt was in Cornwallis's office listening to Smithers, Dominic was in the withdrawing room in Brunswick Gardens talking to Vita Parmenter. The maids had already dusted and swept the room and the fire was beginning to burn up well. It was a bright morning, but cold, and Vita shivered a little as she moved restlessly back and forth, unable to sit.

"I wish I knew what that policeman was thinking," she said, turning and looking at Dominic, her face puckered with distress. "Where is he? Who is he talking to, if not us?"

"I don't know," he said honestly, wishing he could comfort her instead of standing helplessly and watching her fear. "I really know very little of how they work. He may be finding out more about Unity."

"Why?" She was confused. "What difference can it make?" She moved jerkily, one moment spreading her hands wide, the next knotting them together till it must have hurt her, nails digging into her palms. "Do you mean that because she was a loose-living woman in the past, he may think she behaved that way here?"

He was startled. He had not thought Vita knew anything of Unity's past. It was peculiarly disturbing, but he should have realized that she must have heard Unity's talk about moral freedom, the right

146

to follow emotions and appetites, the nonsense she frequently talked about the liberating influence of passions and how commitment stifled people, women in particular. He had once or twice tried to argue with her that commitment actually protected people, most especially women, and she had withered him with her anger and contempt. Thinking of it now, it was foolish to suppose Vita had not seen or heard at least something of such attitudes.

She was standing on the edge of the Aubusson carpet looking at him with real fear in her wide eyes. She looked very vulnerable, for all the inner strength he knew she possessed.

"I don't even know that that is what he is doing," he answered quietly, stepping a little closer to her. "It is just a possibility. It must be common sense to look at the life of someone who has been . . . killed . . . when trying to discover who is responsible."

"I suppose so." Her voice was husky. "Does that mean . . . do you think . . . that it may not be Ramsay?" She stared up at him, her face white, her expression veering between hope and despair.

Without thinking he put out his hand and took hers, holding it gently. Her fingers were limp for an instant, then clung to him desperately.

"I'm so sorry!" he whispered. "I wish there were something I could do. Anything. I owe you so much."

She smiled a very little—it was just a curving at the corners of her lips—but as if it mattered to her.

"Ramsay helped me when I was in the depths," he went on. "And now there seems nothing I can do to help him."

She lowered her eyes. "If he killed Unity, there is nothing any of us can do to help him. It . . ." She gulped. "It is the . . . the not knowing which is unbearable." Then she shook herself. "That is a silly thing to say . . . and weak . . . we have to bear it." Her voice dropped. "But, Dominic, it hurts!"

"I know . . ."

"All sorts of terrible things keep going through my mind." She was still whispering, as if she could not bring herself to say things clearly, although there was no one else in the room. "Is it disloyal of me?" She searched his eyes. "Do you despise me for it? I think perhaps I despise myself. But I wonder if he was attracted to her . . . she . . . was very . . . very vibrant, very . . . full of ideas and emotions. She had beautiful eyes, didn't you think?"

He found himself smiling in spite of the wretchedness of the situation. Unity's eyes were so much less beautiful than Vita's own. Unity had been voluptuous. He remembered her body with a shiver, and her lips.

"Not remarkable," he answered with literal truth. "Far less so than yours." He disregarded the color filling her cheeks. "And it is hard to believe Ramsay found her appealing. He disliked her opinions too much. She was very critical, you know." He still held her hand, and she was gripping his hand. "If she found anyone in a mistake," he went on, "she never refrained from telling them about it, and usually with pleasure. That does not predispose a man towards romantic ideas."

She looked at him steadily for several seconds. "Do you really think not?" she said at last. "She was a little sharp, wasn't she? A little cruel with her tongue . . ."

"Very!" He let his hand fall from hers. "I don't think you should fear that. It is so far from the man we know."

"They worked together a great deal . . ." She could not completely rid herself of the fear. "She was young, and . . . very . . ."

He knew what she meant, even if she was reluctant to use the words. Unity had been physically highly attractive.

"They did not actually work together so much," he pointed out. "Ramsay worked in his study, and she quite often worked in the library. They conferred only when it was necessary. And there were always servants about. And, in fact, almost as long as Unity has been here, so has Mallory, so have I. The house is full of people. Not to mention Clarice and Tryphena. Pitt must know that, too."

She did not look greatly comforted. The furrow of anxiety was still deep between her eyes, and her face was very pale.

"Did you ever see anything to suggest it?" he asked her, almost certain she would say no. He could not imagine Ramsay having any relationship with Unity except the very formal and rather unhappy one he had seen. On every occasion he could recall observing them together they had either been working, and the conversation had been academic and often based on disagreement of one kind or another, or else they had been in public and rather cool. There had been a lot of differences of opinion, carefully concealed beneath outward civility for the most part, but containing a sharp element of Unity's need to prove herself right. Unity had taken distinct pleasure in making her points. She had never let an opportunity slip. She catered to no one's feelings. Possibly it was intellectual integrity. He thought it more likely it was a much more childish desire to win.

Ramsay had taken losing a point, any point, badly. He had masked it with a pretense of indifference, but it was plain enough in his thinned lips and long silences. Any physical passion between them was unimaginable.

"No . . ." Vita shook her head. "No . . . I didn't."

"Then don't believe it," he assured her. "Don't let it even enter your mind. It is not worthy of either of you."

The ghost of a smile touched her mouth again. She took a deep breath and faced him. "You are very kind to me, Dominic. Very gentle. I don't know what any of us would do without your strength to support us. I trust you as I can trust no one else."

"Thank you," he said with a rush of pleasure even the circumstances around them could not dampen. To be trusted was something he had long hungered for. In the past he had not been—and had not deserved to be. He had too often placed his own needs and appetites before anything else. He had seldom been spiteful, simply self-obsessed, thoughtless, behaving on impulse, like a child. Since Ramsay had found him and taught him so much, the things he desired had changed. He had tasted the depths of loneliness in the knowledge that those who valued him did so only for his handsome face and the appetites of theirs he could satisfy. He was like a good meal, hungered for intensely, eaten, and then forgotten. It had all been meaningless, devoid of the things which last.

Now Vita trusted him. She knew countless good and learned men dedicated to helping others, yet she felt he had strength and honor. He found himself smiling back at her.

"There is nothing I want more than to be of comfort to you during this appalling time," he said with profound feeling. "Anything whatever that I can do, you have but to tell me. I cannot say what will happen, but I can promise to give you my support, whatever it is, and to be here to stand beside you."

At last she seemed to relax, her body eased and the tension slipped away from her shoulders. Her back became less rigid. There was even a little color in her cheeks.

"It was a very blessed day for us when you entered this house," she said softly. "I am going to need you, Dominic. I fear very much what that policeman is going to find. Oh, I believe you are right, Ramsay did not have any romantic relationship with Unity." She smiled a little. "The more I think of what you said, the more foolish it seems. He disliked her too much for that."

She was standing very still, about two feet away from him. He could smell her perfume. "In fact, I think he was afraid of her," she continued. "For her quickness of mind and her cruel tongue, but most of all for the things she said about faith. She was terribly destructive, Dominic. I could hate her for that." She drew in her breath and let it out in a shuddering sigh. "It is a wicked thing deliberately to mock someone else's belief and systematically to take it apart and leave them with nothing but the broken pieces. I ought to be sorry she is dead, oughtn't I? But I can't be. Is that very wrong of me?"

"No," he said quickly. "No, it is completely understandable. You have seen the damage she has done, and you are afraid of it. So am I. Life is quite hard enough for most of us. Faith is all that enables us to get through with some dignity and strength. It makes healing and forgiveness possible, and hope when we can see no end to difficulty or grief. To rob people of it is a fearful thing to do, and when the victim is someone you love, how much more must you feel it."

"Thank you." She touched his hand lightly, then straightening her shoulders, she turned and walked away towards the baize door and the butler's quarters. Domestic necessities did not stop because of mourning, or fear, or policemen investigating the tragedies of your life.

Dominic went upstairs to see Ramsay. There must be practical duties with which he could help. Also perhaps there was some way in which he could offer, if not comfort, at least friendship. One thing at least, he could not run away. Ramsay must know he would not be deserted either from suspicion or cowardice.

He put his hand into his pocket for his handkerchief, but it was not there. He must have dropped it—an annoying circumstance because it was a good one, monogrammed linen from his better financial days. Still, it was barely important now.

He knocked on the study door, and when Ramsay answered, he went in.

"Ah, Dominic," Ramsay said with a forced courage. He looked ill, as if he had slept little and his weariness was deeper than the merely physical. There was a hollowness around his eyes, but also within them. "I am glad you came." He moved his hands briskly among the papers on his desk, as though whatever he was looking for was of great importance. "There are one or two people I would like you to see." He looked up with a brief smile. "Old friends, in a sense, parishioners who need a word of comfort or guidance. I should be very obliged if you could find the time today. There it is." He produced a piece of paper on which were written four names and addresses. He passed it across the desk. "None of them is far. You could walk if the weather is pleasant." He glanced at the window. "I think it is."

Dominic took the list, read it, then put it in his pocket.

"Of course I will." He wanted to add something, but now that he was alone with Ramsay he did not know what. There was a generation between them. Ramsay was in every way his senior. He had rescued Dominic when he was in despair, so filled with self-loathing he even contemplated taking his own life. It was Ramsay who had patiently taught him a different and better way, who had introduced a true faith, not the bland, complacent, Sunday-only sort he was used to. How could he now tax Ramsay over this tragedy and press him to speak when he obviously did not wish to?

Or did he? He was sitting awkwardly in his large chair, his hands fiddling with papers, his eyes first on Dominic's, then downcast, then up again.

"Do you wish to speak about it?" Dominic asked, wondering if he were trespassing unforgivably, but to sit in silence was such a cowardly thing to do.

Ramsay did not pretend to misunderstand.

"What is there to say?" He shrugged his shoulders. He looked bemused, and Dominic realized that behind the effort to be busy, to appear normal, he was also very frightened. "I don't know what happened." His face tightened. "We quarreled. She left the room in a temper, shouting back at me. I am ashamed to say I shouted at her equally abusively. Then I returned to my desk. I am not aware of hearing anything more. I disregard many of the household sounds, the occasional bang or squeal." For a moment his concentration on the present was broken. "I recall one of them spilling a bucket of water on the carpet in the library. She had been cleaning the windows. She screamed as if she were being attacked by robbers." He looked bemused. "Such rage. Everyone came running. And then there are always the mice."

"Mice?" Dominic was lost. "Mice are tiny. They squeak."

A flicker of amusement lit Ramsay's eyes for a moment, then died. "Maids scream, Dominic, if they see mice. I thought Nellie would crack the chandeliers."

"Oh, yes, of course." Dominic felt ridiculous. "I didn't think . . ."

Ramsay sighed and leaned back in his chair. "Why should you? You were trying to be helpful. I realize that and appreciate it. You were giving me the opportunity to tell you if I had some appalling burden on my conscience—if, in fact, I did push Unity down the stairs, either intentionally or accidentally. It can't have been easy for you to approach me on the subject, and I am aware of the courage it must have taken." He looked straight back at Dominic. "Perhaps it is a relief to speak about it . . ."

Dominic felt panic rise up inside him. He was not equal to this. What if Ramsay confessed? Was Dominic bound by any oath of confidence, or even an unspoken understanding? What should he do? Persuade Ramsay to confess to Pitt? Why? Help him towards a repentance before God? Did Ramsay even understand what he had done? Surely that was the most important thing? Dominic looked at him and saw no harrowing guilt. Fear, certainly, and some guilt, some awareness of the enormity of the situation. But not the guilt of murder.

"Yes . . ." Dominic swallowed and nearly choked. He clasped his hands together in his lap, below the height of the desk, where Ramsay could not see them.

Ramsay smiled more widely. "Your face is transparent, Dominic. I am not going to lay a burden of guilt upon you. The worst I can confess to is that I am not sorry she is dead . . . not nearly as sorry as I know I should be. She was another human being, young and full of energy and intelligence. I mustn't suppose that, in spite of her behavior to the contrary at times, she was not just as capable of tenderness and hope, love and pain as the rest of us."

He bit his lip, his eyes full of confusion.

"My brain tells me that it is tragic that her life should have been cut off. My emotions tell me I am greatly relieved not to have to hear her arrogant certainty in the superiority of mankind over all else, most especially of Mr. Darwin. Passionately . . . intensely . . ." His fingers locked around his pen so violently he bent the quill. "I do not wish to be a random organism descended from apes!" His voice thickened, close to tears. "I wish to be the creation of God, a God who has created everything around me and cares for it, who will redeem me for my weaknesses, forgive my errors and my sins, and who will somehow sort out the tangles of our human lives and make a kind of sense of them in the end." He dropped to a whisper. "And I can no longer believe it, except for moments when I am alone, at night, and the past seems to come back to me, and I can forget all the books and the arguments and feel as I once used to."

Rain pattered against the window, and the moment after sunlight picked out the bright drops.

"She is not the cause of doubt in the world," Ramsay went on. "Of course she is not. I had heard the arguments before she ever came to Brunswick Gardens. We all had. We had discussed them. I have reassured many a confused and unhappy parishioner, as no doubt you have, and will continue to." He swallowed, pulling his mouth into a line of pain. "But she focused it all. She was so monumentally certain!" He was looking beyond Dominic now, towards the bookcase with the glass fronts shining in the sudden sun. "It is no one thing she said, rather the day-by-day air of being so terribly sure of herself. She never let slip a chance to mock. Her logic was relentless."

He stopped for a moment. Dominic tried to think of something to say, then realized he should not interrupt now.

"She could demolish mine in any argument we had. Her memory was perfect," Ramsay said with a shrug. "There were times when she made me feel ridiculous. I admit, Dominic, I hated her then. But I did not push her, that I swear." He looked at Dominic steadily, pleading to be believed, and yet not willing to embarrass him by asking openly. And perhaps he was afraid to hear the answer.

Dominic was embarrassed. He wanted to believe him, yet how could it be true? Four people had heard Unity cry out "No, no, Reverend!" Had it not been a protest but a cry for help? Then it could only be Mallory who had pushed her.

Why? She had not touched his faith. His beliefs fed on opposition. To him it was only another confirmation that he was right. Every time she mocked him or checked his blind statements with logic, he simply restated them. If she did not understand, it was due to her lack of humility. If his reasoning was faulty, even completely circular, that was the mystery of God, and not supposed to be understood by man. If she made a scientific statement he disliked, he simply contradicted it. He might be angry, but he was never inwardly disturbed.

"Dominic, I did not kill her!" Ramsay repeated, and this time the fear and the loneliness were sharp in his voice, intruding into Dominic's emotions.

This was a debt he must repay. But how, without endangering himself? And surely Ramsay, who had made him what he was, would not want to undo his creation by having him deny his honesty now.

"Then it was Mallory," Dominic said, forcing himself to look at Ramsay's eyes. "Because I did not."

Ramsay covered his face with his hands and leaned forward over the desk.

Dominic sat motionless. He had no idea what to do. Ramsay's distress seemed to fill the room. He could not possibly be unaware of it. To pretend would be inconceivable. Ramsay had never pretended with him, never evaded an issue or offered insincere words. Now, at this moment in this silent room, it was time to repay the obligation he had incurred. It was time to put into effect all the good ideas, the beliefs he had worked for so hard. What was the theory worth if, when he was faced with reality, he was unable or unwilling to meet it? It became a sham, just as hollow and useless as Unity Bellwood had claimed.

He could not allow that to be true!

He thought of reaching across the desk and touching Ramsay's hand, of gripping it, then instantly abandoned the idea. They knew each other so well in some ways. Ramsay had seen the very depth of his own confusion and despair. He had not shrunk then even from holding him.

But that was different. Even as it had placed a bond between them, it had also set them apart, made Ramsay forever the guide, the invulnerable, the rescuer. To try to reverse that now would be to strip from him the last dignity. Dominic would not intrude.

He kept his hands where they were.

"If it was Mallory, we must face it," he said aloud. "We must help him in any and every way possible. We must help him to acknowledge what has happened and, if we can, to understand it. Either he did it by accident or else it was intentional."

His voice sounded cold, terribly rational. It was not what he intended.

"If it was meant, then he must have had a powerful reason. Perhaps she taunted him once too often, and he finally lost his temper. I expect he regrets it bitterly now. Every man has lost his temper at some time in his life. It is easy to understand, certainly with Unity."

Ramsay lifted his head slowly and stared at Dominic. The older man looked ashen, his eyes haunted.

Dominic could barely control his voice. He heard himself speaking as if he were someone else, far away. He still sounded extraordinarily calm.

"Then we shall help him with the police and the law. He must know that we shall not abandon him, nor condemn him. I am sure he understands the difference between condemning the sin and the person who commits it. We shall have to show him the reality of that."

Ramsay breathed in and out very slowly. "He says he did not do it."

Dominic sat quite still. Did Ramsay think that he had? Is that what he was saying? It would be natural. For all their differences, however deep, Mallory was Ramsay's son.

"Do you think Clarice did?" He was struggling to use reason. He must be sensible.

"No, of course not!" Ramsay's face showed how absurd he considered the idea.

"I didn't," Dominic said steadily. "I did not especially like her, but I had no cause to kill her."

"Didn't you?" Ramsay asked with a lift of curiosity in his voice. "I am not blind, Dominic, even if I appear to be absorbed in my books and papers. I saw how she was attracted to you, how she looked at you. She teased Mallory, provoked him, but he was too vulnerable to be a real challenge to her. But you were. You are older, wiser; you have known women before, a great many of them, so you told me when we first met. And I should have guessed it even if you had not told me. It is there in the assurance of your bearing with them. You understand women too well to be a novice. You rejected Unity, didn't you?"

Dominic felt a flush of extreme discomfort. "Yes . . ."

"Then you were the perfect challenge for her," Ramsay concluded. "She loved a battle. Victory was her ultimate delight. Intellectual victory was very sweet, and God knows she sought enough of those over me, and found too many . . ." His face tightened with momentary anger and humiliation, then smoothed out again. "But the power of emotional victory was more complete. Are you sure she did not provoke you too far, and it was you who momentarily lost your temper with her? I could understand your pushing her away from you, literally, physically, and causing the accident which killed her."

"So could I," Dominic agreed, feeling the fear rise inside him. So could Pitt. In fact, Pitt would enjoy believing it. It would let Ramsay escape, and Vita. It would be exactly what Clarice prayed for, escape for both her father and her brother. And, of course, Mallory would welcome it. Tryphena would not care as long as someone was blamed.

Dominic swallowed and found his throat tight. He had not pushed Unity. He had been nowhere near the landing when she fell, and he had no idea who had been. This was even worse than Cater Street. Then it had all been new. He had not known what to expect. He had been numb with the shock of Sarah's death. Now he was very much alive, every nerve aware of the dreadful possibilities. He had seen the pattern before.

"But I did not push her," he said again. "You are right, I am experienced." He swallowed. His mouth was dry. "I know how to refuse a woman without panicking, without provoking a quarrel, let alone violence." That was not strictly true, but this was not a time for going into qualifying explanations.

Ramsay said nothing.

Dominic cast around for what to say next. Ramsay all but stood accused of the crime. If he were innocent he must feel just the same sense of terror that had brushed by Dominic, only worse. Everyone had implicated Ramsay, even his own family. The police seemed to believe them. He must feel so alone it was beyond the imagination to conceive.

Instinctively, Dominic stretched out his hand and put it over Ramsay's wrist, then when he realized what he had done, it was too late to pull away.

"Pitt will get to the truth," he said firmly. "He will not allow an innocent man to be accused or to suffer arrest. That is why they sent him. He will not bow to pressure from anyone, and he never gives up."

Ramsay looked mildly surprised. "How do you know?"

"He is married to my wife's sister. I knew him a long time ago."

"Your wife?"

"She is dead. She was murdered . . . ten years ago."

"Oh . . . yes, of course. I'm sorry. For a moment I forgot," Ramsay apologized. Gently he loosed his hand from Dominic's, ran it over his head as if to brush back the hair which was too thin to need it. "I am afraid I am finding it very difficult to concentrate at the moment. This is like walking through a dark dream. I keep tripping over things."

Dominic rose to his feet. "I will go and visit these people. Please . . . please don't despair . . ."

Ramsay smiled bleakly. "I won't. I suppose I owe you that much, don't I?"

Dominic said nothing. The debt was his, and he knew it. He went out and closed the door softly.

His first call was to Miss Edith Trethowan, a lady whose age it was difficult to determine because ill health had robbed her of the vitality she might normally have enjoyed. Her skin was pale and her hair was almost white. Dominic had at first assumed her to be in her sixties, but one or two references she had made had embarrassed him for his clumsiness, and he had realized she was probably no more than forty-five. It was pain which had marked her face and bent her shoulders and chest, not time.

She was fully dressed, but lying on a chaise longue, as she usually did on her better days. She was obviously pleased to see him.

"Come in, Mr. Corde!" she said quickly, her eyes lighting. She waved a thin blue-veined hand towards the other comfortable chair. "How nice to see you." She peered at him. "But you are looking tired. Have you been doing too much again?"

He smiled and sat down where she invited. It was on the tip of his tongue to tell her why he looked weary, but it would only distress her. She liked to hear of happy things. Her own trials were as much as she could bear.

"Yes, I suppose I have," he agreed with a shrug. "But I don't mind. Perhaps I should use better judgment? But today is for visiting friends. How are you?"

She also hid reality. "Oh, I am very well, thank you, and in excellent spirits. I have just read some beautiful letters from a lady traveler in Egypt and Turkey. What a life she leads! I do enjoy reading about it, but I think I should be fearfully afraid to do it myself." She gave a little shiver. "Aren't we fortunate to be able to partake of all these things through other people? All the interest, and none of the flies and heat and diseases."

"Absolutely," he agreed. "No travel sickness, no lumping or

bumping on the back of mules or camels, and no sleeping on the ground. You know, Miss Trethowan, I confess, above all I like to have decent plumbing . . ."

She giggled happily. "I do so agree. We are not all the stuff of explorers, are we?"

"And if nobody stayed at home, whom would they tell when they returned?" he asked.

She was greatly amused. She lay for half an hour talking of all she had read, and he listened attentively and made appropriate remarks every time she stopped long enough to allow him. He promised to find her more books on similar subjects, and left her feeling well satisfied. He had said nothing of religion to her, but he only thought of it afterwards. It had seemed inappropriate.

Next he visited Mr. Landells, a widower who was finding himself acutely lonely and growing more bitter by the week.

"Good morning, Mr. Landells," Dominic said cheerfully as he was admitted to the chilly sitting room. "How are you?"

"My rheumatism is fearful," Landells replied crossly. "Doctor is no use at all. Wettest year I can remember, and I can remember a fair number. Shouldn't wonder if we have a cold summer, too. Happens as often as not." He sat down stiffly, and Dominic sat opposite him. This was obviously going to be hard work.

"Have you heard from your daughter in Ireland?" Dominic enquired.

"Even wetter there," Landells said with satisfaction. "Don't know what she went for." He leaned forward and put a tiny piece of coal onto the fire.

"I thought you said her husband had a position there. Did I misunderstand?"

Landells glared at him. "I thought you were supposed to cheer me up! Isn't that what the church is for, make us believe all this is somehow for the best? God is going to make it all worth something!" He waved his rheumatic hand irritably at the world in general. "You can't tell me why my Bessie is dead, and I'm sitting here alone with nothing to do and no one to care if I die tomorrow. You come here because it's your duty." He sniffed and glared at Dominic. "You have to. The Reverend comes by now and then because it's his duty. Tells me a lot about God and redemption and the like. Tells me Bessie is resurrected somewhere and we'll meet again, but he doesn't believe it any more than I do!" He curled his lip. "I can see it in his face. We sit opposite each other and talk a lot of nonsense and neither of us believes a word."

He fished for a large handkerchief and blew his nose loudly. "What do you know about growing old, finding your body doesn't work properly anymore and those you love are dead and there's nothing to look forward to except dying yourself? I don't want any of your platitudes about God."

"No," Dominic agreed with a smile, but looking at Landells very directly. "You want someone to blame. You are feeling lonely and frightened, and it is easier to be angry than to admit that. It is a nice releasing sort of emotion. If you can send me away thoroughly crushed, you will feel you have power over somebody . . . even if it is only power to hurt." He did not know why he said it. He heard his words as if they were a stranger's. Ramsay would have been horrified.

Landells was, too. His face flushed scarlet.

"You can't speak to me like that!" he protested. "You're a curate. You've got to be nice to me. It's your job! It's what you're paid for!"

"No, it's not," Dominic contradicted. "I'm paid to tell you the truth, and that is not what you want to hear."

"I'm not frightened," Landells said sharply. "How dare you say that I am. I'll report you to Reverend Parmenter. We'll soon see what he has to say. He comes and prays for me, talks to me with respect, tells me about the resurrection, makes me feel better. He doesn't sit there and criticize."

"You said he doesn't believe it, and neither do you," Dominic pointed out.

"Well, I don't, but that's not the point! He tries."

"I do believe it. I believe we will all be resurrected, you and Bessie," Dominic answered. "From what I hear of her, she was a lovely woman, generous and wise, honest, happy and funny. She laughed a lot . . ." He saw the tears in Landells's eyes and ignored them. "She would have missed you, had you died first, but she would not have sat around getting angrier and angrier and blaming God. Just suppose there is a resurrection . . . Your body will be renewed to its prime, but your spirit will be just the same. Are you ready to meet Bessie like this . . . never mind meeting God?"

Landells stared at him. The fire settled in the grate. It needed stoking again, but there was too little coal in the bucket. "You believe that?" the old man said slowly.

"Yes, I do." Dominic spoke without doubt. He did not know why; it was a certainty inside him. He believed what he had read about Easter Sunday and Mary Magdalene in the garden. He believed the story of the disciples on the road to Emmaeus who had walked with the risen Christ and discovered it only at the last moment, when he had broken bread with them.

"What about Mr. Darwin and his monkeys?" Landells demanded, the expression in his eyes flickering between hope and despair, momentary victory and lasting defeat. Part of him wanted to win the argument; a larger, more honest part was desperate to lose.

"I don't understand it," Dominic confessed. "But he isn't right if he says God did not create the earth and all that is on it, or that we are not special to Him but simply accidental forms of life. Look at the wonder and the beauty of the universe, Mr. Landells, and tell me it is chance and there is no meaning to it."

"There's no meaning to my life now." Landells's face crumpled. He was winning, and he did not want to.

"Since Bessie has gone?" Dominic asked. "Was there before? Was she no more than an accident, a monkey's descendant gone gloriously right?"

"Mr. Darwin . . ." Landells began, then subsided in his chair,

smiling at last. "All right, Mr. Corde. I'll believe you. I don't understand, mind, but I'll believe. You tell me why the Reverend Parmenter didn't say that, eh? He's senior to you . . . a lot senior. You're
only just a beginner, you are."

Dominic knew the answer to that, but he was not going to tell
Landells. Ramsay's faith was rooted in reason, and his reason had
deserted him in the face of an argument more skilled than his own,
growing out of a field of science he did not understand.

"I'm still right," Dominic said firmly, rising to his feet. "Go and
read your Bible, Mr. Landells . . . and smile while you're doing it."

"Yes, Mr. Corde. Will you pass it to me, please? I'm too stiff to get
up out of this chair." There was a flash of humor in the old man's
eyes, a parting shot of victory.

Dominic visited Mr. and Mrs. Norland, had luncheon late, and spent
the rest of the afternoon with Mr. Rendlesham. He returned to
Brunswick Gardens in time for an early dinner, which was quite the
most appalling meal he could remember. Everyone was present and
extremely nervous. The day's silence from the police had told upon
their fears, and tempers were frayed even before the first course was
cleared away and the second served. Conversation went in fits and
starts, often two people speaking at once and then falling silent, no
one continuing.

Vita alone tried to keep some semblance of normality. She sat at
the foot of the table looking pale and frightened, but her hair was
immaculately dressed as always, her gown soft gray trimmed with
black, as was suitable to observe the presence of death in the household but not of a family member. Dominic could not help noticing
once again what a lovely woman she was, how her grace and poise
were better than conventional beauty. Her charm did not fade, nor
had it ever become tedious.

Tryphena, on the other hand, looked terrible. She had taken no
trouble at all with her normally lovely hair. At the moment it looked

dull and disorderly, and her eyes were still puffy and a little pink. She was sullen, as if resenting everyone else's failure to equal her depth of grief. She was dressed in unrelieved black, no ornament at all.

Clarice was also untidy, but then she had never had her mother's sophistication of dress or manner. Her dark hair was often as unruly as it was now, but its natural sheen and wave gave it a certain beauty regardless. She was very pale and kept glaring from one person to another, and spoke to her father unnecessarily often, as if making a tremendous effort to be normal towards him and show she did not believe what everyone else might think. She only succeeded in drawing attention to it.

Mallory was absorbed in thought and answered only when addressed directly. Whatever his preoccupation, he did not allow anyone else to know it.

The table was set as always with the usual crystal and silver, and there were flowers from the conservatory in the center.

Dominic tried to think of anything to say which would not sound too callous, as if there had been no tragedy. They should be able to speak sensibly to one another, to talk of something more than the weather without quarreling. Three of them were men dedicated to the service of God, and yet they all sat at the table avoiding each other's eyes, eating mechanically. The air was filled with fear and suspicion. Everyone knew that one of the three men there had killed Unity, but only one of them knew which, and he carried the burden of guilt and the terror that went with it.

Sitting there chewing meat that was like sawdust in his mouth, wondering how to swallow it, Dominic looked almost under his lashes at Ramsay. He looked older, more tired than usual, perhaps afraid as well, but Dominic could see no trace of guilt in him, nothing to mark him as a man who had killed and was now lying about it, allowing his friend, and worse, his son, to be suspected in his place.

Dominic turned to Mallory and saw his shoulders tense, neck stiff, eyes towards his plate, avoiding anyone else's. He had not once looked at his father. Was that guilt? Dominic did not particularly like Mallory Parmenter, but he had thought him an honest man, if humorless and something of a bore. Perhaps it was largely a matter of callousness. Time would alter that, teach him it was possible to serve God and laugh as well, even to enjoy the beauties and absurdities of life, the richness of nature and of people.

Was he really such a coward as to allow his father to take his punishment for a crime of . . . what . . . passion?

"I suppose it is very hot in Rome?" Clarice's voice cut across his thoughts. "You'll get there in time for summer." She was talking to Mallory.

He looked up, his face dark and angry.

"If I get there at all."

"Why shouldn't you?" Vita asked, her brow puckered as if she did not understand. "I thought everything was arranged."

"It was," he replied. "But I did not 'arrange' for Unity's death. They may view things rather differently now."

"Why should they?" Tryphena said boldly. "It has nothing to do with you. Are they unjust enough to blame you for something you didn't do?" She set down her fork, abandoning her meal. "That's the trouble with your religion; you think everybody is to blame for Adam's sin, and now it looks as if he didn't even exist, but you are still wandering around dipping infants in water to wash it away . . . and they haven't the faintest idea what's going on. All they know is they are dressed up, passed to a strange man who holds them up and talks over them, not to them, and then hands them back again. And that is supposed to make it all all right? I've never heard of such idiotic superstition in my life. It belongs in the Dark Ages, along with trial by ordeal and ducking witches and thinking it is the end of the world if there is a solar eclipse. I don't know how you can be so gullible."

Mallory opened his mouth.

"Tryphena . . ." Vita interrupted, leaning forward.

"When I wanted to wear bloomers to ride a bicycle," Tryphena went on regardless, "because it would be very practical, Papa nearly had an apoplexy."

She waved her hand, only just missing her glass of water.

"But nobody thinks it the least bit odd if you all dress up in long skirts with beads around your neck and sing songs together and drink something you say turns from wine into blood, which sounds absolutely disgusting, not to mention blasphemous. And yet you think cannibals are savages who ought to be—"

Mallory drew in his breath.

"Tryphena! That is enough!" Vita said sharply. She turned to Ramsay, her face creased with irritation. "For goodness sake, say something to her. Defend yourself!"

"I thought it was Mallory she was attacking," Ramsay observed mildly. "The doctrine of the transubstantiation of the host is a Roman belief."

"Then what do you do it for?" Tryphena countered. "You must believe it is something. Or why dress up in embroidered clothes and go through the whole performance?"

Ramsay looked at her sadly but said nothing.

"It is a reminder of who you are and the promises you have made," Dominic said to her as patiently as he could. "And unfortunately we do need reminding."

"Then it wouldn't matter if it were bread and wine or biscuits and milk," she challenged, her eyes bright and victorious.

"Not in the slightest," he agreed with a smile. "If you meant what you said and came with the right spirit. Far more important you come without anger or guile."

She was flushed. The triumph was slipping away from her. "Unity said it was just extremely good theater, designed to impress everyone and keep them obedient and in awe of you," she argued, as if quoting Unity proved something. "It is all show and no substance. It is the desire for power on your part, and superstition on theirs. It makes them feel comfortable if they confess their sins and you forgive them; then they can start over again. And if they don't, then they live in terror of you."

"Unity was a fool!" Mallory said sharply. "And a blasphemer."

Tryphena swung around to face him. "Well, I didn't notice you saying that to her when she was alive. You're suddenly very brave now she's not here anymore and can't reply for herself." Her scorn was devastating. "You were quick enough then to do as she asked you. And I don't recall your ever contradicting her in public in that tone of voice. What conviction you've suddenly developed, and fire to defend your faith."

Mallory's face was white and his eyes hot and defensive. "There was no point in arguing with Unity," he said with a very slight tremor in his voice. "She never listened to anyone because her mind was made up before you began."

"Isn't yours?" Tryphena countered, glaring at him across the white linen and the glass and the dishes.

"Of course it is!" His eyebrows rose. "Mine is a matter of faith. That is quite different."

Tryphena slammed down her fork. She was fortunate not to chip her plate.

"Why does everyone presume that their own belief is based on some virtuous thing like faith, which is all praiseworthy, and Unity's belief is wicked and insincere and based on emotion or ignorance? You are so self-righteous it is sickening . . . and absurd. If you could see yourselves from the outside you'd laugh." She threw the words at them, her face twisted with fury and knowledge of her own helplessness. "You'd think you were a parody. Except you're too cruel to be funny. And you win! That's the unbearable part of it. You win! There's superstition and oppression and ignorance everywhere, and catastrophic injustice." She stood up, glaring at them with tears in her eyes. "You all sit here eating your dinner, and Unity is lying on a cold table in a shroud, waiting to be buried. You'll all dress up—"

"Tryphena!" Vita protested, and was ignored. She turned to Ramsay desperately, but he did nothing.

". . . in your gorgeous gowns and robes," Tryphena went on, her voice choking, "and play the organ and sing your songs and intone prayers over her. Why can't you speak in a proper voice?" She stared at her father challengingly. "How can you speak like that if you really mean a thing you say? You'll carry on like a bad oratorio, and all the time one of you killed her! I keep expecting to wake up and find this is all a nightmare, except I realize it's been going on for years, one way or another. Maybe this is hell?" She flung her arms out, only just missing the top of Dominic's head. "All this . . . hypocrisy! Though hell is supposed to be hot, maybe it isn't. Maybe it's just bright and endless . . . nauseating." She swung around to Vita. "And don't bother to tell me to leave the room . . . I'm going to. If I stayed I should be sick." And she knocked her chair over backwards and stormed out.

Dominic rose and picked up the chair. It would be pointless to try to make excuses for her.

Ramsay looked wretched, eyes cast down towards his plate, skin white around the lips, flushed in patches on his cheeks. Clarice was staring at him with naked distress. Vita kept her gaze steadily ahead of her, as if she could not bear any of it but could not escape.

"For someone who speaks so disparagingly of theater," Clarice said huskily, "she manages to put on a highly dramatic performance. Overacting a bit, though, don't you think? The chair was unnecessary. Nobody likes an actress who upstages the rest of the cast."

"She may be acting," Mallory retorted, "but I'm not!"

Clarice sighed. "What a pity. It would have been your best excuse."

Dominic looked at her quickly, but she was turned towards Ramsay again.

"For what?" Mallory would not let it go.

"Everything," she answered.

"I haven't done anything!" he said defensively, then inclined his head towards his father.

There were two hectic spots of color on Clarice's cheeks. "You mean you didn't push Unity? I've been thinking about that. Maybe she was having an affair with Dominic."

Vita glared at her daughter, her eyes wide and angry. She drew in her breath to say something, but Clarice continued loudly and clearly.

"I can remember lots of things, now I think about it, times when she sought his company, little looks, glances, standing very close to him—"

"That's not true!" Vita interrupted her at last, her voice tight, as if her throat would barely allow the words through. "It's a wretched and irresponsible thing to say, and you will not repeat it. Do you understand me, Clarice?"

Clarice looked at her mother in surprise. "It is all right for Tryphena to imply that Papa murdered Unity, but not to say that Unity was having an affair with Dominic? Why ever not?"

Dominic could feel his own face burning. He remembered those moments, too, with a clarity which horrified him and made him wish he were anywhere but at this table, with Vita looking hurt and dismayed, Mallory's lip curled in loathing, and Ramsay avoiding everyone's eyes, drowning in his own fear and loneliness.

"I suppose he got tired of her," Clarice went on relentlessly. "All that political preaching can become a bit tedious. There are times when it is terribly predictable, and that is a bore. She didn't listen, you see, and men hate a woman who doesn't at least pretend she hangs on their words, even if her mind is miles away. It's an art. Mama is wonderful at it. I've watched her hundreds of times."

Vita blushed and seemed about to say something, but was too frozen in embarrassment.

No one except Dominic noticed the door open and Tryphena appear in the entrance.

"I daresay he found Mama was attractive," Clarice went on in the prickly silence. "That's it. Dominic fell in love with Mama . . ."

"Clarice . . . please . . ." Vita said desperately, but her voice was low, her eyes downcast.

Mallory stared at his sister, his attention at last truly caught.

"I can see it." Clarice warmed to the drama. She sat back with her eyes closed, her chin lifted. She, too, was giving a fine performance. "Unity still besotted with Dominic, but he is bored with her and he's moved on to someone more feminine, more alluring." Her expression was rapt, a fierce concentration filling her. "But she will not give him up. She cannot bear rejection. She blackmails him with their past liaison. She will tell everyone. She will tell Papa; she will tell the church. He will be thrown out."

"That's nonsense!" Dominic protested angrily. "Stop it! You are talking completely irresponsibly, and none of it is true."

"Why not?" She opened her eyes and turned on him. "Why shouldn't someone else be blamed? If it's fair to blame Papa, why not you, or Mallory . . . or me, for that matter? I know I didn't, but I don't know about the rest of you. Isn't that why we are all sitting here wondering about each other, remembering everything we can and trying to make it have meaning? Isn't that what we are all afraid of?" She flung her arms out in an expansive gesture, her eyes wide. "It could be any one of us. How can we protect ourselves except by proving it was somebody else? How well do we really know each other, the secret selves behind the familiar faces? Don't stop me, Mallory!" He had leaned forward. She pushed him away impatiently. "It's true!" She laughed a little wildly. "Maybe Dominic got bored with Unity, fell in love with Mama, and when Unity wouldn't let him go, he killed her. And he's only too happy to see Papa blamed for it, because it not only keeps Dominic from being hanged for it, it gets rid of Papa at the same time. Then Mama is free to marry him, and—"

"That's absurd!" Tryphena said from the doorway, her voice loud and furious. "It's quite impossible."

Clarice swiveled to face her sister. "Why? People have killed for love before now. It makes far more sense than thinking Papa killed her because she was an atheist. Heavens, the world is full of atheists. Christians are supposed to convert them, not kill them."

"Tell that to the Inquisition!" Tryphena snapped back, coming further into the room. "It's impossible because Dominic wouldn't have thrown Unity over. If she'd even have looked at him in that way, which is terribly unlikely, then she'd have been the one to get bored and break it off. And she wouldn't stoop to blackmail. It is infinitely beneath her." She looked at Clarice with loathing. "Everything you say just shows the poverty of your own mind. I came down to apologize, because I disturbed the meal, which was bad manners. But I can see that's all rather pointless now, since Clarice has just accused one of our guests of having an illicit affair with the other and then murdering her in order to blame my father and marry my mother. What is a little thing like upsetting the dinner table?"

"Unity wasn't a guest," Clarice said pedantically. "She was an employee. Papa hired her to help with the translations."

Dominic rose to his feet. He was surprised to find he was shaking. Even his legs felt unsteady. He gripped the back of his chair, knuckles white. He looked from one to another of them.

"One thing Clarice said is true; we are all afraid, and it is making us behave very badly. I do not know what happened to Unity, except that she is dead. Only one person here does know, and there is no purpose in us all protesting innocence or, unless we have some definite fact, in accusing anyone else." He wanted to add that he had not had an affair with Unity, but it would only lead to a round of denials, exactly what he had suggested they do not do. "I am going to study for a while." And he turned and left the table, still trembling inside and aware of a coldness of fear touching his skin. Clarice's suggestion was preposterous, of course it was. But it was not unbelievable. It was a far better motive than anything attributable to Ramsay.

A thoroughly appalling evening was compounded by the arrival of Bishop Underhill at quarter past nine. Both Dominic and Ramsay had no alternative but to go down to the withdrawing room to receive him. He had called in his official capacity to offer his sympathy and support to the whole household during their bereavement and in this most difficult time.

Everyone was gathered together; it was due to his rank in the church. They were all uncomfortable in their different ways. Tryphena glared at him. Vita sat demurely, pale-faced, eyes full of dread. Mallory tried to pretend he was not there. Clarice mercifully kept silent, sitting motionless except for the occasional glance at Dominic.

The bishop stood, awkwardly, uncertain what to do with his hands. One moment he held them together, the next gestured with them wide open, then dropped them, and then started again.

"I am sure all our sympathies are with you during this ordeal," he said resonantly, as if he were addressing an entire congregation. "We shall pray for you in every way . . . in every possible way."

Clarice put her hands up to her face and stifled something which may have been a sneeze. Dominic was sure it was laughter, and he thought he knew what pictures were in her mind. He wished he were free to do the same instead of being obliged to listen seriously and look as if he were full of respect.

"Thank you," Vita murmured. "It is all so horribly confusing."

"Of course it is, my dear Mrs. Parmenter." The bishop seized on something specific to address. "One must seek always for honesty and the guidance of the light of truth to find our way. The Lord has promised to be a lamp unto our path. We must put our trust in Him."

Tryphena rolled her eyes, but the bishop was not looking at her.

Ramsay sat in wretched silence, and Dominic felt agonized for him. He was like a butterfly on a pin, still alive.

"We must have courage," the bishop went on.

Clarice opened her mouth and then closed it again. Her face showed her struggle to keep her temper, and for once Dominic could identify with her utterly. Courage to do what? Not offer the hand of friendship or any promise of loyalty or help. That the bishop had very carefully refrained from doing. He had spoken nothing but the most guarded platitudes.

"We will do all we can," Vita promised, looking up at him. "You are very kind to come to see us. I know how busy you are . . ."

"Nonsense, Mrs. Parmenter," he responded with a smile. "It is the very least I could do . . ."

"The very least," Clarice said under her breath, then she added aloud, "We knew that you would do that, Bishop Underhill."

"Thank you, my dear. Thank you," he accepted.

"I hope you will help us to behave honorably and to have the courage to act only for the best?" Vita went on rather quickly. "Perhaps a word of advice now and then? We should appreciate it so much. I . . ." She left the words hanging between them, the uncompleted sentence witness to her distress.

"Of course," the bishop assured her. "Of course I will. I wish . . . I wish I knew . . . my own experience . . ."

Dominic was embarrassed for them all, and ashamed of himself for how profoundly he loathed the bishop. He should have admired him, should have felt he was a rock of support, wiser than they, stronger, filled with compassion and honor. Instead, the bishop seemed to have hedged and evaded, given general advice they did not need, and scrupulously avoided committing himself to anything.

The bishop's visit dragged out a further half hour, then, to Dominic's intense relief, he left. Vita accompanied him to the door, and Dominic met her in the main hall as she returned. She looked exhausted and almost feverish. How she found the strength to keep her composure as she did, he could not imagine. It would be difficult to think of a more fearful dilemma than that in which she was placed. His admiration for her was boundless. He cast about for some way to tell her so which was not fulsome or merely a further cause for anxiety or embarrassment.

"Your courage is superb," he said gently, standing close enough to her that he could speak softly and be heard by no one else. "We all owe you a great deal. I think perhaps it is your strength which makes this bearable."

She smiled up at him with a sudden rush of pleasure he thought for a moment was absolutely real, as if he had given her a small but precious gift.

"Thank you . . ." she whispered. "Thank you, Dominic."

CHAPTER
SIX

"Do you think it is Ramsay Parmenter?" Charlotte asked, pushing the marmalade across the breakfast table to Pitt. It was now the fourth day since Unity Bellwood's death. Charlotte had, of course, told Pitt about her visit to Brunswick Gardens, and he had not reacted favorably. She had had some considerable explaining to do, and had not been very successful. She knew he was still unhappy about it—not that it was her meddling, which he was more than used to, but because she had gone so quickly to Dominic.

"I don't know," he replied to her question. "It seems most probable from the facts, and least likely from what I can learn of the man."

"People do sometimes behave very out of character." She took a piece of toast herself.

"No, they don't," he argued. "They only behave out of the character you know. If he was a man to do that, it will be there somewhere."

"But if it wasn't him, then it must have been Mallory," she pointed out. "Why would he? The same reason?" She was trying to keep it out of her voice, but at the back of her mind was the cold fear that Dominic would be suspected. The change in him had been so complete, could Pitt believe it? Or would he always see Dominic as he had been in Cater Street, even by his own admission now, selfish, too easily flattered, giving in to appetite at the first whim?

"I doubt it," he replied. "She irritated him with her views, but he was sufficiently certain in his mind it did not trouble him. But he could have been the father of her child, if that is what you mean."

The coldness inside her grew. She tried to recall to her mind the image of Dominic as he had been during their carriage ride to the haberdasher. There was something he was keeping hidden and which troubled him, something to do with Unity.

"Then it probably was Mallory," she said aloud, pouring him more tea without asking. "I spoke quite a lot with Dominic when I visited. I had the opportunity to be alone with him in the carriage. He really has changed utterly, Thomas. He has lost all the old selfishness. He believes in what he is doing now. It is a vocation for him. His whole face lights up when he speaks of it—"

"Does it?" Pitt said dryly, concentrating on his toast.

"You should talk to him yourself," she urged. "You will see how different he is. It is as if he has suddenly grown up into all the best that was possible in him. I don't know what happened, but he was in great despair, and Ramsay Parmenter found him and helped him, and through his pain he discovered a far greater goodness."

He put his knife down. "Charlotte, you have spent the whole breakfast telling me how Dominic has changed. Somebody in that house killed Unity Bellwood, and I shall investigate it until either I discover who it was or there is nothing more to pursue. And that includes Dominic as much as anyone else."

She heard the edge to his voice, but she kept on arguing. "But you don't really think Dominic could have done it, do you?" she persisted. "We knew Dominic, Thomas. He is part of our family." She ignored her tea, which was rapidly going cold. "He might have been foolish in the past, indeed we know he was, but that is a very different thing from murder. He couldn't! He's terribly afraid for Ramsay Parmenter. His whole mind is taken up with his debt of gratitude to him and how he can help now that Ramsay needs him so much."

"None of which means he could not have known Unity far better than he is implying," he answered. "And that she didn't find him extremely attractive and pursue him, perhaps more than he wished, tempt him, and then blackmail him afterwards." He drank the last of his tea and set down the cup. "Taking the cloth forbids a man indulging his natural desires, but it does not stop him feeling them. You are being just as idealistic about Dominic as you used to be in Cater Street. He is a real man, with real weaknesses, like all of us!" He rose from the table, leaving the last two mouthfuls of his toast uneaten. "I am going to see what I can learn about Mallory."

"Thomas!" she called out, but he had gone. She had done the last thing she had meant to. Far from helping Dominic, she had only succeeded in angering Pitt. Of course she knew Dominic was as human and as fallible as anyone else. That was what she was afraid of.

She stood up and started to clear the table.

Gracie came in looking puzzled, her starched apron crisp and clean. She was still so small all her clothes needed taking up, but she had filled out a little and was barely recognizable from the waif she had been when they had taken her in seven years before. Then she had been thirteen and looking for a domestic place, any place at all. She was extremely proud of working for a policeman, and a senior one at that, who solved all kinds of important cases. She never allowed the butcher's boy or the fishmonger to take liberties with her, and told them off soundly if they were impertinent. She was quite capable of giving orders to the woman who came in twice a week to do the heavy scrubbing and laundry.

"Mr. Pitt din't finish 'is breakfast!" she said, looking at the toast.

"I don't think he wanted it," Charlotte replied. There was no point in making up a lie for Gracie. She would not say anything, but she was far too observant to be misled.

"Prob'ly worried about that reverend wot pushed the girl down them stairs," Gracie said with a nod, picking up the teapot and putting it on the tray. " 'Nother nasty one, that. I daresay as she was no better than she should be, an' teasin' a reverend is a wicked fing ter do, seein' as they get undressed or summink if they fall inter sin." She set about clearing the rest of the dishes from the table.

"Undressed?" Charlotte said curiously. "Most people get undressed to—" She stopped. She had no idea how much Gracie knew of the facts of life.

" 'Course they do," Gracie agreed cheerfully, putting the marmalade and the butter onto her tray. "I mean the bishop takes 'em to court an' undresses 'em permanent, like. And then they in't reverends anymore. They can't preach nor nuffink."

"Oh! You mean defrocked!" Charlotte bit her lips to stop herself from laughing. "Yes, that's right. It's very serious indeed." Her heart sank again, thinking of Dominic. "Perhaps Miss Bellwood wasn't a very nice person."

"Some folks like ter do that kind o' thing," Gracie went on, picking up the tray to carry it through to the kitchen. "Yer gonner find out all about 'em, ma'am? I can look arter everyfink 'ere. We gotter 'elp the Master if 'e's got a bad case. 'E depends on us."

Charlotte opened the door for her.

" 'E must be worried," Gracie went on, turning sideways to get through. " 'E's gorn awful early, an' 'e never leaves 'is toast, 'cos of 'is likin' fer marmalade."

Charlotte did not mention that he had gone in anger because of her repeated praise of Dominic and old wounds she had clumsily reopened.

They went into the kitchen, and Gracie set down the tray. A ginger striped cat with a white chest stretched languidly in front of the fire and removed himself from a pile of clean laundry.

"Get orff me dusters, Archie!" Gracie said sharply. "I dunno 'oo's kitchen this is . . . 'is or mine!" She shook her head. "Wot wif 'im an' Angus chasin' each other all over the 'ouse, it's a wonder more don't get broken. I found 'em both asleep in the linen cupboard last week. Often lie there, them two. Black and ginger fur all over everythin', there was."

The front doorbell rang and Gracie went to answer it. Charlotte followed her into the hall and saw Sergeant Tellman. She stopped abruptly, knowing Tellman's complicated emotions regarding Gracie, and her very simple reaction to him.

"If yer lookin' for Mr. Pitt, 'e already went," Gracie said, regarding Tellman's lantern-jawed face, its characteristic dourness softening as he saw her.

Tellman pulled his watch out of his waistcoat pocket.

" 'E went early," Gracie agreed with a nod. " 'E din't say w'y."

Tellman was undecided what to do. Charlotte could see that he wanted to stay longer and talk to Gracie. He had intense feelings about anyone's being a servant to another person. He despised Gracie's acceptance of the role, and she thought he was foolish and impractical not to see the great advantages it held. She was warm and dry every night, had more than sufficient to eat, and never had bailiffs after her, or any of the other trials and indignities of the poor. It was an argument they could have pursued indefinitely, only she considered it too silly to bother with.

"Yer 'ad yer breakfast?" Gracie asked, looking him up and down. "Yer look 'ungry. Not that you never looks like nothin' but a fourpenny rabbit anyway, an' a face like a dog wot's bin shut out."

He decided to ignore the insult, although he did it with difficulty.

"Not yet," he answered.

"Well, if yer wants a couple o' pieces o' toast, there's an 'ot cup o' tea in the kitchen," she offered quite casually. "If yer like?"

"Thank you," he accepted, coming in straightaway. "Then I'd better be going to find Mr. Pitt. I can't stay long."

"I in't askin' yer fer long." She whisked around, flashing her skirts and marching back down the corridor towards the kitchen. "I got work ter do. Can't 'ave the likes o' you clutterin' up me way 'alf the mornin'."

Charlotte returned to the parlor and pretended she had not seen them.

———

She left the house herself a little after nine, and by ten o'clock was at her sister Emily's town house in Mayfair. She knew, of course, that Emily was in Italy. She had received letters from Emily regularly detailing the glories of the Neapolitan spring; the most recent, yesterday evening, had been from Florence. The city was extremely beautiful and full of fascinating people, artists, poets, expatriate English of all sorts, not to mention the native Italians, whom Emily found courteous and more friendly than she had expected.

The very streets of Florence fascinated her. In the straw market, uncharacteristically for her, she was more drawn to the brave beauty of Donatello's statue of the young St. George than to the goods she might have bought.

Charlotte envied her sister that adventure of the body and of the mind. But in Emily's absence Charlotte had promised to call at the very least once or twice to visit with Grandmama, who was there virtually alone, at least as far as family was concerned. Caroline would call occasionally, but she was too busy to come often, and when Joshua was playing outside London, which he did now and then, she went with him.

Grandmama was not yet ready to receive visitors, and the maid asked Charlotte to wait, which was what she had expected. Whatever time she called had to be wrong, and ten in the morning should hardly be too late, therefore it would be too early.

She contented herself with reading the morning newspaper, which the footman brought to her ironed and on a salver. She accepted it with a smile and began to see what comments it had about the death of Unity Bellwood. At least so far it was not a scandal, merely a tragedy without satisfactory explanation. It would probably not have been mentioned at all had it not occurred in the home of the next Bishop of Beverly.

The door opened and the old lady stood in the entrance. She was dressed in black, as was her habit. She had made an occupation of being in mourning ever since her husband's death some thirty-five years since. If it was good enough for the Queen, it was certainly a pattern worthy of her emulation.

"Reading the scandal are you, again?" she said critically. "If this were my house, I shouldn't allow the footman to give you the newspapers. But then it isn't. I don't have a home anymore." Her voice took on a note of acute self-pity. "I am a lodger, a dependent. Nobody takes any notice of what I want."

"I am sure you can please yourself whether you read the newspapers or not, Grandmama," Charlotte replied, folding the paper and setting it aside on the table. She rose to her feet and went towards the old lady. "How are you? You look well."

"Don't be impertinent," the old lady said, bridling a little. "I am not well. I have hardly been sleeping at all."

"Are you tired?" Charlotte enquired.

The old lady glared at her. "If I say yes, you will suggest I return to my bed; if I say no, you will tell me I did not need the sleep," she pointed out. "Whatever I say, it will be wrong. You are most argumentative today. Why did you come, if all you want to do is contradict me? Have you quarreled with your husband?" She looked hopeful. "I daresay he is tired of your meddling in matters that are none of your concern and of which no decent woman would even have heard." She stomped over to Charlotte, waving her stick in front of her, and sat down heavily in one of the chairs near the fire.

Charlotte returned to her chair and sat down also.

"No, I have not quarreled with Thomas," she said smoothly. It was true, in the way Grandmama meant it, if not literally. And even if he had beaten her, she would not have told the old lady so. "I came to visit you."

"Nothing better to do, I suppose!" the old lady remarked.

Charlotte was tempted to say that she had many better things and she had come as a matter of duty, but decided it would achieve nothing she wished for, and refrained.

"Not at the moment," she answered.

"No crimes for you to interfere with?" The old lady raised her eyebrows.

"Dominic has become a minister," Charlotte said, changing the subject.

"Vulgar, I think," the old lady pronounced. "Most of them are corrupt anyway, always currying favor with the public, who don't know any better. Government should be conducted by gentlemen, born to lead, not by people chosen at random by the masses who haven't the faintest idea what it means half the time." She stood her stick up in front of her and crossed her hands over the knot, rather in the manner the Queen was wont to adopt. "I am against electing," she announced. "It only brings out the worst in everybody. And as for women having the vote, that is preposterous! No decent woman would want it, because she would be quite aware that she had no knowledge upon which to base her judgment. Which leaves the rest . . . and who wants the nation's fate in the hands of harlots and 'new women'? Not that they aren't after the same thing anyway."

"A minister in the church, Grandmama, not in the government," Charlotte corrected.

"Oh. Well, that's better, I suppose. Although how he expects to keep Emily on a minister's pay I've no idea." She smiled. "Have to stop wearing those fancy gowns then, won't she? No silks and satins for her. And no unsuitable colors anymore, either." She looked thoroughly satisfied at the prospect.

"Dominic, Grandmama, not Jack."

"What?"

"Dominic, who was married to Sarah, not Emily's Jack."

"Then why didn't you say so? Dominic? That Dominic you used to be so in love with?"

Charlotte controlled herself with an effort. "He is a curate now."

The old lady knew she had scored a point. "Well, well!" She breathed out with a sigh. "Nobody as righteous as a reformed sinner, is there? No more flirting with him, then, eh?" She opened her black eyes very wide. "What brought that about? Lost his looks, has he?

What happened? Did he catch the pox?" She nodded. "Those who live longest see most." Then her eyes narrowed suspiciously. "How did you find out, then? Went looking for him, did you?"

"He knew the woman whose death is Thomas's present case. I went to congratulate him on his vocation," Charlotte replied.

"You went to meddle," the old lady corrected her with satisfaction. "And because you wanted to look at Dominic Corde again. Always said he was no good. Told Sarah that when she wanted to marry him, poor child. Told you, but did you listen? Of course not! You never do. And look what happened to you. Married a policeman. Scrub your own floors, I shouldn't wonder. And get to a lot of places a decent woman wouldn't be seen near. I'd be sorry for your mother if she wasn't even worse! My poor dear Edward's death must have deranged her mind." She nodded again, still keeping her hands on her stick. "Marrying an actor young enough to be her son. I'd be sorry for her if I weren't so ashamed. I daren't go out of the house for the embarrassment of it!"

Unfortunately, there was little to argue about that. Several of Caroline's erstwhile friends had decided not to know her anymore. And she had ceased to care about it in the slightest. She still enjoyed the company of those whose friendship rode the wave of such eccentricity.

"It is most unfortunate for you." Charlotte decided to try a new approach. "I really am very sorry. I don't suppose any of your friends will speak to you now. It is a disgrace."

The old lady stared at her with damning anger. "That is a terrible thing to say. My friends are of the old school. None of this modern selfish way. A friend is a friend for life." She emphasized the last word. "If we did not remain loyal to each other, where would we be?"

She sniffed and leaned a trifle forward over her stick. "I have seen a great deal more of life than you have, and I can tell you this new idea of women trying to become like men is all going to end in tragedy. You should stay at home, my girl, and look after your family. Keep your house clean and well run, and your mind the same." She nodded. "A man has a right to expect that. He provides for you, protects you and instructs you. That is as it should be. If he falls a little short now and then, you must be patient. That is your duty. Everything depends on a man's advantages and strength, and a woman's humility and virtue." She sniffed again. "Your mother should have taught you that, if she were fulfilling her calling," she added meaningfully.

"Yes, Grandmama."

"Don't be impertinent! I know you disagree with me. I can see it in your face. Always thought you knew better, but you don't!"

Charlotte rose to her feet. "I can see that you are very well, Grandmama. If I speak to Dominic again I shall convey your congratulations to him. I am sure you are glad he has found the path of rectitude."

The old lady grunted. "And where are you going?"

"To see Great-Aunt Vespasia. I am to take luncheon with her."

"Are you? You didn't offer to take luncheon with me."

Charlotte looked at her long and carefully. Was there any point in telling her the truth? That her endless criticism made her company burdensome, that the only way to tolerate it without weeping was to laugh? That she had never once felt happier, lighter-hearted, braver or more hopeful because of it?

"One would have thought you would have preferred your own family to some lady who is only related to you by your sister's marriage," Grandmama went on. "That says something for your values, doesn't it?"

"One would have hoped it, certainly," Charlotte agreed. "But Great-Aunt Vespasia likes me, and I don't think you do."

The old lady looked startled, a faint flush of pink in her cheeks.

"I am your grandmother! I am family. That is quite different."

"Absolutely," Charlotte agreed with a smile. "Relationship is a birthright; liking someone has to be acquired. I hope you have a pleasant day. If you want to read the scandal in the newspapers, it's on page eight. Good-bye."

She left feeling guilty, and angry with herself for allowing the old lady to provoke her into retaliation. She took another hansom and sat for the whole journey seething with anger and wondering if Unity Bellwood had suffered with family like Grandmama. She knew the rage within herself and the passion to prove herself right that it engendered. To be continuously thwarted, told she was inadequate to the dream she treasured, that her role was forever limited, brought out the worst in her, a desire to justify herself at almost any cost. She entertained ideas of cruelty which would have horrified her in less-heated moments.

Pitt had told her about the attitudes of the church academic he had spoken to, how he had patronized Unity and belittled her ability, stating, as of a proven matter, that because she was a woman she was necessarily of inferior emotional stability and therefore unsuited to higher learning. The compulsion to prove them wrong in that, and in anything and everything else, must have been overwhelming.

She alighted outside Lady Vespasia Cumming-Gould's home, paid the driver, and walked up the steps just as the maid opened the door for her. Vespasia was the great-aunt of Emily's first husband, but she had developed an affection for both Emily and Charlotte which had long outlasted George's death and had grown with their every meeting. She was well over eighty now. In her youth she had been the greatest beauty of her generation. She was still exquisite and dressed with elegance and flair, but she no longer cared what society thought of her, and spoke her opinions with wit and forthrightness, which inspired admiration in many, anger in some, and downright terror in others.

She was waiting for Charlotte in her spacious withdrawing room with its tall windows letting in the sunlight and the great sense of calm its pale colors and uncluttered surfaces credited. She greeted her with pleasure and interest.

"Come in, my dear, and sit down. I think perhaps to ask you to make yourself comfortable would be foolish." She regarded Charlotte with amusement. "You look in far too high a temper for that. What has occasioned it?" She indicated a carved and upholstered chair for Charlotte, and occupied a chaise longue herself. She was dressed in her favorite shades of ivory and deep cream with long pearls almost to her waist. The entire bodice of her gown was made of guipure lace over silk, with a silk fichu at the throat. The bustle was almost nonexistent, as was so far in fashion as to be all but in advance of it.

"I have been to visit Grandmama," Charlotte replied. "She was appalling, and I behaved badly. I said things I should have kept to myself. I loathe her for bringing out the worst in me."

Vespasia smiled. "A very familiar feeling," she sympathized. "It is remarkable how often one's family can occasion it." A ghost of laughter crossed her silver eyes. "Particularly Eustace."

Charlotte felt the tension ease away from her. Memories of Vespasia'a son-in-law Eustace March were mixed with tragedy, rage and mirth, and most recently high farce and an uneasy alliance which had ended in victory.

"Eustace does have certain redeeming qualities," she said, honesty compelling her. "Grandmama is impossible. I suppose she did concentrate my mind on aspects of Thomas's new case." She stopped, wondering whether Vespasia wished to hear about it or not.

"Your luncheon rests upon it!" Vespasia warned with a glitter in her eyes. "I am very fond of you, my dear, but I refuse to sit and discuss the weather with anyone, even you. And we have no society acquaintances in common whom we may criticize with any degree of entertainment, and I do not care to speak of friends except to pass on news. Emily has written, so I have no need to enquire how she is. I know she is doing excellently."

"Very well," Charlotte agreed with a smile. "Do you think a man whose religious faith is his profession and his status, as well as his moral code, would be so deranged by doubts, the attacks or the mockery of atheists as to lose control of himself and kill . . . in temper?" Had she stated the case fairly?

"No," Vespasia said with barely a hesitation. "If he appears to have done so, I should look for a motive more rooted in the real man, less of the brain and more of the passions. Men kill from fear of losing something they cannot bear to live without, be it love or status or money. Or they kill to gain the same thing." Her expression was filled with interest, but no doubt whatsoever. "Sometimes it is to avenge a wrong they find intolerable or from jealousy of someone who has what they believe should be theirs. Sometimes it is hatred, usually based in those same feelings that somehow they have been robbed of love or honor . . . or money."

She smiled very slightly, just curling the corner of her lips. "They will fight over an idea, but only kill if their status is threatened, their belief as to how they perceive themselves in the world, in a way their life . . . or what makes it valuable to them, their conception of its importance."

"She threatened his faith," Charlotte said with a little shiver. She did not want it to be true, but then there was not any answer that she did want—not one that was possible. "Isn't that his status . . . as a clergyman?"

Vespasia laughed with a slight lift of one thin shoulder under its ivory lace and silk. There was anger and pity in her eyes as well as amusement. "My dear, if every clergyman in England who had doubts were to resign his living there would be precious few churches left open. Those that were would be mostly in villages where the minister is too busy spending his time with the frightened, the sick and the lonely to read anything but the Four Gospels, and no time at all for learned disputations. He does not think about who God is, because he already knows."

Charlotte sat silently. She could not feel that Ramsay Parmenter had any such knowledge. Perhaps it was that absence, that hole at the core of what should have been, which had allowed his faith to collapse in upon itself so tragically.

"It troubles you." Vespasia's voice was gentle. "Why? Is your anxiety for Thomas?"

"Not really. He will do what he has to. It will be unpleasant, of course, but then these things always are."

"Then for whom?"

She had never lied to Vespasia, even by implication or omission. To do so would destroy something which could never be replaced and which was of immeasurable value to her. She shifted her position very slightly on the chair.

"There are three men in the house, any of whom could have been at the bend of the stairs when Unity fell," she said slowly. "The second is Mallory, the son of the house, who is about to become a Roman Catholic priest . . ." She ignored Vespasia's suddenly risen eyebrows, silver, arched and elegant. "The third is the new curate there . . . who is my brother-in-law, Dominic. He was married to my elder sister, Sarah, who was murdered in Cater Street."

"Go on, my dear . . ."

There was no escaping Vespasia's gaze, nor the feeling of heat creeping up her own cheeks.

"I used to think myself in love with him before I met Thomas," she began. "No, that is not quite true . . . I was in love, obsessively. I got over it, of course. I realized how . . . how shallow and fragile Dominic was, how easily he gave in to his appetites." She was talking too quickly, but she did not seem to be able to help it. "He was very handsome indeed. He is even more so now. Something of the smoothness of youth is gone, a callowness. His face is . . . refined . . . by experience."

She met Vespasia's clear, silver-gray eyes. She made herself smile back. "I feel no more than friendship for him now—indeed, I have for a long time. But I am afraid for him. You see, Unity was with child, and I know Dominic's frailty. He wants passionately to succeed in his vocation, I believe that, I can see it and hear it in him. But one cannot cast off the temptations and needs of the body merely at will."

"I see." Vespasia was very grave. "And what of the other two men, Mallory and the man of whom you spoke first? Could they not also be tempted?"

"Mallory . . . I suppose so." Charlotte gave a dismissive little shrug. "But not the Reverend. He's at least sixty!"

Vespasia laughed. It was not an elegant little murmur but a rich gurgle of hilarity.

Charlotte found herself blushing. "I mean . . . I didn't mean . . ." she stammered.

Vespasia leaned forward and put her hand on Charlotte's. "I know precisely what you mean, my dear. And I daresay from thirty-three, sixty seems like dotage, but when you get there it will look quite different. So will seventy—and even eighty, if you are fortunate."

Charlotte's cheeks were still hot. "I don't think the Reverend Parmenter is fortunate. He is as dry as dead wood. He is all arguments in the mind."

"Then if something awakens his passions at last, it will be all the more dangerous," Vespasia answered, sitting back again. "Because he is unused to them and will have little experience in controlling them. That is when it is most likely to end in a disaster such as this."

"I suppose it is . . ." Charlotte said slowly, with a mixture of pain and relief. The realization of such an answer exonerated everyone else, but it left one person with the extra burden to bear. Yet still, for all the rationality of it, she found herself unable to believe it. "I could sense no passion in him," she repeated. "Except the doubt. Although I realize that most of what I know of that comes from Dominic, still I think that is Reverend Parmenter's overriding emotion. He and Unity used to quarrel terribly. They had a fearful row just minutes before she fell. It was overheard by several people. You see, she challenged his belief in everything to which he had given his life. That is an awful thing to do to anybody. It is saying, in effect, that they are worth nothing, that all their ideas are silly and wrong. If you believed that, you could hate them very much."

"If she really was the one to shake his faith, then yes, indeed, he could," Vespasia agreed. "There is nothing quite so frightening as an idea or a freedom which negates your own sacrifice and obedience when it is too late for you to avail yourself of it. But from what you say, your Reverend was not in this position. Surely it is the initiators of the idea he should hate, not the followers?" She sighed. "Although you are quite right, of course. It was the unfortunate young woman who was standing at the top of the stairs, not Mr. Darwin, who was safely out of reach. I am very sorry. It sounds like a sad affair."

She rose to her feet with a little stiffness, and Charlotte stood instantly also, offering her arm to assist, and together they went into the breakfast room. It was filled with sunlight, and the perfume of narcissi blooming in a green glazed pot. Smoked salmon was already served with wafer-thin slices of brown bread, and the butler was waiting to pull out Vespasia's chair for her.

Charlotte felt compelled to go again to Brunswick Gardens. Her brain told her there was little she could accomplish, but she could not simply wait to see what happened. If she went she might learn something more, and knowledge would enable her to act.

She was received somewhat coolly by Vita Parmenter.

"How kind of you to call again, Mrs. Pitt," she said. "It is generous of you to give up so much of your time." "And take up so much of ours" was implied.

"Family loyalties are very important in times of trouble," Charlotte answered, and hated hearing herself mouthing such platitudes.

"I am sure you are a very loyal wife," Vita said with a smile. "But we cannot tell you anything that we did not already tell your husband."

This was dreadful. Charlotte felt herself blushing hot. Vita was a far sharper adversary than she had supposed, and as determined to protect her husband as Charlotte was to protect Dominic. Charlotte ought to have admired her for it, and reluctantly part of her did, in spite of her own discomfort. The two of them stood facing each other in the gracious, very modern withdrawing room, Vita small and elegant in soft patterned blue edged with black, Charlotte at least three inches taller in last year's muted plum, which flattered her warm skin and mahogany-brown hair.

"I did not come to enquire into the details of your tragedy, Mrs. Parmenter," she said very politely. "I came to ask after your well-being and to see if there was anything I could do to be helpful."

"I cannot imagine any help you might give." Vita kept the air of courtesy, but it was very thin. "What had you in mind?"

There was obviously nothing anyone could do, and they both knew it.

Charlotte looked straight back at her and smiled. "I have known Dominic for many years, and we have experienced tragedies and difficulties together in the past. I thought he might find comfort in speaking freely, as one can to friends of long standing, and to people who are not immediately involved and therefore will not be hurt in the same way." She was pleased with that. It sounded very reasonable, and it was almost true.

"I see," Vita said slowly, her face a little harder, a little colder. "Then no doubt we should call him and see if his duties will allow him the time." She reached for the bell rope and pulled it sharply. She did not speak again until the maid appeared, then she simply asked her to inform Mr. Corde that his sister-in-law had called and wished to offer him her companionship, if it was convenient for him.

They discussed the weather until the door opened and Dominic came in. He looked pleased to see Charlotte, his face lighting immediately, but she noticed the shadows around his eyes and the strain in the fine lines beside his mouth.

"How kind of you to come," he said sincerely.

"I was concerned for you," she replied. "You could hardly help being distressed."

"We all are." Vita looked from Charlotte to Dominic. Her expression had altered since he came into the room. There was a softness to it now, a respect bordering on admiration in her eyes. "It has been quite the worst time in any of our lives." She turned to Charlotte as if her previous coldness had not existed. Her face was so innocent Charlotte wondered if her own guilt had manufactured the rebuff.

"But we have also discovered strengths in one another we had not known," Vita went on. "You said, Mrs. Pitt, that you had endured great difficulties yourself some time ago. I daresay you had the same experience? One finds that those one had thought to be friends, and people of unquestioned strength, are not of the . . . the quality one had hoped. And then that others have compassion, courage, and"—her eyes were soft and bright—"a sheer goodness that surpasses all one had imagined." She did not speak any names, but her momentary glance at Dominic made him blush with pleasure.

Charlotte saw it. It was delicate, a flattering directed most precisely where he was vulnerable. He yearned not to be desired, found amusing or romantic or clever, but to be found good. It might be that Vita was simply fortunate in touching on the one hole in his armor, but Charlotte was perfectly sure it owed nothing whatever to chance. And yet even if she had wanted to warn Dominic of it, she could not. It would be both cruel and pointless. It would hurt him and turn him against Charlotte, for the pain. Catching Vita's eye for a moment, she was perfectly certain that Vita knew that also.

"Yes, I did," Charlotte agreed with a forced smile. "It is the one thing that lasts even after all the other mystery is solved, the new knowledge one has gained of people we thought we knew. It can never be exactly the same again."

"I am sure it will not be," Vita agreed. "There are new debts . . . and new loyalties. It is a turning point in all our lives, I think. That is what makes it so frightening . . ." She let the words hang in the air. "One tries hard to hope, and that also hurts, because it matters so very much." She smiled and glanced at Dominic, then away again. Her voice dropped. "Thank heaven one does not have to do it all alone."

"Of course not," Dominic said firmly. "That is about the only good thing we can cling to, and that I promise."

Something in Vita relaxed. She turned to Charlotte and smiled, as if she had made a profound decision.

"Perhaps you would care to stay to tea, Mrs. Pitt. You would be most welcome. Please do."

Charlotte was surprised. It was a sudden change, and although she had every intention of accepting, it also filled her with an awareness of unease.

"Thank you," she said quickly. "That is most generous of you, especially in the circumstances."

Vita smiled, and the expression lit her face with conviction and warmth. It was easy to see that in other circumstances she would be a woman of extraordinary charm, having both intelligence and vitality, and almost certainly a ready wit.

"Now please, you must spend a little time with Dominic, which is what you came for, and I am sure he would appreciate it. Tea will be at four o'clock."

"Thank you," Dominic said earnestly, and there was a light and a gentleness in his face, then he turned to Charlotte. "Shall we walk in the garden?"

She followed him, taking his arm, very conscious of Vita watching them leave. Vita had changed her attitude completely. She was a different woman when Dominic was present. Was that trust, the knowledge that Charlotte was the wife of the policeman investigating Unity's death and therefore inevitably linked with blaming Ramsay with murder? Vita could hardly help being suspicious of Charlotte, even disliking her regardless of every natural personal impulse. Charlotte would have hated anyone who posed a threat to Pitt. Knowing it was unjust would make no difference. It would touch her mind but not her instinct.

And Vita must know Dominic's loyalty to Ramsay, his immense sense of gratitude and debt. She could count on him to do all that was humanly possible to help.

They went out through the side door into the garden, still leafless and dappled with light through the branches. The snowdrops were over and the narcissus spears were high and already bending their heads, ready to open. If Charlotte had had this land she would have planted primroses, celandine and a drift of wood anemones under those trees. The gardeners here had been a trifle unimaginative with periwinkle and ferns, their heads barely through the ground.

Dominic was talking about something and she was not listening. Her mind was filled with memory of the emotion in Vita's face as she had looked at him. There was such admiration in it. Did she cling to him because Ramsay was weaker, a flawed vessel, and she knew it? Charlotte remembered how he had sat at the table and allowed Tryphena to make offensive remarks without defending himself or his beliefs. It was as if he had in some way already surrendered.

Vita did not seem like a woman who gave up. She might be beaten by circumstance, but she would not simply cease to try. It was not surprising she was drawn to Dominic, admiring his spiritual energy and conviction. It matched her own strength of will. Charlotte had seen her flatter those aspects of his nature, and how precious it had been to him. Surely Vita knew that, too?

She made an appropriate reply to Dominic, her mind less than half upon what he was saying. It was of the past, memories shared. It did not need her attention. They were under the trees, looking towards the azaleas. They would not bloom for another two months. They looked miserable, almost dead against the naked earth, but in late spring they would blaze with color, orange, gold and apricot flowers on bare branches. It took an effort of imagination to see it now. But then that was what gardening was about.

They walked together in companionable silence, the occasional remark made not for meaning but simply to establish some sense of being together. All the things that mattered must remain unsaid. They were only too aware of the suspicions and the overshadowing fear, the knowledge that something ugly and irreversible was waiting in the future to be discovered, and coming closer with every hour.

They were still talking when Tryphena came across the grass with a message that Dominic was needed, and he excused himself, leaving the two women together. It was an opportunity for Charlotte to learn a little more of Tryphena, a chance which might not occur again, and too good for her not to seize it.

"I am very sorry for your bereavement, Mrs. Whickham," Charlotte said quietly. "The more I hear from my husband of Miss Bellwood's achievements, the more I realize it may be a loss to women in general."

Tryphena looked at her skeptically. She saw a woman in her early thirties who had adopted the most usual, most comfortable, and by far the easiest role for women. Her contempt for this was clear in her eyes.

"Are you interested in scholarship?" she asked only barely politely.

"Not particularly," Charlotte answered with equal candor and with just as forthright a gaze. "But I am interested in justice. My brother-in-law is a member of Parliament, and I have hopes of influencing his views, but,"—she took a plunge—"I should prefer to have the power to do it more directly, and without being dependent upon a relationship, which is quite chancy and arbitrary."

Now she had Tryphena's interest. "You mean the vote?"

"Why not? Don't you believe women have the intelligence and the judgment of human character to exercise it with at least as much wisdom as men?"

"More so!" Tryphena said instantly, stopping and turning where she stood so she faced Charlotte. "But it is only a tiny beginning. There are far greater freedoms we cannot legislate for. Freedom from the convention of ideas, from other people deciding what we shall want, what we shall think, even what will make us happy." Her voice was rising and sharp with emotion. She stood in the sunlight stiff with anger, her black dress pulling across her shoulders. "It is the whole patriarchal order of society which oppresses us. If we are to be free to use our intellectual and creative abilities, and not merely our physical ones, then we must be freed from the rigid ties of the past and the moral and financial dependence we have suffered for centuries."

Charlotte had seldom felt shackled or dependent, but she was honest enough to know that few women had marriages as satisfying as hers, or that granted them as much freedom. Because of the difference in their social background, she and Pitt were more equal partners than most. Because of Pitt's toleration of her either helping or meddling with his cases, depending upon one's point of view, she had a variety and interest in her life, and a fulfillment of far more sides of her nature than domesticity alone could have given. Even Emily, with her money and position, was frequently bored by the narrowness of her acquaintances and limitations, the sameness of one day to another.

"I think we shall change things only a small step at a time," she said diplomatically and realistically. "But we can ill afford to lose people like Miss Bellwood, if she was all I hear."

"She was far more!" Tryphena responded quickly. "She not only had a vision, she had the courage to live it through, no matter what the cost. And it could cost dearly." The impatience and the contempt crept back into her face, and she started to walk across the grass, not with any direction but simply for the release of movement. "But that is the courage to face life, isn't it? To grasp hold of it and cling to it even if at times it stabs you to the soul."

"You mean her death?" Charlotte kept up with her.

Tryphena turned away, a shadow over her face. "No, I mean life itself, the living of it. She had the bravest heart of anyone I know, but those who love passionately can be hurt in ways lesser people cannot even imagine by those who are unworthy of them." She jerked her body angrily, as if thinking of the people and the lives behind them, and dismissing their feelings as superficial.

Charlotte wanted intensely to say the right thing. She must not anger Tryphena, nor allow her curiosity to betray itself. Had Tryphena known Unity had been with child? She must say something intelligent, sympathetic, something to prompt a continuing confidence. She kept pace with Tryphena, step for step across the grass towards the gravel path by the herbaceous border, its flowers still little more than dark mounds in the damp earth, a few green shoots here and there.

"Well, if there were not pain in it, and no risk," she mused, "then anyone would do it. It would hardly need someone special."

Tryphena said nothing. Her face was sunk deep in thought, and perhaps memory.

"Tell me something about her," Charlotte said at last as they reached the path and their boots crunched on the gravel. Subtlety was not going to work. "She must have been much admired. I expect she had many friends."

"Dozens," Tryphena agreed. "Before she came here she lived with a whole group of like-minded people who believed in freedom to live and love each other as they chose without the superstitions of society, and the hypocrisies, to limit them."

Charlotte thought it sounded more like license, but she refrained from saying so—what was freedom to one person frequently appeared selfishness and irresponsibility to another. Some of the difference was merely the passage of time—and having children of one's own for whom one could see all the dangers of the world; the desire to protect them was overwhelming.

"It takes a lot of courage," she said aloud. "The risks are great."

"Yes." Tryphena stared at the ground as they walked, very slowly, along the path to the shallow steps. "She spoke about it sometimes. She told me of the sense of exhilaration they had, how intense passion could be when it is utterly true, no law binds you, no superstitious dread holds you or inhibits you, no rituals make you wait or try to hold you in an anchor after the fire and the honesty had gone out of it." There was such bitterness in her voice, such a depth of emotion, that Charlotte could not help wondering at Tryphena's own experience of marriage. She glanced at her and saw no softness in her eyes or mouth, no warmth in her memories at all. Had she wanted the marriage herself? Or was it something arranged by her family, and she had agreed to it, willingly or unwillingly?

"It is all so"—Tryphena furrowed her brow, looking for the word—"so . . . clean! There is no pretense." Her eyes became fierce, her lips pressed together. "No ownership by one person of another, no slow eating away of independence, of self-esteem and the knowledge and beliefs of who you are. Nobody says 'You must think this way, because I do.' 'You must believe that, because I do.' 'This is where I want to go, so you must come, too.' A marriage of equals is the only sort that is worth anything! It is the only sort which has honor or decency or any inner cleanliness." Her fists were clenched at her sides, and her arms seemed locked right up to her shoulders. "I will not be second-rate . . . second-class . . . worth only second-best!"

Charlotte wondered if Tryphena had any idea how much of her own hurt she betrayed in her words. Some of this might be Unity's thoughts, but the passion was Tryphena's. "I think if somebody loved you, they would want you to be the best you possibly could," Charlotte said gently, walking up the steps beside her. "Isn't that what love is, wanting someone to fulfill all the best in themselves? But then you would want the same for him, wouldn't you? And be prepared to give something that might cost you quite a lot, to that end?"

"What?" Tryphena turned her head, looking surprised.

"If you love, you stay, even when it isn't convenient, or fun, or easy," Charlotte elaborated. "If you leave the moment you no longer feel like staying, isn't that simply selfishness? You are talking about freedom to please yourself, freedom from hurt or boredom or duty. Life is about giving and being vulnerable, which is precisely why it needs both courage and self-discipline."

Tryphena stared at her, stopping on the gravel close to the glasshouse. "I don't think you understand at all, Mrs. Pitt. You may think you are a fighter for freedom, but you sound just like a traditional woman who is prepared to do exactly as her father and then her husband tell her to." Her words were so angry they had to come from her own experience. "People like you are the ones who really hold us back. Unity truly loved, and she was terribly hurt. I could see it in her eyes, and sometimes catch it in her voice." She looked at

Charlotte accusingly. "You are speaking as if she were selfish, as if her kind of love were less than yours, just because you are married and she wasn't. But that is blind and false and utterly wrong. You don't win great victories by playing safe!"

The scorn in her face now was as plain as the sunlight across the grass. "I am sure you meant to be kind, and I daresay you thought you supported the women of the new age, but you really haven't any understanding whatever." She shook her head sharply, the wind catching the stray pieces of her fair hair. "You want to be safe . . . and you can't be . . . not if you are fighting a great battle. Unity was one of the finest and the best . . . and she fell. Pardon me, but I don't want to talk about her to you anymore." And with that she turned and walked stiffly into the rose arbor, head high as if she were struggling against tears.

Charlotte remained where she was for several minutes, thinking over the conversation. Did Tryphena know of one real tragedy in Unity's past, or was she being melodramatic? Had Unity loved someone intensely, and was the result of that love the child she had been carrying when she died? The child of one of the three men in this house?

Had she been hurt by this man? If so, she would not be the first to retaliate blindly out of pain and fear. Was she afraid? Most women would be terrified of the ruin unmarried motherhood would bring them, but Charlotte had no idea whether that was true of Unity or not. If Pitt had explored that, he had not told her. But then perhaps he could not imagine the emotions a woman might feel: the mixture of elation at knowing of the life within her, that it was part of the man she loved, in a sense an indissoluble bond between them; and yet also a reminder of him she would never lose, and with it a reminder of his betrayal of her . . . if he had betrayed her!

And then there was the fear of childbirth itself, of being left alone at one's most vulnerable both emotionally and physically. Charlotte could remember how she had felt when carrying each of her children. She had been radiantly happy one day, and plunged into misery another. She remembered the excitement, the aching back, the tired-ness, the clumsiness, the pride, the self-consciousness. And she had had parents who were steady and calm, and a husband who made her laugh and kept his patience most of the time, when it mattered—and the approval of society.

Unity would have been alone. That was altogether different.

Had she tried to blackmail him? It would be understandable.

Charlotte started to walk back to the house, wondering about Dominic and about the love by which Unity had apparently been so hurt in the past. Perhaps knowing that would prove who the father was—and that it was not Dominic.

Or that it was.

That was a cold, sickening thought. What did she think of Dominic that she feared to find that out? And, she was afraid, the feeling was sharp and far too familiar to deny. She could remember being in love with him herself, and behaving stupidly, feeling so vul-nerable, hurting when he seemed to ignore her, floating on air if he smiled or spoke, being consumed with jealousy if he favored someone else, dreaming, imagining all kinds of things. She blushed hot to think of it now.

But that was what obsession was like, the kind of love which is all in one's own mind, not the kind that is sure and sweet, as she had with Pitt. That had its pain and its darkness as well, its racing pulse and burning embarrassment, but it was rooted in reality, in sharing thoughts and ideas and, above all, feelings about the things that cut the deepest.

She came through the side door into the short passage to the hall. At this point the floor was carpeted, and her feet made no sound. She saw Dominic and Vita standing near the foot of the stairs, close together, almost touching. They stood just about where Unity must have lain when she fell. Vita was looking up at him, her eyes wide, her expression filled with softness as if she had just said something private and very tender. He moved his hand to touch her, then changed his mind and smiled, then he stepped back. She hesitated a moment, then, with a little shrug, went lightly up the stairs.

Charlotte's mind raced. How could Dominic be so incredibly foolish, so dishonest? Vita was older than he, but she was also charming, beautiful, and acutely intelligent, a woman of passion and wit. He could not possibly be considering having an affair with her, could he? Not the wife of his mentor, his friend, the man in whose home he now lived?

Was it possible?

The past crowded in on her too closely with all its remembered pain and disillusion. It was imaginable . . . it was possible. Was it Dominic that Unity had fought with at the top of the stairs? Was it conceivable Vita would lie to protect him?

No. No, because others had heard Unity cry out to Ramsay. Tryphena had heard it, as had both the maid and the valet. She felt relief flood through her.

Dominic turned around. There was no embarrassment in his face, not even any awareness that he had been seen in a situation far better to have remained private.

"I'm sorry I left you," he said with a slight smile. "It was an urgent matter. I am afraid the Reverend Parmenter is not able to care for things as he does normally." His face was shadowed with concern. "Mrs. Parmenter says he is not at all well. He has the most severe headaches. I suppose that is not to be wondered at, poor man." He looked at her ruefully. "It's odd, but I can remember the Cater Street tragedies in retrospect with far more understanding than I think I had at the time." He was close to her now and spoke very quietly. "I wish I could go back and improve the way I behaved then, show more sensitivity to other people's fears and pain." He sighed. "And that's absurd, because I don't even know how to help this now. The only thing I can say is that I am trying, whereas I thought only of myself then."

She did not know what to say. She longed to believe him, but that look on Vita Parmenter's face prevented her . . . she hesitated now to use the word *love*.

She turned away so he should not read her eyes, and started to walk towards the withdrawing room. It was five minutes before teatime.

Tea was actually served nearly ten minutes late, and Vita was not present. It was left to Clarice to host the small gathering and to try to make some sort of conversation. Tryphena was there, but she made no effort to entertain Charlotte. Mallory came in, picked up a dainty sandwich and ate it in two mouthfuls, not bothering with a cup of tea. He stood restlessly by the window, as if feeling restricted in the room but obliged to stay. It was almost certainly not the house but the circumstances which imprisoned him, but those were beyond escape.

Clarice surprised Charlotte by talking both tactfully and interestingly on a number of subjects. She touched on the theater as if the recent death in the house were a normal happening, to be expected in the course of events of life, and there was no need or purpose in speaking in hushed voices or avoiding any mention of happiness or glamour. She referred to a recent visit of foreign royalty written of extensively in the *London Illustrated News*. She drew Charlotte into the conversation, and for nearly three quarters of an hour it would have been perfectly possible to mistake the occasion for a most agreeable afternoon call between people who were newly discovering each other and might become friends.

Several times Charlotte looked at Dominic and saw the same surprise in his eyes, and also a growing respect for Clarice which apparently he had not hitherto felt.

It was after five when the door flew open and Vita stood in the entrance, her hair disheveled, most of it actually out of its pins and falling over one shoulder. Her face was cut across the cheek and her left eye was swollen and fast showing fearful bruising.

Mallory was aghast.

Dominic rose to his feet immediately, face white.

"What happened? What is it?" he demanded, going over to her.

She shrank back, her eyes wide with horror. She was shaking and looked on the verge of hysteria. She swayed as if she might fall at any moment.

Charlotte got up quickly, skirting around the tea table to avoid knocking it over.

"Come and sit down," she ordered, taking Vita by the shoulders and with an arm around her for support, guiding her to the nearest chair. "Pour some more tea and a little brandy," she said to Dominic. "And you'd better find her maid and tell her."

Dominic hesitated a moment, swinging around to look at Mallory.

"What happened?" Tryphena demanded. "Mama? You look as if somebody hit you. Did you fall?"

"Of course she fell!" Clarice snapped. "Don't be absurd! Who would hit her? Anyway, we're all here."

Tryphena looked around, her eyes wide, and suddenly everyone was aware that the only member of the family not present was Ramsay. One by one they looked back to Vita.

She was trembling violently now, sitting huddled up, her face ashen except for the darkening bruises around her eye and the scarlet slash oozing blood on her cheek. Charlotte held the cup for her; she was shaking too badly to hold it herself.

"What happened?" Mallory asked, his voice rising sharply.

Dominic stood by the door, waiting to hear before he would leave.

Vita drew in her breath and tried to speak, but gulped back a sob.

Charlotte put her arms around her very gently, not to hurt what else must surely be damaged in such an injury. "Perhaps you had better send for your doctor?" She turned to Clarice as being the most likely to be in command of herself and the situation.

Clarice stared back at her without moving.

Tryphena swiveled from one to the other of them, her eyes accusing.

Mallory made as if to move, and then froze.

"Please!" Charlotte urged.

Vita raised her head. "No . . ." she said hoarsely. "No . . . don't do that! I . . . it is only . . . a little cut . . ."

"It is more than that," Charlotte said seriously. "That bruising may be pretty unpleasant, and one cannot tell how widespread it may be. I am sure a little arnica will help, but I think you should call your doctor all the same."

"No." Vita was resolute. She was struggling fiercely to regain control of herself. Tears spilled over her cheeks and she ignored them. Her face was probably too sore to touch. Her whole body still shuddered. "No . . . I do not want the doctor to be informed."

"Mama, you must!" Clarice insisted, coming forward for the first time and standing only five or six feet away. "Why ever should you not? He won't think you foolish, if that is what you are worrying about. People do fall . . . accidentally. It is easy enough."

Vita closed her eyes, wincing as the pain struck her. "I did not fall," she whispered. "The doctor may know that if he comes. I . . . couldn't bear it . . . especially now. We must . . ." She took a deep breath and almost choked. "We must show . . . loyalty . . ."

"Loyalty!" Tryphena exploded. "To what? To whom? When you say loyalty, you mean lie! Cover up the truth . . ."

Vita started to weep quietly, retreating into herself in misery.

"Stop it!" Dominic was back from the doorway, glancing at Tryphena. "Words like that are not helping anyone." He knelt down in front of Vita, staring at her earnestly. "Mrs. Parmenter, I think you had better tell us the truth. We can then decide what is best to do about it. But while it is all imagination or suspicion, we are likely to make mistakes. You did not fall . . . What *did* happen?"

Slowly Vita raised her head again. "I quarreled with Ramsay," she said huskily. "It was terrible, Dominic. I don't even know how it happened. One moment we were talking quite agreeably, then he went to look at his letters which the butler had left on his desk, and without any warning at all he flew into a rage. He seemed to lose all control of himself." She kept her eyes on Dominic's all the time she spoke, but she must have been acutely aware of Mallory standing at the edge of the group, his shoulders tight, his face drawn into faint lines of anger and confusion.

Clarice made as if to interrupt and then stopped.

Vita was gripping Charlotte's hand so tightly it was painful, but Charlotte did not pull away.

"He accused me of opening his letters . . . which is ridiculous. I would never touch anything addressed to him. But one must have been torn in the delivery, and he just lost his temper and started to say it was I who had done it." Her voice was low and urgent, sharp with fear. Now that she had started she could not stop herself. The words were tumbling out full of confusion. "He shouted at me, not loudly . . . *shout* is the wrong word. He was so furious it was more like a snarl." Her teeth chattered so she was in danger of biting her tongue.

"Drink some tea," Charlotte said quietly. "It will help a little. You are terribly shocked. It is only natural."

"Thank you," Vita accepted, putting her hands over Charlotte's to steady the cup for herself. "You are very kind, Mrs. Pitt."

"I will call the doctor," Mallory insisted, starting towards the door.

"No!" Vita insisted. "I forbid it! Do you hear me, Mallory? I absolutely forbid it." Her voice was so strained, her face so full of anguish, he stopped where he stood, reluctant to obey and yet not wishing to defy her.

Dominic started saying something, then caught Mallory's glare of fury and stopped.

Vita closed her eyes. "Thank you," she murmured. "I am sure I will be all right. I shall just go and lie down for a while. Braithwaite can look after me." She made as if to rise to her feet, but her knees would not support her. "I'm sorry," she apologized. "I feel so . . . foolish. I just don't know what to do. He accused me of undermining his authority, of belittling him, of questioning his judgment. I denied it. I never have . . . ever in my life! And he . . . he struck me."

Clarice stared at her for a moment, then brushed past Tryphena and Dominic and went to the door. She threw it open and they heard her footsteps cross the hallway and go up the stairs, loud on the black, uncarpeted wood.

"This is appalling!" Mallory said in anguish. "He's mad! He must be. He's taken leave of his wits."

Dominic looked acutely distressed, but after only a moment's hesitation he mastered his own feelings and turned to Mallory.

"We must abide by her wishes. We should not say anything further about it."

"You can't do that!" Tryphena protested. "Are you going to wait until he kills her, too? Is that what you want? I thought you cared about her! In fact, I thought you cared a great deal."

Vita looked at her desperately. "Tryphena! Please . . ."

Dominic bent and picked Vita up in his arms and walked over to the door.

Charlotte hastened to open it wider for him, and he went through without looking back. Charlotte faced the room.

"I think there is nothing I can do to help except leave you some privacy to make whatever decisions you believe best. I am so sorry this should have happened."

Mallory recollected his duty as host in his parents' absence, and hastened to the door after her.

"Thank you, Mrs. Pitt. I . . . I hardly know what to say to you. You came to call upon us out of kindness, and we have embarrassed you dreadfully . . ." He looked acutely uncomfortable, his face white except for blotches of pink in his cheeks. He stood awkwardly, not knowing how to rest his weight or what to do with his hands.

"I do not think of being embarrassed," she said with something less than the truth. "I have had tragedy in my own family, and I know how it can change everything. Please do not think of it again." She was at the front door. She tried to smile as he opened the door for her, and for a moment she met his eyes and was sharply aware of the fear in him, almost panic, and that it lay barely beneath the surface, threatening to break through if there were one more tear in the fabric of his life, however small.

She wished she could have comforted him, but she could not promise it would get better. It probably would not.

"Thank you, Mr. Parmenter," she said quietly. "I hope next time we meet the worst will be over." Then she turned and went down the steps and along the pavement to look for a hansom.

Earlier that day Cornwallis had received an unexpected visitor in his office. The constable outside told him that Mrs. Underhill had asked to see him.

"Yes . . . yes, of course . . ." He rose to his feet and accidentally knocked over a pen with his cuff. He set it right. "Ask her to come in. Did . . . did she say what it was about?"

"No sir. Didn't like to ask her, her bein' a bishop's wife an' all. Shall I go an' ask her now, sir?"

"No! No, please show her in." Unconsciously he straightened his jacket and pulled at his tie, actually setting it crooked.

Isadora came in a moment after. She was dressed in a dark shade somewhere between blue and green. It reminded him of the color of ducks' tails. It suited her pale skin and almost black hair, with its wing of white at the brow. He had not realized it before, but she was beautiful. There was an inner peace in her face which made it remarkable. It was a face he could look at without growing tired of it, or feeling as if he had learned every expression and could predict its next light or shadow.

He swallowed. "Good morning, Mrs. Underhill. How may I help you?"

A smile flickered across her face and vanished. She obviously felt some awkwardness about the matter, whatever it was, and disliked having to broach it with him.

"Please sit down," he offered, indicating the large chair near his desk.

"Thank you." She glanced around his office, noticing the ship's sextant on the shelf and looking quickly at the titles of the books.

"I'm sorry. I should not waste your time, Mr. Cornwallis." She brought her attention back to him. "I think perhaps I was foolish to have come and disturbed you. It is a personal matter, not official. But I felt that we left a most unfortunate impression upon you the evening you came to dinner. The Bishop . . ." She gave his title rather than calling him "my husband," as he would have expected. He noticed the hesitation. "The Bishop was deeply distressed about the whole incident," she went on quickly. "And fearful that the wider repercussions could damage so many people, I think he may have seemed less concerned with Ramsay Parmenter's own . . . welfare . . . than he really is."

She was obviously finding it extremely difficult to talk, and studying her face, her shadowed eyes avoiding his, he felt that she was as deeply offended by the bishop's behavior as he was himself. Only for her it was also a profound shame, because she could not dissociate herself from it without disloyalty. She had come here now to try to improve her husband's image in Cornwallis's eyes, and she must hate doing it and feel a terrible inner anger at the necessity. Did she wish to tell him her true emotion, but honor forbade her?

"I understand," he said in awkward silence. "He has many considerations beyond the purely personal. All men with great responsibility have." He smiled, keeping his eyes very steadily on hers. "I have commanded a ship myself, and no matter what my feelings towards any individual member of the crew, what like or dislike, what pity or respect, the ship itself always had to come first or we should all perish. They are hard decisions to make, and not always thought fair by others." He did not think those rules applied to Bishop Underhill. His "ship" was a moral one, fighting the elements of cowardice and dishonor, not of wood and canvas struggling against the ocean's power. Cornwallis's commission had included safeguarding the lives of his men. Underhill's was to safeguard their souls.

But he could say none of this to her. She must know it as well as he . . . at least—looking at her, the awkwardness of her hands knotted together in her lap, the way her eyes avoided his—he believed she did, and he did not wish to remind her.

"We must all make whatever decisions we feel to be the best in difficult circumstances," he went on. "It is easier to judge others than to be in that position oneself. Please do not feel I misunderstand."

She looked up at him quickly. Was she aware that he was trying to be kind rather than honest? He was unused to women. He had only the vaguest idea how they thought, what they believed or felt. Perhaps she saw right through him and despised him for it? That possibility was startlingly unpleasant.

She smiled at him. "I think you are being very generous, Mr. Cornwallis, and I am grateful to you for that." She glanced around the room. "Were you at sea for long?"

"A little over thirty years," he replied, still looking at her.

"You must miss it."

"Yes . . ." The answer came instantly and with a depth which he had not expected. He smiled self-consciously. "In some ways it was a great deal simpler. I am afraid I am not used to politics. Pitt tries to keep instructing me in the nature of intrigue and the possibilities of diplomacy—and more often the impossibilities."

"I don't suppose there has to be much diplomacy at sea," she said thoughtfully, looking away again, the shadow returning to her face. "You are in command. You simply have the terrible burden of being right, because everyone depends upon it. Great power brings its equal responsibility." Her voice was thoughtful, as if she were talking as much to herself as to him. "I used to imagine the church was like that . . . a magnificent proclaiming of the truth, like John the Baptist before Herod." She laughed at herself. "About as undiplomatic as it would be possible to be . . . telling the king publicly that he is an adulterer and his marriage is illegal, and to repent and ask God's forgiveness. He can hardly have been surprised to lose his head."

His body relaxed. His hands lay easy on the desk. "How do you say such a thing diplomatically?" he asked with a grin. "Your Majesty,

I think maybe your conjugal relations are a trifle irregular, and you may wish to reconsider them or counsel with the Almighty?"

She laughed, a sudden ripple of joy at absurdity.

"And he would say, 'I am sorry, but I am quite satisfied with arrangements as they are, thank you. And if you repeat this suggestion in public, I shall be obliged to incarcerate you. And when I have the appropriate excuse, I shall bring your life to a premature end. It would be better if you were to acknowledge to everyone that it is all in order and meets with your approval.'" She stood up, suddenly serious again, her voice charged with emotion. "I should far rather go out with all guns blazing than be branded by the enemy and marred by his crime, for his purposes. I apologize for the mixed metaphors and for usurping your naval imagery."

"I consider it a compliment," he returned.

"Thank you." She moved to the door. "At first I felt very foolish coming, but you have made me at ease. You are very gracious. Good day."

"Good day, Mrs. Underhill." He opened the door for her and watched her leave with regret. He nearly spoke, to detain her a moment longer, but realized how ridiculous that would be.

He closed the door and went back to his desk, but he sat for nearly a quarter of an hour without moving or taking up his papers again.

CHAPTER
SEVEN

Pitt sat in the hansom as it clattered through the early morning traffic. It was just after eight, and he had been up late the evening before listening to Charlotte's account of her day. She had said little about Grandmama, and only touched on her luncheon with Aunt Vespasia, but she had repeated Vespasia's opinion that men did not murder over ideas but over passions.

A brewer's dray lumbered past them, the horses magnificent with their plumed manes and gleaming brasses. The air seemed loud with the sound of hooves, the cries of street traders. A dog barked and someone shouted to a cabby. The hansom jolted forward again and then came to a sharp stop. There was a crack of a whip, and then they set off at a brisker pace.

Pitt could imagine Vespasia saying that. He could see her still-beautiful face clearly in his mind. She would probably be dressed in ivory, silver-gray or lilac, and she usually wore pearls in the daytime.

She was right. People killed because they cared about something so fiercely they lost all sense of reason and proportion. For a time their own need eclipsed everyone else's, even drowned out their sense of self-preservation. Sometimes it was carefully-thought-out greed. Sometimes it was a momentary fear, even a physical one. Seldom was it revenge. That could be exacted in so many other ways. On rare occasions he had come across crimes resulting from blind, insensate rage.

But as Vespasia said, it was always a passion of some sort, even if only the cold hunger of greed.

Which was why, in spite of the evidence, he found it hard to believe that Ramsay Parmenter would have killed Unity deliberately. Pitt had to learn who the father of her child was. Fear would be a highly understandable motive. Was she a woman who would have blackmailed him, or even betrayed him and ruined his career?

Why not? Hers was ruined. There was very little purpose to be gained, but there was a kind of justice.

Charlotte had told him of Tryphena's emotional and rather disconnected account of Unity's past and of the hurt of some tragedy in it, and of a love which had been far more than a slight romance, a hope and a dream. Apparently it had left Unity deeply marked.

She had been a complex woman. After all, as it transpired he did need to know more of her. If Ramsay were the father, why had she entered into such a relationship with him? What in his dry, pedantic character could possibly have attracted her?

Or was it not personal but rather his position which tempted her? Was exposing his frailty a kind of revenge for her, for all the years of bigotry she had suffered at the hands of men like him? Pitt tried for a moment to imagine himself in her place, an outstanding intellect, a hunger to work, an ambition; all thwarted and denied by prejudice, confronted in every direction by polite, blind condescension. He had tasted a little of it himself, because of his birth and his father's misfortune. He knew injustice, bitter and fatal in his father's case. He had lain alone in his small room under the eaves and burned with rage and misery for him after his deportation for a theft he did not commit. Pitt and his mother might well have starved had it not been for Sir Arthur Desmond's kindness. It was the tutor that he shared with Desmond's son who had taught him to speak well, and that had marked the difference in his career.

But he understood discrimination, even if he had been taught most of the arts which enabled him to overcome the greater part of it. Unity Bellwood never could, because she would always be a woman. If there was a deep, ineradicable anger in her, he could understand it.

He could probably arrest Ramsay Parmenter on the evidence he had, including the previous night's extraordinary attack. But any lawyer worthy of his calling would have the case dismissed when it reached court, if it ever did. And once the case had been tried, even if he could thereafter prove Ramsay's guilt, he could not bring the charge a second time. It must be proved now or not at all.

He needed to know more about both Dominic and Unity Bellwood. Their pasts might teach him something to explain it all or to alter his perception entirely. It was something he dared not overlook. Events, as he knew them, were incomplete. They made no sense. He must at the very least know who was the father of Unity's child. He winced within himself as he thought how it would hurt Charlotte if it were Dominic. There was a shabby, mean-spirited part of himself which would be pleased if it were. He was ashamed of that.

He arrived at Brunswick Gardens, paid the cabby and ignored the paperboy crying out the latest news, which was a heated discussion which had been raging as to whether there was land, ice or sea at the North Pole. A device had been created by two Frenchmen, a Monsieur Besançon and a Monsieur Hermite, to settle the matter once and for all. It was a hot air balloon of sufficient size to carry five men, with excellent accommodation and provisions, a number of dogs to draw a sledge, and even a small boat. The death of Unity Bellwood paled in comparison. Pitt went up to the front door with a ghost of a smile. The door was opened by Emsley, looking extremely unhappy.

"Good morning, sir," he said without surprise. His expression suggested that Pitt was the realization of his worst fears.

"Good morning, Emsley," Pitt replied, stepping inside to the vestibule, then the extraordinary hallway where Unity had met her death. "May I speak with Mrs. Parmenter, please?"

Emsley must already have decided what he would do in the event of Pitt's arriving.

"I shall inform Mrs. Parmenter you are here, sir," he announced gravely. "Of course, I cannot say whether she is able to see you."

Pitt waited in the morning room with its strongly Middle Eastern flavor, but he was only peripherally aware of it. It was no more than ten minutes before Vita opened the door and came in, closing it behind her. She looked fragile and ill with worry. There was an enormous bruise purpling around her right eye and a scar still shining red with spots of blood on her cheek. No art of powder or rouge could have hidden it, even had she been a woman who used such things.

He tried not to stare at it, but it was such a startling blemish on an otherwise lovely face, that it was almost impossible not to.

"Good morning, Mrs. Parmenter," he said. He had no need to affect pity or shock; both were too deep in him to have hidden. "I am sorry to have to disturb you on such a matter, but I cannot leave it unexplained."

Instinctively her hand moved to her cheek. It must have been extremely painful.

"I am afraid your journey is wasted, Superintendent," she answered very quietly. He could only just hear her words, her voice was so low and husky. "There is nothing for you to do, and I have no statement to make. Of course, I realize that Mrs. Pitt will have told you what she observed yesterday evening. In her position she could hardly have done otherwise." She made an effort to smile, but it was thin and close to tears, a defense rather than a politeness. "But it is a personal matter between my husband and myself, and will remain so." She stopped abruptly, staring up at him as if uncertain how to continue.

He was not surprised. He would have been surprised had she told him freely what had happened and accused Ramsay. She had too much dignity and loyalty to speak openly of her injuries, most especially now. He wondered what violence she might have suffered in the past. Sometimes women did, considering it part of their situation of dependence and obedience. Misbehavior earned the right of a husband to beat his wife. The law acknowledged it, and a woman had no recourse. It was within Pitt's memory when it had been illegal for a wife to run away from home to avoid anything her husband might choose to do, short of inflicting a crippling or fatal injury.

"I know I cannot force you, Mrs. Parmenter," he replied quietly. "And I respect your desire to protect your family and what you may feel to be your duty. But violence has resulted in death in this house a few days ago. This is no longer entirely a personal quarrel which can be dismissed and forgotten. Have you seen a doctor?"

Again her hand rose to her cheek, but she did not touch the inflamed skin. "No. I do not think it is necessary. What could he do? It will heal by itself in time. I shall treat it with cold compresses and a little feverfew for headache. Oil of lavender is excellent also. There is no permanant damage."

"To the cheek, or to your marriage?" he asked.

"To my cheek," she replied, not taking her eyes from his. "I thank you for concerning yourself with my marriage. You are a man of kindness and good manners. But to you as a policeman, I have no complaint to make, and therefore it does not enter into your professional sphere." She sat down a little wearily in one of the chairs and looked up at him. "It was a domestic incident, such as happens all over England every day of the week. It was a misunderstanding. I am sure it will not happen again. We have all been under a great pressure since Unity's death."

She drew in her breath and waited while Pitt sat opposite her. "It has affected my husband most of all, quite naturally," she went on, her voice quiet, confidential. "He worked closely with her and . . . and—" She stopped. The rest of the truth hung between them in a chasm of the unknown and the feared. She must be as aware as he was of the implications of Ramsay's violence towards her the previous evening. He had only to look at her to see the extent and the viciousness of it. Ramsay had not merely slapped her. That might have left a weal, fingermarks, never the bruising that disfigured her now, or the slashing cut. He must have struck her with a closed fist, and a great deal of weight behind it. The cut made by his signet ring was plain. To protest otherwise could deceive no one. Whatever she chose to say, he had seen the wound and could come to only one conclusion.

"I understand, Mrs. Parmenter," he said with a tight smile, not for her silence but for the tragedy which lay behind it. "Now I would like to speak to the Reverend Parmenter, if I may." It was not really a question, only a demand courteously phrased.

She misunderstood him. "Please don't!" she said urgently. She stood up and took a step towards him. He stood also.

"I could not bear him to think I had called you!" She went on urgently. "I didn't! I forbade any of the family from mentioning the incident at all, and he may not even know that Mrs. Pitt was here at that time." She shook her head vigorously. "I certainly did not tell him. Please, Superintendent. This is a completely private matter, and unless I complain you cannot involve yourself." Her voice rose and her eyes were wide and dark. "I shall tell you I walked into a door. I slipped and fell. I caught myself on a piece of furniture. It was a ridiculous accident. There was no one else present at the time, so no one can contradict me. If Mrs. Pitt thought otherwise, I shall deny it. She misunderstood. I was hysterical and did not know what I said. There! There is nothing for you to do." She looked at him with defiance, even the shadow of a smile. "You cannot possibly make evidence of it because no one saw anything. If I deny it, then it never happened."

"I wish to see him about Miss Bellwood's past academic career, Mrs. Parmenter," he said gently. "And what he may know of her personal life. As you say, whatever happened yesterday evening is not a public matter but a private one."

"Oh. Oh, I see." She looked taken aback and a trifle embarrassed. "Of course. I'm sorry. I leaped to a conclusion. Please forgive me."

"Perhaps I should have explained," he said sincerely. "It is my fault."

She shot him a dazzling smile, then winced as her cheek hurt. But even her bruising and the swelling across her cheekbone could not mar the radiance of her look.

"Please come upstairs. He is in his study. I expect he can tell you quite a lot about her. He did learn a great deal before he employed her." She led him to the bottom of the stairs, then turned and said very softly, "Actually, I think he would have been far wiser not to have chosen her, Mr. Pitt. I am sure she was brilliant in her skills, very gifted, so I hear. But her personal life was . . ." She gave a little shrug. "I was going to say questionable, but I am afraid there were very few questions that were not unfortunately answered . . . and not in her favor. Still . . . Ramsay can tell you the details. I cannot. But he was more tolerant than I think he should have been. And look at the tragedy it has brought him." She started up the stairs again, running her hand up the shining, black banister rail. In spite of the heaviness which lay over the house, she walked straight-backed, her head high, and with a very slight sway which was extraordinarily graceful. Not even this oppression could rob her of her courage or the qualities of her character.

Ramsay greeted Pitt with mild surprise, rising from his seat behind a desk scattered with papers. Vita left, closing the door behind her, and Pitt accepted the chair offered him.

"What can I do for you, Superintendent?" Ramsay asked, his brow puckered, his eyes anxious. He looked at Pitt as though he could not quite focus upon him.

Pitt had an extraordinary sense of unreality. It was as if Ramsay had forgotten his wife's injury. It did not seem to occur to him that Pitt could have called with regard to that, or even that he had noticed it. Was Ramsay so familiar with the idea of striking a woman, albeit in his notion of proper discipline, that he felt no discomfort that a stranger should be aware of it?

Pitt found it difficult to force his attention to the reason he had given for coming, and indeed it was his secondary purpose.

"I need to know more about Miss Bellwood's past, before she came to Brunswick Gardens," he answered. "Mrs. Parmenter tells me you made the usual enquiries about her, both as to her professional abilities and to her character. I should like to know what you learned about the latter."

"Oh . . . would you?" Ramsay looked surprised. He seemed preoccupied with something else. "Do you really think it will help? Well, I suppose it might. Yes, naturally I enquired for some references and asked various people I knew. After all, you do not take people lightly when the work is of importance and you expect to associate with them closely. What is it you would like to know?" He did not offer anything, as if he had little idea what Pitt was seeking.

"What was her position immediately prior to coming here?" Pitt began.

"Oh . . . she was assisting Dr. Marway with his library," Ramsay replied straightaway. "He specializes in translations of ancient works, and he has many of them in the original Latin and Greek, of course. It was a matter of classifying and reorganizing."

"And he found her satisfactory?" This was an extraordinary conversation. Ramsay was talking about a woman with whom it seemed he had had an affair, and then murdered, and he looked absent-minded about it, as if it were only of peripheral importance to him, something else consumed his real attention, and yet he did not wish to be discourteous or unhelpful, so he was prepared to do his best to answer.

"Oh, commendably so. He said she was exceptionally gifted," he said sincerely. Was it to justify his choice? He certainly had not liked her personally. Or was he seeking to deflect suspicion away from himself now?

"And before then?" Pitt persisted.

"If I remember correctly, she was coaching Reverend Daventry's daughters in Latin," Ramsay said with a frown. "He told Unity they improved quite beyond his highest expectations. Before you ask me, prior to that she translated some Hebrew scrolls for Professor Allbright. I did not enquire further than that. I felt no necessity."

Pitt smiled but saw no answering light in Ramsey's face. "And her personal life, her standards of conduct?"

Ramsay looked away. Obviously the questions disturbed him. His voice was quiet and troubled, as if he blamed himself. "There were some remarks about her manner, her political views were rather extreme and unattractive, but I discounted that. I did not wish to judge when it was not my place. In my opinion, the church should not be political . . . at least not in a discriminatory sense. I am afraid I have since come to regret my decision." His hands on the top of the desk were clenched uncomfortably, fingers locked around each other.

"I think in my desire to be tolerant, I failed to defend what I believe in," he continued, examining his hands without appearing to see them. "I . . . I had not met anyone like Miss Bellwood before, anyone so . . . so aggressive in their desire to change the established order, so full of anger against what she perceived to be unjust. Of course, she was quite unbalanced in her views. No doubt they sprang from personal experience of some unhappy sort. Perhaps she had sought some position for which she was unsuited, and rejection had embittered her. Possibly it was a love affair. She did not confide in me, and naturally I did not ask." He looked up at Pitt again. His eyes were shadowed, and all the lines of his face tense, as if inside himself he were locked in an almost uncontrollable emotion.

"What were her relationships with the rest of the household?" Pitt asked. There was no purpose in trying to appear casual. They both knew why he asked and what implications would follow from any answer, no matter how carefully worded.

Ramsay stared at him. He was weighing all the possibilities of what he might say, what evasions he could escape with. It was clear in his face.

"She was a very complex person," he said slowly, watching Pitt's reaction. "There were times when she would be charming and made most of us laugh with the readiness of her wit, although on occasion it could be cruel. There was an . . . an anger in her." His mouth tightened, and his hands fiddled with a penknife on the desk top in front of him. "Of course, she was opinionated." He gave a tiny, rueful laugh, hardly any sound at all. "And she had no reluctance in expressing herself. She quarreled with my son about his religious opinions, as she did with me . . . and with Mr. Corde. I am afraid it was in her nature. I do not know what else I can add." He looked at Pitt in a kind of desperation.

Pitt thought of Vespasia's words. He wished he knew more about these quarrels, but Ramsay was not going to tell him.

"Were they ever personal, Reverend Parmenter, or always to do with religious faith or opinion?" He did not expect a useful answer, but he was interested in watching how Ramsay would choose to reply. They both knew that one of them in the house must have pushed her.

"Ah . . ." Ramsay's hands tightened on the knife. He began tapping it rapidly on the blotting paper, a nervous, almost twitching motion. "Mallory was worst. He takes his calling very seriously, and I am afraid he does not have a developed sense of humor. Dominic, Mr. Corde, is older and a trifle more accustomed to dealing with . . . women. He did not fall so . . . readily." He regarded Pitt with undisguised distress. "Superintendent, you are asking me to make statements which may incriminate either my son or my curate, a man I have taught and cared for for many years, and now a guest in my home. I cannot do it. I simply don't know! I . . . I am a scholar. I do not observe personal relationships a great deal, not closely. My wife . . ." He changed his mind; the retreat was clear in his expression. "My wife will tell you that. I am a theologian."

"Is that not based on the understanding of people?" Pitt enquired.

"No. No, not at all. On the contrary, it is the understanding of God."

"What use is that if you do not also understand people?"

Ramsay was perplexed. "I beg your pardon?"

Pitt looked at him and saw confusion in his face, not the superficial failure to understand what Pitt had said, but the far deeper darkness of corroding doubt that he understood himself. Ramsay Parmenter was tormented by a void of uncertainty, fear of wasted time and passion, of years spent pursuing the wrong path.

And all that came into focus in Unity Bellwood, in her sharp tongue and incisive mind, her questions, her mockery. In one terrible moment had rage at his own futility exploded in physical violence? To destroy self-belief was perhaps the greatest threat of all. Was his crime a defense of the inmost man?

But the more he knew of Ramsay Parmenter, the less did Pitt find it possible to imagine that he had once been Unity's lover. Did he know who was? Mallory or Dominic? His son or his protégé?

"Unity Bellwood was almost three months with child," he said aloud.

Ramsay froze. Nothing in the room made the slightest motion or sound. From outside a dog barked, and the wind moved very faintly in the branches of the tree close to the window.

"I'm sorry," Ramsay said finally. "That is extremely sad."

It was the last response Pitt had expected. Looking at Ramsay's face, amazement and sorrow were all he saw. There was certainly no embarrassment—and no guilt.

"Did you say three months?" Ramsay asked. Now there was fear as he realized the implications. The little color there was drained from his cheeks. "Then . . . are you saying . . . ?"

"It is most likely," Pitt replied.

Ramsay bent his head. "Oh dear," he said very quietly. He seemed to be struggling for breath. He was obviously in acute distress, and Pitt wished there were something he could do to help him, at least physically if not emotionally. He was as helpless as if there were a thick wall of glass between them. The longer he knew Ramsay, the less he understood him and the less could he believe unequivocally in his guilt for Unity's death. The only explanation lay in some kind of madness, a division in his mind which managed to divorce the act, and the persons which had driven it, from the man he was now.

He looked up at Pitt. "I suppose you think it must have been someone in this house, which means either my son or Dominic Corde?"

"It seems extremely likely." Pitt did not mention Ramsay himself.

"I see." He folded his hands carefully and stared at Pitt, his eyes full of distress. "Well, I cannot help you, Superintendent. Either possibility is unbelievable to me, and I think I should say nothing further to you that might prejudice your judgment. I do not wish to wrong either man. I am sorry. I realize that is no help to you, but I find myself too . . . too disturbed in my mind to think or act clearly. This is . . . overwhelming."

"Can you at least tell me where Dominic Corde was living when you first met him?"

"The address? Yes. I suppose so. Although I do not know what assistance that will be. It is several years ago now."

"I know. I should still like it."

"Very well." Ramsay opened one of the desk drawers and produced a piece of paper. He copied what was written on it onto another piece and pushed it across the polished surface of the wood towards Pitt.

Pitt thanked him and took his leave.

He did not go back to the police station for Tellman, who was occupied on the final details of their previous case. There was so little to follow in Unity's death that Pitt could find nothing for Tellman to do. It was all so insubstantial. It depended upon emotion and opinion. All the facts he had were that Unity Bellwood was three months with child and that the father was probably one of the three men in the Parmenter house, any one of whom would be ruined by the fact, were it known. She had been overheard to quarrel with Ramsay on several occasions, the last immediately prior to the fall down the stairs which had killed her. He denied having left his study. Mrs. Parmenter, her daughter Tryphena, the maid and the valet had all heard Unity cry out to him the moment before she fell.

Other minor facts, perhaps relevant, perhaps not, were that Mallory Parmenter had been alone in the conservatory and denied seeing

Unity, but she had a stain on her shoe which could only have been obtained by crossing the conservatory floor within the short space of time when he was there. There had been no stain on the hem of her dress, but she had probably lifted that instinctively against the possibility of dust or soil on the path. Was Mallory's denial guilt or simply fear?

It all added up to suspicion, but certainly not the sort of proof Pitt could present to a court. He must have that to proceed, and yet he did not even know what he was looking for, or even if it existed.

He hailed a hansom and gave the driver the address Ramsay had given to him.

"All the way, guv?" the driver said in surprise.

Pitt collected his wits. "No . . . no, you had better take me to the station. I'll catch a train."

"Right y'are then." The man looked relieved. "In yer get."

Pitt got off the train at Chislehurst Station and walked through a bright, windy late morning towards the crossroads by the cricket ground. There he made enquiries as to the nearest public house and was directed to take the right-hand road and follow it about five hundred yards to where he would find St. Nicholas's Church and the fire station on his left, and the Tiger's Head public house on his right.

There he had an excellent luncheon of fresh bread, crumbly Lancashire cheese, rhubarb pickle and a glass of cider. On further enquiry he was told where to find Icehouse Wood and the house there which was still occupied by the group of eccentric and unhappy people whom, apparently, he sought.

He thanked the landlord and went on his way. It took him no more than twenty minutes to find the place. It was situated deep among the bare trees and should have been beautiful. The blackthorn was in blossom in drifts of white, and the earth was starred with pale windflowers, but the house itself had an air of dilapidation which spoke of years of misery and neglect.

How on earth had the elegant and sophisticated Dominic Corde come to be here? And what had brought Ramsay Parmenter to cross his path?

Pitt walked across the overgrown lawn and knocked on the door, heavily overhung by honeysuckle not yet in bud.

His knock was answered by a young man in ill-fitting trousers and a waistcoat which had lost several of its buttons. His long hair hung over his brow, but his expression was agreeable enough.

"Have you come to mend the pump?" he asked, looking at Pitt hopefully.

Pitt remembered his early experience on the estate farm.

"No, but I can try, if you are having trouble."

"Would you? That's terribly decent of you." The young man opened the door wide and led Pitt through untidy and chilly corridors to the kitchen, where piles of dishes sat on the wooden bench and in a large earthenware sink. The young man seemed oblivious of the mess. He pointed to the iron pump, which was obviously jammed. He did not seem to have the faintest idea what to do about it.

"Do you live here alone?" Pitt asked conversationally as he began to examine the pump.

"No," the young man said easily, sitting sideways on the table and watching with interest. "There are five or six of us. It varies. People come and go, you know?"

"How long have you had this pump?"

"Oh, years. It's been here longer than I have."

Pitt looked up and smiled. "Which would be?"

"Oh, seven or eight years, as far as I recall. Do we need a new one? God, I hope not. We can't afford it."

Seeing the general state of disrepair, Pitt could believe that. "It's rather rusted," he observed. "It looks some time since it was cleaned. Have you any emery?"

"What?"

"Emery," Pitt repeated. "Fine gray-black powder for polishing metal. You might have it on cloth or paper."

"Oh. Peter might have. It will be on the cupboard over here if he has." And obediently he looked and came up with a piece of cloth, holding it triumphantly.

Pitt took it and began to work on the rusted pieces.

"I'm looking for a friend—a relative, actually," he remarked as he rubbed. "He was here almost four years ago, I believe. His name is Dominic Corde. Do you remember him?"

"Certainly," the young man answered without hesitation. "In a rare state when he came. Never seen a man more despairing of himself and the world . . . except Monte, and he drowned himself, poor devil." He smiled suddenly. "But don't worry about Dominic. He was fine when he left. Some clergyman came here looking for Monte, and he and Dominic got on marvelously well. Took a while, of course. These things do. Talk the leg off an iron pot, that clergyman, but it seemed to be what Dominic needed."

Pitt had taken off his jacket and rolled up his sleeves. He was working hard on the pump.

"I say, that's awfully decent of you," the young man said admiringly.

"How did Dominic get into that state?" Pitt asked, sounding as casual as he could.

The young man shrugged.

"Don't know. Something to do with a woman, I think. It wasn't money, I know that, and it wasn't drink or gambling, because you don't stop those instantly, and he didn't do either when he was here. No, I'm pretty sure it was a woman. He'd been living in Maida Vale with a whole lot of other people, men and women. He didn't talk about it much."

"You don't know where, do you?"

"Hall Road, I believe. Can't tell which number. Sorry."

"Never mind. I expect I can find it."

"Brother, is he? Cousin?"

"Brother-in-law. Can you pass me that cloth?"

"Are you going to get that working? That would be marvelous."

"I think so. Hold that for me."

It was late by the time Pitt returned home, and he told Charlotte nothing about his expedition to Chislehurst. The following day, the sixth since Unity's death, he took Tellman with him and went to search for the house in Maida Vale where Dominic had lived before meeting Ramsay Parmenter and finding his vocation in the church.

"I don't know what you expect to learn," Tellman said dourly. "What difference does it make what he did five years ago, or who he knew?"

"I don't know," Pitt said sharply as they walked towards the railway station. It was a fairly direct route to St. John's Wood Station, and then a short distance from there to Hall Road. "But it must have been one of the three of them."

"It was the Reverend," Tellman said, keeping step with him with difficulty. Pitt was three inches taller, and his stride was considerably longer. "You just don't want it to be him because of the trouble it will cause. Anyway, I thought Corde was your brother-in-law. You don't think your brother-in-law murdered Miss Bellwood, do you?" He looked sideways at Pitt, anxiety and a certain disgust in his lantern-jawed face.

Pitt was jolted. He realized how significant a part of him would find it very acceptable that Dominic should be guilty.

"No, I don't!" he snapped. "But are you suggesting I should not bother to investigate him because he is a relation . . . by marriage?"

"So that's what this is, is it?" Tellman's voice was heavy with incredulity. "Duty?"

They crossed the platform and climbed onto the train. Tellman slammed the door shut behind them.

"Has it occurred to you that I might be just as eager to prove him innocent?" Pitt asked as they sat down, facing each other across an empty compartment.

"No." Tellman looked back at him. "You haven't got a sister, so who is he? Mrs. Pitt's brother?"

"Her elder sister's husband. She is dead. She was murdered ten years ago."

"Not by him?"

"Of course not! But his behavior was far from admirable."

"And you don't believe he's reformed? Become a minister and all." Tellman's voice was ambivalent. He was not sure what he thought of the church. Part of him believed it was the Establishment. He preferred a nonconformist preacher, if he went to church at all. But religion was still sacred, any Christian religion . . . maybe any religion at all. He might despise some of its show and resent its authority, but respect for it was part of the dignity of man.

"I don't know," Pitt replied, staring out of the window as a cloud of steam drifted past and the train launched forward.

It took them until early afternoon to find the right house in Hall Road. It was still occupied by a group of artists and writers. It was difficult to tell how many, and there seemed to be several children, as well. They were all dressed in a Bohemian way, bits of costume of different styles, even some oriental clothing, startling in this quiet and very English suburb.

A tall woman who introduced herself simply as Morgan assumed the leadership and answered Pitt's questions.

"Yes, Dominic Corde did live here for a short while, but it was several years ago. I am afraid I have no idea where he is now. We have not heard from him since he left." Her face with its wide eyes and fine lips showed a shadow of sadness. She had a mane of fair hair which she wore loose, except for a woven ribbon band around her brow, like a green crown.

"It is the past I am interested in, not the present," Pitt explained.

He saw Tellman disappear along the corridor and assumed he was, as had been previously agreed, going to speak to some of the other inhabitants.

"Why?" She looked at him very directly. She had been working on a painting, which stood on a large easel behind her, when he had interrupted. It appeared to be a self-portrait, the face peering through leaves, the body half hidden by them. It was enigmatic and in its way very beautiful.

"Because present events make it necessary I know what happened to several people in order that an innocent man may not be blamed for a crime," he answered. It was oblique, and something less than the truth.

"And you want to blame Dominic for it?" she assumed. "Well, I shan't help you. We don't talk about each other, especially to outsiders. Our way of life and our tragedies are private, and no concern of yours, Superintendent. No crime was committed here. Mistakes, perhaps, but they are ours to mend, or not."

"And if it is Dominic I am trying to absolve?" he asked.

She looked at him steadily. She was beautiful, in a wild way, although she was well past forty and there was something in her which still held all the unfinished rebellion of youth. There was no peace in her face. He wondered what her relationship with Dominic had been. They seemed as different from each other as possible, and yet he had changed almost completely in the last few years. Perhaps during his time there they had complemented each other in some way. He had been restless then, incomplete, and she might have fed his needs.

"From what crime?" she asked, her brilliant eyes steady and almost unblinking.

He had to remind himself that he was the interrogator, not she. He pushed his hands into his pockets and relaxed a little. With his shaggy hair and crooked tie, pockets full of odds and ends, he did not look nearly as out of place in this house as Tellman did.

"But he did live here for some time?" he repeated calmly.

"Yes. We have no reason to deny that. But there is nothing here to concern the police." Her jaw tightened. "We live very ordinary lives. The only thing about us which is unusual is that we share a large house, seven of us and the children, and we are all artists of one sort or another. We weave, paint, sculpt and write."

"Did Dominic practice any of these things?" he asked with surprise. He had never imagined him to possess any sort of talent.

"No," she said reluctantly, as if it were an admission. "You still have not told me what crime you are investigating or why I should answer any of your questions."

Footsteps passed along the corridor, hesitated, then continued.

"No, I haven't," he agreed. "Something happened here which distressed him very much—so much, in fact, that he was close to despair. What was it?"

She hesitated. The indecision was mirrored in her eyes.

He waited.

"One of our number died," she said at length. "We were all distressed. She was young, and we were very fond of her."

"Was Dominic in love with her?"

Again she waited before she answered. He knew she was weighing what to tell him, how much of the truth she could conceal without leading him to other things, more deeply secret.

"Yes," she said, still looking directly at him. Her eyes were extraordinary, light blue and burningly clear.

He did not disbelieve her, but he was sure that somehow her reply covered something unsaid and more important.

"How did she die?" He would not know if she told him the truth, but he could ask neighbors and make enquiries at the local police station. There would be a record of it. "What was her name?"

The resentment was stiff in her face and the set of her square shoulders and long back.

"Why do you want to know? What can it possibly have to do with your present enquiry? She was young and sad, and she hurt no one. Leave her in peace."

He caught the intonation of tragedy in her voice, and of defensiveness. If she did not tell him, he would certainly enquire. It would not be difficult to find out, only time-consuming.

"Another tragedy has occurred, Miss Morgan," he said gravely. "Another young woman is dead." He saw the blight in her face, as if he had struck her. She seemed scarcely able to believe him.

"Another . . . How?" She stared at him. "What . . . what happened? I don't believe it could be . . ." But obviously she did. It was too painfully clear.

"I think you should tell me what happened here."

"I have told you." Her hands clenched. "She died."

"Of what cause?" he insisted. "Either you can tell me, Miss Morgan, or I can make enquiries and find out through the local police station, doctor, church—"

"Of an overdose of laudanum," she said angrily. "She took it to sleep, and one night she took too much."

"How old was she?"

"Twenty." She dared him to construe meaning into that, but even as she did so she knew she was defeated.

"Why?" he asked quietly. "Please don't make me draw this out of you, Miss Morgan. I am going to have to find the answer. It takes longer this way, but it will not alter anything."

She turned from him, staring at her vivid painting, examining every leaf and flower in it. When she spoke her voice was low and fierce with emotion. "We used to believe that for love to be real, its highest and noblest form, it must be free, unfettered by any restrictions or bonds, any . . . any unnatural curbs upon its will and its honesty. I still believe that."

He waited. The constructive arguments that came to his lips had no place here.

"We tried to practice it," she went on, her head bent a little, the light shining on her hair, pale like early wheat. "We were not all strong enough. Love should be like a butterfly. If you close your hand on it, you kill it!" She clenched her fist. She had surprisingly powerful hands, square-fingered, smudged with green paint. She jerked her hand open. "If you love someone, you should be prepared to let them go, too!" She stared at him challengingly, waiting for him to comment.

"Would you leave your child if it became boring to you or interrupted what you wanted to do?" he asked.

"No, of course not!" she said sharply. "That is entirely different."

"I don't think it is," he answered quite seriously. "Pleasure is about coming and going as you like. Love is about doing what is sometimes difficult, or expensive in time and emotion, for someone else's sake, and finding that if it adds to their happiness, then it does to yours also."

"You sound very pompous," she stated. "I suppose you are married."

"You disapprove of marriage?"

"I think it is unnecessary."

"How condescending."

Suddenly she laughed. It lit her face, softening the hard angles and making her beautiful. Then as quickly it vanished, leaving her sad and defensive as before.

"Actually, I think it is necessary for some people," she conceded unwillingly. "Jenny was one of them. She was not strong enough to let go when the time came."

"She killed herself . . ." he guessed.

She looked away again. "Perhaps. No one can be certain."

"Dominic was certain, and that is why he blamed himself and left in despair." He was sure that what he said was the truth, or close to it. "He would not marry her?"

"He couldn't marry both of them!" she said scornfully, anger in her eyes as she faced him. "Jenny couldn't cope with sharing. She became—" She stopped again, looking away.

"With child," he finished for her. "Vulnerable. Needing more for herself than someone who came when they felt like it and left equally selfishly." He thought sharply and with overwhelming sweetness of

Charlotte. "She began to understand that love is commitment," he said quietly. "Making promises and keeping them, being there when people need you, whether it suits you or not. She grew up . . . and the rest of you didn't. You were still playing. Poor Jenny."

"That's unfair!" Her voice was raised and angry. "You weren't here! You don't know anything about it!"

"I know Jenny is dead, because you just told me, and I know Dominic felt the height of his guilt, because I know where he went after here."

"Where did he go?" she demanded. "Is he all right?"

"You care?" He raised his eyebrows.

She snatched her hand back as if she would like to hit him but did not dare to. He wondered if she had been the other woman. He thought probably not.

"Was Unity Bellwood ever here?" he asked instead.

She looked totally blank. "I've never heard of her. Is she the girl who is dead this time?" In spite of herself there was an edge of sorrow in her voice, and perhaps guilt, too.

"Yes. Only she didn't kill herself. She was murdered. She was with child as well."

She looked down. "I'm sorry. I would have staked anything I had he would never do anything like that again."

"Perhaps he hasn't. I don't know. Thank you for being honest with me."

"I had no choice," she said grudgingly.

He smiled, a wide smile of both humor and victory.

It was late when he arrived home. Tellman had told him a little more about the establishment in Hall Road, all of which was much as he might have guessed. A group of people had begun pursuing a kind of freedom they believed passionately would bring them happiness. It had instead brought them confusion and tragedy. They had changed at least some of their ways, but were loath to admit error or let go of the dream. Jenny was seldom spoken of. Tellman had learned of her from one of the children, a ten-year-old boy with a less-guarded tongue who found lurid tales of London's Whitechapel District too fascinating to miss, in exchange for a little factual information about his own, to him very boring, household.

"Immoral," Tellman had said damningly. "They should know better. They aren't poor or ignorant." He had great compassion for the old or the sick, the very poor, although he was reluctant to let anyone see it. But from those he considered his betters, or who thought they were, he expected high standards, and when they fell below them, he had only contempt. "No respect," he added. "No decency."

Pitt had sat all the way on the train wondering what he was going to tell Charlotte. She would be bound to ask. Anything to do with Dominic she would naturally care about intensely. His behavior to Jenny had been close to inexcusable. The fact that she had thought she could live with sharing him with another woman was no answer. He was twice her age. He had been married to Sarah and knew perfectly well that such liberty was almost certain to fail. He had been as shallow thinking and as indulgent as when he had lived in Cater Street, taking pleasure where it was offered and thinking no further than the moment.

Could people really change? Of course it was possible. But was it probable?

There was a cold unhappiness inside Pitt, because part of him wanted to think this case was Dominic all over again, the old Dominic he had known before. And Dominic was surely far more likely to be guilty than Ramsay Parmenter, dry, ascetic, intellectual, tormented Ramsay, filled with doubts and arguments, seeking immortality by writing some abstruse interpretation of theology.

Tellman had said very little throughout the journey. He had seen a glimpse of a world which disturbed him, and he needed to think about it alone.

As soon as Pitt was inside the door Charlotte asked him.

"Yes," he answered, taking off his coat and following her through to the parlor. She was so concerned she had barely touched him, and left him to hang up his coat and scarf himself.

"Well?" She turned and faced him. "What happened? What did you find out?"

"I've had a long journey and I'd like a cup of tea," he replied, stung by her eagerness. The old care for Dominic was just as sharp.

She looked surprised. "Gracie is getting you one. It will be here in a moment. Would you like something to eat as well? I've got fresh bread and cold mutton."

"No. Thank you." He was being ungracious, and he knew it. What should he tell her about Dominic? If he lied, and Dominic were guilty, she would blame him for not having been honest. "I found the house where Dominic lived before he went to Icehouse Wood."

"Icehouse Wood?" she questioned. "You didn't tell me about Ice-house Wood. Where is it? It sounds horrible."

"Chislehurst. It isn't nice. It could be, if it weren't neglected." He sat down by the fire, stretching his feet out and leaving her standing.

She stared down at him. "Thomas! What is wrong? What is it you won't tell me?"

He was too locked up in anger and indecision to smile at her illogic.

"What did you find out about Dominic?" Her voice was sharper and he could hear the fear behind it. He turned to look up at her. It was the end of the day and she was tired, too. There was very little color in her cheeks and her hair was coming out of its pins. She had been too preoccupied to tidy herself up for his return. The anxiety was written plainly on her face, the fine lines around her eyes, the shadows in them, the tightness of her mouth.

He loved her too much to be invulnerable. He despised part of himself even as he answered.

"He lived in a large house in Maida Vale with several other people. They believed in love without commitment, more or less do-as-you-please. He had two mistresses. One was a girl called Jenny, who was twenty . . ." He saw her wince, but ignored it. "He got her with child. She felt frightened and alone. She was no longer able to share him. He wouldn't choose between the two. She took an overdose of laudanum and killed herself. He knew he was to blame, and he ran away in despair . . . to Icehouse Wood . . . which is where Ramsay Parmenter found him, close to suicide."

"Poor Dominic," she said softly. "He must have felt as if there was nothing left in life."

"Well, for Jenny and her child . . . there wasn't!" he lashed back instantly. Suddenly his anger was overwhelming. The sheer useless, horrible tragedy of it was more than he could bear. And now Dominic was wearing a clerical collar and convincing little old ladies like Alice Cadwaller that he was a shepherd for the weak and the innocent. Not to mention Vita Parmenter, who seemed to think him the strength and the conscience of the house, and heaven only knew what Unity Bellwood had felt for him. And now here was Charlotte, of all people, who had known what he was like, had seen him hurting her own sister, instead of despising him and pitying Jenny, saying "Poor Dominic."

Charlotte was white-faced. "That was a terrible thing to say, Thomas!" She was trembling.

Gracie opened the door with a tray of tea and neither of them noticed her.

"It was a terrible thing to do." He could not draw back now. "I did not want to tell you, but you asked me."

"Yes, you did!" she accused, not loudly now but very quietly, her voice low and angry and hurt. "You wanted me to know that Dominic had done something so wretched I could never forget it."

That was true. He had wanted her to know. He had wanted to break the false, idealized notion she had of him and make her see him as he had had to: real, shallow, selfish, tortured with guilt . . . but for how long? Long enough to change . . . or not?

Gracie put the tray on the table. She looked like a frightened child. This was the only home she knew, and she could not bear quarrels in it.

Charlotte turned around to her. "Thank you. You'd better pour it out. I'm afraid we have had some rather unpleasant news about Mr. Corde, my brother-in-law. Things I would rather were not true, but it seems they are."

"Oh," Gracie said with a gulp. "I'm sorry."

Charlotte tried to smile at her but did not succeed. "I shouldn't really be so upset. I've known him long enough it should not surprise me." She watched Gracie pour out the tea and, after a moment's hesitation, take a cup over to Pitt.

"Thank you," he accepted.

Gracie put Charlotte's cup near her and went out.

"I suppose you think he was the father of Unity's child and that she was blackmailing him, so he killed her," she said flatly.

"Well, you have no right to say that," he retorted, stung by the unfairness of it. "I have not concluded anything of the sort. I have no proof which of them killed Unity, nor any hope of getting any practical evidence of the act itself. All I can do is find out more about each of them and hope it shows something or absolves one of them. What would you have me do . . . assume Dominic's innocence?"

She turned away. "No, of course not. I'm not angry that you found this out, just that it pleases you. I want you to be as hurt and as miserable about it as I am." She stood stiff-backed, staring away from him out of the darkened window.

He felt excluded, because he understood what she meant, and yet the dark, cold little voice inside him still almost wished Dominic to be guilty.

He slept very badly and woke late in the morning. He went downstairs and found Tellman drinking tea in the kitchen, talking to Gracie. He stood up the moment Pitt came in, his face coloring slightly.

"You might as well finish it," Pitt said curtly. "I have no intention of going out without breakfast. Where is Mrs. Pitt?"

"Upstairs, sir," Gracie replied, watching him carefully. "Sorting the linen."

"I see. Thank you." He sat down at the kitchen table.

Gracie put a bowl of porridge in front of him and started to warm the frying pan for kippers. He wanted to say something to comfort her, to tell her that this unease in the house was only a passing thing. But he could think of nothing. And half an hour later, when he left, he still had not mentioned it, nor had he been upstairs to speak to Charlotte.

He sent Tellman off to learn what he could of Mallory Parmenter's past, his conversion to the Church of Rome, and his personal habits and relationships.

He began to seek more of Unity Bellwood's past, and spent a miserable Saturday interrupting the brief leisure time of people who had known her in a more personal way. He found out her previous address from Ramsay Parmenter, and now he called upon the house in Bloomsbury, less than fifteen minutes from his own home. He walked rapidly, striding out and passing neighbors without recognizing them, still consumed in his own anger and unhappiness.

There was an air to the house not unlike the one he had been to in Maida Vale. There were similar works of art on the walls, piles of books in and out of cases, a sense of being intentionally different. He was received ungraciously by a bearded man of about fifty who agreed that, yes, Unity Bellwood had lived there some three or four months ago and had left to go to a position which he knew nothing about.

"How long did she live here?" Pitt asked. He was not going to be put off because he was a nuisance and was disturbing a quiet Saturday morning when people wished to relax and not be bothered with strangers.

"Two years," the man replied. "She had rooms upstairs. They are relet now to a nice young couple from Leicestershire. She can't have them back, and I've nothing else." He looked at Pitt belligerently. His regard towards Unity was plain.

Pitt pressed him until he lost his temper, and then went on to speak to all the other residents of the house who were at home, forming a picture of Unity which added little to what he already knew. She was academically outstanding, but her arrogance and her passion had both caused fierce reactions in people. Those who admired her had done so intensely, and felt her death to be both a public and a personal loss. She had represented great courage in the fight against oppression of all kinds, of bigotry, of narrow and unjust laws, and against those limitations of the mind which seek to regiment the emotions and restrict the true liberty of thought and ideas. He heard in her echoes of Morgan's cry for the nobility of free love.

From those who hated her he heard the notes of envy and fear. They were frightened of her. She disrupted what they knew and understood. She threatened their peace of mind and unsettled thought.

He also detected through their stories, of both those who admired her and those who scorned her, a consistent thread of manipulation, a love of power and the will to use it, even for its own sake.

He pursued it until after dark. His back ached, he was exhausted and hungry, and had found he still knew little he could not have guessed. He could no longer put off going home. He walked along the footpath in Gower Street, crossed the intersection at Francis Street and Torrington Place, and went on. His feet hurt. Perhaps that was why he was walking more and more slowly.

There was damp in the air and a slight haze around the new moon above the bare branches of the trees. It was possible they had not seen the very last of the frost. What should he say to Charlotte? She had been so angry this morning she had refused to be present so she would not have to speak to him.

Did she care for Dominic so very much . . . even now? He was part of a past Pitt could never share in, because it had happened before he had known her. It was part of the life she was born to, of sufficient money and beautiful dresses, not hand-me-downs from Aunt Vespasia or gifts from Emily. It was parties and dances, soirees, the theater, having one's own carriage instead of using a hansom on the rare occasions one went out. It was being known in fashionable circles, never having to explain yourself, to conceal the fact that your husband worked for a living, that you had only one resident maid and no manservant. It was the whole world of leisure.

It was the whole world of idleness, of seeking petty occupations with which to fill your day, and at the end wondering why you were still unsatisfied. Even Dominic had grown tired of it and chosen, with a passion, to do something difficult and consuming with his life. That was what Charlotte admired in him, not his handsome face or his charm or his social position. He had no social position.

She had said "Poor Dominic." Did he ever want to hear her say "Poor Thomas" like that?

Never! The thought made his stomach hurt.

He turned the corner into Keppel Street. He was a hundred yards from home. He lengthened his stride. He turned up his own step and opened the front door. He would pretend nothing had happened.

The lights were on. He heard no sound. She could not be out. Could she?

He swallowed hard. He wanted to shout. He could feel panic welling up inside him. This was ridiculous. He had been wrong to be pleased about Dominic, but it was not a sin so grievous as—

He heard laughter from the kitchen, women's laughter, light and happy.

He strode down the corridor, his feet heavy on the linoleum, and threw the door open.

Charlotte was standing beside the flour bin near the dresser and Gracie was next to the sink with a tray of small cakes. There was milk all over the floor. He looked at the mess, then at Gracie, lastly at Charlotte.

"Don't step on it!" she warned. "You'll slip. Don't worry, it isn't all I have. It's only half a pint. It looks terrible like that, but it isn't really bad."

Gracie put down the cakes and reached for a cloth. Charlotte took a mop and squeezed it out, then began to swab up, looking at

Pitt as she did and sending the milk in even wider circles. "You must be tired. Have you had anything to eat?"

"No." Was it going to be all right?

"Would you like scrambled eggs? I've got enough milk for that . . . I think. Perhaps it had better be an omelette. I can do that with water. And I have a confession to make."

He sat down, keeping his feet out of the way of the mop.

"Have you?" He tried to sound light, unafraid.

She looked down at the mop, guiding it back to the right place. "Daniel put his foot through one of the sheets," she said. "I looked at them all. They're all on their way out. I bought four new pairs, and pillow slips to go with them. Two pairs for us, one each for Daniel and Jemima." She looked up to see what he would say.

Relief overwhelmed him like a tidal wave. He found he was smiling, even though he had not meant to. "Excellent!" He did not even care how much they had cost. "A very good thing. Are they linen?"

She still looked a little cautious. "Yes . . . I'm afraid so. Irish linen. It was a good bargain."

"Even better. Yes, I would like an omelette. And have we any pickle left?"

"Yes, of course." She smiled slowly. "I never run out of pickle. I wouldn't dare," she added under her breath.

"Neither should you." He tried to sound sincere, but he was too happy. He almost wanted to laugh, just because what he had was so precious. Happiness was not in taking what you pleased, as Morgan thought, but in knowing the infinite value of what you had, of being able to look at it with gratitude and joy. "Never run out of pickle," he reaffirmed.

She looked at him under her eyelashes and smiled.

That Sunday, John Cornwallis was invited to dine yet again at the house of Bishop Underhill. It never occurred to him not to accept. He knew why the bishop had sent the invitation. It was entirely to do with the matter of Unity Bellwood's death. He wanted to know if there was further progress—and to urge Cornwallis to avoid scandal at any cost.

Cornwallis had no desire to allow the church to come into disrepute, even among those who were ignorant or insincere enough to judge the message of the Gospel by the failure of one of its servants to live up to even the ordinary laws of the land, let alone the higher laws of God. But neither did he intend to allow an actual wrong to be committed in order to hide an apparent one. He had nothing else to say to Bishop Underhill. He would have sent a polite note of apology except he wanted to go to dinner, to see the bishop's wife again. If he refused, she might think he imagined the bishop's expediency was hers also and that she shared in his cowardice. He had never thought it for a moment. The shame in her eyes had haunted him, her helplessness to deny the bishop without disloyalty.

He dressed very carefully. He wished to appear at his best. He told himself it was because the bishop was in a sense the enemy. He was fighting for a different cause. When sailing into conflict one flew all the flags on the masthead, colors streaming in the wind. There must not be a speck of dust on the black broadcloth of his jacket, and neither on his white collar or shirtfront. Cuff links and studs must gleam. Boots must be without dullness or smear.

He presented himself at exactly the hour stated, neither five minutes before nor five minutes after. He was welcomed by the footman and shown into the withdrawing room, where Isadora was waiting for him. She was dressed in very dark blue, soft as the night at sea. He could remember just that sort of sky after twilight in the Caribbean. She looked pleased to see him. She was smiling.

"I am so sorry, Mr. Cornwallis, the Bishop has been detained, but he will not be long, perhaps half an hour at most."

He was delighted. His spirits soared immediately. He had to stop himself from allowing it to show in his face. What should he say?

What would be honest, and not too bold, yet polite? He must say something!

"I'm sure it won't matter." Was that a foolish thing to say? As far as he was concerned if the bishop never came, so much the better! "I—I have no real news to tell him. It is all . . . insubstantial."

"I imagine it will be," she agreed. A shadow crossed her face. "Do you think they will be able to prove it?"

"I don't know." He knew what she was worrying about. At least he thought he did. A darkness would hang over Parmenter forever, his guilt neither proved nor disproved. He would always be suspect. It was almost a worse sentence than guilt outright, because there was a resentment as well, the feeling he had cheated justice. "But if there is anyone who can solve it, it will be Pitt," he added.

"You think very highly of him, don't you?" she said with a smile touched by anxiety.

"Yes I do." There was no equivocation in his mind.

"I hope it is capable of proof. Some things aren't." She glanced towards the French doors and the garden, where the light was fading, casting deep shadows under the tangled branches of the trees, although they were still bare. "Would you like to walk?"

"Yes," he said without hesitation. He loved gardens at twilight. "Yes, I would."

She led the way, stopping to allow him to open the door for her, then stepping through into the soft night air, rapidly cooling after the fragile warmth of the day. But if she felt cold through the thin fabric of her dress, she ignored it.

"There is not much to see, I'm afraid," she said as she walked over the grass. "Just a glimmer of crocuses under the elms." She pointed towards the far end of the lawn, and he could make out the blur of white and purple and gold across the bare earth. "I think I've brought you under false pretenses. But you can smell the narcissi."

He could. There was a delicate sweetness in the air, clean and sharp as only white flowers can be.

"I love the change between day and night," he said, lifting his face to look up at the sky. "Everything between sunset and darkness. There is so much room for imagination. You see things in a different way from the glare of daylight. There's a richer beauty, and an awareness of how fleeting it all is, how ephemeral. It makes everything infinitely more precious, and there is a sense of regret in it, an understanding of time, and loss, that heightens everything." He was talking dreadful nonsense. In the morning he would be mortified with embarrassment when he remembered.

And yet it was what he meant, and he did not stop. "And at dawn, from the first white fin of light in the east, right through until the clean, cold white daylight, its pale mists clearing across the fields, the dew over everything, there is an unreasoning hope you cannot explain—or feel at any other time." He ceased abruptly. She must be thinking him a complete fool. He should never have come. He should have stayed inside, talking polite rubbish until the bishop arrived and tried to coerce him into arresting Ramsay Parmenter and having him declared insane.

"Have you noticed how many flowers have their best perfume at dusk?" she asked, still walking a little ahead of him, as if she also were reluctant to go back to the warm room and the lights and the fire. "If I could have anything I wanted, I would live overlooking water, a lake or the sea, and watch the light on it every evening. The earth consumes the light. The water gives it back." She turned to him. He could see the faint glimmer of her fair skin. "It must be marvelous to watch the dawn or the sunset at sea," she said softly. "Are you afloat in an ocean of light? Please don't tell me you aren't! Don't you feel as if you are half in the sky, a part of it all?"

He smiled widely. "I hadn't put it in such excellent words, but yes, that is exactly it. I watch the seabirds, and feel as if I am doing almost the same thing, as if the sails are my wings."

"Do you miss it terribly?" Her voice came out of the near darkness, close to him.

"Yes," he said with a smile. "And then when I was at sea I missed the smell of the damp earth, the wind in the leaves and the colors of autumn. Perhaps you can have everything, but you certainly cannot have it all at once."

She gave a little laugh. "That is what memories are for."

They were walking close together. He was very aware of her beside him. He would have liked to touch her, to offer her his arm, but it would have been too obvious. It would break the delicacy of the moment. The cloud bank was deepening over the west. He could barely see her, and yet he had never felt more aware of anyone.

Suddenly the lights from the house shone out over the grass. Someone had opened the French windows. The bishop was silhouetted against the warm color of the room, staring out at them.

"Isadora! What on earth are you doing out there? It's pitch-dark!"

"No, it isn't," she contradicted him. "It's only late twilight." Her eyes were used to it, and she had not been aware of the change.

"It's pitch-dark!" he repeated crossly. "I don't know what made you take our guest out at this hour. There's nothing whatever to see. It was most thoughtless of you, my dear."

The addition of the words *my dear* somehow added insult to the injury of rudeness. There were so obviously not meant, except to disguise the irritation behind them. Cornwallis controlled his temper because the man was a bishop and this was his house—or more accurately, his garden.

"It is my fault," he said very clearly. "I was taking great pleasure in the smell of the evening flowers. I am still not used to the feeling of the earth under my feet."

"Where are you accustomed to finding it?" the bishop said tartly.

Isadora stifled a giggle. Cornwallis heard it distinctly, but the bishop was too far away to be sure.

"You see!" he challenged, mistaking the noise for a sneeze. "You will catch cold. Most foolish, and if I may say so, self-indulgent. Others will have to care for you and perform your duties. Please come in at once."

Cornwallis was livid. He was glad his face was still hidden until he crossed into the bar of light.

"I am accustomed to finding the land many miles away," he said almost between his teeth. "I apologize for prevailing upon Mrs. Underhill's good nature as hostess in asking her to allow me the pleasure of walking in her garden at twilight. I fear I have trespassed upon your hospitality too much and caused an ill feeling I did not intend. Perhaps I should take my leave before I do further damage."

The bishop was obliged to swallow his anger. That was the last thing he wished. He had not yet even broached the subject which was the purpose of the evening, let alone concluded a satisfactory understanding.

"I would not hear of it," he said hastily, forcing a sickly smile to his lips. "I am sure there is no damage done at all. I daresay I worry about my wife's health too much. A single sneeze means nothing whatsoever. It was most remiss of me to mention it. I forget how much a man of the sea must miss such a thing as a garden. One takes it for granted when it is there all the time. I am delighted you enjoyed it. Please come in and warm yourself."

He stood back while Isadora, then Cornwallis, stepped through the doorway inside, then he closed the door behind them. He even made the grudging sacrifice of offering Cornwallis the position closest to the fire. He did not think of offering it to Isadora. His concern for her health stretched only so far.

He did not raise the subject of Ramsay Parmenter until they were well into the second course of the meal, an excellent fish pie.

"How is your man proceeding with the tragedy in Brunswick Gardens? Has he had success in excluding anyone from suspicion yet?"

Cornwallis wished he could answer with some assurance.

"Unfortunately not. It is a subject in which it is extremely difficult to find proof." He took another mouthful of the pie.

The bishop's face darkened. "What is your considered judgment as to whether he will succeed before so much damage is done to the Reverend Parmenter's reputation that he is effectively unable to continue?" he demanded.

"So far there is no suspicion outside the immediate family," Cornwallis replied carefully.

"But you have said his miserable daughter is perfectly prepared to testify against him!" the bishop pointed out. "It cannot be long before she makes some catastrophic remark and the word spreads like fire. Then think of the damage that will be done by such rumors. How will we check it, when we have no proof?" The strength of his fear was sharp-edged in his voice. "We shall be seen to condone his act. We shall appear to be trying to conceal it, to protect him from the consequences of his crime. No, Captain Cornwallis, it is entirely unacceptable. I cannot afford the risk of such indecision." He sat up very straight. "I am speaking for the church. This is not leadership, this is allowing events to dictate to us, not us to be master of events."

Isadora cringed under his tone. She opened her mouth, but there was nothing she could say which would not make it worse. She looked from Cornwallis to her husband, and back again.

Cornwallis did not want to quarrel with a bishop, any bishop, least of all with one who was Isadora's husband. But if he were to behave with honor he had no choice.

"I will not act until I know the truth," he said steadily. "If I charge Ramsay Parmenter, and I cannot prove it in court, then he is free, and suspicion rests either on Mallory Parmenter or Dominic Corde, regardless of whether they are guilty or not. And if I then find proof of Ramsay's guilt, I can do nothing about it."

"I do not want you to charge him, for God's sake!" the bishop said furiously, leaning forward with elbows on the table. "Use your brains, man! That would be disastrous. Think what it would do to the reputation of the church. Your duty is to find moral proof of his guilt, not physical. Then we can have him committed to an asylum, where he can hurt no one and be cared for in privacy and decency. His family will not suffer, and Corde can continue with his no doubt promising career in the church unlimited by any implication of scandal. What happens to Mallory is not our concern. He has chosen the Church of Rome."

Cornwallis was revolted. He could not keep it from his face.

"I am a policeman, not a physician to the insane," he said icily. "I have no idea whether a man is mad or not. All I can deal in is whether he is proven to have committed a given act. And I do not know whether Ramsay Parmenter pushed Unity Bellwood to her death or whether it was someone else. Until I do, I am not prepared to make any statement on the subject. That will have to be acceptable to you, because there is no alternative." He laid down his knife and fork as if he would eat no more.

The bishop stared at him. "I am sure," he said slowly, "that when you have had time to consider the matter more fully, and the implications of what your attitude will do to a church towards which I believe you have some loyalty, then you will reconsider your situation." He gestured to the footman waiting near the door. "Peters, will you remove the plates and bring in the meat."

Isadora closed her eyes and drew a deep breath. Her hands were shaking. She set down her glass before she spilled it.

For her sake only, Cornwallis stayed for the remainder of the meal.

CHAPTER
EIGHT

An hour or so after breakfast on Monday, Dominic was walking up the stairs feeling annoyed because he could not find his penknife. He kept putting things down and forgetting where. It must be part of the strain they were all feeling. He was halfway up when he heard raised voices coming from Ramsay's study. He could not distinguish the words, but it was clearly Ramsay himself and Mallory, and the discussion was acrimonious in the extreme. There seemed to be accusations and denial on both parts. Before he reached the top, the study door flew open and Mallory stormed out, slamming the door behind him. His face was flushed and his lips tight in a thin, furious line.

Dominic made as if to walk past him, but Mallory obviously wanted to continue a battle, and Dominic was an excellent target.

"Shouldn't you be out with parishioners or something?" he demanded. "That would be more use than waiting around here trying to comfort Mother. There's nothing you can say or do that will make any difference." His eyebrows rose high. "Unless, of course, you can confess to having killed Unity? That would be really useful."

"Only temporarily," Dominic replied tartly. There were times when Mallory annoyed him intensely, and this was one of them. Mallory was very superior about belonging to the "one true faith," and yet he allowed himself to be extraordinarily petty-minded and motivated by malice. "Because the police will almost certainly find out the truth in a while. Pitt is very good indeed." He said it spitefully, and was rewarded with seeing the color ebb from Mallory's face. He had intended to frighten him. At least half his mind believed Mallory was guilty of Unity's death . . . more than he believed it could be Ramsay.

"Oh, yes," Mallory said with as much sarcasm as he could muster and control. "I forgot you were related to the police. Your late wife, wasn't it? What an odd family for you to marry into. Not a very good move for your career. I am surprised at you, seeing how ambitious you are, and keen to curry favor."

They were standing at the stairhead. A maid passed below them across the hall carrying a mop and bucket of water. Dominic could just see the lace cap on her head. He turned back to Mallory.

"I married Sarah for love," he said levelly. "It was several years before her sister married a policeman. And yes, it was an odd thing for her to do. But then Charlotte never did things to advance her social position. I don't expect you to understand that."

"A family of that sort, it would have to be love," Mallory observed. "You would still be better employed now in going out and being some use in the parish. There is nothing here that I couldn't do better."

"Indeed?" Dominic affected surprise. "Then why haven't you? All I have observed you doing so far is retreating into your room to study books."

"Great truths are to be found in books," Mallory replied loftily.

"Of course they are. And precious little good they do if that's where they remain," Dominic responded. "Your family needs your comfort, your reassurance and loyalty, not quotations out of books, however wise or true."

"Reassurance?" Mallory's voice rose sharply. "Of what? What can I reassure them about?" His mouth twisted in a smile that failed. "That Father did not kill Unity? I don't know that. I wish to God I did. But someone killed her, and it wasn't me. I assume it was you . . . I certainly want to think it was you!" Suddenly there was real terror in his voice. "She followed you around often enough, always arguing with you, mocking you, making intrusive, cruel little remarks." He nodded. "I caught her eye more than once when she was looking at you. She knew something about you, and she was letting you understand that. I don't know anything about you before you came here, but she did."

Dominic felt the blood drain from his face, and he knew Mallory saw it. The victory was bright in the younger man's eyes.

"It is you who should be afraid of Pitt," Mallory said triumphantly. "If he is anything like as clever as you suggest, whatever it is Unity knew, he'll dig it up."

"You look as if you would like that, Mal." Clarice's voice cut across them from the stairs, below and behind them both. Neither of them had heard her come up, even though the wood was uncarpeted. "Isn't that rather unchristian of you?" She opened her eyes wide as if the question were innocent.

Mallory colored, but it was temper more than shame.

"I suppose you would like it to be me?" he continued, his voice brittle. "That would suit you nicely, wouldn't it? Not your beloved father you are so quick to protect all the time, and not the curate he created out of God knows what. Only your brother. Does that fit in with whatever your morality is?"

"It is not you believing it is Dominic I object to," she replied quite calmly. "That may be honest, I don't know. It is your pleasure in it, your sense of some kind of victory that you still find him entangled in darkness and tragedy. I had not realized you hated him so much."

"I—I don't hate him!" Mallory protested, but now he was defending himself, backed into a corner. "That's a terrible thing to say . . . wrong—and . . . quite untrue."

"No, it isn't," she said, coming up to the top step and onto the landing. "If you could have seen your own face as you spoke just now, you wouldn't bother denying it. You are so afraid for yourself, you'll blame everyone, and this is a wonderful chance to get back at Dominic because Unity found him so attractive, more attractive than you."

Mallory laughed. It was an ugly, jerky sound, and there was no real amusement in it, only a tearing kind of humor at something that hurt, and that he could not share.

"You are stupid, Clarice!" he accused her. "You think you are so clever, but in reality you have always been stupid. You think you stand back and watch, and see everything. And you see nothing. You're blind to Dominic's real nature." His voice was rising and getting louder. "Have you ever asked him where he was before he came here? Have you asked about his wife or why he chose to join the church now, at forty-five, and not in the beginning? Haven't you ever wondered?"

Her face was grim and pale, but she did not look away from him. "I don't take the same pleasure in unearthing people's past weaknesses and grief as you do," she answered unflinchingly. "I never even thought about it." It was a lie. Dominic could see that in her eyes, and that she was hurt by it. He had not realized before that she was vulnerable. It had never occurred to him that, under the wild humor and the family loyalties, there was a woman capable of such feeling.

"I don't believe you," Mallory said flatly. "You are so desperate to have it be anyone but Father, you must have thought of Dominic."

"I've thought of everyone," she agreed very quietly. "But mostly I've thought about how we are going to cope with it when we do know. How are we going to treat that person? How are we going to treat each other? How are we going to make up for the things we have thought unjustly, the things we've said and can't take back and can't forget?" She frowned very slightly. "How are we going to live with the knowledge of what we have seen in each other this last week that is ugly and self-serving and cowardly, but we hadn't ever had reason to see before? I know you better than I ever wanted to, Mal; and I don't like all of it."

He was angry, but much more deeply than that, he was hurt. He tried to find something to say to justify himself, and nothing was good enough.

She must have seen the wound in him. "It isn't over yet," she said with a little shrug. "You can always change . . . if you want to. At least . . . maybe you can."

"I don't want anyone to be guilty," he said stiffly, his cheeks pink. "But I must face the truth. Confession and repentance are the only way back. I know I didn't kill her, therefore it was either Dominic or Father . . . or you! And why on earth would you kill her?"

"I wouldn't." She lowered her eyes, and her face was full of confusion and fear. "Will you let me pass, please? You are blocking the way, and I want to go and see Papa."

"What for?" he asked. "You can't help. And don't go in there telling him comfortable lies. It will only make it worse in the end."

Suddenly she lost her temper, swinging around on him furiously. "I'm not going to tell him anything, except that I love him! It is a pity that you can't do that! You would be a lot more use to everyone if you could!" And she whirled away, banging her elbow against the newel, and oblivious of it, marched across the landing to the far corridor and up to Ramsay's door. She threw it open without knocking and disappeared inside.

"Perhaps you had better go and read another book," Dominic said acidly. "Try the Bible. You could look for the bit which says 'A new commandment I give, that ye love one another'!" And he started down the stairs towards the hall.

He met Vita coming out of the morning room with a bowl of hyacinths in her hands. She stopped in front of him, her eyes steady, wide and searching. He knew she must have overheard at least some of the quarrel, if only the raised voices.

"They're getting dry in here," she said pointlessly, not looking at the hyacinths. "I suppose it's the fire. I think I should put them back in the conservatory for a while. Maybe there's something else in there that would do." She started to walk across the hall, and he went after her.

"May I carry that for you?"

She passed the bowl to him, and together they went into the conservatory. She closed the glass doors and led him to the garden end, where there were other pots of flowers on the bench. He put the hyacinths down.

"How much longer is it going to go on?" she said softly. She looked close to tears, as if she were mastering herself only with difficulty. "It is breaking us, Dominic!"

"I know." He longed to be able to help. He could feel her pain and fear in the air as tangibly as the scent of the winter lilies and the paper-whites.

"You were quarreling with Mallory, weren't you?" She spoke still looking down at the flowers.

"Yes. But it was nothing important, just nerves getting both of us."

She turned and smiled at him, but there was reproof in her expression. "That's kind of you, Dominic," she said gently. "But I know that is not true. Please don't try to protect me. I can see what is happening to us. We are frightened of the police, frightened of each other . . . frightened of what we may learn which will change the world we know forever." She closed her eyes tightly; her voice trembled. "Something has started which we cannot stop, cannot control, and none of us can see the end of it. Sometimes I am so afraid I feel as if my heart will stop."

What could he possibly say or do that would not make it worse, sound stupid or insensitive, offer false comfort neither of them believed?

"Vita!" He used her Christian name without realizing it. "There is only one thing we can do. Live each hour as it comes and do the very best we can. Behave with honesty and kindness, and trust in God that somehow in the end it will be bearable."

She stared up at him. "Will it, Dominic? I think Ramsay is having some kind of breakdown." She gulped. "One moment he is the man we are all used to, patient and calm and so reasonable it is . . . almost boring." She shivered. "The next he loses his temper completely and is a different person. It is as if there is a terrible rage inside him against the world, against . . . I'm not sure . . . against God . . . because He is not there and Ramsay has spent so many years, so much time and energy, thinking He was."

"I haven't seen . . . anger," he said slowly, trying to remember the times he had talked with Ramsay and the emotions there had been. "I think he's disappointed because it isn't as he thought. If he were angry, it would only be with people, those he may feel misled him. But if they did, then they were misled themselves. That can only make one sad . . . you cannot blame them."

"You can't, because you are honest," she continued, a twisted little smile on her lips. "Ramsay is very confused, very . . . I am not sure. I think in a way frightened." She searched Dominic's face to see if he understood what she meant. "I feel so sorry for him. Does that sound arrogant of me? I don't mean to be. But sometimes I can see the fear in his eyes. He is so alone . . . and I think also ashamed, although he would never admit it."

"Doubt is nothing to be ashamed of," he answered, keeping his voice very low. He did not want some passing servant to hear. "In fact, it takes a special kind of courage to keep behaving as if one believed when one can't anymore. I don't think there is any more ter-rible loneliness in the world than to lose one's faith when one has once had it."

"Poor Ramsay," she whispered, knotting her hands together, looking down at them. "When people are afraid they do strange things, far outside the character you think you know. I remember my brother once, when he was afraid . . ."

"I didn't know you had a brother."

She gave a little laugh. "Why should you? I don't speak of him very often. He was older than I, and he did not behave very well some of the time. My father was very upset and terribly disappointed. When Clive got into debt gambling once, and couldn't pay, he lost his head completely and took silver from the house and sold it. Of course, he didn't get nearly as much as it was worth, and Papa had to pay twice as much to redeem it. It was all horrible, and not like Clive at all. But he did it because he was frightened."

Dominic felt a great heaviness inside him.

"You think Ramsay killed Unity, don't you?"

She shut her eyes tightly. "I am afraid of it . . . yes. I know it could not have been you." She made it a simple statement of fact, unquestionable. "And I don't believe it was Mallory. I . . . Dominic, I heard her call out!" She gave a little shudder. "That in itself wouldn't be enough, but I've seen him lose his temper." Almost unconsciously her hand went up to her cheek, where the bruises were still dark and painful. "He had no control at all. He was a different person. He would never have done that to me in—in his normal self. He has never raised a hand to me in all our lives." She shuddered. "Something is happening to him, Dominic. Something very terrible . . . as if there is something inside him which is broken. I—I don't know what to do!"

"Neither do I," Dominic admitted unhappily. "Perhaps I should try talking to him again?" It was the last thing he wanted to do, and he felt intrusive even thinking of it, but how could he leave her to face this alone? Ramsay was the man she loved, and she was watching him drown in some emotional vortex she could neither understand nor help. He was being sucked away from her, from them all. Dominic knew only too well what it was like to be dragged down and suffocated by despair. He had wanted to kill himself during those few weeks at Icehouse Farm. It was only cowardice which had held him back, not any love of life, or hope. But Ramsay had not backed away from him or allowed embarrassment to keep him from stretching out his hand.

"No . . ." Vita said gently. "Not yet, anyway. He will only deny it, and it will make him upset. I am sure you have tried already . . . haven't you?"

"Yes—but . . ."

She laid her hand on his arm. "Then, my dear, the kindest thing you can do is visit people who are expecting him. Do his duties that he is at present incapable of doing for himself. Keep up the dignity and respect he used to have for people, and do not let them see what has become of him. Do it for their sakes also. They need what he could do for them if he were himself. There are things to be organized, decisions to be made which are beyond him at the moment. Do it for him . . . for all of us."

He hesitated. "I don't really have the authority . . ."

She spoke with absolute certainty, her head high, her voice clear. "You must take it."

He wanted to do that, to find an honorable excuse to leave the house with its suspicion and anger, the fear that seemed to permeate everything like a coldness into the bones. He did not want to quarrel with Mallory again, or face Tryphena's grief, or try to think of a way to approach Ramsay without badgering or being intrusive or accusatory, and leaving him feeling even more alone than before.

The only person he found he could think of with any sense of relief, surprisingly, was Clarice. She was outrageous. Some of the things she said were appalling. But he could understand why she said them, and in spite of his better judgment, he did think they were funny, even if no one else did. There was an honesty of emotion in her which he respected.

"Yes," he said decisively. "Yes, that would be the best." And without allowing time for any further discussion he bade Vita good-bye and collected the necessary addresses and information, then took his hat and coat and left.

It was one of those spring days when the wind drives the clouds across the skies so that one moment everything is bathed in light and the next there is chill and shadow, and the moment after, silver and gold again as the sun slants on falling rain. He walked briskly. He would have run had it not been ridiculous, such was his sense of momentary freedom.

He fulfilled all his errands, extending them where possible. Even so, at half past five he had no further reason to remain away from Brunswick Gardens, and was home again by six.

The first person he encountered was Clarice. She was alone on the terrace in the early evening light. The terrace was sheltered and warm, out of the wind, and she was enjoying a few moments of solitude. His immediate thought was that he had intruded.

"I'm sorry," he apologized, and was about to turn and leave.

"No!" she said hastily. She was dressed in muslin, near white, with a green-and-white shawl over her shoulders. He was surprised how it became her. It made him think of summer, cool shaded mornings when the light is clear, before anyone thinks of what will be done in the day.

She smiled. "Please stay. How were your visits?"

"Unremarkable," he replied honestly. He never thought of being other than honest with Clarice.

"But nice to be out," she said perceptively. "I wish I had some reason to escape. Waiting is the worst of it, isn't it?" She turned away and stared at the lawn and the fir trees. "I sometimes think hell is not actually something awful happening, it's waiting for something and never absolutely sure if it will happen, so you soar on hope, and then plunge into despair, and then up again, and down again. You get too exhausted to care for a while, then it all starts over. Permanent despair would almost be a relief. You could get on with it. It takes so much energy to hope."

He said nothing, trying to think.

She looked at him. "Aren't you going to tell me it will all be over soon?"

"I don't know that it will." Then he was ashamed of being so candid. He should have tried to comfort her, instead of unburdening himself. He was behaving like a child, and he was nearly twenty years older than she. She deserved better of him than that. Why did he think of her as stronger? If he could protect Vita, then he should far more try to protect Clarice. "I'm sorry," he apologized. "I expect it will. Pitt will discover the truth."

She smiled at him. "You are lying . . . not in a bad way! A white lie." She shrugged a little, pulling her shawl tighter. "Please don't. I know you mean to be kind. You are doing your pastoral duty. But take off your priest's collar for a few minutes and be an ordinary man.

Pitt may find the truth. He may not. We might have to live like this forever. I know that." Her mouth curved very slightly, as if mocking herself. "I have already decided what to believe, I mean what I shall live with, so I don't lie awake at night torturing myself, turning it over and over in my mind. I have to have a way to function."

Half a dozen starlings flew up out of the trees at the end of the lawn and spiraled upward on the wind, black against the sky.

"Even if it isn't true?" he said incredulously.

"I think it probably is," she answered, staring ahead of her. "But either way, we have to go on. We can't simply stop everything else and go round and round the same wretched puzzle. It was one of us. That is inescapable. We can't run anymore; we are better accepting it. There is no point in thinking how dreadful it is. I have been lying awake a lot, turning it over and over. Whoever did it is someone I know and love. I can't just stop loving them because of it. Anyway, you don't! If you didn't love someone anymore because they did something you found ugly, no love would last. None of us would be loved, because we all do things that are shabby, stupid, vicious from time to time. You need to love from understanding, or even without it."

She was not looking at him but at the fading sunlight and lengthening shadows across the grass.

"And what have you decided?" he said quietly. Suddenly he dreaded that she was going to say it was he. He was amazed at how it would hurt. He cared intensely that she should not think he had had an affair with Unity here, under her father's roof, and then, in a moment of rage and panic, pushed her to her death, even if she could believe he had not meant it. Certainly he would be intentionally allowing Ramsay to be blamed. And after all Ramsay had done for him, that was inconceivable.

He waited with the sweat prickling on his skin.

"I have decided that Mallory had an affair with Unity," she said quietly. "Not love. I think for him it was a temptation. She wanted him, because he had sworn to be celibate and to believe something she found preposterous."

The starlings wheeled back again and disappeared behind the poplar.

"She wished to show him he could not do it, and that it was all pointless anyway," she went on. "She set out to seduce him from his path, and she succeeded. It was a kind of triumph for her . . . not only over Mallory himself but over all the male-dominated church that patronized her and shut her out because she was a woman." She sighed. "And the terrible thing is that I can't entirely blame her for that. It was stupid and destructive, but if you are rejected often enough, it hurts so much you lash out wherever you can. You pick the vulnerable people, not necessarily the ones that attacked you. In a way Mallory represents religion's most easily wounded point: human vanity and appetite. She tried Papa's doubt as well, but the victory over that was so much harder to see or measure."

He watched her as if in a strange state of disbelief, and yet there was sense in what she said. It was the fact she said it which was extraordinary.

"Why would Mallory kill her?" he asked, his voice catching in a cough, his mouth dry.

"Because she was blackmailing him, of course," she said as if the answer had been obvious. "She was with child. Pitt told Papa, and he told me. I daresay everyone knows now." A gust of wind blew her hair and tugged at the loose ends of her shawl. She hugged it closer. "It would ruin him, wouldn't it?" she went on. "I mean, you cannot start out in a great career as a Catholic priest leaving behind a pregnant woman you have seduced and then deserted. Even if it was really she who did the seducing."

"Does he want a great career?" he said with surprise. It was irrelevant, but he had never thought of Mallory as ambitious. He had believed the contrary, that he was using the Catholic faith as a prop to hold him up, to fill the void in certainty and authority where he thought his father's church had let him down—let them all down.

"Perhaps not," she agreed. "But with that behind him, he wouldn't even have a mediocre one."

"Have you any reason for this belief?" he asked, uncertain what he expected her to say. He realized in some ways how little he knew her. Was she clutching at straws, being wildly brave or quite practical? He had been in the house for months, and he had known Ramsay for years. He had taken Clarice too much for granted. "If you have a fact . . ." he started, without thinking, moving closer to her. Then he realized that Mallory was her brother. Her loyalties could only be desperately tangled. He could see the complexity and the pain of it in her eyes.

"The way he behaves," she said quickly. "He has quite changed since Unity's death, which isn't very intelligent. But then I don't think Mallory is, in the ordinary living from day to day and dealing with people." She looked down at her arms, huddled in the shawl. She was obviously cold. The sun had gone down behind the poplars. "He's very good at books, like Papa," she said as if to herself. "I can't see it's going to be the remotest use to him as a priest. But then there is a lot about the church that I can't see. I'm sure she was making him do things." She was obviously referring to Unity again. "She enjoyed it. I could see it in her face. The less he liked whatever it was, the more satisfaction it gave her. I can understand it." She was struggling to be fair. "He can be impossibly pompous at times, and so condescending one would want to scream. I would probably have made him squirm a bit myself if I'd known how to."

The wind was sighing in the trees, and neither of them had heard Tryphena come through the withdrawing room door onto the stones. She was wearing black, and she looked sickly pale. She was obviously extremely angry.

"I believe you would very easily have made him squirm," Tryphena said bitterly. "You've always been envious, because you don't know what to do with yourself. Mallory has found something he cares about passionately, something to give his life to. I know it's ridiculous, but it matters to him." She came forward onto the terrace. "And so have I. You have nothing. All the education you insisted Papa give you, and you do nothing but wander around criticizing and getting in the way."

"There's very little I can do with it!" Clarice retaliated, turning to face her sister. "What can a woman do, except be a governess? There are generations of us, each teaching the next generation, and nobody doing anything with the knowledge except passing it on again. It's like that stupid party game of Pass the Parcel. Nobody ever unwraps it and uses what is inside."

"Then why don't you fight for freedom, as Unity did?" Tryphena asked, stepping further onto the terrace. She had changed into a wool dress and was not cold. "Because you haven't the courage!" she answered her own question. "You just want somebody else to do it all for you and hand it to you when the battle's over. Just because you think you were as good as Mallory in the schoolroom—"

"I was! In fact, I was better."

"No, you weren't. You were just quicker."

"I was better. My exam marks were higher than his."

"It doesn't matter, because the most you could ever be would be a minister's wife, if you could find a minister who would have you. But you don't need any learning for that." She dismissed it as worthless with a wave of her hand. "Only tact, a sweet smile and the ability to listen to everybody and look interested no matter how daft it is or how boring—and to never repeat anything anybody says to you. And you couldn't do that if your life depended on it!" Tryphena's look was withering. "No minister wants a wife who could write his sermons for him. And you can hardly teach theology—you aren't supposed to be able to know about it. If you had any intestinal fortitude, you would fight for the right of women to be accepted as equals, on their own terms, instead of trying to blame Mallory for something that's utterly ridiculous." She was staring out at the dying light. "Unity would never have stooped to blackmailing anybody. That just shows how little you know of her."

"It shows how little one of us knows of her," Clarice said point-edly. "Somebody fathered her child. If you knew her so very well, I assume you knew who it was?"

Tryphena's face tightened, the lines hardening. If the color had still been in the light one would have seen her blush. "We didn't dis-cuss that sort of thing! Our conversations were on a much higher level. I don't expect you to understand that."

Clarice started to laugh, a slightly hysterical note creeping into it.

"You mean she didn't tell you she seduced Mallory, and then blackmailed him, for fun," she jeered. "That hardly surprises me. It wouldn't fall in with your hero-worshipping idea of her, would it? That isn't the stuff great women martyrs are made of. Let the side down rather hard—it's even a trifle grubby. When it comes down to it—"

"You are disgusting!" Tryphena said between her teeth. "You will blame anyone but your precious Papa. You've always been his favor-ite, and you hate Mallory because you think he betrayed Papa by joining the Church of Rome." She gave a sharp little laugh. "It threw back all his love in his face. It showed up how weak his own faith really is, that he couldn't even convince his own son, let alone a whole flock of his congregation. You can't stand the truth! So you'll even try to get our brother hanged rather than face it. You've never forgiven him because you think he had the chances you should have had and you could have used them so much better. You would never have disappointed Papa. It's easy enough to think that when you didn't have to live up to it and actually do anything!"

Clarice bit her lip, and Dominic could see that she kept her com-posure only with the greatest difficulty, and perhaps for the first moment she was too shocked to find words. Such rage was almost like a physical blow.

Dominic himself was shaking, as if he too had been attacked. He intervened without thinking first. His argument had nothing to do with reason or morality, simply outrage and a passion to protect. He turned on Tryphena.

"Whatever happened in the schoolroom has nothing to do with Unity! Whoever got her with child, it wasn't Clarice. You are just furious because you thought she told you everything, and obviously she didn't. There was something absolutely fundamental she omitted." He was aware as he spoke that he was approaching extremely dangerous territory, but he rushed in anyway. "You feel left out because she didn't trust you enough to tell you, so you are trying to blame everyone else."

Tryphena looked at him with eyes blazing. "Not everyone!" she said very pointedly. "I knew her better than to imagine she would blackmail anyone. She wouldn't stoop so low. None of you had anything she wanted. She despised you! She wouldn't have . . . have soiled herself!"

"Of course," Clarice said scathingly. "The Second Coming. Another Immaculate Conception? But if you'd read a little more theology, if you were as good a student as Mal, let alone as I was, you'd know the Lord is coming down out of the heavens next time, not being born again. Even to Unity Bellwood!"

"Don't be ridiculous!" Tryphena snapped. "And blasphemous! You may have studied theology, but you haven't the faintest understanding of ethics."

"And you haven't of love!" Clarice retorted. "All you know is hysteria and self-indulgence and—and obsession."

"Whom did you ever love?" Tryphena laughed, her voice rising out of control. "Unity knew what love was, and passion and betrayal, and sacrifice! She loved more in her life, cut off as it was, than you'll ever know. You're only half alive. You're pathetic, full of envy. I despise you."

"You despise everyone," Clarice pointed out, catching at her shawl as the wind tugged it. Her hair was coming undone. "Your whole philosophy is based on the fact that you imagine you are better than anyone else. I can imagine how Unity hated being with child— to a mere mortal man. She probably threw herself downstairs hoping to lose it."

Tryphena whirled around, eyes wide open, and slapped Clarice so hard across the face she knocked her off balance, made her stumble against Dominic.

"You evil woman!" Tryphena said. "You despicable creature! You'd say anything, wouldn't you, to protect someone you love, whatever he's done? You have no honor, no truth. Haven't you asked yourself where Papa found your precious Dominic?" She waved her hand in his direction but without looking at him. "What was he doing there? Why would a man his age suddenly want to join the church and become a minister, eh? What has he done that is so terrible he wants to spend the rest of his life in penance? Look at him!" She jabbed her finger towards Dominic again. "Look at his face. Do you think he really gave up women and pleasure? Well, do you? It's time you looked at the world as it is, Clarice, and not as your theological studies told you!"

Dominic could feel himself shivering, the fear icelike inside him. What had Unity told Tryphena? What would Clarice believe of him? And far worse in its real and terrible danger, what would Pitt learn? He could not keep the delusion anymore that Pitt would not at least find a part of him only too glad to be able to blame Dominic. He had never truly forgotten Charlotte's early romantic dreams about him, though dreams were all they had been.

He wanted to fight back, but how could he? Where were the weapons?

Tryphena began to laugh, her voice high with hysteria.

"That's why you are an atheist," Clarice said quite calmly, cutting across the laughter. "You don't like people, and you don't believe that they can change and put the old things away. You don't really believe in hope. You don't understand it. I have no idea where Papa found Dominic or what he was doing, and I don't care. All I care about is what he is like now. If his change was enough for Papa, it is enough for me. I don't need to know about it. It is none of my business. Somebody got Unity with child—somebody in the last three months. About the only places she went outside here were the library or the concert hall or those dreadful meetings about politics. And you went to all of those. So it is almost certainly someone in this house. You knew Unity. Who do you think it was?"

Tryphena stared back at her, her eyes suddenly filled with tears. She was utterly alone again, the rage gone, swallowed up in loss. Anger did not drive the emptiness away for long, and when the anger evaporated she was left with even less than before.

"I'm sorry," Clarice said very quietly, taking a step closer. "I said it was Mallory only because some kind of certainty is better than tormenting ourselves from one fear to another. I think he is the most likely. And if you wish to know what I think actually happened, I think it was an accident. I expect they quarreled and it ran away with them, and now Mallory is terrified to admit it."

Tryphena sniffed, her eyes red-rimmed. "But I heard her call out 'No, no! Reverend!'" She gulped.

Dominic passed her a handkerchief, and she took it without looking at him.

"She was calling for help," Clarice said decisively.

Tryphena blinked. She gave a tiny shrug, more a gesture of pain than acceptance, and turned and left without glancing at Dominic.

"I'm sorry." Clarice looked at Dominic. "I don't suppose she meant most of it. Don't—don't think about it. If you don't mind, I think I shall go up and see Papa." And without waiting for an answer, she went through the withdrawing room door also.

Dominic stepped off the terrace and walked slowly across the grass in the growing darkness. The dew was heavy and soaked his shoes, and at the edges where the lawn had not been mown, it caught the bottoms of his trousers as well. He was barely aware of it. He should not be surprised at the sudden flash of temper tearing the skin off old wounds. Fear did that. It exposed all sorts of ugly emotions which might otherwise have lain unknown all life long. It showed resentments no one wanted to own. It brought to the tongue thoughts that in wiser or kinder times would have been suppressed and anyway were only partially true, born of his own fear and need as much as any truth.

There were things better not known.

He had not realized how hurt Tryphena was, how isolated she felt herself to be, how alone now that Unity had gone. Clarice had seen it. She was frightened, too, for her father and for Mallory, but she was kinder. She struck to defend, not to hurt for any pleasure in it. And she had certainly defended him. He had not expected her to. It gave him a sharp realization of pleasure that she should wish to.

He looked up as the clouds parted and a pale, three-quarter moon made him realize how dark it was. He could only just see the grass behind him, and the branches were black against the sky, the house a silhouette, the color gone.

Clarice surprised him. But then thinking back on the time he had known her, he had very seldom been able to predict what she was going to say or do. Her sense of the ridiculous was alarming. She would make outrageous remarks, laugh at embarrassing things, appalling things, see humor where no one else did.

He remembered individual instances, wincing at some of them, standing in the gathering darkness unaware that he was smiling. Once or twice he even laughed aloud. They were excruciating. Absurd. But when he thought of them, none he recalled had been made simply to draw attention to herself or to make herself seem superior. Certainly they were not always kind; if she thought someone a hypocrite, she exposed him without mercy. Laughter could destroy as well as heal.

He put his hands in his pockets and turned and walked back towards the house and the lights across the terrace. He went upstairs to his own room with the intention of studying. He preferred to be alone and it was the best excuse. However, when the door was closed and he picked up a book he found his eyes did not focus on the page. He was thinking about Mallory, and the more he turned over in his mind what Clarice had said, the more did it seem the likely answer.

He knew he himself was not the father of Unity's child, and he could not believe it was Ramsay. It was not that he imagined Ramsay to be too ascetic or too self-disciplined ever to feel the hungers for physical comfort, or that Unity could not possibly have tempted him. He believed that if Ramsay had yielded to such a thing, he would have felt so different afterwards that Dominic at least would have noticed. And frankly, he thought Unity would have been different also. The constant need to attain small victories over Ramsay would not have remained so sharp. She would have proved his vulnerability to both of them. It would never need testing again to that degree.

And when he looked back now, he could recall—even the day before she died—the look of pleasure in her face when she had found an error in one of his translations. It had been tiny, and something a second glance would have found and corrected, but her need to point it out had been there. And there were other instances. He could see her face in his mind's eye so clearly, every expression of it familiar; it was difficult to realize she was dead. She had been so positive, so sure of everything she felt and thought she knew.

What did he feel now that she was gone? Certainly there was sadness. She had been so urgently alive. Any death was a loss, a diminishing. Death itself was a frightening change, a reminder of the fragility of all things, of all those one loved, above all of oneself.

But there was undeniable relief in him also. It was there in the relaxing of the muscles that had unconsciously been held tight for so long. There was even ease in the mind, in spite of the fears, as if a shadow had passed.

He stood up and went to the door. It could not simply be left, in the hope that they would settle to life as it had been before and somehow Pitt would find an answer and prove it. He might. He might allow his doubts of Dominic, and the evidence—and he was certainly clever enough to find it—to convince him of Dominic's guilt.

He went along the passage and knocked on Mallory's door. He was doing it in part for himself, but he also owed Ramsay all he could do to find the truth, whatever he did about it afterwards.

He knocked again. There was no answer.

He turned away, not sure if he was relieved or disappointed.

Braithwaite, Vita's maid, was coming along the corridor. Her face was lined with strain, as if she had slept little in the last nine days. Her graying hair was pulled a little tight, as if she had dressed it without care. He wondered if she wished now that she had not spoken of what she had heard.

"Mr. Mallory is in the conservatory, Mr. Corde," she said helpfully. "He took his books down there."

"Oh." Now there was no escape. "Thank you." He turned and went down the stairs and across the hall. He could never pass this way without thinking of Unity and wondering. He hesitated only a moment, then went into the conservatory. Here it was dark, but he could see light through the leaves and knew it came from the iron table at the far end, where Mallory must be sitting.

He pushed past the palm fronds and lily leaves, his footsteps making very little sound on the slightly damp bricks, and what little there was was covered by the gurgle of water from the pool.

Mallory looked up when Dominic was almost there. He was sitting in the same chair he must have been in when Unity met her death, if he had told the truth. But there was the mark on Unity's shoe which made a liar of him at least in his denial that he had seen her that morning.

"What do you want?" Mallory asked. He made no pretense at friendship. He resented Dominic's favor with Ramsay, and he resented the way Dominic had taken over a certain leadership since the tragedy. The fact that he was older, and that Mallory himself had not wished for it, meant nothing.

Dominic wondered if Tryphena had told Mallory of their quarrel, and what Clarice had said. In the yellow light of the lamp, with its heavy shadows, he should have been able to read it in Mallory's face, but he could not. There was too much emotion in it already: fear, anger, resentment, striving after a peace he felt he should have had, and guilt because he did not. His faith had not been equal to the test he had placed upon it. Dominic knew that from the missal he held open in his hand.

Dominic sat on the edge of the planting bench, ignoring the fact that it could be damp or dirty, or both.

"Pitt is going to find out," he said gravely.

Mallory stared at him, and Dominic knew in an instant that he was going to bluff.

"Probably," Mallory agreed. "But if you are expecting me to help you protect Father somehow, I can't. It isn't only a matter of whether I think it is right to do so, I don't believe it would accomplish anything for more than a short time. In the end it would only make things worse." He sat up a little straighter, his mouth tight, dark eyes defensive. "Face the truth, Dominic. I know you admire Father, probably because he held out a hand to you when you desperately needed it, and heaven knows, gratitude is a virtue we see too little of. But it cannot take the place of honesty or justice. It will always have to be at someone else's expense."

It was on the edge of Dominic's tongue to say "You mean yours," then he realized it was equally easily his own, and he said nothing.

"We have different faiths," Mallory went on. "But something of the core of them must be the same. You cannot pass your sins on to another person. Christ is the only one who can take sins for another; we must each bear our own. That includes you and me, and Father. The law is not the only concern, and it shouldn't even be our main one. Can't we at least agree on that much?"

"We can." Dominic leaned forward, elbows on his knees. The pool of lamplight was yellow around them, islanding them amid the leaves. The rest of the house could have been a world away. "Do you believe your father was Unity's lover?"

Mallory hesitated, and the guilt was hot in his eyes. For an instant he wavered, but he knew Dominic had seen it. It was already too late to retreat.

"No." He looked down at his hands.

There was silence except for the bubbling of the water in the pool and a slight, steady dripping somewhere on the leaves.

"Was she blackmailing you over it?" Dominic asked.

Mallory looked up slowly. His face was for once wiped of all conscious expression but fear.

"I didn't kill her, Dominic! I swear! I wasn't anywhere near the top of the stairs when she fell. I was in here, as I said I was. I don't know what happened, and I don't know why it happened. I honestly thought it was Father. I still do. And if it was not, then it must have been you."

"It was not me," Dominic said very quietly. "Did anyone else know she was blackmailing you?"

"Who?" Mallory looked surprised. "Clarice? She is the only other member of the family, because I can't imagine any of the servants being responsible for Unity's death."

"They weren't," Dominic said unhappily. "We know where all of them were. And no, I don't think Clarice would have."

"Not to protect me, anyway," Mallory said dryly. "Tryph might have, but she wouldn't. She's always thought she would make a better priest than I. She is cleverer, but that's only a tiny part of what is needed. I've tried to show her that, but she doesn't want to know. It's a matter of faith. More than that, it's obedience. She hasn't any obedience."

It was not the time to argue the relative merits of obedience and charity.

"Could it not have been an accident?" Dominic suggested, trying to offer him a way to admit to something lesser.

"It could have," Mallory agreed. "Of course it could have." He jerked up. "My God, it wasn't me . . . accident or intentional." His voice rose. "I wasn't there, Dominic! If it was an accident, then it was still Father!" His long fingers opened and closed again. "See if you can get him to admit to it. I can't, and heaven knows I've tried. He doesn't even listen to me. It is as if he has shut himself off from the rest of us. All that seems to matter to him is his wretched book. He works away at those translations as if they were the most important thing in his life. I know he wants to publish before Dr. Spelling, but it hardly matters compared with murder in the house, and when one of us is responsible." He looked wretched. For once there was no thought for himself, no pretense or guardedness at all. He looked almost boyish with his smooth cheeks and brow in the lamplight amid the shining, slanting leaves of the man-made jungle. "Dominic, I think he has had some mental collapse. He is no longer in reality—"

He got no further. There was a thin, high scream, cut off suddenly.

They both froze, waiting for it to come again.

But there was no sound other than the water.

Mallory gulped and swore, rising to his feet clumsily, knocking the missal onto the floor with his elbow.

Dominic started after him along the brick pathway back towards the hall. Mallory threw the door open and left it swinging as he strode across the black-and-white mosaic to where the withdrawing room door stood wide. Dominic was at his heels.

Inside, Vita was huddled over in one of the chairs. Her dark gray gown was soaked in blood all down the bosom and onto the skirt. Her arms and shoulders were dark with it, and even her hands were scarlet.

Tryphena had collapsed on the floor, but no one was trying to assist her. Perhaps it was she who had screamed.

Clarice was on her knees in front of her mother, holding her by the arms. They were both shaking violently. Vita seemed to be attempting to speak, but she could not catch her breath, all she could do was sob and gasp.

"Oh God!" Mallory stumbled as if he too might lose his balance. "Mama! What happened? Has somebody sent for the doctor? Get bandages—water—something!" Instinctively he turned to Dominic.

Dominic bent to Clarice, taking her by the shoulders.

"Let us see, my dear," he said gently. "We must see where the wound is to stop it bleeding."

Reluctantly, still shuddering, Clarice allowed herself to be helped up by Mallory, who clung onto her, his knuckles white. Still no one went to Tryphena.

"Let me see," Dominic ordered, looking at Vita's ash-white face.

"I'm not hurt," she whispered, her voice grating in her throat. "At least—not much. Just—bruises, I think. I don't even know. But—" She stopped and looked down at the blood all over herself, almost as if she had not really seen it before. Then she looked up at Dominic again. "Dominic—Dominic . . . he tried to kill me! I—I had to . . . defend myself! I only meant . . ." She swallowed with such a constriction of her throat that she choked, and he had to hold her while she coughed until she could find her breath again. "I only meant to fight him off . . . just so I could get away. But he was insane!" She held up her right arm, where the imprint of a bloody hand showed clearly around her wrist. "He had hold of me!" She seemed amazed, as if she could still hardly believe it. "I . . ." She swallowed again. "I managed to reach for the paper knife. I thought if I could stab his arm, he would have to let go of me and I could escape." Her eyes were fixed on his, wide and almost black. "He moved . . . he moved, Dominic! I only meant to stab his arm."

He felt sick. "What happened?"

"He moved!" she repeated. "His arm was there! He was holding me. His hands were around my throat! The look in his face! It wasn't the man I know at all. It wasn't Ramsay! He was terrible, full of hate and such—such anger!"

"What happened?" he repeated more firmly.

Her voice sank. "I struck at his arm, to make him let go of me, and he moved. The knife caught his neck . . . his . . . throat, Dominic—I think he's dead!"

They all remained frozen for seconds. A log blazed up in the fireplace in a shower of sparks.

Clarice turned her head and leaned against Mallory's shoulder, and wept. He clung to her, burying his cheek in her hair.

On the floor, Tryphena started to sit up.

Dominic left Vita and went over to the bell rope and pulled it, far harder than he had intended, but his hands were tingling as if they were numb, and he was trembling.

"Get Emsley to bring some brandy and fetch the doctor," he said to Mallory. "I'll go upstairs." He did not bother to ask Vita if it was the study. He assumed it was. Ramsay had barely left it in the last week.

He went along the top corridor and opened the study door.

Ramsay was lying near the desk, half on his back, one leg a little crooked under him. There was a gash on his throat and a wide, deep pool of crimson blood puddling on the carpet beside him. There was nothing in his hands, but there were smears of blood on them, staining his cuffs. His eyes were wide open, and he looked surprised.

Dominic knelt down and felt a desperate sadness engulf him. Ramsay had been his friend, had held out kindness and hope when he had needed it. Now he had drowned in an ocean Dominic had not even comprehended. He had watched it happen, and not been able to save him. His sense of loss filled him with pain—and a bitter knowledge of having failed.

CHAPTER
NINE

Pitt was sitting by the fire in the parlor with his feet on the fender when the telephone rang. It was so unusual an occurrence that he never left Gracie to answer.

Charlotte looked up from her sewing with surprise, meeting his eyes questioningly.

He shrugged and stood up. The instrument was in the hall, and he had to go out into the comparative chill, but he found himself shivering even before his feet were on the linoleum. He picked up the speaker.

"Hello? Thomas Pitt here."

He barely recognized the voice on the other end. "Thomas? Is that you?"

"Yes. Who is it? Dominic?"

"Yes." There was a gasp and a breath of relief. "Thomas . . . I'm in Ramsay Parmenter's study. Thank God for the telephone here. He's dead."

The first thought that came to Pitt's mind was suicide. Ramsay had felt the inevitable truth closing around him and he had taken the way out he felt most honorable. Perhaps he imagined it would save the church embarrassment. The bishop would be pleased. At that thought Pitt found himself suddenly almost speechless with rage.

"Dominic!"

"Yes? Thomas . . . you'd better come—immediately. I . . ."

"Are you all right?" There was no point in asking. There was nothing he could do to help the shock and the distress he heard through Dominic's voice. He had misjudged him. Dominic had not been to blame—probably not for anything. Charlotte would be happy.

"Yes—yes, I am." Dominic sounded wretched. "But, Thomas . . . it was an—an accident. I suppose you could say . . ." His voice trailed off.

Pitt's first thought was to refuse to say anything of the sort. He would not lie to protect the bishop's interest. He cared for duty to truth, to the law, to Unity Bellwood. But there was no good to Unity served by exposing her tragedy, or Ramsay Parmenter's.

"Thomas . . . ?" Dominic's voice was urgent, uncertain.

"Yes," Pitt replied. "I don't know yet. How did he do it?"

"Do it?" For a moment Dominic sounded confused. "Oh . . . he— Thomas, he didn't kill himself! He attacked Vita—Mrs. Parmenter. He had some sort of . . . I don't know . . . brainstorm. He lost control of himself and tried to strangle her. She defended herself with a paper knife which was on the desk—it happened in his study—and in the struggle it slipped . . . and stabbed him. I'm afraid it was fatal."

"What?" Pitt was astounded. "You mean— Dominic, I can't cover that up!"

"I'm not asking you to!" Dominic was amazed. "Just come here before we have to call in the local constable . . . please!"

"Yes—of course. I'll come right away. Hold on." Without realizing what he had said, he put the earpiece back on its hook, missing it the first time because his hands were shaking. He walked back into the parlor.

"What is it?" Charlotte said immediately. "What's happened?" Her voice rose sharply with fear, and she was already getting to her feet.

"No." He shook his head. "It's all right. It's Parmenter. It was

Dominic on the telephone. Parmenter tried to kill his wife, and in the struggle he was killed himself. I have to go there. Will you call the station to send for Tellman to meet me at Brunswick Gardens?"

Charlotte stared at him. "Mrs. Parmenter killed him in a struggle when he was trying to kill her?" Her voice rose to a squeak. "That's ridiculous! She's tiny! Well—she's small. She couldn't possibly kill him."

"With a knife," he explained.

"I don't care what with. She couldn't have taken a knife from him if he were trying to kill her with it."

"He wasn't. He was trying to strangle her. He must have utterly lost his sanity, poor man. Thank God he didn't succeed." He stopped, facing her for a long moment's silence. "At least this proves Dominic had no guilt in it."

She smiled at him very slightly. "Yes, there is that," she agreed. "Now, you had better go, and I'll get the message to Tellman."

He hesitated, as if to add something else, but there really was nothing more to say. He turned on his heel and went to the hall, putting his boots on and collecting his coat from its hook, and went out.

When he reached Brunswick Gardens there was already a carriage outside at the curb. The coachman was huddled up under his coat as if he had been there for some time, and lights streamed from the windows of the house below the half-lowered blinds, as if no one had bothered to draw the front curtains.

Pitt alighted, paid the cabby and told him not to wait. Emsley greeted him at the door, his hair wild from where he had run his hands through it, his face so pale it looked gray around the eyes.

"Come in, sir," he said hoarsely. "The mistress is upstairs lying down, and Mr. Mallory is with her—and the doctor, of course. Miss Tryphena is—is gone to her room, I think. Poor Miss Clarice is trying to take care of everything, and Mr. Corde is upstairs in the study. He told me to send you up, if you'd be so good, sir. I don't know what everything is coming to . . . Just a few days ago everything was as usual, and now suddenly—this." The man looked close to weeping as he thought of the ruin of all he found familiar and precious, the daily life that created his world and was his purpose.

Pitt put his hand on Emsley's arm and gripped it. "Thank you. Perhaps it would be best if you were to close the door and all the downstairs curtains, then see if you can help Miss Clarice keep the servants calm. They are bound to be deeply distressed, but the house must still be run. People will need to eat, fires be kept going, the place cleaned and tidied. The more people can be busy, the less they will have time to be upset."

"Oh . . . yes." Emsley nodded. "Yes sir. Of course, you are quite right. We don't want people losing control of themselves, getting hysterical. Helps nobody. I'll see to it, sir." And he went off looking purposeful.

Pitt climbed the now-familiar black staircase and went along the landing corridor to Ramsay Parmenter's study. He opened the door and saw Dominic sitting behind the desk, white-faced, his dark hair, flecked with tiny threads of gray, falling forward over his brow. He looked ill.

"Thank God you're here." He stood up shakily, turning sideways, compelled to stare beyond the desk and down, where Pitt could not see.

Pitt closed the door behind him and walked around the chair. Ramsay Parmenter was crumpled on the floor where he had fallen, a huge pool of blood soaked deep into the carpet near his neck, which was gashed with a fearful wound. It must have been a very violent struggle. His shirt was torn at the front, and there were two buttons ripped off his jacket, as if someone had tried desperately to pull him by his clothes. His eyes were closed, but there was no peace in his face, only a sense of amazement, as if at the very last moment he had realized what he was doing and the horror of it had over-whelmed him.

"I—I closed his eyes," Dominic said apologetically. "Perhaps I shouldn't have, but I couldn't bear to leave him lying staring like that. They were open. Does it matter?"

"I don't think so. Did the doctor see him? Emsley said the doctor was here."

"No . . . not yet. He's with Vita . . . Mrs. Parmenter."

"How is she?"

"I don't know. She seemed to be all right; I mean, she wasn't injured, at least not seriously. I'm sorry, I am not being very lucid." He looked at Pitt desperately. "I feel as if I failed about as thoroughly as I could." His face puckered. "Why couldn't I help him before it got to this? What happened? Why didn't I see it was so—so . . . that he was drowning? I should have been able to give him enough faith to hold on, to let someone understand. We shouldn't any of us, least of all me, who professes to be a pastor of souls, we shouldn't let anyone be this utterly alone!" He shook his head a little. "What's the matter with us? How can we live in the same house, sit at the same table, for God's sake, and let one of us die of loneliness?"

"'That is usually where it happens," Pitt said realistically. "It is in being hemmed in by others who see only the outside of you, the image of you they have painted from their own minds, that you suffocate. Shepherds and woodsmen don't die of loneliness; it's people in cities. It is the invisible walls that we can't see that prevent us touching. Don't blame yourself." He looked at Dominic closely. "Sit down. Perhaps you had better take a good stiff brandy. It won't help anyone if you are taken ill."

Dominic retreated to the chair beyond the desk and sat down heavily. "Can you keep the details out of the newspapers? I suppose I shall have to tell the bishop."

"No, you won't. We'll let Commissioner Cornwallis do that." Pitt was still standing over Ramsay's body. "What was the quarrel about, do you know?"

"No. I can't remember whether she said."

"Did anybody hear it?"

"No. No, the first thing we knew was when Mrs. Parmenter came into the withdrawing room. Or more exactly"—he screwed up his face with the effort to clear his mind and speak coherently—"I was in the conservatory with Mallory. We were talking. I heard—we heard . . . a scream. We both got up and went back to the withdrawing room. It was Tryphena who had screamed, but she had fainted by then . . . at seeing the blood, I suppose."

"I was thinking of the servants."

"Oh. I don't know. It was close to the time the servants have dinner. I expect they were in their hall. I didn't think to ask."

"Probably just as well. I'll come to it fresh." Pitt turned and looked at the door. There was a key in the lock. "If you would prefer to go to your own room, or see if you can help downstairs, I'll secure it here."

"Oh." Dominic hesitated, staring down at Ramsay on the floor. "I feel . . . can't we move him now you've seen him?"

"Not until the doctor has."

"Well, cover him up, at least," Dominic protested. "What can the doctor tell you? It's pretty obvious what happened, isn't it?" He was taking his jacket off as he spoke.

Pitt put out his hand to restrain him. "When the doctor's seen him. Then you can take him to his own room and lay him out properly. Not yet. Come out and leave him. You've done everything you can. It's time to care for the living."

Dominic replied, "Yes, of course. Clarice must be feeling terrible . . . so grieved, so hurt."

"And Tryphena as well, I imagine." Pitt opened the door for Dominic.

Dominic turned in the doorway. "Tryphena didn't love him the way Clarice did."

Before Pitt could answer that, Tellman came up to the top of the stairs and across the landing. He looked tired and unshaven. He had already had a long and miserable day.

Pitt indicated the study door. "In there," he said tersely. "I'll send the doctor in a moment. Apparently it was an accident. When you've finished in here, and the doctor's been, secure it and return the key."

Tellman's face betrayed deep skepticism, but he said nothing. He glanced at Dominic, muttered something—possibly an attempt at sympathy—and disappeared into the study.

Dominic told Pitt which was Vita's room, then went downstairs. Pitt knocked. The door was opened after a moment or two by the same doctor he had seen at Unity's death. The doctor's face was pale and bleak, his eyes reflecting profound distress.

"Terrible business," he said quietly. "I had no idea it was so serious. I honestly thought he was simply a little . . . overwrought, depressed by the way public perception of religion had changed since Darwin's theories on evolution became known to the general reader . . . I daresay by word of mouth, in garbled fashion, to just about everyone." His voice betrayed his own view of it. "I had no idea it had disturbed the balance of his mind. I feel very guilty. I noticed nothing. He always seemed perfectly natural to me, simply . . . unhappy." He sighed. "It is not unusual, in my experience, for men in the church to have their periods of doubt and confusion. It is a heavy calling. One may put on a brave face to the world and preach a sermon every Sunday; it does not mean you cannot be lost in a desert of this sort yourself . . . for a period." His face was full of sadness. "I'm really very sorry."

"No one saw it coming," Pitt assured him, sharing the blame. "Where is Mrs. Parmenter? Is she injured?"

The doctor met his eyes steadily.

"A few bruises. I daresay they will be painful for a while, and disfiguring, but nothing that will last. Her left shoulder is rather wrenched, but it will mend with time." He still looked surprised and confused. "Thank heaven she is a supple woman, in good health, and of considerable courage. She must have fought hard for her life." His lips tightened. "As for her emotional state, that is another matter. I cannot answer for that. She has extraordinary courage, but I have left a sedative for her, which she refused to take until she had spoken with you, knowing that you would have to question her about the tragedy. But do please be as brief as you can. Exercise whatever pity and discretion your duty allows."

"I will," Pitt promised. "Now, I would appreciate it if you would look at the body of the Reverend Parmenter and tell me all you can of his death. My sergeant is in the study. He'll let you in and lock up after you."

"I doubt I can offer you any assistance, but of course I'll look. There will have to be an inquest, I presume?"

"Yes, of course there will, but please do it anyway." Pitt stood back to allow the doctor to pass, then went in and closed the door.

It was a large room, beautifully furnished, feminine and less exotic than the more public areas of the house. Nevertheless there were marks of Vita's individual and daring taste, splashes of oriental color: peacock blue, lacquer red.

Vita Parmenter was sitting on her bed, propped up by pillows. The first thing Pitt was aware of was the blood. It soaked the front of her gown and splashed scarlet on the pale skin of her throat. It made the more obvious her ashen, almost gray face, with feverish eyes. Her maid, Braithwaite, was standing a few feet away, a glass in her hand. She looked exhausted.

"I am sorry to have to intrude upon you, Mrs. Parmenter," Pitt began. "If there were any alternative I would not."

"I understand," she said very quietly. "You are only doing your duty. Anyway, I think it is probably easier to speak of it now than to start again tomorrow morning. There is something about telling someone—outside the family—which relieves one of some of the burden. Does that sound . . . selfish?" She looked at him earnestly.

"No." He sat down on the dressing chair without waiting for her to invite him. "It makes excellent sense. Please tell me what happened as exactly as you can remember."

"Where shall I begin?"

"Wherever you wish."

She considered for several moments, then drew a deep breath. "I am not sure what time it was." She cleared her throat with difficulty. "I had just changed for dinner. Braithwaite had left me and gone downstairs. It was the hour the servants eat. They dine before us, but I expect you know that? Yes, of course you do." She blinked. "I'm sorry. I am rambling. I am finding it very difficult to think properly." Her hands were opening and closing on the bedclothes. "I decided to go and see how Ramsay was, see if perhaps I could talk to him. He had been very . . . alone. He seldom came out of his room. I thought perhaps I could persuade him to take dinner with us, at least." Her eyes searched Pitt's face. "If you ask me why, I am not sure now. It seemed quite natural then, quite a good idea." She started to cough, and Braithwaite handed her the glass again. "Thank you," she murmured, taking a sip from it.

Pitt waited.

She cleared her throat again and resumed with a tiny smile of thanks. "I knocked on the study door, and when he answered I went in. He was sitting at his desk with a lot of papers spread out. I enquired how his work was proceeding. It seemed a harmless sort of thing to say . . . and quite natural." She looked at him, her eyes pleading for acceptance.

"Quite natural," he agreed.

"I—I walked over to the desk and picked up one of the papers." Her voice had dropped and become very hoarse. "It was a love letter, Superintendent. Very . . . passionate and very . . . very graphic. I have never read anything like it in my life. I didn't know people . . . women . . . used such language, or even thought in such terms." She gave a high, nervous little laugh. She was clearly embarrassed. "I confess, I was shocked. I suppose it showed in my face. It must have."

"It was a letter from a woman to a man?" he asked.

"Oh, yes. The . . . content of it made that quite plain. As I said, Mr. Pitt, it was very . . . explicit."

"I see."

She looked down, then up again quickly, staring at him. "It was in

Unity Bellwood's hand. I know it well enough. There is much of her writing in the house. It was what she was employed for."

"I see," he said again. "Go on."

"Then I saw other letters, in my husband's hand. They were love letters also, but much more . . . restrained. More spiritual, if you like . . . much . . ." She gave a jerky, painful little laugh. "Much more in his style . . . roundabout, meaning the same sort of thing but never really coming to the point. Ramsay always preferred to be . . . metaphorical, to conceal the physical and emotional behind something paraphrased as spiritual. But stripped of its euphemisms, it was much the same."

Pitt should not have been surprised. Ramsay's death should have prepared him for something like this. A suppressed passion, a need long smothered and denied, when it does break out, is wild, beyond control, perhaps inevitably destructive not only of the pattern of safe and productive life but of previous morality and convention, even of the curbs of taste. And yet he was surprised. He had seen nothing in Ramsay but a middle-aged churchman crowded by spiritual doubt, old before his time because he saw nothing ahead but a desert of the soul. How wrong he had been.

"I'm sorry," he said softly.

She smiled at him. "Thank you. You are very kind, Superintendent; far kinder than your duty necessitates." She shivered a little, drawing her shoulders in, hunching herself amid the piled pillows. "Ramsay must have seen my expression. I did not conceal my feelings . . . my amazement . . . and my . . . my revulsion. Perhaps if I had . . ." She lowered her eyes and for a moment seemed unable to continue.

Braithwaite stood beside her helplessly, raising and lowering the glass in her hands, not knowing what to do. Her face vividly reflected her anguish.

Vita regained her control with an effort. "I'm sorry," she whispered. "I can't remember what I said to him. Perhaps it was not tactful, or prudent. We had a fearful quarrel. He seemed to lose all . . . sanity! His whole bearing altered until he was like a madman." Her hands gripped at the embroidered linen of the sheet. "He threw himself at me, saying I had no right to violate his privacy by looking at his personal letters." Her voice dropped even lower. "He called me all sorts of . . . frightful things: a thief, a philistine, an intruder. He said I had spoiled his life, dried up his passion and his inspiration, that I was a . . . a leech, a drain on his spirit, unworthy of him." She stopped abruptly. It was a moment or two before she could continue. "He was almost incoherent with rage. He seemed to have lost all control of himself. He threw himself at me, with his hands out, and caught me by the neck." She put her fingers up towards her throat but did not touch it. It was red where his hands had been and was already beginning to darken into bruising.

"Go on," Pitt said gently.

She lowered her hands slowly, watching his face. "I couldn't argue with him, I couldn't speak. I tried to fight him off, but of course he was far stronger than I." She was breathing very hard, gulping. He could see her breast rise and fall. "We struggled back and forth. I don't remember exactly now. His grip was getting tighter all the time. I could hardly breathe. I was afraid he meant to kill me. I . . . I saw the paper knife on the desk. I reached for it and struck at him. I meant to stab his arm, so the pain of it would make him let go of me and I could escape." She shook her head, her eyes wide. "I couldn't cry out. I couldn't make a sound!" She stopped again.

"Of course," Pitt agreed.

"I . . . I struck at his arm, at his shoulder, where I wouldn't miss. If I struck lower down I was afraid I would only catch sleeve." She took a very deep breath and let it out silently. "I drove it with all my strength, before I fainted from lack of air. He must have moved." She looked paper white. "I caught his neck." Her voice was so low it was barely a whisper, as if the strangling hands were still choking her. "It was terrible. It was the worst moment of my life. He fell back . . . staring at me as if he couldn't believe it. For an instant he was himself again, the old Ramsay, sane and wise and full of tenderness. There was . . . blood . . . everywhere." Her eyes filled with tears. "I don't know what I did then. I was so filled with horror . . . I—I think I went to kneel where he fell. I don't know. It was all a blur of horror, of grief. . . . Time stood still." She swallowed, her throat tightening. It must have hurt. "Then I went downstairs to get help."

"Thank you, Mrs. Parmenter," he acknowledged gravely. While she had been speaking he had been watching her face, her hands, and looking discreetly at the deep bloodstains on her dress. Everything he saw was consistent with her account of what had happened and with what he had seen in the study. There was no cause to doubt the tragedy as she had told it to him. "I am sure you would now like to bathe and change your clothes, and perhaps take the sedative the doctor left for you. I shall not need to disturb you further tonight."

"Yes. Yes, I should." She gave a little shiver and pulled the sheet higher up over her, but she did not say anything else.

Pitt left her and went back to the study. He must speak to the doctor, to both her daughters, and either he or Tellman should speak to the servants. Somebody might have heard something. Not that it would help if they had; it was simply a matter of being thorough.

It was nearly midnight when he arrived at Cornwallis's rooms and the manservant let him in. The man had already retired and had been awakened by the doorbell. He had a dressing robe on over hastily donned trousers, and his hair stood on end at the back where his comb had not reached it.

"Yes sir?" he said a little stiffly.

Pitt apologized. "I imagine Mr. Cornwallis has gone to bed, but I am afraid I need to see him urgently. I'm sorry."

"Yes sir, he has. May I deliver a message, sir?"

"You may," Pitt agreed. "Tell him Superintendent Pitt is downstairs and needs to give him news which will not wait until morning."

The man winced, but he did not argue. As he passed the telephone instrument hanging on the wall, he glanced meaningfully at it but forbore from recommending its use. He left Pitt in the sitting room, a comfortable, highly masculine place filled with padded leather chairs, books, mementos such as a giant conch shell from the Indies, its curved heart glowing with color, a polished brass miniature cannon, a wooden cleat from a ship's rigging, two or three pieces of ambergris and a porcelain dish full of musket balls. There were several paintings of the sea. The books were of a wide variety, novels and poetry as well as biography, science and history. Pitt smiled when he saw Jane Austen's *Emma*, Eliot's *Silas Marner* and the three books of Dante's *Divine Comedy*.

Cornwallis came in less than ten minutes later fully dressed and carrying two glasses of brandy and soda.

"What is it?" he asked, pushing the door closed behind him and passing Pitt one of the glasses. "Something terrible, to judge by your face and to bring you here at this time of night."

"I am afraid Parmenter lost his head completely and attacked his wife. She fought him off, but she killed him in the struggle."

Cornwallis looked astounded.

"Yes, I know," Pitt agreed. "It sounds absurd, but he tried to strangle her, and when she could feel herself suffocating, she grasped the paper knife from the desk and attempted to stab his arm. She said he moved, in order to keep the grip on her throat, and she drove with all her strength at his shoulder and caught his neck." He sipped the brandy and soda.

Cornwallis looked wretched, his face creased with unhappiness, his body stiff as if braced against a blow. He stood still for several moments. Pitt wondered if he was thinking of the bishop and his reaction, and how he would now be able to have the whole matter kept private and dealt with exactly as he had wanted.

"Damn!" Cornwallis said at last. "I had no idea he was so . . . his sanity was so fragile. Had you?"

"No," Pitt confessed. "Neither did his doctor. He had been called for Mrs. Parmenter, and I asked him. He looked at the body, too, of course, but there was nothing he could do, and nothing of any help to say."

"Sit down!" Cornwallis waved at the chairs and Pitt accepted gratefully. He had had no idea he was so tired.

"I suppose there is no doubt that is what happened?" Cornwallis went on, looking at Pitt curiously. "It wasn't a suicide the wife was trying to disguise?"

"Suicide?" Pitt was puzzled. "No."

"Well, she might," Cornwallis argued. "After all, we haven't proved he killed the Bellwood woman, not beyond doubt. But suicide is a crime in the eyes of the church."

"Well, trying to murder your wife isn't well regarded, either," Pitt pointed out.

Cornwallis's face was tight in spite of the flash of humor in his eyes. "But he didn't succeed in that. He may have intended the crime, but you cannot punish him for it . . . not when he is dead anyway."

"You cannot punish a person for suicide, either," Pitt said dryly.

"Yes, you can," Cornwallis contradicted. "You can bury them in unhallowed ground. And the family suffers."

"Well, this was not suicide."

"Are you certain?"

"Yes. The knife must have been in her hand, not his."

"Left side of the throat or right?" Cornwallis asked.

"Left . . . her right hand. They were facing each other, the way she described it."

"So it could have been in his hand?"

"I don't think so, not at that angle."

Cornwallis pursed his lips. He pushed his fists deep into his pockets and stared at Pitt unhappily. "Are you satisfied that he killed Unity Bellwood?"

Pitt was about to answer, then realized that if he were honest, he was still troubled by an incompleteness to it. "I can't think of any better answer, but I feel there is something important I've missed," he admitted. "I suppose we'll never know. Perhaps the letters will explain."

"What letters?" Cornwallis demanded.

"That's what provoked this quarrel, a collection of love letters between Unity and Parmenter, very graphic on Unity's part, according to Mrs. Parmenter. When he realized she had seen them he completely lost control of himself."

"Love letters?" Cornwallis was confused. "Why would they write letters to each other? They were in the same house. They worked together every day. Are you saying they knew each other before he employed her?"

It did seem in need of explanation. It should have occurred to him before, but he was too surprised at the nature of the letters to have considered it.

"I don't know. I didn't ask Mrs. Parmenter if the letters were dated . . . or for that matter why they were all together. One would expect her to have his, and he to have hers."

"So he was the father of her child," Cornwallis concluded, his voice dropping with a low, harsh note of disappointment. Perhaps in a young man he would have found it easier to understand and forgive, though age was no protection against the passion, the need, the vulnerability or the confusion of falling in love, or of the storms of physical hunger, even if when they subside they leave a wreckage of injury and shame. Was Cornwallis so detached from life ashore, with both men and women, that he did not know that?

"It would seem so," Pitt conceded. "We shall never know beyond question, since they are both dead now."

"What a mess," Cornwallis said more quietly. His face was pinched with sadness, as if he could suddenly see all the futility of it spread out plainly in front of him. "It was all so . . . unnecessary. What was it for? A few hours' indulgence of . . . what?" He shrugged. "Not love. They despised each other. They agreed on nothing. And look what it has cost!" He glanced up, searching Pitt's face. "What happens to a man that he so loses his balance as to throw away a lifetime's work and trust . . . for something he must know is going to last only a few weeks and in the end be worth nothing? Why? Was he mad, in some way a doctor would recognize? Or was the whole of his life until then a lie?"

"I don't know," Pitt said honestly. "I don't understand it any more than you do. It doesn't seem like the man I saw and spoke to. It is as if there were some division in his mind, as if he were two men inside."

"But you are satisfied it was he who pushed Unity, whether he meant to kill her or not? I mean, this proves it, doesn't it?"

Pitt looked at him. He was not certain from Cornwallis's face whether he was asking for reassurance, so he could forget the matter, or if he was asking an open question to which the answer could possibly be in the negative. He knew how it galled Cornwallis to concede to the bishop, and therefore also to Smithers, but he would not have allowed that to affect his decision.

"You don't answer," Cornwallis prompted.

"Because I suppose I am not sure," Pitt replied. "It doesn't feel right, because I don't understand it. But I assume it must be."

Cornwallis hunched his shoulders. "Thank you for coming to tell me. I'll go and report to the bishop in the morning . . . first thing!"

As a young man, Reginald Underhill had risen early and pursued his duty with a diligence appropriate to his considerable ambition. Now that his place was assured he felt he could lie in bed a great deal longer, be brought tea and possibly the newspapers. Therefore he was not pleased when his valet came to him at eight o'clock with the news that Mr. Cornwallis was downstairs to see him.

"What, now?" he said irritably.

"Yes sir, I am afraid so." The valet also knew how inconvenient it was. The bishop was not washed, shaved, or dressed, and he hated hurrying. The only thing worse was to be caught looking disheveled and ill prepared. It robbed one of any dignity whatsoever. It was difficult to keep people in their place when dressed in one's nightshirt and with gray stubble all over one's cheeks and chin.

"What does he want, for heaven's sake?" the bishop asked sharply. "Can't he come back at a more suitable time?"

"Shall I ask him to, my lord?"

The bishop slid down a little further in the warm bed. "Yes. Do that. Did he say what he wanted?"

"Yes sir, it was to do with the Reverend Parmenter. I believe there has been a very dramatic development in the case. He felt you should know immediately." The shadow of a smile crossed the man's face. "Before he took any action you might feel ill advised."

The bishop gritted his teeth and suppressed a word he would not care to have his valet hear him use. He threw the covers back and climbed out of bed in an extremely bad temper, added to by the fact that he was now also afraid.

Isadora had risen early. The hours before Reginald was up were frequently her favorites of the day. Sunrise was coming sooner with every passing week as the year strengthened. This particular morning was bright, and the sharp light fell in dazzling bars across the dining room floor. She enjoyed breakfasting alone. It was extraordinarily peaceful.

When the maid told her that Mr. Cornwallis was in the hall she was amazed, but in spite of herself, and the knowledge that if he had called at this hour it could not be for any happy reason, she felt a quickening of excitement.

"Do ask him if he will join me," she said hastily, with less dignity than she had intended. "I mean, ask him if he would care for a cup of tea."

"Yes, ma'am," the maid acknowledged obediently, and a few moments later Cornwallis came in. Isadora saw the unhappiness in his face immediately. It was not the simple grief of a tragedy but the complex distress of indecision and embarrassment.

"Good morning, Mr. Cornwallis. I am afraid the Bishop is not yet down," she said unnecessarily. "Please join me for breakfast, if you should care to? Would you like tea?"

"Good morning, Mrs. Underhill. Thank you," he accepted, sitting opposite her, avoiding the chair at the head of the table.

She poured for him from the large silver pot, and offered milk and sugar.

"Would you like some toast as well? There is honey, marmalade or apricot preserve."

Again he accepted, taking the toast from the rack self-consciously and spreading it with butter. He chose the apricot preserve.

"I am sorry to intrude so early in the morning," he apologized after a moment. "I really think perhaps I should have waited. I did not wish the Bishop to hear in some other way. It would have been unfortunate." He looked up at her quickly. He had clear, hazel eyes, extremely direct. She could imagine all sorts of expressions in them, but never evasion or deceit. But that was not something she should be thinking. After this wretched business with poor Parmenter was over, she would probably not see him again. Suddenly she felt terribly isolated, as if the sun had gone in, although in fact it was still shining across the table. Now the light was hard, lonely, revealing an emptiness.

She looked down at her plate. She no longer had any desire to finish the toast which a moment ago had seemed delicious.

"I assume that something of importance has happened," she said, and was ashamed that her voice sounded so hoarse.

"I am afraid so," he answered. "I—I am sorry to intrude upon you in this way, and before you have even begun your day. It was clumsy of me . . ."

He was embarrassed. She could hear it in his words and almost feel it for him. She forced herself to look up and smile.

"Not at all. If there is news you have to tell, this is as good an hour as any. At least there is time to think about it and to make whatever decisions are necessary. Can you tell me what has happened?"

The tension slipped away from him, in spite of the fact that he was about to discuss whatever it was that had brought him here. He sipped his tea and met her eyes steadily. Gently he told her what had happened.

She was horrified. "Oh dear! Is he badly hurt?"

"I am afraid he is dead." He watched her anxiously. "I'm sorry. Perhaps I should not have told you until the Bishop came." Now he looked thoroughly distressed. He half rose to his feet, as if he feared she might faint and need physical assistance. "I'm so sorry . . ."

"Oh, please sit down, Mr. Cornwallis," she said hastily, although in truth she did feel a trifle shaky. It was so preposterous. "I assure you I am quite all right. Really!"

"Are you?" His face was creased with worry, his eyes bright. He remained standing awkwardly.

"Of course I am. Perhaps you do not realize how many times a bishop's wife is called upon to face situations of bereavement? It is a far larger part of my life than I could wish, but if you cannot turn to your church in times of extremity and grief, then where is there left?"

He sat down again.

"I had not thought of that. I still should have been more considerate."

"Poor Ramsay," she said slowly. "I thought I knew him, but I cannot have known him at all. There must have been a storm of darkness gathering inside him that none of us had the slightest knowledge of. How bitterly alone he must have been, carrying that burden."

He was looking at her with a gentleness that was almost luminous. She saw it in his face, and the warmth blossomed up inside her until without thinking she was smiling at him.

The dining room door opened and the bishop came in, closing it with a bang.

"You had better excuse us, Isadora," he said abruptly, glancing at her plate and almost-empty teacup. He took his place at the head of the table. "Mr. Cornwallis has some news, I gather."

"I already know it," she said without moving. "Would you like tea, Reginald?"

"I should like breakfast!" he said waspishly. "But first I suppose I had better hear whatever it is that has brought Mr. Cornwallis here at this hour of the day."

Cornwallis's face was bleak, the skin across his smooth cheekbones tight. "Ramsay Parmenter tried to strangle his wife yesterday evening, and in defending herself, she killed him," he said brutally.

"Good God!" The bishop was aghast. He stared at Cornwallis as if he had struck him physically. "How . . ." He drew in his breath in a gulp. "How . . ." he repeated, then stopped. "Oh dear."

Isadora looked at him, trying to read his expression, to see in it the reflection of the sadness and sense of failure that she felt. He looked bland, as if he were thinking rather than feeling. She was aware of a gulf between them she had no idea how to cross, and far worse than that, she was not nearly sure enough that she even wished to.

"Oh dear," the bishop repeated, turning his body a little further towards Cornwallis. "What a tragic ending to this whole unfortunate business. Thank you for coming so swiftly to inform me. It was most considerate of you. Most civil. I shall not forget it." He smiled slightly, his earlier irritation forgotten in relief.

And it was relief. She could read it in him, not in his eyes or his mouth, he was too careful for that, but in the set of his shoulders and the way his hands moved across the tablecloth, no longer tense but loose-fingered. She was overcome by a wave of revulsion and then anger. She glanced at Cornwallis. His mouth was tight, and he sat upright, as if facing some threat from which he must guard himself. With a flash of insight she thought she knew what he was feeling: the same confusion as she was, a rage and a disgust he did not want, which embarrassed him but which he could not escape.

"Have some more tea," the bishop offered, holding up the pot after he had helped himself.

"No, thank you," Cornwallis declined without giving it a moment's thought.

A servant came in silently and placed a hot dish of bacon, eggs, potatoes and sausage in front of the bishop. He nodded acceptance and she left.

"It was obviously as we feared," the bishop went on, taking up his knife and fork. "Poor Parmenter. He was suffering from a steadily increasing insanity. Very tragic. Thanks be to God he did not succeed in killing his wife, poor woman." He looked up suddenly, his fork balanced with sausage and potato. "I assume she is not seriously injured?" He had only just thought of it.

"I believe not," Cornwallis replied tersely.

"I shall visit her in due course." The bishop put the food into his mouth.

"She must be shattered," Isadora said, turning to Cornwallis. "One can hardly imagine anything worse. I wonder if she had any idea he was so . . . ill."

"It hardly matters now, my dear," the bishop said with his mouth full. "It is all over and we need not harrow our minds with questions we cannot answer." He swallowed. "We are in a position to protect her from further grief and distress at the intrusion of others into her bereavement and its causes. There will be no more police investigation. The tragedy has explained itself. There is no justice to be sought . . . it is already accomplished in the perfect economy of the Almighty."

Cornwallis winced.

"The Almighty!" Isadora exploded, disregarding Cornwallis's widened eyes and the bishop's hiss of indrawn breath. "God didn't do this! Ramsay Parmenter must have been sinking into despair and madness for months, probably years, and none of us saw it! None of us had the slightest idea!" She leaned forward over the table, staring at both of them. "He employed a young woman and had an affair with her. She became with child and he murdered her, whether he meant to or not. Now he attacks his wife, trying to strangle her, and instead is killed himself. And you sit there saying it is all over—in the economy of God!" Her outrage was withering. "It has nothing to do with God! It is human suffering and failure. And with two people dead, and a child never to be born . . . it is hardly economical!"

"Isadora, please take control of yourself," the bishop said between his teeth. "I can quite understand your distress, but we must keep calm. Hysteria will help no one." He was talking too quickly. "I merely meant that the matter has come to a natural conclusion and there is nothing to be served by pressing it any further. And that God will take care of the judgment necessary."

"That is not what you meant," she said bitterly. "You meant that now it can all be put away without any effort on our part to conceal a scandal. The real scandal is that we want to. That we knew Ramsay Parmenter all those years and we never noticed his misery."

The bishop smiled apologetically at Cornwallis. "I am so sorry." He shook his head very slightly. "My wife is deeply distressed at this turn of events. Please excuse her unguarded outburst." He turned to Isadora, his lips a thin line. "Perhaps you should go and lie down for a little, my dear. See if you can compose yourself. You will feel better shortly. Have Collard bring you a tisane."

Isadora was livid. He spoke to her as if she were mentally incompetent.

"I am not ill! I am considering our responsibility in the violent death of one of our clergy, and trying to examine in my heart whether we could and should have done more to help when there was still time."

"Really—" the bishop started, his face pink.

"We all should have," Cornwallis cut across him. "We knew someone in that house killed Unity Bellwood. We should have found a way of preventing a second tragedy."

The bishop glared at him. "Since the poor man was obviously incurably insane, it is not a tragedy that he should have died, and thank the Lord, not by his own hand," he corrected. "Given the already irreparable circumstances, this is the least appalling outcome we could expect. I believe I have already thanked you for coming to inform me, Mr. Cornwallis. I do not believe there is anything further I can tell you that will assist you in any other matter, and this one is mercifully closed."

Cornwallis rose to his feet, his expression a mixture of embarrassment and confusion, as if he were struggling to reconcile warring emotions, both of which hurt him.

Isadora knew how he felt. She was filled with the same conflict of anger and shame.

Cornwallis turned to her. "Thank you for your hospitality, Mrs. Underhill. Good day, Bishop." And without extending his hand he swiveled around and went out of the dining room door.

"I think you had better retire for a while until you can compose yourself," the bishop said to Isadora. "Your behavior in this matter has been something rather less than I had hoped for."

She looked at him steadily and with a detachment of which she had not expected herself to be capable. Now that the moment had come, there was a calm center of warmth inside her, quite steady.

"I think we are both disappointed, Reginald," she replied. "You hoped for discretion from me, and I cannot be discreet about this. I hoped for compassion and honesty from you, and a little self-examination as to whether we could and should have done more to understand before this happened. And it seems you have neither the pity nor the humility to be capable of that. Perhaps you had a right to be surprised in me. I gave too little sign of what I felt. I had no right to be surprised in you. You have always been like this. I simply refused to see it." She walked to the door and opened it. She heard him gasp, and he started to speak as she went into the hall, but she did not listen. She went across the floor and through the baize door into the kitchens, where she knew he would not follow.

Pitt returned to Brunswick Gardens to clear up the last details of Ramsay Parmenter's death. He did not expect to achieve anything, it was merely necessary.

He was let in by Emsley, looking red-eyed and exhausted.

"There is no need to trouble Mrs. Parmenter," Pitt said as he crossed the hall. "I don't think I have any further questions to ask."

"No sir," Emsley said dutifully. He seemed to hesitate. If so dignified and unhappy a figure could be said to do so, he dithered.

"What is it?" Pitt asked gently.

"It is not my place to ask, sir," Emsley said miserably, "but is it necessary to allow those in the newspapers to know all this, sir? I mean, I . . . I mean, could you just say Mr. Parmenter died in an accident? He was . . ." He took a shaky breath and attempted to control himself. "He was such a quiet gentleman, Mr. Pitt, never a rough word to anyone all the time I knew him. And I've served in this house above twenty years. Kindest man, he was, sir. Always had time . . . and patience. The worst you could say of him was that he was a bit remote . . . like absentminded. Forgot things. But that's hardly a sin. Most of us can be forgetful. Terrible worried, he was, lately." Emsley swallowed and sniffed. "All that stuff about Darwin and monkeys and all that. Got him down terribly." His face puckered. "I tried to tell him it was all nonsense, but it's not my place to say things like that . . . not to the likes of the Master, him being a proper churchman."

"I don't think it matters who says it, if it is true," Pitt answered. "And I will certainly not volunteer any unnecessary information to anyone. I cannot imagine that Mrs. Parmenter will. How is she this morning?"

"I haven't seen her myself, sir, but Braithwaite says she's very upset, naturally, and feeling the shock of it now. But she's very brave. Did you need to see anybody, sir? I can tell Mr. Mallory you're here, or Mr. Corde."

"You could tell Mrs. Parmenter I'm here, as a courtesy," Pitt answered. "But I don't need to speak to anyone, thank you. I need to go back to the study."

"Yes sir. It's locked up. I suppose you have the key?"

"Yes, I have, thank you."

"Right sir. Will you be wanting anything? A cup of tea, perhaps?"

"In an hour or so, thank you," Pitt accepted, then excused himself and went up the black staircase, along the passage and unlocked the study door.

The room was exactly as he had left it. There were still dark bloodstains on the floor beside the desk. The paper knife was in the farther corner, where it had fallen. There had never been any question of its not being the weapon, or of anyone else's having touched it. It was evidence, but there was nothing to dispute.

He stood staring at it, trying to picture in his mind what had happened. Physically it was easy, but what had happened between Ramsay and Vita in the years leading up to it? Or more correctly, what had happened to him? How had his doubts so distorted his thinking, his feeling, that he had moved from being a loving husband dedicated to the care of other people's souls to being a man whose own weaknesses so overwhelmed him he made love to a woman he despised, under his own roof, and when she blackmailed him with her pregnancy, killed her—and then tried to kill his wife?

Perhaps the answer was simply madness—as clear and as incomprehensible as that.

He went to the desk and started to look through the papers lying in piles. If Ramsay and Vita had quarreled over love letters, they must have been where she could easily see them. He had been in the room when she went in, so she had not searched for them; her eye had caught them by chance. And she would have had no opportunity to move them since then.

There was a paper on St. Paul. Half folded was the draft of a sermon on the Epistle of St. James titled "If any man lack wisdom, let him ask of God, who giveth liberally, and upbraideth not!" Under that were two short letters from missions abroad, one in Africa, one in China. He put them in a pile again and looked at the surface of the desk. There was a red leather-bound copy of the Meditations of Marcus Aurelius. A Stoic philosopher, albeit an emperor of Rome, was odd reading for a cleric of the Church of England, but not perhaps for what he had first believed Ramsay to be. Its dry, brave, rather

comfortless wisdom would be exactly what would echo his own philosophy. It would be a companion voice. He looked beside it and saw
half a dozen papers written in two quite different sets of handwriting.
He picked up the first.

It was a neat, exact hand with open Greek *E*'s. Ramsay's writing.
Pitt knew that from other papers on the desk. He began to read it.

> You who are dearest to me, how can I express to you the
> sense of loneliness I feel when we are separated? The distance
> between us is immeasurable, and yet thoughts may fly across
> it and I can reach you in heart and mind in as short a space as
> it takes for one to find some solitary corner where I can
> summon you to my heart's eye.
>
> Then time vanishes and once more we can walk and talk
> as of old. I can share with you my dreams, the explorations of
> all truth and meaning which is surely our greatest treasure. I
> am no longer a wanderer among strangers, but am at home in
> you. We breathe the same air, our understanding is but two
> halves of the same whole . . .

He continued down to the end of the page and turned it over. It
was all in the same vein, about loneliness and separation, about unity
of thought and heart, symbolized by unity of person.

The second was in the same hand, and while dealing with a different subject, it was of the same nature. Again loneliness was a con-
tinuous thread running through it, the desire to be together again, to
remove all difficulties and barriers that kept them apart. The under-
lying emotion was obviously deeply felt, but it was couched in
metaphor, a trifle pedantic, drawing back from the ultimate of verbal
commitment. Pitt could hear Ramsay Parmenter's careful, slightly dry
voice all the way through it.

The third was in a different hand, rapid, exuberant, full of confidence. Here the meaning was undisguised. It began instantly and
passionately.

My own beloved, my hunger for you is inexpressible. When we are apart I drown in a void of loneliness, engulfed in the night. Infinity yawns between us. And yet I have but to think of you and neither heaven nor hell could bar my way. The void disappears and you are with me. I touch you, hold you again. We are one heart and one flesh. I drown in you. All pain is forgotten as a dream.

The sweetness of times past returns with all its echoes of passion and hopes and terrors shared. We climb together the starry heights of truth and leap beyond into the unknown deeps of faith, life's greatest gift, eternity's crowning glory. All my grief is in the past, slipping from me like shadows before the rising sun. We melt into one another in eternal ecstasy . . .

There were three more in the same dashing hand. Little wonder Vita Parmenter had been amazed and had challenged her husband to explain them. What could he possibly say?

Pitt set them down again in the place where they had been. He felt confused, overtaken by his own sense of not being equal to the task given him. He had failed to understand Ramsay while he was alive, and thus to prevent his death. And he could not dismiss the fact that Ramsay could have succeeded in hurting Vita. Then Pitt would have been responsible for that, too. Now he understood even less. He had read the love letters, and anyone could see how they would precipitate a quarrel. It was inevitable the moment Vita saw them . . . or for that matter if anyone else in the family had, or even Dominic. But why had Ramsay left them out on the desk where they must be seen? Why did he have both his and hers? Presumably he must have retrieved them from her belongings after her death. With any sense at all he would have destroyed them.

Did he still love her, or was he so obsessed with her, that he could not, in spite of the risk they represented? Had he abandoned hope of escape for the result of his act? Was he only waiting for the inevitable?

And yet looking at the unbridled passion in the letters, Pitt could see neither Ramsay nor Unity in them. The wording was characteristic of what he had seen of him and heard of her. But the emotion was not. He still could not imagine them in love with each other at all, let alone so wildly.

Which showed the depth to which he had failed in this case.

He sighed and started to look through the drawers of the desk. There were the usual personal accounts and trivial letters regarding Ramsay's profession. He read them all as a matter of duty. They were even drier than he had expected, the same pedantic phrases repeated in each one. Perhaps they were meant sincerely, but there was a stiffness about them which made it difficult to believe.

In the next drawer down there were more letters. They were from various people, colleagues, parishioners, friends. He glanced at them. Most of them were several years old, apparently kept because they were of emotional value. Among them he found one from Dominic. It was an invasion of privacy to read it, yet he found he had done so even while the thought was in his mind.

Dear Ramsay,

I know I have said so many times to you when we have spoken, still I wished to put on paper, my gratitude to you for your unending patience with me. I must have tried you sorely at times. I remember in guilt and embarrassment how long you argued with me, and I repeated the same selfish objections over and over. Yet you never lost your kindness towards me nor allowed me to think you valued your time more than you valued me.

Perhaps more than anything you said was your example of what it is to minister to those in need. If I could so follow in your footsteps that one day anyone might feel the joy I do, because of something I have done for them, then my whole life will have a completeness and a happiness I can now only aspire to.

The best thanks I can offer, and which I know would be of the most value to you, will be to try to be as you are.

My gratitude will not fade.

Your devoted friend, Dominic Corde

Pitt refolded it with an overwhelming sadness. For a moment he was at one with Dominic in a way he had never imagined possible. He could understand his hurt now, the lost opportunity that could not be retrieved. The reproach would never leave.

And the letter must have been precious to Ramsay, because he had kept it among the few other tokens of friendship over the years. Some had dates as far back as his university days.

There were none from Vita. Perhaps they had not written to each other, or if they had, then he had kept them somewhere else, possibly in his bedroom. It hardly mattered.

He looked at the drawer below. There were only more letters to do with his profession. Several of them concerned the book he was currently working on. Pitt leafed through them rapidly. They were all brief and exceedingly dry. Then he came upon one in Unity's hand. He recognized it instantly. It was dated from the end of 1890, just over three months before. It was her application for the position she had occupied.

Dear Reverend Parmenter,

I have read your earlier work with the greatest interest, and a deep regard for your scholarship and your lucid and enlightening explanations of matters hitherto not clearly understood by me, and I must say in honesty, by those more learned than I, to whom I had addressed my questions.

I hear you are to write another work which will require research and translation of early classical letters and papers. I am a scholar in Aramaic and Greek and have a working knowledge of Hebrew. I enclose copies of my qualifications in these subjects, and references from past employment, with

names and addresses of those who would confirm my abilities
to you.

I would humbly, but with as much urgency as may be
judged not too immodest, request that you consider me for
the position of assistant to you in this most important under-
taking. I believe I have the necessary scholastic skills, and you
will not anywhere find a person who has a greater belief in the
work, or admiration for you as the only man capable of doing
it justice.

I write with the greatest hope, and remain yours faithfully,

Unity Bellwood

He folded that also and put it in with the love letters. It was one
thing more which confused him. She had written as a stranger, and
yet that was only six or eight weeks before she had become pregnant,
at the outside. It was a short time for such passion to explode.

There was one more thing. Ramsay had kept a notebook, a brown
leather-bound volume about an inch thick. Glancing through it, Pitt
saw that it did not seem to be a diary so much as a journal of occasional thoughts. He looked at one page, then another, and found it
too difficult to understand. Some of it seemed to be in Latin, some in
almost a shorthand of Ramsay's own devising. He would take it with
him and study it and the letter later, when he had time.

There was nothing more to be done here. He should speak to
Vita, and perhaps Dominic, and then check finally with Tellman and
attend to the formalities. The cases of Unity Bellwood and Ramsay
Parmenter were closed—not satisfactorily, but still closed, for all that.

CHAPTER
TEN

Pitt went home early. It was good to have some time to spend with his family. The verdict of the inquest on Ramsay Parmenter had been exactly what he'd expected. While the balance of his mind was turned he had attacked his wife, and she had defended herself. Death by misadventure.

Now Pitt forced the matter out of his mind and simply put on his oldest clothes and pottered in the garden. There was not a great deal to be done. The growing season had barely begun. The weeds had not established themselves, but there was always tidying of one sort or another, things to mend. And perhaps it was not too cold to sow the first seeds.

Daniel and Jemima helped him. They each had their own marked-out pieces of earth where they could grow what they pleased. Daniel's was largely designed with stones, which he had taken to collecting, but there was a small fuchsia bush in it, at the moment looking rotted and very sad.

"It's dead!" Daniel said tragically. He reached to yank it out by the roots. Jemima watched, feet together, face glowering, full of sympathy.

"Probably not," Pitt said, restraining Daniel with one hand, bending down to examine the offending plant. "They do that in winter. Sort of snuggle down. It will waken up when it gets warmer, and grow some more leaves."

"Will it?" Daniel said doubtfully. "It looks dead to me. Where would it get new leaves from?"

"It will grow them. It will feed out of the soil, if we look after it."

"Shall I water it?" Daniel said helpfully.

"No, I think the rain will do that," Pitt put in before Daniel could go further than a step.

"Well, what shall I do?" Daniel asked.

Pitt thought. "Put a little compost around the roots. That'll keep it warm and give it something to eat," he suggested.

"Will it?" Daniel's expression was hopeful at last.

They worked happily until nearly seven o'clock, then Daniel and Jemima went in to supper and hot baths, now extremely necessary, and Pitt changed out of his gardening clothes and went to the parlor. He ate yesterday's potato, cabbage and onions, refried till it was hot and full of crisp pieces, along with cold mutton and a little of last summer's rhubarb chutney, then apple pie with a flaky crust, and cream.

At about quarter to nine Charlotte picked up Emily's latest letter.

"Shall I read it to you?" she offered. Emily's handwriting was not of the neatest, and it became more idiosyncratic the more enthused she was.

Pitt smiled, sliding down a little further in his chair and preparing to be entertained, if not by Emily's actual travels, at least by her comments upon them.

Charlotte began: " 'My dear Charlotte and Thomas.

" 'I suppose I should begin by saying I miss you all. There is a sense in which I do. I think a dozen times a day how I would love to share with you the marvelous things I am seeing and the enormous variety of people I meet. The Italians themselves are superb, so full of the love of life and beauty, and far more welcoming of foreigners than I had expected. At least on the outside. Sometimes I catch a glimpse of something else, a look between two of them with their wonderful eyes, which makes me wonder if they secretly find us very gauche and a bit tedious. I hope I am not of that sort! I try to behave with dignity, not as if this is the first time I have ever seen such ravishing love-liness: the light on the landscape, ancient buildings, the sense of history.

" 'After all, what could be lovelier than England in the spring? Or the summer? Or especially the autumn?

" 'Yesterday we went for a drive to Fiesole. I wish there was time to do it again. The views! We came back via Settignano, and there was a place on the road where we could see Florence, which was quite breathtaking. It made me think of old Mr. Lawrence and his stories of Dante on the bridge. At that moment nothing seemed impossible, or even unlikely.

" 'But tomorrow we are off to Rome! "O Rome! My country! City of the soul!" as Lord Byron says. I can hardly wait! If it is all I dream and hope, then one day, regardless of who has been murdered or how or why, then you must both pack up everything and come as well! What is money worth if one cannot spend it seeing the glories of the world? I have been reading too much Byron! If there can be such a thing. Do I make any sense?

" 'I shall write you from there! All my love, Emily. P. S. Jack sends his love as well, of course!' "

Charlotte smiled at him over the papers.

"How very Emily," he answered with deep satisfaction.

"I must write to her." Charlotte folded it up and put it back into the envelope. "I have nothing so exotic to tell her. May I relate the wretched situation here? I shall tell her about Dominic, of course. That is barely a secret."

"Yes, tell her about poor Ramsay Parmenter, if you like," he agreed. There seemed no harm in it. And Emily could keep her own counsel if need be.

Mention of Ramsay Parmenter made him think again of the note-book. The notes in it seemed to make no sense, and yet they must have done, at least to Ramsay himself. It did not matter any longer.

The case was over. But he could not let his mind rest until he had done his best to understand his failure. How else could he salvage at least the wisdom to do better next time?

He picked up the book and opened it to the first entry. There was no date. It seemed to concern a fisherman, or someone whose name was Fisherman, and an ill-fated expedition, or holiday, to somewhere described as "summer-clime." The next two pages were on the same subject. Then there followed what appeared to be jottings of ideas for an essay or a sermon on life and disappointment. It did not seem very promising.

Half a dozen pages on he found a reference to "the master" and "the ringer," and a comment with an exclamation mark—"What a carillon that must have been!"—and then the question "But when?" Then: "A peal of bells, but what time? A funeral knell, a burial of other things, did the call to prayer come from that, I wonder!" And on the following page: "Poor soul!" and "But who is the walking dead?"

Charlotte looked up, her expression curious.

"Send my love to Emily," he offered.

"I will. What are you reading?"

"Ramsay Parmenter's notebook."

"What does he say? Does it explain anything?"

"Nothing at all. It doesn't even appear to be sense, just odd words and phrases."

"For example?"

"A whole lot about 'the master' and 'the ringer,' different peals of bells, and the walking dead. I assume that must be metaphorical."

She smiled. "Well, it certainly isn't literal, I hope!"

"No, of course not."

"Maybe it is metaphorical," she agreed. "Although the peals of bells sounds bland enough. Perhaps they are all notes on services and sermons and that sort of thing. I should think you have to have ideas far in advance in order to give a decent sermon every week. You can't just hope it will come by Saturday afternoon."

"Possibly. There were notes earlier on life and disappointment."

"Miserable subject. Perhaps he was going to say something about real values, or faith, or something?" she suggested, her pen still in the air.

"Nothing about faith so far. I'll read some more. Don't let me interrupt your letter to Emily."

She smiled brightly. "You mean don't interrupt you anymore. I take your point, so subtly put."

He pulled a slight face at her and returned to Ramsay's notebook. There was more about the fisherman. Apparently Ramsay did not like him and considered him in a sense to have been a thief, but the object stolen was not specified.

Then he returned to the master and the ringer again. The writing was becoming very jerky, as if written under great emotional pressure: "The ringer!! Where did it all begin? That was it! What a damnable thing. The same tune played over . . . is that it? Oh Master, Master, what have you done? In God's name why?"

Pitt stared at the page. There was such passion in it. It could not possibly be written of bell ringing. No one would care so fiercely about such a thing. And why write about it? Who was the master? It did not seem to be a religious reference.

Did "ringer" mean a double, a look-alike, one person mistaken for another?

But who? There had been no questions of identity in this case. The only people who were not members of the Parmenter family, known to each other for years, were Unity Bellwood and Dominic. And Pitt was perfectly certain about Dominic.

And that left Unity. But how did her identity matter? What difference would it make if she were who she said or not?

Ringer . . . for whom? Or was it bell ringing after all?

Or Bellwood? Was it a mildly oblique way of referring to Unity Bellwood?

Master! There were Latin phrases here and there in the notes. Master . . . *dominus* . . . "Dominic!"

He did not realize he had spoken aloud until Charlotte looked up, her eyes wide, her brow furrowed with alarm.

"What?"

"I just understood what one of these references meant," he explained.

"What does he say?" she demanded, her own letter now totally ignored.

"I don't know yet. I've only just begun to decipher it." It was not very subtle really. The notes were never meant for anyone else's eyes, certainly not to fool Mallory or Dominic himself, or Unity.

Now the references took on a very different meaning. It made excellent sense . . . sense that chilled him and sent a coldness running through his mind till it seemed almost like a physical thing in the warm, familiar room. He would tell Charlotte nothing of it yet.

He read on. It was inescapable now. Ramsay believed Dominic to have known Unity in the past. The references to tragedy were easy to see, although not specifically what it had been, only that its nature was personal and inspired a deep guilt in one or both of them. Ramsay concluded that Unity had lost Dominic for some time, perhaps years, and on discovering where he was, had sought the position in Brunswick Gardens solely in order to follow him there. Thinking again of the urgency of her application for the position, when her qualifications were so high, that was not difficult to believe.

There was a very clear mention of blackmail in order to force Dominic to reestablish the old relationship between them, regardless of his wishes, which, since he had run away in the first place, it was safe to presume he did not want.

There were brief, rather jagged notes, Ramsay's writing becoming less even, far less controlled, as if his hand had shaken and he had gripped the pen too hard. There were occasional scratches and blots. They expressed fear not only in the words but in the black, spiky letters on the page. Ramsay thought Dominic had killed Unity rather than allow her to break up his new life with its public respect and hope of dignity and gentle progress towards acceptance and advancement.

He had not intended anyone else to read this. To judge from the different tones of the ink, even different colors in some places, it had been written over a space of time. There was no reason to doubt it had been written contemporarily with the events themselves. Pitt could not escape the conviction that Ramsay had genuinely thought Dominic guilty of Unity's death, and it had caused him pain and a deep and terrible sense of his own failure. If he had considered his own death, it would not have been from guilt over Unity but from despair because his life had seemed to him devoid of purpose or success. Everything he had attempted had turned to ashes. Dominic was the last blow, and the worst. There were undeniable accents of the desire to escape, to find an end, becoming stronger. Pitt could not evade them.

He closed the book with the chill inside him consuming.

The room around him was so comfortable it jarred against his inner misery, making him more acutely conscious of the world of difference between the physical and the reality of the mind and the heart. The flames flickered gently in the hearth, sending a wavering light onto Charlotte's skirt, her arms and shoulder and cheek. It made her hair almost copper and shadowed the hollow of her neck. Her hands moved rhythmically as she wrote. There was no sound but the clock on the mantelpiece, the flames and the movement of her pen over the paper, and the very faint burning of the gas lamp. It was all so familiar, comfortable, a trifle worn with use. Some of the things had been secondhand, part of someone else's life before theirs, but probably just as loved. He took the safety of it all for granted. He had always been happy here. There were no darknesses, no regrets.

As if sensing his stillness, Charlotte looked up.

"What is it? What have you found now?"

"I'm not completely sure," he prevaricated.

She was not to be so easily put off. "Well, what is it you think?"

"I think perhaps Ramsay Parmenter was not guilty of pushing Unity down the stairs . . ." he said slowly, watching her face.

She understood. "Then who was?" she said hesitantly, her eyes on his.

"It's only a thought." He was being evasive.

She was not to be put off.

"Why? What has he written in that book?" she demanded.

"It's all in a kind of code, not very obscure if you understand that he's using a sort of dog Latin, puns and so on . . ."

"Thomas!" Now her voice was sharp. "You are frightening me. Is it so bad you can't bring yourself to be honest with me?"

"Yes . . ." he said quietly.

Her face paled. She stared at him with hollow eyes. "Dominic?"

"Yes." He had thought he would get some kind of satisfaction from being able to show her Dominic's weakness, but now that he had not only the chance but no escape from the necessity, there was nothing but sadness. And he felt it not only for her but within himself as well. He had believed the letter of gratitude in Ramsay's desk, and it had brought him surprising warmth.

"What does it say?" Charlotte pressed. "What does Ramsay say that makes you think it was Dominic? Couldn't he be wrong? Or trying to put blame from himself?" There was no accusation in her voice or in her eyes. She knew he was not enjoying it this time. She was only looking for escape.

He opened the book and read out the first relevant passage to her. Her schoolroom Latin was quite quick enough to understand.

"Go on," she said huskily.

He obeyed, reading the second and the third, right through to the last.

"Does that have to mean he was right?" she asked.

"No. But it does mean he can't have done it himself."

She did not mention Mallory, but it hung unspoken between them, possible, but only a hope, too fragile to cling to.

"What are you going to do?" she said at last.

"I'm not sure."

Again she sat silently for several moments. The fire settled down, flames brilliant as it consumed the unburnt coal, then sinking again. Pitt reached forward for the tongs and put on half a dozen more pieces.

"You can't leave it," she said at last. "Even if we didn't have to know, you can't allow Ramsay Parmenter to be blamed for something he didn't do."

"He is dead," he pointed out.

"His family isn't. Clarice isn't. Anyway, don't you have to know? I shall always be afraid it was Dominic. Maybe it isn't. Isn't the truth better, whatever it is?"

"Not always."

She put her pen and ink away, even though the letter was unfinished. She lifted her feet and tucked them beside her on the sofa. It was a position she adopted when she was cold, frightened, or deeply miserable.

"Even so, I think you had better find out all you can. You can look . . . can't you?"

"Yes. There's enough in Ramsay's notebook to start."

"Tomorrow?"

"I suppose so."

She said nothing else, but hugged her arms around herself and shivered.

Pitt set out with Ramsay's notebook in his coat pocket. It made the right side bulge and hang crookedly, but that hardly mattered. He walked rapidly. Now that he had determined to do it there was no point in hesitating. It was raining quite hard, although over the roofs to the west there were gleaming patches of blue in the sky . . . "enough to make trousers for one sailor," as his mother used to say.

He took a cab to Maida Vale, back to the house in Hall Road.

"I don't know anything about it," Morgan said fiercely. She was dressed in green and white and looked quaintly regal with a crown of leaves in her hair. She was quite unself-conscious of any absurdity. As before, they were in her studio, cluttered with canvases, but this time the light was flat, draining the color, and rain beat against the windows. She had been painting before he came in, but there were only greens and yellows on her palette, which now sat on a stool a yard away.

"I have never heard of Unity Bellwood," she denied. "And we have had no tragedy here, except Jenny's death, and you already know all about that." Her face darkened. "You did not need to have sent your man behind my back to ask the boy. That was devious."

Pitt smiled at her naive indignation; it was the only sensible reaction.

"Why are you laughing at me?" she demanded, but he could see in her eyes that she half understood. "I don't discuss other people's affairs, least of all with police," she went on. "It is not wrong to protect people from inquisitive strangers, it is wrong not to. It is part of the nature of friendship not to betray, especially whatever you think or fear might be a weakness." Her light blue eyes were clear. Whatever she knew or suspected, at least this sentiment was honest.

"Do you place the interests of your friends before those of others?" he asked, leaning his weight against the mantel.

"Of course," she replied, staring at him.

"Always?"

She did not answer.

"Does it matter how little your friend loses, or how much the other person does? Is your friend always right, no matter the issue or the price?"

"Well . . . no . . ."

"Dominic's embarrassment against Ramsay Parmenter's life? What about your own morality? Do you have a faith to yourself as well?"

Her neck stiffened. "Of course I do. Is it Ramsay Parmenter's life?"

"No. It is just a question, to see where your judgment is."

"Why do you pick Ramsay Parmenter?" She did not believe him, and it was clear in her face.

"His life is not in the balance. He is already dead."

That jolted her. The color faded from her skin, leaving her looking tired. "If he's dead, why do you need to know?"

"Can't you guess?"

"Are you trying to say Dominic killed him?" She was very white now. "I don't believe that!" But the raw edge to her voice showed that she could not dismiss it from her mind so completely.

"Where was he living before he was here?" he pressed. "You must know. He didn't appear from nowhere. He had clothes, belongings, letters, at least acquaintances. He always dressed well. What about his tailor? Where did his money come from? Or did you keep him?"

She flushed. "No, I did not keep him! I don't know all those things. I didn't ask. We don't ask questions of one another. It is part of friendship, and trust."

"Did he leave anything behind when he went to Icehouse Wood?"

"I don't know. But if he did, it is long since cleared away. Anyway, it wouldn't tell you anything."

"What about clothes? Did he buy any new clothes while he was here?"

She thought about it for a moment. "A coat, a brown overcoat."

"Didn't he have one before?"

She smiled. "Yes, of course he did. Can't a man have two coats? Anyway, he didn't keep the old one. He gave it to Peter Wesley, next door. He hadn't one."

"Is Peter Wesley still there, next door?"

"No. He moved."

"Where to?"

"What does it matter?" She shrugged. "I don't know."

He pressed her further and learned nothing except that Dominic seemed to have been very secretive about his immediate past, and she had gained the impression, never substantiated, that there was someone he would prefer did not find him there.

"Did he receive any letters?" Pitt asked her.

"No, never that I remember." She thought for a moment. "No, I am sure he never did. And what he purchased he would have paid for at the time, because there were no bills, either, not even from his tailor, bootmaker, or shirtmaker."

It completed a picture of a man who feared pursuit and was anxious to conceal all signs of where he was. Why? Who wished to find him, and for what reason?

He thanked her and went to search for the brown overcoat, which might at least offer him a tailor's name.

But no one at the next house knew where Peter Wesley had gone to. Pitt was left on the doorstep looking out at a now-busy street which offered nothing further to tell where Dominic Corde had been before this place, or what had driven him from it.

An open carriage passed, ladies braving the sharp air to display their fashionable hats and pretty faces. They were shivering with cold but smiling brightly. He could not help smiling back, half in pleasure, half in amusement at their youthful vanity and optimism.

A coal cart passed, horses leaning forward into the harness against the weight. A newsboy shouted the headlines, mostly political. There was disturbing news from Africa, something about Cecil Rhodes and diamonds in Mashonaland, and settlers in Dutch South Africa. No one cared about the death of one not particularly fashionable cleric in what, so far as they knew, was a domestic accident.

A costermonger walked along the side of the street pushing a barrow, his shoulders straining against a coat a size too small but of very good cut and cloth. It reminded Pitt again of Dominic's coat. A tailor would have been a good place to start. A man often did not change his tailor, even if he moved his accommodation. And if that were true of Dominic, then perhaps four or five years ago he had still had the same tailor as when he had lived in Cater Street. Pitt had no idea who that had been, and probably Charlotte had not. But Caroline might!

He had already walked rapidly to the main cross street and hailed a cab, and was sitting down in it when he realized it was quite possible Caroline was not at home. These days, if Joshua were touring with a play, she would go with him. She could be anywhere in England.

He fidgeted all the way to Cater Street, trying to think what to do next if Caroline were away or if she had not the slightest idea who Dominic's tailor had been. Of course, the best person to ask would be the valet, only she had let him go when Edward died. Joshua would have brought his own man. But Maddock, the butler, might know. There would hardly be household accounts left from a decade ago, and a tailor's account was personal anyway.

He was rattling through quiet, house-lined streets, passing delivery wagons, private carriages, other hansoms, all the routine traffic of any residential district. There were three million people in London. It was the largest and busiest city in the world, the heart of an empire that covered continents—India, Africa and Asia—the Pacific, the vast prairies and mountains of Canada from one ocean to another, and islands uncountable in every body of water known to man. How did you look for one private individual who wanted to be lost five years ago?

Except that a man is a creature of habit. One clings to identity. In all the upheaval and strangeness of tragedy or of guilt, physical things that are familiar are perhaps the only comfort left. If we lose places and people, then possessions become the more valuable.

They were in Cater Street. The cab stopped, and within moments Pitt was on the doorstep waiting for someone to answer. The minutes seemed to drag. There must be someone, even if Caroline and Joshua were away.

Maddock was on the step, looking older and quite a bit grayer. It made Pitt realize how long it had been since he had been there.

Caroline had so often visited them in Keppel Street instead, and although Charlotte had been there recently, it was alone, when he had been busy.

"Good morning, Mr. Pitt, sir," Maddock said, concealing his surprise. "Is all well, sir?"

"Very well, thank you, Maddock," Pitt answered him. "Is Mrs. Fielding at home?"

"Yes sir. If you care to come in, I shall inform her you are here." He stood aside, and Pitt stepped into the familiar hallway. In one sweep it took him back ten years to the first time he had come following the first Cater Street garottings. He had met Charlotte when she was the middle daughter, seeming to her own social class so rebellious and different, and to him so exactly what he expected a well-bred unmarried young lady to be. He smiled at the memory.

Dominic Corde had been married to Sarah then, before her murder by the same hand as all the others. What would Caroline know of him?

He had only a few moments to wait in the morning room before she came in. She had changed utterly since her respectable widowhood from pleasant and predictable Edward and her scandalous marriage to charming and desperately unsuitable Joshua, an actor seventeen years her junior. She looked radiant. She had always been a handsome woman, not as much as Charlotte—at least not to Pitt's eye—but very good-looking, nonetheless. He admired her warm coloring and nicely curved figure. She was wearing a morning gown with roses on it, something she would have considered in Edward's time as being far too showy and self-indulgent.

"Good morning, Thomas," she said with a slight frown. "Maddock said everything was all right, but are you sure? Charlotte is not ill or troubled?"

"Not in the slightest," he assured her, "except that there is an unpleasantness where Dominic is now living, and it may concern him. But that is all. The children are very well."

"Are you?" She regarded him still with a trace of seriousness.

He smiled. "I am up against a difficulty I am hoping you can help me solve," he replied honestly.

She sat down on the sofa, draping her flowing skirts around her. He noticed that she carried herself with less dignity and more grace than before she had known Joshua. *Theatrical* was too strong a word to use, but certainly she had a more dramatic flare than before. Years of behaving modestly and appropriately had fallen away, revealing a more colorful woman.

"I?" she said with surprise. "What could I do? What is this difficulty?"

"Do you know where Dominic went after he left here?"

She looked at him very steadily, her eyes shadowed. "You said that the unpleasantness may concern him. You do not waste your time with petty thefts, Thomas. It must be very unpleasant indeed to warrant your attention. Just how much does it concern Dominic? And please don't fob me off with a comforting story that is not true."

"I don't know how much it concerns him," he said, meeting her eyes without pretense. "I hope not at all. He appears to have changed completely from the rather shallow, charming young man he used to be."

"But . . ." she prompted.

"But the case is murder." He hated having to say it. He saw her face tighten and the shadows cross her eyes.

"You don't think he did it . . . surely . . ."

"I hope not." He surprised himself by how much he meant that. He really wanted to prove that it was not Dominic.

"Then how can I help?" she asked gravely. "I don't know where he went after Burton Street, and I don't think he was there long."

"Burton Street?" he asked.

"He took rooms there after he left here. He didn't feel he could remain after Sarah . . . died." The pain was there in her eyes for a moment, the anguish of memory, the shock and the grief that never really left. Then she forced her attention to the present again. Sarah was beyond any ability to help now, or any need for it. Dominic was still here, and open to injury and fear. "Why do you want to know? Surely you know where he is at present?"

"Yes, in Brunswick Gardens," he replied. "But I need the past, between Cater Street and Maida Vale."

"Maida Vale? I didn't know he had lived there." She looked surprised.

"For a while. Do you know the address in Burton Street? I might be able to find someone who could help me there."

"I don't remember it, but I'm sure I have it somewhere. I used to forward mail for him. I presume you don't believe whatever he has told you?"

He smiled a little self-consciously. He had not actually asked Dominic. Perhaps if he had Dominic would have told him the truth, but he doubted it. If Dominic had really known Unity Bellwood in some circumstance so personally tragic that Ramsay had believed it had provoked her murder, if he were going to confess it, he would have done so at the time, not allowed Ramsay to be suspected and to suffer the fear and isolation which it seemed in the end had broken him. That was a dark thought, and one which had not occurred to Pitt in precisely that form before. It was painful.

Caroline was staring at him and sensing his newer, sharper unhappiness.

"I need to know for myself," he said with slight evasion. "What sort of letters did you forward?" He saw her raised eyebrows. "I mean, were they personal or tradesmen's accounts?"

She relaxed a little. "Mostly tradesmen's accounts, I think. There were very few of them anyway."

"A tailor's bill perhaps?"

"Why? Do his clothes matter in this . . . crime?"

"Not at all. But if I were to find the tailor, he might know where Dominic went afterwards. A man quite often keeps the same tailor for years, if he is happy with him."

In spite of every intention of good manners, Caroline could not help smiling. Pitt had never in the decade she had known him looked as if his clothes were the right size, let alone ever tailored for him.

He read the thought in her eyes, and laughed.

"I'm sorry." Caroline blushed. "I really did not mean to hurt your feelings. . . ."

"You didn't."

"Are you sure?"

"Yes. One day perhaps I shall have a coat made to fit me, but there are other things a hundred times more important. Dominic's tailor?"

"I can't remember his name, but he bought his shirts at Gieves, off Piccadilly. Is that any help?"

"It may be. Thank you. Thank you very much." He made as if to rise.

"Thomas!"

"Yes?"

"Please tell me when you know. If—if Dominic is guilty, Charlotte is going to be so hurt. Whatever his faults, he was part of our family . . . for many years. I was very fond of him. I did not realize how much until after he had gone. He was very grieved by Sarah's death, more than he realized to begin with. I think he felt in some way he should have done something to prevent it." She gave a little shake of her head. "I know that is foolish, and it is extremely self-important to imagine we could have prevented fate . . . but when a thing is hard to bear we look for ways in which it need not have happened. We think that perhaps we can prevent anything like it again . . . and if we can, then it follows we could have the first time."

"I know," he said gently. "I will tell you what happens, and of course I shall make it as easy for Charlotte as I can."

"Thank you, Thomas." She rose also, seemed to want to add something, then realized they had already said all there was.

He told her a few pleasant details about the children, and they parted at the door. He walked to the corner, found another cab, and went back to the center of the city. In Piccadilly, he found the shirtmakers, and after showing the proof of who he was and explaining the gravity of the case, he enquired if indeed they had served Dominic Corde in the past. It took some five minutes to acquire the address where Dominic had been staying when he had last ordered from them, approximately six years before. Possibly since then his income had decreased and he had reduced his taste in fine shirts.

The address was on Prince of Wales Road in Haverstock Hill, a considerable journey to the north and west. It was late afternoon by the time he found the right house. It was large and a trifle shabby, the sort of place which was originally built to accommodate an abundant family and had since been broken up into a series of apartments or rooms for a dozen or so individuals without dependents or companions.

He knocked at the door, noticing the paint peeling on the edges of the panels and a few spots of corrosion on the knocker itself.

His knock was answered by a middle-aged man with a ragged beard and clothes faded to an agreeable nondescript color by the bleaching effect of the sun and too-frequent laundering. He looked at Pitt with surprise.

"Yes? Forgive me, but do I know you, sir?"

"No. My name is Thomas Pitt. I am enquiring after a Mr. Dominic Corde, who used to live here several years ago." He left no doubt in his voice, no room for argument.

The man's face shadowed slightly, so very little that, had he not been facing the light, Pitt might not have seen it at all.

"I'm sorry. He left here a long time ago. I cannot tell you where he is now; I have no idea. And he left no forwarding address." That too was a statement which permitted no space for further speech on the subject.

"I know," Pitt said firmly. "I am quite aware of where he is now. It is the past which concerns me."

The first few spots of rain spattered on the footpath.

The man's face was bland but firm, his expression closed. "I am sorry, I can be of no assistance, sir. I bid you good day." He made as if to close the door. Everything in his body, the faint droop of his shoulders, the heavy solidity of his stance, spoke of exhaustion and a weight of sadness rather than anger. Watching him, Pitt felt cold, in spite of the softness of the evening light and the fact that the air was still mild. This was where it had happened, whatever it was.

"I am sorry, sir," he said gravely. "But I cannot allow the matter to be closed. I am from the police, in command of the Bow Street station, and the assistant commissioner has directed me to investigate a case of murder." He saw the man wince and his pale blue eyes open wide. He was surprised, but not incredulous.

The coldness sharpened inside Pitt. He could see Charlotte's face in his mind when he had to tell her. It would be the last dream from girlhood gone, a certain innocence of belief would go with it, and he would have given a lot not to do this. He even hesitated before he began again.

A few spots of rain fell.

"I know something happened while Mr. Corde was living here," he said after a moment. "I need to know what it was."

The man stared at him. He was obviously weighing in his mind what he should say, how much he could deny and be believed, or if he was not believed, at least get away with.

Pitt did not move his gaze.

The man's shoulders slumped. "I suppose you had better come inside," he said at last, turning away. "Although I'm not sure what I can tell you."

Pitt followed him, closing the door behind himself. The last protest had been merely a gesture, and he knew it. He allowed the man the pretense that it had a meaning.

The room he led them into was untidy in a homely way. Books and papers littered the surfaces of the tables and chairs and spilled over onto the floor. There were several rather good pictures on the wall, most of them at least an inch crooked. There was a piece of wood on a side table, a frog emerging from it, polished to a rich, almost wet-looking brown. Even unfinished, it was a beautiful piece of work. Looking at it, Pitt was not sure if it would not be of greater power left as it was. Completing every detail might reduce it to some-thing far more mundane, a thing anyone might have conceived.

"Are you going to do anything more to it?" he asked.

"You want it finished?" the man asked, almost challengingly.

"No!" Pitt replied quickly, making up his mind in that instant. "No, I don't. It is right as it is."

The man smiled at last. "I apologize, sir. You are not quite the philistine I presumed. Clear yourself a space and sit down." He waved towards one of the crowded chairs. There was a very old white cat on it. "Never mind him," the man said casually. "Lewis! Get off!"

The cat opened one eye and remained where it was.

"Lewis!" the man repeated, clapping his hands loudly.

The cat went back to sleep again.

Pitt picked him up, sat down, and replaced him in the same posi-tion on his lap. "Dominic Corde," he said unwaveringly.

The man took a very deep breath and began his story.

Pitt arrived home shortly before midnight. The house was quiet, and there was only the hall light on downstairs. He crept up, wincing at each step that creaked. He dreaded what he was going to have to say, but there was no alternative and no escape. At least it would be able to wait until morning, not that he would sleep . . . knowing what lay ahead and how Charlotte would feel. He felt wretched himself, and for her it would be far worse.

But when he reached the landing he saw the crack of light beneath the door. She was still awake. There was no putting it off. Perhaps that was almost a relief. He would not have to lie awake in the dark room, feeling her beside him and waiting, silent and mis-erable, to tell her when she awoke.

He opened the door.

She was sitting up against the pillows with her eyes closed, her hair spread around her. He closed the door without letting the latch go and tiptoed across the room.

She opened her eyes. "Thomas! Where have you been? What did you find?" She saw his face and froze, her eyes wide and dark in the lamplight.

"I'm sorry . . ." he whispered.

"What?" She spoke jerkily, swallowing on nothing. Her voice lowered. "What is it?"

He sat on the edge of the bed. He was tired and cold, and he wanted to undress and feel the fleecy warmth of his nightshirt next to his skin, and wriggle down under the blankets beside her. But that was not the way to say what he had to. This must be done face-to-face.

"I found where Dominic lived before he went to Maida Vale. I went to Cater Street and saw your mother. She gave me the name of his shirtmaker . . ."

"Gieves," she said huskily. "I could have told you that. How did that help?"

"They had his address on record . . ."

"Oh. Where was it?"

He was putting off the time when he would have to tell her the part that mattered, that would hurt.

"Haverstock Hill."

"I didn't know that."

"Of course not. You didn't know Dominic then."

"What was he doing there?"

Should he answer the question she meant? What was his occupation? He could tell her about his financial affairs, his speculation, his banking advice. It was irrelevant. He was tired and cold. It was midnight already.

"He was having an affair with Unity Bellwood, who lived in Hampstead and was working for one of his clients."

Her face was very white. "Oh." She took a deep breath and let it out slowly. "I suppose it matters, or you wouldn't be having to tell me." She searched his eyes. Her voice dropped even lower. "And you wouldn't look like that. What is it, Thomas? Did—did Dominic kill her?" She looked as if she were waiting to be physically struck.

"I don't know." He put his hand on her shoulder and ran it gently down her arm, holding her. "But he lied by implication and omission, and it seems he had pretty good cause. She took the affair very seriously. He got her with child, but for whatever reason, she had it aborted."

Her face crumpled with pain and confusion, and her eyes filled with tears. She bent her head into his shoulder, and he tightened both his arms around her. There was no point in stopping now. Best to tell her all of it, far better than stopping and having to start again.

"He ran away, fled, leaving her behind." His voice was soft and hollow in the silence. "Apparently he panicked. He was very upset indeed. Whether he was upset that she was with child, and demanded she have it aborted, or whether he was distressed she aborted it, and ran away because he couldn't face that, no one seemed to know. But he went one night, without telling anyone or leaving any clue as to where he was going. I don't know where he did go. But a few months later he turned up in Maida Vale without any belongings except his clothes, and no mail was forwarded from Haverstock Hill."

Charlotte pulled back from him, but her eyes were closed and her jaw was clenched. He could feel her body clenched also.

"And he had an affair with the girl Jenny, and she was with child as well . . . and she took her own life," she said very quietly, her voice thick with pain. "Then he ran away to Icehouse Wood, where Ramsay Parmenter found him."

"Yes."

"And then the terrible coincidence that Unity took a job with Ramsay—"

"It wasn't a coincidence. She saw the job advertised in an academic journal, and Dominic's name was mentioned. She knew he was there. That was why she wanted the job so very much."

"To be with Dominic again?" She shivered. "How he must have

felt when he saw her arrive!" She stopped abruptly, her face pinched. "Was that why he . . . are you sure he did, Thomas? Absolutely sure?"

"No. But she was with child again . . . and can you believe it was Ramsay Parmenter? You met him. Do you believe he made love to her almost as soon as she was in the house? And more to the point, can you believe she made love with him, when Dominic was there?"

"No . . ." She looked down, away from him. "No."

They sat together, huddled closely in silence as the minutes ticked by.

"What are you going to do?" she said at last.

"Face him," he answered. "If Unity's child wasn't Ramsay's then Ramsay had no reason to kill her, and I can't accept blindly that he did."

"Then why did he try to kill Vita?"

"God knows! Perhaps by then he really was mad. I don't understand it. It doesn't make any sense. Perhaps he felt the net closing around him and he committed suicide, and she lied about it to protect him. She probably thinks he was guilty. She won't know anything about Dominic and Unity."

She looked at him with a slight frown. "You don't suppose she thought he was guilty and killed him, do you?"

"No, of course not! She found the love letters he and Unity—" He had temporarily forgotten them.

She stared at him, wide-eyed. "But they were real! You said yourself they were in his handwriting—and hers! Thomas, it makes no sense at all. Did . . . was she carrying Dominic's child, and then fell in love with Ramsay? Could she possibly do that? Could anybody? And Dominic killed her in jealousy . . . Oh, Thomas! She was calling out to Ramsay to help her!" She closed her eyes very slowly and buried her face in his shoulder. Her hand reached across the bedclothes and found his. She clung to him so hard she bruised his fingers.

"I can't let it go," he said, bending his cheek to touch her hair.

"I know," she answered. "I know you can't."

CHAPTER

ELEVEN

A strange peace had settled over the house in Brunswick Gardens. It was the kind of relief death brings when the illness has been long and filled with pain. The bereavement is there, the sense of loneliness and loss, but it is momentarily dulled by sheer exhaustion. For a little while all one can feel is that at last one can sleep without fear, without the gnawing anxiety and the guilt if even for a moment one relaxes and forgets to be watchful and afraid.

On the evening when Pitt was listening to the man in Haverstock Hill, Clarice and Tryphena had both retired early, Tryphena because she still preferred to mourn Unity alone, knowing no one else shared her feelings, and Clarice because she was hurt beyond bearing by her father's death. Mallory chose to study. It was an escape from the present world, which he found too oppressive and in which he felt he had little place.

Vita had not wished to retire. She was dressed entirely in black and had behaved all day with solemnity, but there was a kind of ease about her, as if at last she had been able to let go of the foreboding which had gripped her ever since Unity's fall. The color had returned to her face. She looked vulnerable as she sat on the large, overpadded sofa, and extraordinarily young in the soft gaslight.

"Would you prefer to be alone?" Dominic asked with concern. "I should understand perfectly if—"

"No!" she answered before he had finished speaking, looking up at him with her amazing eyes wide. "No—please! I should greatly prefer not to be alone. It is the very last thing I want." She smiled with a trace of self-mockery, a shadow of laughter in her eyes. "I want to pretend for a little while that none of this has happened. I would like to talk about other things, ordinary things, just as if we were two friends with no tragedy between us. Does that sound miserably selfish?"

He was startled, uncertain how to answer. He did not want to sound dismissive of her grief, or as if he could take it lightly on her behalf, or indeed on his own. Was she thinking of herself, as she implied, or was it her generosity, knowing his own sense of failure, the near despair which weighed upon him because he had watched Ramsay drowning in pain and done nothing?

"Dominic?" she said gently, reaching up towards him and putting her fingers on his arm. Her touch was so light he saw it rather than felt it. He looked at her.

She smiled, and there was extraordinary warmth in it. "Grieve for Ramsay, my dear, but please don't blame yourself. You and I are in the same position, only I even more. We must both believe we could have done something, how could we not? Failure is a bitter thing to bear." She lifted her hand in a tiny movement of denial. "There is little else which hurts so constantly, which clouds everything else we try to do, which cripples other effort and in the end makes us doubt ourselves in everything, and finally even hate ourselves. Please don't let that happen to us. It is the last thing Ramsay, in his true self, would have wanted."

He did not answer, thinking of what she had said. It was profoundly true. She was right, and he wanted and needed to believe her. And yet it was not the entire truth. He could not walk away from the memory of Ramsay lying on the study floor in his own blood. That would be irredeemably callous. Decency owed more than that, let alone friendship—and gratitude.

"Dominic!" She repeated his name very softly. She was standing now, only a couple of feet away. There was no sound except the flickering of the fire. He could smell the fragrance of her skin and hair and some flower delicacy she wore. "Dominic, the kindest thing you can do for Ramsay is to remember him as he used to be, at his best, his wisest and kindest, when he had control of himself and was the man he wished to be . . . before he was ill."

He smiled, a little halfheartedly.

"My dear," she continued. "If you were in his place, if you were to become ill in your mind, would you want those you had loved to think of you as you were then, in the extremity of your illness, or as you had been at your best, your very finest?"

"At my best," he said without hesitation, looking at her clearly at last.

Her face eased, the lines of anxiety disappearing from her brow. Her body relaxed, but she did not take her hand from his arm.

"Of course. So would I." Her voice was urgent, charged with emotion so intense he was aware of nothing else in the room. "I should want it passionately," she went on. "It would be the greatest kindness anyone could do for me, and from those whose opinion I valued the most, I should most want it. And he did care about you, you know. He thought you were going to be a great minister to the people, but far above that, he thought you were going to be a leader." There was a warmth in her eyes and a faint flush of color to her cheeks. "We desperately need leadership, Dominic. You must know that! Everywhere there is increasing worldliness. All sorts of people are only too eager to step forward and proclaim themselves in politics or exploration or arts and ideas, but no one has the conviction to lead us in religion anymore. It is as if all the fire had gone out of everyone. . . ."

Unconsciously she clenched her fingers, and her body was rigid with the power of her own feelings and the frustration that she could not lead herself. "Where are the voices of passion and certainty that we need, Dominic? Where are the men no new theories can shake, no worldly wisdom can make afraid or undermine, the men who have the courage to face them all and defy them, and lead us as we should be led?"

She gave a little gasp. "There are new scientific inventions almost every day, certainly every week. Because we can do so much now, we imagine we can do everything. We can't! We shouldn't!"

It was true. He knew exactly what she meant. There was a feeling not just of euphoria—that would have been all right. It was the arro-gance, the delusion that man was supreme and all problems were capable of a purely human solution. There was a driving hunger to learn but little capacity to be taught.

"You will need all your courage," Vita was saying urgently, her hand tightening on his arm. "There will be times when it will be ter-ribly difficult, so many people will be against you, and they will be so sure they are right, your own faith will have to be a rock against all weathers, even the greatest storms. But I am sure you can do that. You have a strength poor Ramsay did not." A smile of certainty crossed her mouth. "Your faith is rooted in goodness, in knowledge and understanding. You know what it is to suffer, to make mistakes and to find the courage and the trust in God to climb up again and go onward. It has given you the power to forgive both others and your-self." Her hand was so tight now it hurt him. "You can be all the things Ramsay believed of you. You can take the place he was unable to. Is that not the best thing, the finest gift you could give him? Does that not make his life worthwhile?"

The chill inside him started to ease away. Some of the pain dis-solved. Perhaps something was retrievable after all?

"Yes . . . yes, it would," he answered her with immense gratitude. "It could be the best way possible, the only way with real meaning."

"Then come and sit down," she offered, letting go of his arm and leading the way towards the sofas by the fire. The flames burned up brightly, filling the room with a soft, yellow glow, reflecting on the table beside one of the sofas and making the wood seem even richer than it was. Vita sat gracefully, one hand flicking her skirt almost as if she were only half aware of it. The light was warm on her cheek, blending away the lines of tiredness and grief. She looked as if she could have obeyed her own injunction and for a few hours forgotten all memory of tragedy.

He sat down opposite her, relaxing at last. There was no sound in the room but the fire, the ormolu clock on the mantel with its enamel sides painted with cherubs, and the very faint rustle of the wind and tap as a branch bumped against the window. The rest of the household need not have existed for any intrusion of its presence upon the peace in the room.

Vita wriggled a little deeper into her seat, smiling. "Shall we talk of something that doesn't matter at all?"

"What would you like?" he asked, falling into the mood.

"Well . . ." She thought for a moment. "I know! If you could go for a holiday anywhere you wished—expense making no difference at all—where would you choose?" She sat still, watching him, her eyes calm and happy, intent upon his face.

He gave himself over to dreaming. "Persia," he said after a moment. "I would love to see ancient cities like Persepolis or Isfahan. I would love to hear camel bells in the night and smell the desert wind."

Her smile widened. "Tell me more."

He elaborated, describing what little he knew and all he imagined. Now and again he quoted verses of Fitzgerald's translation of Omar Khayyam. He lost count of time. All their present griefs and suspicions disappeared. When at last they said good-night and parted at quarter to one, he was physically almost asleep where he stood on the landing near her bedroom door, but he felt less weary to the core than he had since Unity's death—in fact, since long before that, perhaps since her arrival at Brunswick Gardens and the first awful horror of seeing her again.

———

He slept deeply and without stirring until morning, and woke with the room full of sunlight. It was late, after eight o'clock, and it took him a moment or two to remember why he had slept in. Of course! He had sat up for hours talking to Vita. It had been most pleasant. She was excellent company. She gave her attention completely, as few people did. It was as if for that space of time no one else existed for her. It was very flattering.

He rose, washed, shaved and dressed. By the time he got to the dining room Mallory had already been and gone. Tryphena was taking breakfast in her room. Clarice and Vita were at the table.

"Good morning." Clarice regarded him sadly and with a faintly hostile look.

He replied, then turned to Vita. She was still wearing black, of course, but she looked wonderful in it.

"Good morning, Dominic," she said gently, smiling at him, her eyes very direct.

Suddenly he felt self-conscious. He mumbled his reply and helped himself to breakfast, unintentionally taking more than he really wanted. He sat down and began to eat.

"You look as if you've barely slept," Clarice said pointedly.

"We were up rather late," Vita explained, her smile widening slightly. She looked calm, very much in control of herself. Dominic admired her courage. It must be an immeasurable help to her family. How much harder their grief would be to bear were they having to support her also, instead of the other way around.

Clarice had obviously been weeping. Her face was pale and her eyes pink-rimmed.

" 'We'?" she asked sharply, looking from Vita to Dominic.

"We were just sitting talking, my dear," Vita replied, passing her the butter although she had not asked for it. "I am afraid we rather forgot how late it was."

"What is there left to talk about?" Clarice said miserably, pushing the butter away. "It has all been said, and none of it helped. I would have thought a little silence might have been advisable now. We have said too much as it is."

"We didn't talk about the things that have happened here," Vita tried to explain. "We spoke of hopes and dreams, ideas, beautiful things we could share together."

Clarice's eyes were wide and hard. "You what?"

It had sounded too bold, far too insensitive. It was not at all how Dominic had seen it or intended it.

"What your mother means is that we spoke of travel and other countries and cultures," he amended. "We escaped the present tragedy for an hour or two."

Clarice barely regarded him. Her food was forgotten. She looked at Vita again, waiting.

Vita smiled in memory. "We simply sat by the fire and dreamed aloud of where we might travel if we were free to."

"What do you mean 'free'?" Clarice pressed. "Free in what way?" Her brows drew down, and she looked frightened and angry. "What sort of freedom are you talking about?"

"Nothing specific," Dominic interrupted, rather too quickly. The conversation was becoming uncomfortable. An innocent evening was being misconstrued into something quite different. He could feel his face warm at the thought. And it surprised him how painful it was that Clarice, of all people, should be the one to misunderstand. "Only a little daydreaming," he rushed on. "After all, one cannot simply throw away all one's responsibilities and go careering off to Persia, or Kashmir, or wherever one has in mind. It would be expensive and probably dangerous . . ." He trailed off, looking at her face.

"And you spent all evening talking about it?" she said blankly. Her eyes were full of misery.

"And similar sorts of things," Vita agreed. "My dear, you should not allow it to disturb you. Why should it? It was only a little happiness in the midst of all our troubles. We must remain as close as we can to each other. I cannot begin to say how grateful I am to Dominic for his understanding and the courage and the strength he has shown throughout this nightmare. For a while it was a perfect companionship. Is it strange that I should be happy to share beautiful ideas with him?"

Clarice swallowed. She seemed to have to force herself to speak. "No . . ."

"Of course not." Vita reached over and patted her hand. It was a familiar gesture, gentle, comforting, and yet oddly condescending as well, as if Clarice had been a child, on the periphery of things.

Dominic was suddenly acutely uncomfortable. Somehow the conversation had run from his control, but it was impossible to cancel the misimpression without churlishness. To say it had meant nothing personal would be absurd. It would be denying something no one but Clarice had thought. It would embarrass Vita, and that would be inexcusable. It must be the last thing she had thought.

Clarice pushed her plate away, the toast half eaten.

"I have things to do. Letters to write." And without further excuse she went out, closing the door behind her with a sharp snap.

"Oh dear," Vita said with a sigh. She gave a quick little shrug. "Was I indiscreet?"

He was confused. It was not what he had expected her to say, and momentarily he could think of no answer.

Vita was looking at him with a faint flicker of amusement and tolerance. "I am afraid she is a little jealous, my dear. I suppose it had to happen, but it is most unfortunate it should be now."

"Jealous?" He was lost.

Now she was really amused. It was plain in her eyes.

"You are too modest. It is one of your virtues, I know, but can you really be so blind? She is extremely . . . fond of you. She is bound to feel . . . excluded."

He did not know what to say. It was ridiculous. It had not been a romantic evening—how could it be? Vita was Ramsay's wife! At least she was his widow—of barely a couple of days! Clarice could not be so foolish. She had once suggested that Dominic was in love with

Vita, but that had been a desperate and totally flippant attempt to distract them all from blaming her father for Unity's death. No one could have thought it anything but a joke in extraordinarily poor taste. That was all it was. Wasn't it?

"Oh, I'm sure . . ." he began. Then he was not sure. He started to rise to his feet. "I must go and explain to her. . . ."

Vita reached across and took his hand. "Don't! Please?"

"But . . ."

"No, my dear," she said softly. "It is better this way, believe me. You cannot alter the way things are. It is kinder to be honest. Leave her to grieve for her father the way she needs to. Later she will understand. They all will. Just be true to yourself; never fail in that, never waver."

He felt confused. Somewhere he had made a mistake, and he was not sure where; only there was a deepening fear in him that it had been a serious one.

"If you think so," he accepted, loosening himself from her hand. "I had better go and start making the arrangements for the service. The bishop asked me to. I wish I could like him more." And before she could chide him for lack of charity, he made his escape.

But upstairs in his room he could not compose his mind to the subject of Ramsay's funeral. What could he say of him? Where did compassion and gratitude end and hypocrisy begin? If he excluded what seemed to be the truth of his death, might not the whole event descend into farce? What did he owe, and to whom? To Ramsay himself? To his children, especially Clarice, and Clarice was more and more often on his mind lately. What Vita had said about her was absurd. She liked him, most of the time, but it was certainly not love. The idea was foolish. Clarice was not that sort of person. If she loved it would be totally, with extravagant generosity. She would be honest, too honest.

He sat back in his chair, smiling at the thought, his papers forgotten. How could any man with ambitions in the church even consider marrying a woman like Clarice Parmenter? She was devastatingly outspoken; her humor was lethal. Clarice was . . . unconventional. She had beautiful eyes, and with a little attention her hair could be dressed quite well. It was thick and shiny. And he rather liked dark hair. And her mouth was pretty—very pretty.

But Vita was wrong.

The thought of Vita made him extremely uncomfortable. There was something in her face, in her eyes, which alarmed him. She seemed to have misunderstood his friendship and read it as . . . he was not sure what. Something for Clarice to be jealous of.

He was still sitting turning it over in his mind, trying to escape from a feeling of being hemmed in, almost claustrophobically so, his thoughts in increasing turmoil, when there was a knock on the door.

"Come in," he said, his voice almost a squeak with nervous tension in case it was Vita.

But it was Emsley who stood in the entrance. The relief was intense. He could feel the sweat prickle over his skin.

"Yes?" he asked.

Emsley looked apologetic. "I'm sorry, Mr. Corde, but Superintendent Pitt is back again, and says he would like to see you, sir."

"Oh. All right." He rose and followed Emsley without any sense of foreboding. It would only be final details to tidy up. He did not wish to discuss the tragedy. He still felt the pain of loss sharply. He was realizing only now how much he had liked Ramsay. Certainly Ramsay had been a little dry, full of doubts and haunted by a sense of his own weaknesses. But he had also been gentle, extremely patient, tolerant of the shortcomings of others, and sometimes his humor had been startling, far quicker than Dominic had expected, and irreverent. Clarice was not unlike him, except she had a stronger will for life, less doubt of herself. And she seemed to have a more emotional faith, rather than intellectual, as Ramsay's had been. Although she could argue theology with anyone. Dominic knew that to his cost. Her knowledge was both wider and deeper than his own.

Pitt was in the withdrawing room, standing alone in front of the fire, which had been lit early. He looked profoundly unhappy. In fact,

Dominic could not remember ever having seen him look so wretched, not since Sarah's death. His face was white, his whole body stiff.

Dominic closed the door with a sinking feeling so overwhelming the room seemed to waver around him.

"What is it?" he said hoarsely. He had no idea what Pitt was going to say. Was it something to do with Charlotte? Had there been some fearful accident? "What's happened?" he demanded, going forward quickly now.

"You had better sit." Pitt waved his hand at a chair.

"Why?" Dominic remained where he was. "What is it?" His voice was growing louder. He could hear the fear in it himself, but he could not control it.

Pitt's face tightened; his eyes looked almost black. "I've been to Haverstock Hill."

Dominic's stomach knotted, and for a moment he thought he was actually going to be sick. The sweat broke out on his skin. Even as the fear gripped him, part of his conscious mind was telling him it was absurd. Why should he be terrified? He had not killed Unity. He was not even the father of her child—not this time. The thought of that other time still hurt like a raw wound. He'd thought it had healed, that time had covered the scar. He had found new hopes, new things to care about, labor for. He could laugh as easily as before. One day perhaps he would love, more than he had loved Sarah. Certainly more than he had loved Unity—if he could honestly say he had loved her at all. It was the child that tore at him, leaving that awful emptiness inside. It was his greatest task, to forgive her for that. He had not succeeded yet.

Pitt was staring at him. There was misery and contempt in his eyes.

Dominic wanted to be angry. How dare Pitt feel such superiority. He had no idea of the temptations Dominic had faced. He sat at home smug and safe with his beautiful, warm and happy wife. No real difficulty crossed his path. He who is never tempted can very easily be righteous.

But he knew all that was a lie which would not deceive Pitt. It did not even deceive him. He had behaved appallingly to Jenny. It had been as much stupidity as malice, but that pardoned nothing. If a parishioner had offered excuses like that, he would have torn him to shreds for the dishonesty they were.

Why should it hurt to see that scorn in Pitt's face? What did he care what a gamekeeper's son turned policeman should think of him?

A great deal. He cared very much what Pitt thought. Pitt was a man Dominic liked, in spite of the fact Pitt did not like him. He understood why. In Pitt's place he would have felt the same.

"I assume from that that you have found out I knew Unity Bell-wood in the past," he said, stumbling over the words more than he wished to. He would like to have been icily dignified, not stiff-tongued, dry-lipped.

"Yes," Pitt agreed. "Intimately, apparently."

There was no point in trying to deny any of it. It would only add cowardice to everything else.

"I did then . . . not since. I don't suppose you will believe that, but it is true." He squared his shoulders and clenched his hands to stop them from shaking. Should he tell Pitt that Mallory was the father? How could he believe that, knowing what he did about the past? No one would. It would sound cowardly and self-serving. And there was no proof, only Mallory's word, which he could easily take back. When he knew about Dominic and Unity he probably would. She could have lain with either of them, or both. Unity would do that. Anyone looking at her history would find that easy to accept.

"Who killed her, Dominic?" Pitt said grimly.

It had to come. For a moment his voice was strangled in his throat. He had to try twice to speak.

"I don't know. I thought it was Ramsay."

"Why? Are you going to tell me he was the father of her child?" Pitt's voice was only mildly sarcastic. He still looked more hurt than angry.

"No." Dominic swallowed. Why was his mouth still so dry? "No, I thought it was because of her constant erosion of his faith. She under-mined him all the time. She was one of those women who made a crusade of proving people wrong and showing them every occasion. She never let an error slip." His hands were clammy. He clenched and unclenched them. "I thought . . . I thought in the end he lost his temper and pushed her, without meaning even to injure her, let alone kill her. I thought that afterwards he was so horrified he refused to believe what he had done. Then it preyed on his mind and drove him to suicide in the end."

"Suicide?" Pitt's eyebrows shot up. "That's hardly what Mrs. Par-menter said."

"I know." Dominic shifted his weight, not because he was lying but because his legs were cramping, his muscles were so tense. "I thought she made up that story to cover for him. Suicide is a crime in the eyes of the church."

"So is murder."

"I know that! But nobody's proved murder against him. We could still say it was an accident."

"His death . . . or Unity's? Or both?"

Dominic shifted his weight again. "Both, I suppose. I know no one would believe that . . . but there would be nothing they could do. It—it is hardly a good answer, but it is all I can think of." He was stammering, and that was ridiculous, because he was speaking the truth. "It's the only thing that makes any kind of sense," he went on desperately. "I can understand how she would defend him the only way she could think of. I know it's hopeless."

"I don't think Ramsay killed Unity, accidentally or with intent," Pitt replied. He seemed able to stand in the same spot without needing to move. His face was implacable. However much he hated this, he was not going to evade it or to stop until he was finished. "I think it was either Mallory or you."

Dominic could hear the blood rushing in his ears. He could think of nothing to say except denial.

"I didn't . . ." It was not much more than a whisper.

"Ramsay thought you did."

"Wh-why?" It was a blow so hard it left him reeling. Ramsay had believed that of him? That he had killed Unity, which could be an accident, or at least an understandable crime? Heaven knew, she provoked people to the limits. It was almost a surprise, when one thought of it, that no one had hurt her physically before.

But he had never acknowledged, even in his worst thoughts, that Ramsay believed he was guilty. How it must have crushed him. He had hoped so much of Dominic, believed so much. It was his one real success, the achievement no one could take from him, no one would draw doubt on or call into question. He could no longer believe in God. His fragile faith could not stand up to Darwin's ruthless reasoning. Evolution had swept away the foundation of his theology, leaving nothing behind. If God did not exist, how could one love Him? He had been left alone in a dark universe. But he had loved people—not all of them, but some. He had truly loved some. Dominic was one of them. That final failure must have been more than he could bear. Clarice was the only one who had never let him down, and in the end that was not enough.

"I didn't," he repeated helplessly. "I can't say I didn't have reason, if one can have reason for killing another person. She tried to manipulate me back into the old relationship, but I refused. There was nothing she could do except make a nuisance of herself, and she did that. But she couldn't afford to lose this position, and she knew I knew that." He smiled bitterly. There was a sour humor in it. "We had an equal power over each other."

"Was she in love with Ramsay?" Pitt asked.

"What?" It was an incredible question. Pitt could have understood nothing about Unity to have asked that. Or was he playing some devious game?

The sunlight faded at the far side of the room and rain spattered against the windows. Pitt moved to the ornate chair beside the fire and sat down at last.

"Could she have been in love with Ramsay?" he said again, carefully. He was watching Dominic's face for the tiniest change in his expression.

Dominic could have laughed, but he was too close to losing control of himself.

"No," he said more levelly than he had thought he was capable of. He sat down as well, a little sharply, as if his legs were not entirely in his control. "If you think that, then you don't understand Unity. Ramsay had qualities which might have made a woman love him, but she didn't see that sort of integrity as interesting or exciting." He loathed having to say this, but it was the truth, and Pitt had to understand. "She thought he was a bore, because she never saw his emotions. He didn't like her, so he never showed her his humor or his imagination or his warmth. She was always criticizing." A score of instances came to his mind. He could see the sneer on her face, the triumph in her eyes as if it had been only a moment ago. "She prevented the best in him from even showing itself in her company. I don't think she realized that, but it doesn't make any difference. He wasn't even worth a challenge. He was unobtainable, perhaps because to her there was nothing to obtain."

"A challenge?" Pitt lifted his eyebrows. "To destroy?"

"Yes . . . I suppose so. She resented the closed world of academia, which was entirely male dominated, to the exclusion of women no matter how excellent their scholarship—and hers was excellent." This also was true, and he could remember the finer part of her in saying it. "In her own field she was brilliant, far better than most men. I—I can't blame her for hating them. Their patronizing was insufferable, and in the end they paid lip service to her intellect and her talent, and then denied her the real chances. Appetite of the flesh was their one vulnerability, where she could beat them, wound them, even destroy them."

"Including Ramsay Parmenter?"

"I don't think so. I doubt she was a match for Vita, even had she wanted to be." He was reluctant to say this, but he had left himself no choice. "No. Her challenge here was Mallory. He was far more vulnerable, and a better victory anyway. Much more personable in the taking, and a deeper wound for Ramsay and to the Establishment. After all, he is not only sworn to chastity but to celibacy as well."

Pitt said nothing, but Dominic could see in his eyes that that at least he could believe.

Dominic swallowed. His tongue was sticking to his teeth. "I did not kill her," he said again. He could feel the panic welling up inside him to the verge of hysteria. He must control himself. He must keep his grip. It would pass. There would be a way out.

He rose to his feet, barely realizing he was doing it. The rain was beating against the windows now, a sudden spring storm.

There was no way out. It was tightening around him. The panic was there again, high in his throat. His heart was beating too fast. His skin was clammy. Pitt did not believe him. Why should he? Why should anyone? The judge would not; the jury would not.

They would hang him! How long was it from trial to the rope? Three weeks . . . three short weeks. The last day would come, the last hour . . . and then the pain . . . and nothing.

"Dominic!" Pitt's voice was sharp.

"Yes . . ." Pitt must be aware of his terror. He must be able to see it, even smell it. Would he believe it could be in an innocent man?

"You'd better sit down. You look dreadful."

"No . . . no. I'll be all right." Why had he said that? He was not all right. "Is that all you wanted?"

Pitt was still watching him closely. "For the moment. But I don't believe Ramsay killed her, and I mean to find out who did."

"Yes . . . of course." Dominic turned to leave.

"Oh . . ."

Dominic stopped. "What?"

"I found love letters between Ramsay and Unity, very passionate, very graphic. Do you know anything about those?"

"Love letters?" Dominic was amazed. Had the circumstances

been any different he would have suspected Pitt of making a bad joke, but he searched Pitt's face and saw no humor at all, only pain and harsh disappointment. "Are you sure?"

"They were in his study on the desk, in his writing and hers," Pitt replied. "They mirror each other. There was no question they are letter and reply. Mrs. Parmenter saw them when she went in to speak to him. That was what precipitated the quarrel and why he attacked her. It was obviously something about which he felt violently."

Dominic was lost for words. It was incredible. If it were true, then all his perceptions were false, everything he thought he knew was not so. It was as if he had touched snow and it had burned him.

"I can see you don't know anything," Pitt said dryly. "I wish I could say it cleared you of suspicion, but I am afraid it doesn't." He rose to his feet. "The fact that they wrote love letters suggests there was much for you to be jealous of, whether you loved her or not. And if Mallory was the father of her child—this time— there was that as well. She was a dangerous woman, both foolish and destructive. Perhaps it was only a matter of time before there was a tragedy. Don't leave Brunswick Gardens, Dominic." And with a bleak and unhappy little gesture, Pitt turned and went to the door.

When Pitt had left, Dominic stood alone in the room for minutes he did not count. He was unaware of the fire collapsing in a shower of sparks, and it was only when he heard the clock on the mantel strike the hour that the thought occurred to him that someone should have muffled it. He must tell Emsley. He was surprised that Clarice had not done so. Had Vita omitted it because she knew it had been suicide, and one part of her regarded that as a sin?

He refused to harbor that thought. It was filled with too much pain, a great tangle of it which seemed to touch everything.

He moved suddenly, striding out of the room, and almost bumped into Emsley in the hall.

"Where is Mallory?" he demanded.

Emsley looked startled. His hair stood out in wisps at the crown where his brush had missed it. The pink had gone from his skin, and he looked unbearably tired.

"I'm sorry," Dominic said quickly. "I did not mean to speak so abruptly."

Emsley's eyes opened wide. He was not used to anyone's apologizing to him. One did not apologize to servants. He did not know what to say.

"Do you know where Mr. Mallory is?" Dominic asked. He could not bring himself to say "Mr. Parmenter." That was still Ramsay. "And no one has muffled the clock in the withdrawing room. Would you do that, please?"

"Yes sir. I'm sorry, sir. It slipped my mind. I—I really am sorry."

"I daresay you had a lot of other things to care for, more important things, like seeing that the rest of the staff are coping." He looked at the older man closely. "Are they?"

"Oh yes, sir," Emsley replied, and Dominic knew he was lying.

"I'm sorry," he apologized again. "I haven't even been through to see them. I—I am too upset. It was very selfish of me. When I've seen Mr. Mallory, I'll come."

"Perhaps, sir, if you could come for grace before the evening meal, that would be a good time?" Emsley suggested. "It might be better after the day's work is over. Some of the maids could be . . . well, a bit emotional, if you understand me."

"Yes, of course." Dominic made a mental note to go, regardless of whatever else happened. They must be shocked by two deaths within days of each other, confused by the guilt and suspicion in the house, and the certain knowledge that one of the people they had served and depended upon, probably looked up to, was guilty of murder and now a death which was to them inexplicable. They must be wondering if it was accident, murder or suicide. The whole order they had grown up with, the safety that had surrounded them and provided all their physical needs, had collapsed. They must wonder whether they even had a home for the future. In the aftermath of Ramsay's death the household would break up, and they might easily be homeless. Vita could not remain in church property now. The house would automatically pass to the next incumbent. It was something he had not even thought of. His own emotions had taken over his mind completely, driving out everything else.

"Mr. Mallory is in the library, sir," Emsley told him. "Sir, Mr. Corde . . ."

Dominic waited, already half turned to face the library door.

"Thank you . . ."

Dominic forced a quick smile, then strode across the mosaic, his feet surprisingly loud. He would never get used to the sound of it. He flung the library door open without even bothering to knock. He closed it behind him.

Mallory was on his knees beside the lowest bookshelf. He looked up, irritated at the intrusion, then surprised to see who it was. He arose slowly, his back to the brown velvet curtains and the wet windows, gleaming now as the sun struck them.

"What is it?" There was a thin thread of rancor in his voice. He was the master now. The sooner Dominic realized it the better. Things would not continue as they had been in the past. "Did you want me?" he added.

"Pitt has just been here," Dominic said peremptorily. "This can't go on. I won't permit it."

"Then tell him to go." Mallory's face showed his impatience. "If you can't deal with that, I will." He moved forward as if to do so that moment.

Dominic remained with his back to the door.

"Pitt is police. He'll come here as often as he wants to until the case is solved to his satisfaction . . ."

"It is solved." Mallory stopped a couple of yards in front of Dominic. "I can't think of anything further to say. It is a tragedy best left to sink into as much forgetfulness as we can manage. If that is all you have come for, then please allow me to continue studying. That at least serves some purpose."

"It is not solved. Your father did not kill Unity . . ."

Mallory's face was tight and bleak. "Yes, he did. For God's sake, Dominic, this is hard enough for the family without raking it over and trying to find ways to escape the truth. There is no escape! Have the courage and the honor to accept that, and if the word applies to you, the faith."

"I am trying to." Dominic heard the anger in his own voice, and the contempt which was for himself as well as for Mallory, standing looking so sullen and defiant. "One of the truths to acknowledge is that Ramsay thought I killed her."

Mallory's eyes opened very wide. "Is that a confession?" His face was full of doubt and new pain as well. "Aren't you a little late? Father is dead. You cannot bring him back now. It's not much use being honest, or sorry . . ."

"No, it's not a confession!" Dominic snapped. "I am pointing out that if Ramsay thought I killed her, then it follows that he could not have, and I didn't. That only leaves you, and you had reason enough."

Mallory was suddenly white. "I didn't!" His body was stiff, shoulders raised high. "I did not kill her!" But there was an unmistakable edge of fear in his voice.

"You had every reason," Dominic insisted. "It was your child! What would it do to your career, your ambitions—"

"The priesthood is not an ambition!" Mallory burst out, anger flushing up his cheeks. He was standing in front of the large desk, the sunlight making patterns on the oak floor. He looked very young. "It is a calling," he said critically. "A service to God, a way of life. You may do it to earn yourself money, recognition, even fame, I don't know. But I do it because I know it is the truth."

"Don't be childish," Dominic said angrily, turning away. "We each do it for lots of reasons. It may be pure one day, and arrogant or cowardly or simply stupid another. That is not the point." He stared back at Mallory. "Unity was carrying your child. She was, if not blackmailing you, certainly using pressure to make you do what she wanted, and enjoying the power. Did she threaten to tell your bishop?" He shook his head. "No, don't bother to answer that. It wasn't worth it. Whatever she said, you must have known she could."

Mallory was sweating. "I didn't kill her!" he said yet again. "She wasn't going to ruin me. She just—just liked the power. She thought it was funny. She laughed, because she knew . . ." He closed his eyes, realizing what he had said and how much it condemned him. "I didn't kill her!"

"Then why did you lie about seeing her that morning?" Dominic challenged him.

"I didn't! I was in the conservatory . . . studying! I didn't see her!" Mallory's voice was high and indignant, but the fear was a sharp note behind it all the time, and Dominic could see and feel it in the air. He must be lying. If Ramsay had not killed her, it could only be Mallory. Dominic knew he was innocent at least of that. Guilty of having got her with child before, certainly guilty of every tragedy of Jenny's, guilty of failing to help Ramsay, of letting him die of misery, loneliness and despair . . . but not of Unity's death.

"If she wasn't in the conservatory, how did she get the stain on her shoe?" he said coldly. He could understand the terror which made Mallory lie even now, when it was hopeless, but he also hated it. It robbed him of the last shred of dignity. It stretched out the pain of this more than it had to be. And he could not forgive him for having allowed Ramsay to be blamed for his guilt. Fear was one thing, even cowardice, but to stand by and watch someone else suffer for your sin was of a different order.

"I don't know!" Mallory was shaking. "It doesn't make any sense. I can't explain it. I only know I didn't leave the conservatory and she didn't come in."

"She must have," Dominic said wearily. "She couldn't have got that on her shoe anywhere else. She trod in it on the conservatory floor as she left."

"Then why didn't I?" There was a sudden surge of hope in Mallory's voice, and he waved his arm as if the movement somehow released him. "Why was there no stain on my shoes?"

"Wasn't there?" Dominic raised his eyebrows. "I don't know that."

"Well, go and look!" Mallory shouted at him, jerking his head towards the door. "Go and look at all my shoes! You won't find any stain on any of them."

"Why not? Did you clean it off? Or did you destroy the shoes?"

"Neither, damn you! I never left the conservatory."

Dominic said nothing. Could that conceivably be true? How could it be possible? If it was not Mallory, then it must have been Ramsay after all. Had he been really, truly mad? So mad he had blanked from his mind what he had done, and believed himself innocent?

"Go and look!" Mallory repeated. "Ask Stander, he'll tell you I haven't thrown away any shoes."

"Or cleaned it off?" Dominic could not easily let go. It meant Ramsay must have been guilty after all, and after the reprieve Pitt had given him, it was too difficult to go back and accept his guilt and the madness that had to go with it. There was something very frightening about madness, something unreachable, something there was no way of dealing with.

"I don't know!" Mallory slashed the air, his voice high and loud. Any servants in the hall must be able to hear him. "I never tried! I never saw the stuff! But probably not—not if it was a stain. It would go into the leather. You can't get chemical stains out of things. Ordinary stains are bad enough, according to Stander."

There was nothing to do but go and look. There was certainly no point in remaining there in the library confronting Mallory.

"I will look." He made it a challenge, then turned and went back into the hall and up the stairs. "Stander!" he called brusquely. "Stander!"

The valet was nowhere to be seen, which in the circumstances was hardly surprising.

Braithwaite appeared. "Can I help you, sir?" She looked tired and frightened. She had been with the family for years, since she was a young woman. Had anyone bothered to think about the servants' emotions, their grief and sense of shock and confusion, their fears for the future?

"I need to look at Mr. Mallory's shoes . . . with his permission. It is important."

"All his shoes?" She was totally confused.

"Yes. Will you find Stander for me, please? Immediately."

She agreed with some obvious misgiving, and Dominic had to wait nearly ten minutes before Stander came up the stairs looking deeply unhappy. Apparently he had checked with Mallory, because he made no demur but went straight to Mallory's dressing room and opened both wardrobes to show the neat rows of shoes with their trees all in place.

"Do you know which ones he was wearing the day Miss Bellwood died?" Dominic asked.

"I'm not sure, sir. It would be either these"—he pointed to a pair of fairly well worn black leather boots—"or these." He indicated another pair, rather newer.

"Thank you." Dominic reached forward and picked up the first pair, taking them over to the window and holding them to the sunlight. They were immaculate. The soles were thin with use, but there were no stains on them, nor any marks of recent scraping such as might be needed to remove a chemical.

He put them down and picked up the other pair Stander had indicated. He examined them in the same way. They also were perfectly clean.

"Had he any more he might have worn that day?" he asked.

"No sir, I believe not." Stander looked totally mystified.

"I'll look at them all anyway." Dominic made it a statement. He was not asking permission. Certainly he would not be diverted now from finding the truth or be misled by the wrong pair of shoes. He picked them up one by one and searched the entire collection, not that there were so many. Mallory was far from extravagant, seven pairs in all, including a very old pair of riding boots. None of them had any chemical stains.

"Did you find what you were looking for, sir?" Stander asked anxiously.

"No. But then I don't think I wanted to." He did not explain what he meant. He was not even sure if it were true. "Are these all? I mean, there isn't a pair missing? In the last two weeks?"

Stander was confused and unhappy, his normally smooth face puckered with concern.

"No sir. These are all the shoes Mr. Mallory has owned since he has been home again, so far as I know. Apart from those he has on, of course."

"Oh . . . yes. I forgot about those. Thank you." Dominic closed the wardrobe door. There were two more things to do, check the shoes that Mallory was wearing at the moment, and speak to the gardener's boy and find out exactly where the chemical was spilled, what it was and how long it would have remained wet enough to have marked anything that touched it.

"I dunno wot it's called, sir," the boy answered with a frown. "Yer'd 'ave ter ask Mr. Bostwick about that. But it don't stay wet more'n an hour, outside. I stood in it meself arter that, an' it din't mark nothin'."

"Are you sure?" Dominic pressed him. They were standing on the stone paving just outside the conservatory. It was bright sunlight through an ever-widening rent in the clouds, but every leaf and blade of grass was tremulous with drops of rain.

"Yes sir, pos'tive sure," the boy replied.

"Do you know what time you spilled it?"

"No . . . not really . . ."

"Even a guess? Before Miss Bellwood fell down the stairs, but how long before? You remember that?" Dominic stood on the wet stones, oblivious of the beauty around him, his mind filled only with times and stains.

"Oh, yes sir! 'Course I do." The boy looked shocked at the idea that anyone could think he might forget such a thing.

"Think back to what you were doing, and what you did after that, until you heard about the—the death," Dominic urged.

The boy considered for several moments. "Well, I were cleaning out the pots for the ferns. That's w'y I 'ad the stuff," he said seriously. "Gotter be terrible careful o' red mites an' them little spiders. Eats leaves summink rotten, they do." His face expressed his opinion of such things. "Never get rid o' them. Then I watered the narcissuses and the 'yacinths. Smell lovely, they do. Them ones wi' the little orange centers is me favorites—narcissuses, I mean. Mr. Mallory were studyin', so I couldn't sweep up 'is end. 'E don' like ter be interrupted." He did not comment as to what a nuisance this was, but his expression was eloquent. Theological studies were all very well in their place, but their place was not the conservatory, where people were busy attending to growing things.

"Did you sweep the rest?" Dominic persisted.

"Yes sir, I did."

"Did Mr. Mallory leave at all?"

"I dunno, sir. I went out ter work in the garden fer a while, seein' as I couldn't finish inside. S'pose I must'a spilt the stuff about 'alf an hour afore Miss Bellwood fell, mebbe a few minutes more'n that."

"Not an hour?"

"No sir," he said vehemently. "Mr. Bostwick 'd 'ave 'ad me fer dinner if I'd took an hour ter do that!"

"So it must have been still wet when Miss Bellwood fell down the stairs."

"Yes sir, must 'ave."

"Thank you."

There was only one thing left to do, although he was sure in his mind that it would yield nothing, and so it proved. The shoes Mallory was wearing were as clean as all those in his wardrobes.

"Thank you," Dominic said bleakly, without explaining himself any further, and went back to his own room feeling wretched.

Mallory was not guilty. He believed it. He was not sure whether he was glad or not. It meant Ramsay had been, and that hurt deeply. But at least Ramsay himself was beyond pain now, beyond earthly pain anyway. What lay farther than that was more than he dared imagine.

But Pitt believed Ramsay was innocent. Which meant he would have to believe Dominic guilty.

He paced back and forth from the window to the bookcase, and to the window, turned and back to the bookcase. The sunlight was bright across the floor and he barely noticed it.

Pitt would be hurt. He would hate having to arrest Dominic, for Charlotte's sake. But he would do it! Part of him would even find satisfaction in it. It would vindicate his judgment of all those years ago in Cater Street.

Charlotte would be terribly grieved. She had been so happy for him that he had found a vocation. There had been no shadow in her pleasure. This would crush her. But she would not believe Pitt had made a mistake. Perhaps that was something she could not afford to believe. And if she did, it would not help Dominic. All it would do would be to tear her emotions.

But what cut him the most deeply was what Clarice would feel. She had loved her father, and she had believed in Dominic. Now she would think of him with loathing and the kind of contempt he could not bear to imagine. It took his breath away even to stand in this familiar room—with its red Turkish carpet, polished wooden clock on the mantel, and the sound of leaves beyond the window—and think of it. And it had not even happened yet! He had never realized before how much Clarice's opinion of him mattered. There was no reason why it should. It should be Vita he thought of. Ramsay had been her husband. This was her home. She was the one who had turned to him in her anxiety, her grief. She was the one who trusted him, saw in him a good man, full of strength and courage, honor, faith. She even believed he could make a great leader in the church, a beacon to guide others.

Clarice had never professed to think him destined for any kind of greatness. It was Vita whose dreams he would break, whose disillusion would be crippling on top of her bereavement and the total loss of not only what her husband was but of what he had been. She would have to believe that Dominic had killed Unity. Pitt would surely tell her why. At least what he thought was why: about their past love affair—if *love* was the word?

Had Unity loved him? Or merely been in love, that consuming need for another person which might include gentleness, generosity, patience and the ability to give of the heart, but also might not. It could so easily be simply a mixture of enchantment and hunger, a loneliness temporarily kept at bay.

Had Unity loved him?

Had he loved her?

He thought back on it, trying to remember it honestly. It hurt for many reasons, but mostly because he was ashamed of it. No, he had not loved her. He had been fascinated, excited, challenged. When she had responded it had been uniquely exhilarating. She was different from all his past acquaintances, more intensely alive than any other woman he had known, and certainly cleverer. And she was passionate.

She had also been possessive and at times cruel. He could think more sharply now of her cruelty to other people than to him. He had felt no gentleness, and nothing like the kind of pity that would have satisfied his present need. With the harsh honesty of hindsight, everything he had felt for her had been innately selfish.

He stood at the window staring at the new, unfolding leaf buds.

Had he ever truly loved anyone?

He had cared for Sarah. There had been far more tenderness in that, more sense of sharing. But he had also become bored by her, because he was concerned primarily with his own appetite, his desire for excitement, change, flattery, the sense of power in new conquests.

How childish he had been.

He could retrieve something now by going to Pitt and telling him that Mallory was innocent. Pitt might well decide to check the stain on the conservatory floor for himself. But he might not. Mallory would tell him, as he had told Dominic. Would he be believed?

The shadow of the noose was already forming over Dominic, and it would take real and tangible shape soon enough. He was innocent. Ramsay believed himself innocent.

Mallory was innocent.

What could Pitt believe? The only other person in the house unaccounted for was Clarice. Vita and Tryphena had been together downstairs. It was physically impossible they could be guilty. The servants had all been within each other's sight, or so occupied as to have been unable to leave their positions unobserved.

He simply could not bring himself to think Clarice guilty. Why would she? She had no possible reason.

Except to save Mallory, if she knew the truth about Unity's child and her power to ruin Mallory because of it.

Or if she had read the love letters Pitt spoke of, which defied explanation, and she panicked. Had Unity even told her, and threatened to ruin Ramsay?

He could not believe it. Perhaps Clarice, like everyone he knew, could have gone into a moment's rage or pain, a fear beyond her to master or in which to think clearly or see beyond the terrible, overwhelming moment?

But Clarice would never have allowed Ramsay to have been blamed. Whatever the cost would have been to herself, she would have come forward and told the truth.

Would she? He believed it. He had not realized he held her in such extraordinary esteem, but he did. Suddenly it filled his mind. There was pain in it, but also a kind of elation which was more than simply a recognition of truth.

Still he was startled some time later when there was a knock on his door and she stood in the entrance, white-faced. He found himself stammering slightly.

"Wh-what is it? Has something—"

"No," she said quickly, attempting a smile. "Everyone is alive and well—at least I believe so. There have been no screams in the last half hour."

"Please, Clarice!" He spoke impulsively. "Don't . . ."

"I know." She came in and closed the door behind her, but stood with both hands still on the knob, leaning against it. "It is a time to be deadly serious—I mean . . . grave." She shut her eyes. "Oh, God!" she whispered. "I can't get it right, can I?"

He was obliged to smile in spite of himself. "No," he agreed gently. "It would seem not. Do you want to try again?"

"Thank you." She opened her eyes wide. They were clear and very dark gray. "Are you all right? I know you had another visit from that policeman. He's your brother-in-law, but . . ."

He meant to be discreet, not to burden her with the decisions he had to make, the uncertainties, the cost.

"You aren't all right, are you?" she said softly. "Did Mallory do it?"

He could not lie. He had struggled for hours with what to do, what to say to Pitt, with the fear of what would happen, what his own conscience would do to him if he did nothing. Now the decision was taken from him.

"No, he didn't," he answered. "He couldn't have."

"Couldn't he?" She was uncertain. She knew it was not necessarily good news. There was apprehension in her eyes, not relief.

He did not look away. "No. The chemical that was spilled across the conservatory path was wet at the time Unity was killed. It was on her shoes, but it wasn't on his. I checked it all with the garden boy, and with Stander. I looked at all Mallory's shoes. He's still lying about her going in there to speak to him. I don't know why. It is completely pointless. But he didn't come out, so he couldn't have been at the top of the stairs."

"So it was Papa . . ." She looked stricken. It was a truth almost more than she knew how to bear.

He responded instinctively, reaching out and taking her hands in his.

"He believed it was me," he said, dreading her response, the moment when she would pull away from him in revulsion, as she must. But he could not let the lie build itself between them. "Pitt found his journal and deciphered it. He really believed I had killed Unity . . ."

She looked puzzled. "Why? Because you knew her before?"

He felt a numbness creep through him, a prickling.

"You knew that?" His voice was hoarse.

"She told me." A smile flickered over her face. "She thought I was in love with you, and she wanted to stop me from doing anything about it. She thought it would anger me or make me dislike you." She gave a jerky little laugh. "She told me you had been lovers and that you had left her." She waited for him to respond.

At that instant he would have given anything he possessed to be able to tell her it was untrue, the fabrication of a jealous woman. But one lie necessitated another, and he would destroy the only relationship he had which had a cleanness to it, an unselfishness not spoiled by appetite, illusion or deceit. When it was shattered, at least it would be by the past, not the present. He would not sacrifice the future for a few days, or hours, until Pitt broke it.

"I did leave her," he admitted. "She aborted our child, and I was so horrified, and grieved, I ran away. I realized we did not love each other, only ourselves, our own hungers. That doesn't justify any of it, or what I did afterwards. I didn't set out to be dishonest, but I was. I had other loves, was innocent enough to believe a woman could share a man with another woman. And then when she was . . . vulnerable . . . to discover she couldn't." He still could not put the true words to it. "I should have known that. I could have, had I been honest. I was old enough and experienced enough not to have believed that lie. I allowed myself because I wanted to."

She was staring at him unwaveringly.

He would like to have stopped, but he would only have to tell her later, begin all over again. Better to complete it now, no matter how hard it was. He let go of her hands. He would not allow himself to feel her pull away.

"I did not want the commitment of one love, of responsibility during the hard times as well as the easy ones," he said, hearing his voice sounding flat and mundane for such terrible words. "It was your father who pulled me out of my despair after Jenny killed herself and I knew I was to blame for it. He taught me courage and forgiveness. He taught me there is no going back, only forward. If I wanted to make anything of my life, of myself, then I must work my way out of the slough I had dug myself into." He swallowed. "And then when he needed me, I was not able to do anything. I stood by helplessly and watched him drown."

"We all did," she whispered, her voice thick with tears. "I did, too. I had no idea what was happening, or why. I believe, and I couldn't help his unbelief. I loved him, and I couldn't see what was happening with Unity. I still don't understand. Did he love her, or simply need something she could give him?"

"I don't know. I don't understand either." Without thinking he took her hands again, and his fingers tightened around hers. "But I must tell Pitt it wasn't Mallory, and he already believes it wasn't your father. That only leaves me, and I can't prove to him I didn't. I think he may arrest me."

She drew in her breath sharply and seemed about to say something, then she did not.

What else was there to say? A score of things poured into his mind. He should apologize for all the hurt he had caused her, for all he had been which was shallow and in the end self-serving and pointless, for all the promises he had made, implicitly, and had failed to live up to, and for what was yet to come. He wanted to tell her how much she mattered to him, that he cared intensely what she thought of him, what she felt in return. But that would be unfair. It would only place another burden on her, when she already had so much.

"I'm sorry," he said, lowering his eyes. "I wanted to be so much better than I have been. I suppose I started really trying much too late."

"You didn't kill Unity, did you?" It was barely a question, more of a statement, and her voice was not tremulous, seeking help, rather demanding confirmation.

"No."

"Then I will do everything I can to see you are not blamed for it. I'll fight everybody I have to!" she answered fiercely.

He looked at her.

Slowly the color filled her face. Her eyes had betrayed her, and she knew it. She avoided him for an instant, then gave up a hopeless task.

"I love you," she admitted. "You don't have to say anything, except for heaven's sake, don't be grateful. I couldn't bear it!"

He started to laugh, because what she feared was so far from anything he felt. Gratitude certainly, overwhelming, joyous gratitude, even if it was too late and there could never be anything ahead of them but struggle and grief. It was the most precious thing to know, and whatever Pitt said or did, whatever he believed, he could not take that away.

"Why are you laughing?" she demanded hotly.

He held on to her hands although she was pulling away.

"Because that is about the only thing on earth that could make me happy just at the moment," he answered. "It is the only good and clean and sweet thing in all this tragedy. I didn't realize it until just before you came in. I seem to see everything really precious when it is too late, but I love you, too."

"Do you?" she said with surprise.

"Yes. Yes, I do!"

"Really?" She frowned for a moment, searching his face, his eyes, his mouth. Then when she saw the truth of it, she reached up and very delicately kissed his lips.

He hesitated, then closed his arms around her and held her, kissed her, and then again, and again. He would go and speak to Pitt . . . but later. This hour might be all there was; he must make it last so he could remember it forever.

CHAPTER
TWELVE

Pitt lay in bed and thought about the evening with a sense of surprise still keeping him wide awake. Dominic had been to see him to tell him that Mallory was not guilty, that he could not be. Pitt already knew the facts and their meaning; Tellman had investigated them on his instruction days before.

What startled him was that Dominic should have seen the proof himself and should have brought it to Pitt, knowing how it had to affect his own position. And yet he had done so, clear-eyed and without equivocation. It had cost him dearly, that much had been very plain in his face. He had looked as if he expected Pitt to take him into custody there and then. He had flinched, but kept his head high. He had searched Pitt's eyes for the contempt he foresaw . . . and he had not found it. Curiously, the emotion that came to Pitt was respect. For the first time since they had met each other, as far back as Cater Street, Pitt had felt a surge of deep and quite genuine admiration for him.

For an instant Dominic had seen it and a faint flush of pleasure had colored his face. Then it had gone again as the truth of his situation returned to him.

Pitt had acknowledged what he had said without telling him he

359

already knew. He had thanked Dominic and allowed him to depart, saying only that he would continue to investigate the matter.

Now he lay close to sleep, but still as confused as he had been at the very beginning. The matter was not solved. It could not have been Mallory. He did not believe it was Dominic, although he had had every reason and every opportunity. There were too many contradictions in Ramsay's guilt for Pitt to accept that with any ease. And yet could it really be Clarice? That was the only other answer, and that did not seem right, either. When he had suggested it to Charlotte she had dismissed it out of hand as totally ridiculous. Not that that was an argument against its possibility, only against its likelihood.

He drifted into restless sleep, half waking every hour or two, and then finally a little before five he was wide awake and his mind turned again to the love letters between Ramsay and Unity Bellwood. He could not understand them. They fitted in with nothing that he knew of either person.

He lay in the dark for half an hour trying to think of anything that would make sense of them, trying to imagine the circumstances in which they could have been composed. What could Ramsay have been feeling to have risked putting pen to paper with such words? He must have been in so great a heat of passion all sense of his own danger had left him. And why write to her when she was there in the house and he could see her within hours, if not minutes? It was the action of a man who had lost all sense of proportion, a man verging on madness.

It came back to that again and again: madness.

Had Ramsay been mad? Was the answer as simple and as tragic as that?

He slipped out of bed, shivering as his bare feet touched the cold floor. He must look at those letters again. Perhaps they would contain some explanation if he studied them enough.

He picked up his clothes. He would dress in the kitchen, so as not to waken Charlotte. It was far too early to disturb her. He tiptoed across the room and pulled the door open. It made a slight squeak, but he managed to close it again silently, or almost.

Downstairs was chilly. The warmth of the evening before had dissipated and only immediately next to the stove could he still feel any heat. At least Gracie had left the scuttle full, to save herself this morning. He lit the lamp and dressed first, then riddled the dead cinders through and after a few moments managed to get the fire going again. He put coals on it very carefully. If he swamped it he would put it out completely. It was definitely a skill.

While it was catching and burning up he filled the kettle and looked out the teapot and fetched the caddy from the cupboard. He took the largest breakfast cup off the hook on the dresser, with its saucer. The fire was burning quite well. He put two more pieces of coal on, then closed the lid. Within moments the stove was beginning to warm. He set the kettle on it, then went through to the parlor and found the letters and the journal again.

Back in the kitchen, he sat down at the table and started to read.

He had been through them all once and was beginning a second time when the sound of the boiling kettle penetrated his thoughts and he put them down and made himself a pot of tea. He had forgotten milk, so he went to the larder and fetched a jug, carefully taking off the little circle of muslin with its trim of beads which kept it covered. He poured the tea and sipped it gingerly. It was too hot.

The letters still made no sense in the pattern of things as he knew them. He sat with the papers spread in front of him and stared, still sipping at the tea and blowing at it now and then. He was achieving nothing, and he knew it.

He did not know how long he sat there, but his cup was nearly empty when he heard Charlotte come in. He looked around. She was wearing her nightgown and a thick dressing robe. He had bought it for her when the children were very small and she had had to get up and down several times during the night, but it still looked soft and very flattering wrapped around her. There were only one or two small mends in it, and a little discoloration on one shoulder where Jemima had been sick, but it could only be seen in a certain light; otherwise it looked like the natural shading of the fabric.

"Are these the love letters?" she asked.

"Yes. Would you like a cup of tea? It's still hot."

"Yes, please." She sat down, leaving him to fetch another cup and pour it for her. She started to read the letter nearest to her, frowning as she did.

He put the tea beside her but she was too absorbed to notice. She picked up a second letter, and a third, and a fourth and fifth. He watched her face and saw incredulity and amazement deepen into a fierce concentration as she read faster and faster.

"Your tea's getting cold," he observed.

"Mm . . ." she replied absently.

"Extraordinary, aren't they?" he went on.

"Mm . . ."

"Can you think why he would write such things?" he asked.

"What?" She looked up for the first time. She put her hand out absently for the cup and sipped from it. She pulled a face. "It's cold!"

"I told you."

"What?"

"I told you it was getting cold."

"Oh. Did you?"

He stood up patiently, took the cup from her and poured the tepid tea down the sink, then took the kettle and topped up the teapot, left it a moment, then poured her a fresh cup.

"Thank you." She smiled and took it.

"Waited on hand and foot," he murmured, sitting down again and refilling his own cup.

"Thomas . . ." She was thinking deeply. She had not even heard what he had said. She was placing the letters in pairs.

"Letter and answer?" he asked. "They do seem to go in twos, don't they?"

"No . . ." she said with rising intensity in her voice. "No, they're not letters and answers. Look at them! Look at them carefully. Look at the way this one begins." She started to read.

" 'You who are dearest to me, how can I express to you the loneliness I feel when we are separated? The distance between us is immeasurable, and yet thoughts may fly across it, and I can reach you in heart and mind—' "

"I know what it says," he interrupted. "It's nonsense. The distance between them was nothing at all, a different room in the same house, at the most."

She dismissed him with an impatient little jerk of her head. "And look at this: 'My own beloved, my hunger for you is inexpressible. When we are apart I drown in a void of loneliness, engulfed in the night. Infinity yawns between us. And yet I have but to think of you and neither heaven nor hell could bar my way. The void disappears and you are with me.' " She stopped, staring at him. "Well, don't you see?"

"No," he admitted. "It is still absurd, just more dramatically put. All her letters are more intense than his, and phrased a great deal more graphically. I told you that before."

"No!" she said urgently, leaning forward over the table. "I mean, it is almost exactly the same thought—just more passionately worded! They all fall into pairs, Thomas. Idea for idea. Even in the same order."

He put down his cup. "What are you saying?"

"I don't think they're love letters at all—I mean, not in the sense that they wrote them to each other," she answered eagerly. "They were both students of ancient literature: he only of theological things, but she of all sorts. I think these are two different translations of the same originals."

"What?"

"The rather drier ones are his, in his hand." She pointed to them. "The more graphic, more passionate ones are hers. She saw the sexual connotations in them, or put it there herself; he was much more metaphorical or spiritual. I'd lay a wager with you that if we search the house, probably the study, we'll find the original Latin or Greek or Hebrew, or whatever, of these letters." Again she waved her hand at them, touching her cup with the sleeve of her gown. "They were probably written by some early saint who fell away, or was drawn into temptation by some wretched woman, no doubt branded an eternal sinner for her ability to draw the said saint away from the path of sanctity. But whoever he was, we'll find one original from which each pair of these is taken." She pushed them across to him, her face shining with certainty.

He took them slowly and placed them side by side, comparing the passages as she pointed to them. She was right. All through they were essentially the same ideas expressed in different ways, or by two personalities who were utterly unlike in all their perceptions, their emotions, their use of words, every way in which they saw the world both without and within.

"Yes . . ." he said with rapidly growing assurance also. "Yes . . . they are! Ramsay and Unity were never in love. These are only one more issue over which they couldn't agree. He saw them as declarations of divine love; she saw them as passionate love between a man and a woman, and interpreted them as such. He kept them all because they were part of whatever it was he was working on."

She smiled back at him. "Exactly. It makes infinitely more sense. The idea of Ramsay being the father of her child can be forgotten completely." She made a sweeping movement with her hand and nearly knocked the milk jug onto the floor.

Pitt moved it to a safer place.

"Which leaves Mallory," she said with a frown. "And he swears he did not leave the conservatory, and yet that he didn't see Unity, either. And we know she went in there while he was there, because of the stain on her shoe."

"And he didn't leave the conservatory during that time," he agreed, "because there was no stain on his shoes."

"You checked?"

"Of course I checked. So did Tellman."

"So she went in . . . and he didn't leave . . . so he lied. Why? If he could prove he didn't leave the conservatory, what difference does it make if she went in and spoke to him or not?"

"None," he conceded. He drank his tea. Actually, he was getting hungry. "I'll make some toast." He stood up.

"You'll burn it," she observed, standing also. "Perhaps I should make breakfast? Would you like eggs?"

"Yes, please." He sat down again quickly, smiling.

She gave him a look of swift understanding of exactly what he had done, but was quite happy to cook, after directing him to stoke the fire again.

It was about half an hour later when they were enjoying bacon, eggs, toast and marmalade and a fresh pot of tea that she returned to the subject.

"It doesn't make a great deal of sense as it is," she said with her mouth full. "But if we could find the originals of those letters, we could at least be sure there was no affair between Ramsay and Unity. Apart from coming closer to the truth, don't you think in honor we should do that? Her family must be heartbroken. Mrs. Parmenter must feel utterly betrayed. I couldn't bear it if I thought you could write letters like that to someone else."

He nearly swallowed his bacon whole.

She burst into laughter. "All right, they are not quite your way of putting things," she agreed.

"Not quite . . ." He gulped with difficulty.

"But we should go and look," she urged, reaching for the teapot.

"Yes, I'll have Tellman do it tomorrow."

"Tellman! He wouldn't know a clerical love letter if it landed on his breakfast table in front of him."

"Not very likely," he said dryly.

"I think we should go. Today would be a good time."

"It's Sunday!" he protested.

"I know that. There will probably be no one at home."

"There'll be everybody at home!"

"No, there won't. They are a church family. They'll all be at the Sunday service. There'll probably be a memorial for Ramsay. They'll be bound to be there."

He hesitated. He wanted to spend the day quietly at home with his wife and children. On the other hand, if they could find the letters it would prove that Ramsay was innocent at least of that. Which would not help a great deal.

But the longer he thought of it, the more he was driven to seek the truth immediately. He could put it off until tomorrow and do it when the whole family was at home. It would be more open and more distressing for them then. And he would have no pleasure today because his mind would be still on Ramsay Parmenter until the question was answered.

"Yes . . . I suppose so," he agreed, finishing the last of his bacon and stretching across for the toast and marmalade. "We might as well do it now as wait until tomorrow."

Charlotte never even contemplated the possibility of being left in Keppel Street while Pitt went to Brunswick Gardens. He could not conduct a satisfactory search without her. The matter did not arise.

They reached the front door at a quarter to eleven, an excellent time to find everyone away from home, either already at church or on their way. Emsley let them in, registering only the faintest surprise at seeing Charlotte.

"Good morning, Emsley," Pitt said with a brief smile. "It came to me at the breakfast table this morning how certain letters which seemed to implicate Mr. Parmenter in unfortunate conduct might actually have a very different, and quite innocent, explanation."

"Indeed, sir?" Emsley's face brightened.

"Yes. It was Mrs. Pitt who prompted the idea. It is something with which she is familiar, so I brought her with me in order to recognize it the more certainly. If I may go into Mr. Parmenter's study, I shall search through his papers for the original. That will prove the matter."

"Yes, yes, of course, sir!" Emsley said eagerly. "I am afraid the family are all at church, Mr. Pitt. It is a memorial service for Mr. Parmenter, and likely to take some little while. I'm sorry, sir. May I offer you any refreshment?" He turned to Charlotte. "Ma'am?"

She smiled at him charmingly. "No, thank you. But I think we should begin with the matter at hand. If we can conclude it before anyone returns, it would be the most heartening news we could offer them."

"Indeed, ma'am. I do hope so!" Emsley backed towards the stairs even as he spoke, eager to have them on their way, and bowed slightly, excusing himself.

Pitt started up and Charlotte followed him, glancing at the extraordinary hall with its mosaic floor and rich colored tiles on the wall along the first stage, and the Corinthian pillars supporting the landing. It really was most unusual. The huge potted palm at the bottom beneath the upper newel seemed almost ordinary by comparison. It was directly beneath where Unity would have stood when she was pushed. Charlotte hesitated as Pitt strode across the landing towards the study. She would follow him in a moment.

She turned and looked down the stairs at the hallway. It was beautiful, but she could not imagine it as home. What a seething passion there must have been in this house to cause so violent an eruption and two deaths . . . what love—and hate.

Pitt and Dominic between them had told her much of Unity, and she was fairly sure that she would not have liked her. But there were certain aspects of her character that Charlotte admired, and she understood something of Unity's frustration, the arrogance and the condescension which had made her strike back. The injustice was intolerable.

But she had aborted Dominic's child. That Charlotte could never understand, when Dominic was there and prepared to marry her. It was not done from fear, desperation, or the feeling of having been betrayed.

What of the child she had been carrying when she died? Had she intended to abort this one also? She was at least three months into the pregnancy. She must have been well aware of her condition. Charlotte remembered her own pregnancies—first with Jemima, then with Daniel. She had been sick only a little, but the giddiness and the nausea had been too pronounced ever to doubt or to ignore. At first she had not put on any weight, but by the third month there was a pronounced thickening around her waist, and other alterations of a more intimate nature.

Pitt came back out of the study door, looking for her.

She went up the last step and across the landing.

"Sorry," she apologized hastily, following him in and closing the door.

He looked at her. "Are you all right?"

"Yes. Yes, I was just thinking . . . about Unity, how she felt."

He touched her very gently, holding her arm for a moment, meeting her eyes, then went back to the bookcases, where he had already started searching for the originals of the letters.

She began with the lower shelves and flipped through one book after another, setting each aside as it proved irrelevant.

"I'm going to look in the library," she said after about fifteen minutes. "If she was working down there, it could be there rather than here."

"Good idea," he agreed. "I'll finish all these and the ones behind the desk."

But when she was outside, another thought seized her, and glancing around to make sure no one was in sight, she slipped along the corridor towards the bedrooms. She tried the first one, and guessed it was Tryphena's from the book by Mary Wollstonecraft on the bedside table. The furniture was mainly in pinks, which somehow suited Tryphena's soft coloring.

The next room was far larger and extremely feminine, even

though the colors were bolder and it had an exotic and very modern air, rather like the main reception room of the house. This was Vita's taste—touches of the Arabic, the Turkish, and even a Chinese lacquered box by the window.

She stepped in and closed the door, her heart beating high in her chest. There was no earthly excuse if she were caught here. Please heaven the maids were all at the service!

She tiptoed across to the dressing table, glanced at the jars of lavender water, attar of roses, the hairbrushes and combs. Then she opened the top drawer. There were several little pillboxes, some gilded and enameled, one of carved soapstone, one of ivory. She unscrewed the first. Half a dozen pills. They could have been anything. She undid the second. A pair of gold cuff links with initials engraved on them—D.C. Dominic Corde!

She replaced the top with hands trembling a little. She searched further. She found a handkerchief with a *D* embroidered on it. There was a pearl-faced collar stud, a small penknife, a single glove, a note for a sermon written on the back of a menu but in Dominic's writing. She knew it from years ago. It had not changed.

She closed the drawer with both hands shaking so visibly she had to sit still and breathe deeply for several moments before she could compose herself sufficiently to stand up and cross back to the door. She could feel her face burning with memory. Ten years ago she had been obsessed with Dominic, so in love with him she could repeat everything he said to her days afterwards. When he came into the room she was almost tongue-tied with emotion. She knew every gesture of his hands, every glance or expression of his face. She followed where he had walked, touched the things he had touched, as if they held some imprint of him even after he had gone. She collected small things that he had lost or no longer wanted—a handkerchief, a sixpence, a pen he had thrown away.

She did not need any deductions to know exactly what Vita had done, and why.

She opened the door slowly and looked around. There was no

one. She slipped out and closed the door, going back to the head of the stairs again. Apart from Tryphena, Vita was the only one who could not possibly have pushed Unity. Had Dominic any idea how Vita felt about him?

Anyone else might think it beyond belief that he could not. But Charlotte knew absolutely that he had had no idea how she herself had felt. She recalled vividly his horror and incredulity when he had learned.

Once was possible . . . but was that ignorance possible twice? Had he known and been . . . What? Flattered, frightened, embarrassed? Or was it Unity who had seen it and threatened to make it public, to tell Ramsay?

She stood at the top of the stairs again and looked down. The house was silent. Emsley would be waiting somewhere not very far away, in case Pitt called, probably wherever the bells rang, which would be in the servants' hall and the butler's pantry. There might be a kitchen maid somewhere, preparing a cold midday meal. There seemed to be no one else, except Pitt in the study.

Unity had quarreled with Ramsay, as had happened so often before. She had stormed out, come along the corridor and across the landing to go downstairs. She had stood there, where Charlotte was now. Perhaps she had shouted one more thing back towards Ramsay, then turned again to go downstairs. She would have held on to the banister rail probably. What if she had slipped?

But there was nothing to slip on or to trip over.

What if she had broken a heel?

But she hadn't. Her shoes had been perfect, except for the stain from the conservatory floor.

Could she have been dizzy? She was three months with child. Dizzy enough to fall downstairs?

Not very likely.

Charlotte leaned a little over the banister rail and looked down. The potted palm was directly below her. She found it rather an ugly thing. She did not like palms inside the house. They always looked a trifle dusty, and this particular one was full of spikes where old fronds had been cut off. There were probably spiders in it, and dead flies. Disgusting! But how could anyone clean such a thing?

There was something caught in it now! Something about an inch and a half square, and pale. Heaven only knew what that could be!

She went down the stairs slowly, tiptoeing again without knowing why. She peered at the palm from a closer vantage point. The object was wedged between the main trunk and one of the shorn-off spikes. It was cube shaped, or almost.

She moved a little to try to see it from a different angle. The top of it looked like raw wood. But when she bent down to peer through the banisters, the side caught the light, as if it were satin. What on earth could it be?

She went all the way down and squeezed behind the huge brass pot and put her hand in among the fronds, gritting her teeth against the risk of spiders. She had to fumble for several moments before her fingers found the object and pulled it out. It was the heel of a woman's shoe.

How long had it been there?

Since Unity broke it in falling? Perhaps she had been a little dizzy, turned too quickly, broke the heel and then, losing her balance, called out instinctively, even as she pitched down, a cry of terror as she realized what was happening?

But when she was found her shoe had not been broken!

And then an answer came to her which satisfied it all. She clutched the heel in her hand and ran back up the stairs and across the landing and into the study.

"I've got it!" Pitt said before she could speak. He held up a slim book, his face triumphant. "They're here."

She opened her hand and showed him the heel.

"I found it in the potted palm at the bottom of the stairs," she said, watching his face. "And that is not all. I . . . I went into Vita's bedroom. I know I shouldn't have, you don't have to tell me! Thomas . . . Thomas, she's hoarded all sorts of little things of

Dominic's, personal things." She could feel the heat of shame creeping up her face. She would infinitely rather not have had to admit this to him, but there was no alternative now. "Thomas—she is in love with him. Obsessively in love."

"Is she . . . ?" he said slowly. "Is she?"

Charlotte nodded. She held out the heel towards him.

He took it and turned it over carefully. "In the palm at the bottom of the stairs?" he asked.

"Yes."

"Directly below the top newel?"

"Yes."

"You're saying Unity broke her heel and fell?"

"She could have. She could have been dizzy at that stage in pregnancy."

He looked at her very steadily. "What you mean is that when Vita found her she hid that fact by changing shoes with her! It was Vita who went into the conservatory and stepped into the chemical. Mallory told the truth. Unity died by accident and Vita made it look like murder, to blame Ramsay."

"And Unity herself half gave her the idea by calling out to Ramsay—for help," she added.

"Possibly. More likely Vita cried out herself," he corrected her, "when she saw Unity's body at the bottom of the stairs."

"Oh!" She was appalled. It was so calculated, so intentionally cruel. What a cold nerve she must have had to be so opportunist, to seize the moment without needing to stop and think. If she had, it would have gone. She stared at Pitt as a chasm of icelike cold opened up in front of her, a selfishness so deep it truly frightened her.

He must have seen it, too; the reflection of her horror was in his eyes.

"Do you really think she did that?" she whispered. "She meant Ramsay to be blamed. But how about his attacks on her? Did she drive him mad with fear? Do you think he knew what she was doing? Then why didn't he say anything? Because he couldn't prove it and he thought no one would believe him? Poor Ramsay . . . he lost his head and lashed out at her. Of course, we'll never know what she said, how she may have taunted him . . ." Her voice trailed away into silence.

"Perhaps . . ." he said slowly, his brow creased with thought. "But maybe not. Let us reenact it."

"What? Ramsay's death?"

"Yes. Let's do it together. You take Vita's part and I'll take his. I never doubted it before because there was no reason to. I'll sit behind the desk." He suited the actions to the words, pointing towards the door. "You come in over there."

"What about the paper knife?" she asked.

"We have it at the station." He glanced around the desk and picked up a pen. "Use this. Pretend, for the time being. We'll ask the maid if she knows exactly where it was afterwards. Do this first."

She went to the door obediently, as if she had just come in. She must think of something to say. What would Vita have said when she came in? Anything would do. It was only conversation until she saw the letters.

"I think it would be a good thing if you had breakfast with us all tomorrow morning," she began.

He looked at her in momentary surprise, then realized.

"Oh. No, I don't think so. I shall be busy. I have a great deal of work to do on my book."

"What are you doing now?" She moved towards the desk.

"Translations of letters," he answered, watching her. "Of course, it may have taken a lot longer than this."

"I know." She picked up a paper and looked at it. It was simply a note of a meeting with the parish council. She affected amazement and hurt. "What's this, Ramsay?"

Pitt frowned. "It's the translation of a letter from an early saint," he replied. "It's what we are working on. What did you think it was?"

She tried to think of something with which to make the argument worse.

"It's a love letter. Saints didn't write letters like this."

"It's metaphorical," he replied. "For goodness' sake, it isn't meant to be taken romantically."

"And this?" She picked up another piece of paper and brandished it furiously. It was a letter from the bishop about a change in the time of Evensong. "Another spiritual letter, I suppose?" She added heavy sarcasm to her tone.

"It's Unity's translation of the same letter," he said reasonably. "I disagree with her profoundly. As you can see from my translation, she has misinterpreted the meaning."

"It isn't working," Charlotte said with a shrug. "I can't quarrel with that. No one could. It would be ridiculous. It must have been about something else."

He stood up. "Well, let us say it was about something else, maybe too personal for her to wish to tell us, and she picked on the letters as an alternative."

"I don't believe that," Charlotte replied.

"Neither do I, but whatever it was, let's try the fight. You had better stand near enough to the desk to reach for the knife."

"It might not work," she pointed out. "You are several inches taller than Ramsay."

"About three, I should think," he agreed. "And you are about three inches taller than Vita. It should be right, to within a fraction." He put up his hands and placed them around her neck, gently, but forcing her back until she was bent against the desk. She tried pushing, but with his greater height, weight and strength she was at such a disadvantage it was pointless. And he was not tightening his hands around her at all.

"Pick up the knife," he instructed.

She put her hand behind her, fumbling over the desk top. She could not find the pen, but that was chance.

He reached over for it and gave it to her.

"Thank you," she said dryly.

He pushed her back a fraction further.

She raised the pen and held it for a moment to give him warning so he could move, as Vita had said Ramsay did, then she brought it down hard, but holding it close to the nib, so it was actually her hand which struck him. She caught his cheek and he winced, but it could have been his throat. She tried again and touched his neck below the ear.

He stood back and put his hand up to rub where she had hit him, perhaps a little harder than she had meant to.

"It's possible," he said unhappily. "But the quarrel isn't. That doesn't make any sense. Do you think he really tried to kill her? Why would he? There was nothing incriminating in the letters, once you know what they are, and when you have the originals it's easy enough to see. Even without these, there are other copies. It is in a sense public knowledge. Any classical expert could find them. He knew his defense was sure."

"Was it something else?" she asked, meeting his eyes.

"Perhaps not," he answered very slowly. "Perhaps she always meant to kill him. We only have her word he ever struck her then or the first time." He reached for the bell cord and pulled it.

"What are you going to do?" She was surprised.

"Find out where the paper knife was," he replied. "From where Ramsay fell, it had to have been within this space here." He pointed to one end of the desk. "Which is at his left-hand side. Ramsay was right-handed. It's not a natural place to keep it. It's awkward. If he stood in front of her, which he must have done to have fallen where he did, then she was leaning backwards exactly where you were. The knife must have been right to her hand, because she would have had no opportunity to turn and look for it. You can't possibly turn if someone has his hands around your throat and is trying to kill you, or is doing anything you could mistake for trying to kill you. So it can only have been on the front edge, the farthest edge from Ramsay if he was sitting in his chair, which is where you would use a paper knife."

"So where was it?" she asked.

"I don't know, but not, I think, where she said."

The door opened and Emsley looked in enquiringly. "Yes sir?"

"You must come into this room regularly, Emsley?"

"Yes sir, several times a day . . . when Mr. Parmenter was alive." A shadow of pain crossed his face.

"Where was the paper knife usually kept, exactly? Show me, will you?"

"Which one, sir?"

"What?"

"Which one, sir?" Emsley repeated. "There's one in the hall, one in the library, and one in here."

"The one in here," Pitt said with a trace of impatience.

"On the desk, sir."

"Where on the desk?"

"There, sir." Emsley pointed to the far right-hand corner. "It was rather handsome, a model supposed to represent Excalibur . . . King Arthur's sword."

"Yes, I know. It looked more like a French saber to me."

"A French saber, sir? Oh no, sir, if you'll pardon me; it is quite definitely an old English sword, sir, quite straight and with a Celtic kind of hilt. A knight's sword. Nothing French about it." He was indignant, two spots of color on his pale cheeks.

"Have you two sword paper knives?"

"Yes sir. The library one looks a little more like you describe."

"You are sure? Absolutely certain?"

"Yes sir. I was a great reader as a boy, sir. Read the *Morte D'Arthur* a number of times." Unconsciously he straightened his shoulders a fraction. "I know a knight's sword from a French saber."

"But you are sure the saber was kept in the library and the knight's sword up here? They couldn't have been changed at some time?"

"They could have, sir, but they weren't. I remember seeing King Arthur's sword on the desk here that day. Actually, Mr. Parmenter and I had a conversation about it."

"You are sure it was that day?" Pitt pressed.

"Yes sir. It was the day Mr. Parmenter died. I will never forget that, sir. Why do you ask? Does it mean something?"

"Yes, Emsley, it does. Thank you. Mrs. Pitt and I will be leaving. Thank you for your assistance."

"Thank you, sir. Ma'am."

Outside in the street in the sun and wind, Charlotte turned to Pitt.

"She took it up with her, didn't she? She intended to kill him. There never was a quarrel. She chose a time when the servants were all at dinner and the family were either in the conservatory or the withdrawing room. Even had there been a shouting match, no one would have expected to hear it."

He moved to walk on the outside of her, along towards the church. "Yes, I think so. I think from the moment she saw Unity lying at the bottom of the stairs, even before she knew for certain that she was dead, she planned to blame Ramsay. She orchestrated everything to make it seem as if he was losing control of himself, until finally his sanity slipped away from him altogether and he tried to kill her. Then she could kill him, in self-defense, and emerge as the innocent and grieving widow. In time she thought she could marry Dominic, and everything would be as she wanted."

"But Dominic doesn't love her!" Charlotte protested, walking a little faster to keep up with him.

"I don't think she believed that." He looked at her quickly. "When one is in love, passionately, obsessively, one sees what one wants to see." He forbore from reminding her of her own feelings in the past.

She kept her eyes straight ahead of her, only the faintest heat in her cheeks.

"That isn't love," she said quietly. "She might have deceived herself into thinking she had Dominic's well-being at heart, but she didn't. She never allowed him to know what she planned, or gave him the chance to say what he wanted or did not want. Everything she did was really for herself. That's obsession."

"I know."

They walked in silence the last hundred yards to the church doors.

"I can't go in this hat," she said in sudden alarm. "We aren't dressed for church. We should be in black. It's a memorial."

"It's too late now." He strode up the steps, Charlotte following quickly behind.

An usher stepped forward, a mildly disapproving look on his face as he saw Pitt's untidy appearance and Charlotte's blue, feather-decorated hat.

"Superintendent and Mrs. Pitt," Pitt said imperiously. "It is police business, and something of an urgency, or I should not have come."

"Oh . . . oh, I see," the usher responded, obviously not seeing at all. But he stood aside for them.

The church was about half full. It seemed many people had been uncertain whether to come or not, and some had remained away. Naturally, there had been gossip and speculation as to exactly what had happened and, even more, as to why. However, Pitt noticed several of the parishioners he had visited, notable among them Miss Cadwaller, sitting very upright in a back pew, dressed in a black coat and with a black, beautifully veiled hat—which Charlotte could have told him was at least fifteen years old. Mr. Landells was there as well, his face tremulous as if close to tears. Perhaps he remembered another death too clearly.

Bishop Underhill was in the pulpit, dressed in magnificent robes, almost shimmering in glory. If he had debated whether he should treat Ramsay's memorial with full clerical honor or as a disgrace to be kept as private as possible, he had obviously decided in favor of pomp and bravado. He was saying nothing of any personal meaning, nothing peculiar to Ramsay Parmenter, but his sonorous voice boomed out over the heads of the tense congregation and seemed to fill the echoing spaces in the vaults above.

Isadora sat in the front row, at a glance seeming grave and very composed. She was beautifully dressed, with a wide black hat whose brim swept up one side, adorned with black feathers. But on closer regard, her face was troubled. There was a tension in her shoulders, and she held herself as if some inner pain threatened and was about to explode. Her eyes were steady on the bishop's face, completely unwavering, not as if she were interested in what he was saying but as if she dared not look elsewhere.

Across the aisle from her the slanting light through the high windows shed a prism of colors on Cornwallis's head. He too kept his gaze fixedly in front of him, looking neither to right nor left.

Charlotte searched for Dominic's dark head. He should be close to the front. Then she remembered with a jolt that he was part of the clergy, not of the congregation. He would surely have some official duty to perform. Until they called someone to replace Ramsay, this was his church.

Then she saw him. He was dressed in the robes of his office, and it startled her. He looked so natural, as if he belonged in them, not as if they were put on for Sundays only. She realized in that moment how deep had been the change in him. He was not the Dominic she had known, only playing a new part; he was a different person, changed inside and almost a stranger. She was filled with admiration for him, and a bright, soaring kind of hope.

Clarice also was watching him. Charlotte could see her face only in profile, and naturally she wore a veil, but it was a very fine one, and the light glinted through it, catching the tears on her cheeks. There was a defiance in the angle of her head, and a very considerable courage.

Tryphena sat more sullenly, her fair skin making her black clothes and lace veil even more dramatic. She seemed to stare straight ahead of her towards the bishop, who was still speaking.

But it was Vita who was unmissable. Like her daughters, she was in black, but her dress was exquisitely cut, fitting her slender figure perfectly, and on her it had an elegance and a flair which was unique.

The angle of the huge brim of her hat was perfect. It conveyed indi-
viduality, grace and distinction without being ostentatious. The
veiling was quite obvious, and yet so sheer it shadowed her face rather
than concealing it. Like Clarice, she too was watching Dominic, not
the bishop.

The bishop finally wound to a close. It had all been predictable,
very general. He had spoken Ramsay's name only once. Apart from
that initial reference, he could have been speaking about anyone, or
everyone, the frailty of mankind, the trust in the resurrection from
death to a life in God. It was impossible to judge from his bland,
almost expressionless face what his own feelings were, or even if he
believed any part of what he was saying.

Charlotte felt a surge of intense dislike for him. His message
should have been glorious, and yet it was oddly without heart. There
was no comfort in it, let alone joy.

When he sat down, Dominic rose to speak. He came to the
pulpit. He stood erect, head high, a half smile on his face.

"I have not much to add to what has been said," he began. His
voice was rich and full of certainty. "Ramsay Parmenter was my
friend. He held out the hand of love towards me when I was desperately in need. It was love unfeigned, love that knows no selfishness or
impatience, love that looks gently on failure and takes no satisfaction
in punishment. He judged my weaknesses in order to help me overcome them, but he did not judge me, except to find me worth saving
and worth loving."

There was not a sound in the whole congregation, not even a
rustle of satin or scrape of broadcloth on barathea.

Charlotte had never felt prouder of anyone in her life, and the
tears prickled sharp in her eyes.

Dominic's voice dropped a little, but was still clear even to the
very back pew.

"Ramsay deserves that we should extend to him that same kind of
love; and if we are to ask it of God for ourselves, as in the end we all

will, then can we, for our own soul's sake, offer anyone else less than that? My friends . . . you may not have been blessed by Ramsay as I was, but please join me in prayer for his rest, and his eternal joy in heaven hereafter, when we shall know God as He has always known us, and we shall see all things clearly." He waited a moment, then bent his head and began the familiar prayer, in which the congregation joined.

When the final hymns were sung and the benediction was pronounced, everyone rose to their feet.

"What are you going to do?" Charlotte murmured to Pitt. "You can't arrest her here."

"I'm not going to," he muttered half under his breath. "I shall wait and follow her back to the house. But I won't let her out of my sight, in case she speaks to anyone, persuades Emsley to change his evidence about the knife or even to destroy the originals of the letters . . . or gets rid of Dominic's things out of her bedroom drawer. I can't . . ."

"I know."

Vita was coming down the aisle towards them, magnificent in widow's weeds, and yet processing more like a bride, her head high, her shoulders straight. She walked with extraordinary grace, refusing to lean on Mallory's arm and completely ignoring her daughters, who came behind her. She stopped at the door and began to accept the condolences of the congregation as they filed past her in ones and twos.

Charlotte and Pitt were close enough to hear what was said. It was a bravura performance.

"I'm so sorry, Mrs. Parmenter," an elderly lady said awkwardly, not knowing what else to add. "How you must grieve . . . I simply don't know . . ."

"You are very kind," Vita replied with a smile. "Of course, it has been dreadful, but we all have our dark nights to endure, each in our own way. I am most fortunate in the love and support of my family.

And no woman could ask for better friends." She glanced momentarily at Dominic, who was approaching. "For stronger, more devoted or more loyal friends than I have."

The elderly lady looked a trifle puzzled, but grateful to be relieved of what she had feared would be a nearly impossible situation.

"I'm so glad, " she murmured, not seeing the look of incredulity in Tryphena's eyes. "I'm so very glad, my dear." And she hastened away.

Her place was taken by Mr. Landells. He had regained his composure and spoke well. "I am very sorry, Mrs. Parmenter. I know what it is like to lose a beloved companion. Nothing can ever make up for it, but I am sure you will have the strength and the comfort of time to help you find peace of heart."

Vita needed a moment or two to formulate an answer for that. She looked to where the bishop was moving towards her along the aisle, then back to Mr. Landells.

"Of course," she said, lifting her chin a little. "We must all trust in the future, however hard that may be. But I have no doubt whatever that God will provide not only all that we need but all that is best for His purposes."

Mr. Landells's eyes opened wide with surprise. "I admire you more than I can say, Mrs. Parmenter. You are an example to us all of fortitude and faith."

She smiled her thanks. Tryphena was standing on the outside of her now, her back to the great doors, and Clarice stood on the other side, nearer the body of the church. Mallory hung back, obviously feeling guilty for even attending a Protestant service. He did not want to abuse the latitude which had granted him permission in the first place. It was worse than alien to him, it was all too familiar—and laden with memories of indecision, faith that was incomplete, argument and ritual without passion, statements equivocal and made without certainty. Charlotte also imagined she saw in the line of his lips a certain resentment, as if, while he did not wish to be there, he also was angry that Dominic should officiate even partially in something which should have been his. He had a long way to grow before he began to understand the kind of love Dominic had spoken of. She considered what injuries had been done to his belief in youth that it was such an easily damaged thing now. How many times did he think he had been let down?

Half a dozen more people passed by, each offering stammered sympathies and hastening away as soon as decency allowed them.

Another elderly lady came, nodding and smiling first to Dominic.

"I could not think what anyone could say which would ease my mind, Mr. Corde, but you did it perfectly. I shall remember your words next time I grieve and feel confused at anyone's actions. I am so glad you were here to speak for poor Reverend Parmenter."

"Thank you," Dominic said with an answering smile. "Your approval means a great deal to me, Mrs. Gardiner. I know the Reverend Parmenter had a great regard for you."

She looked pleased, and turned to Clarice and then Tryphena. Mallory hung back, as if he did not wish to be included.

The bishop was not part of the group. He nodded unctuously.

"Very kind of you to come, Mrs. . . . . er . . ."

"I did not come out of kindness," she said dryly. "I came to pay my last respects to a man I greatly admired for his gentleness. The manner of his death is irrelevant. When he was alive he showed me much generosity. He spent time with me and offered me what support he could." She dismissed the bishop, leaving him pink-faced. She did not notice Isadora's eyes lighten or her glance towards Cornwallis and see the answering softness in his face.

"I am sorry for your loss, Mrs. Parmenter," Mrs. Gardiner continued, looking directly at Vita. "I am sure you will feel it profoundly, and I wish there were some way in which I could help, but I fear that would be intrusive. I can only assure you that we, too, shall miss him, in our own way, and shall think of you with all the goodwill we have."

"Thank you," Vita said softly, her voice little more than a whisper. "You are very kind. As I have said to others, the only comfort is that I have such wonderful friends." Her face softened into a sweet, faraway smile, but on this occasion she did not look at Dominic. "Time will heal all hurts. We must go on with our duty and we shall be made whole again. I know this as surely as I know anything." She nodded. "You will see. We must go forward, ever forward. The past cannot be changed, only learned from. And I have no doubt whatever that other great leaders will come in the church, leaders whose words will inspire us all to reaffirm our faith. There will be a man whose fire and passion will disperse all our doubts and teach us again what it is to belong to the church."

"That is very true," Mrs. Gardiner said sincerely. "I do hope that all things work together for good for you."

Vita smiled. "I have absolute faith that they will, Mrs. Gardiner," she answered, and her voice rang with a conviction that made heads turn towards her.

The bishop looked startled and considerably disconcerted. In fact, he seemed on the point of openly disagreeing with her, only Isadora glared at him so fiercely he closed his mouth again, not obedient so much as alarmed in case she had observed something he had not.

Cornwallis looked across at Isadora, and for an instant Charlotte saw a tenderness, unmasked by discretion, which made her catch her breath with the awareness of a world of emotion within yards of her, and to which the rest of the congregation was utterly blind.

More sympathizers passed Vita, each murmuring civilized words, fumbling for something to say, anything, and then escape.

When the last one had gone, Vita turned to Dominic, her face glowing.

"Now, my dear, I think we may go home again and consider this tragedy well conducted, and this part of it closed."

"I—I suppose so." Dominic was unhappy with her choice of words.

She held out her hand to him, as if she would take his arm, and he was a trifle dilatory in offering it.

He glanced at Pitt and Charlotte. There was fear in his eyes, but he did not retreat.

"Does it have to be here?" he said hoarsely. Instinctively, he had reached for Clarice's hand. She moved closer to him and linked her arm in his, standing beside him, staring at Pitt not quite defiantly, but with a fierce protection which did not permit misunderstanding.

Vita looked at them with a frown. "Clarice, you are behaving very inappropriately, my dear. Please try to have a little more control of yourself."

Clarice glared at her mother. "They have come to arrest Dominic," she said between her teeth. "What do you think would be appropriate? I can't imagine anything. My whole world is coming to an end. Perhaps I should just plant another white cross in the ground and carve on it, 'Here lie my dreams' and then take to my bed? I'm not sure how to go into a decline, but I expect there is a book on etiquette for young ladies which will tell me."

"Don't be ridiculous!" Vita snapped. "You are making a spectacle of yourself. Superintendent Pitt is here to pay his respects to your father, not to arrest anyone. We all know who was guilty, but I find it deplorable—in fact, close to inexcusable—that you should choose his memorial service to raise the issue." She swung around to face Pitt. "Thank you for coming, Superintendent. It was very gracious of you. Now, if you will forgive me, it has been a most trying experience, and I should like to return to my home. Dominic?"

Dominic stared at Pitt, his eyes wide with amazement and hope. Clarice still had hold of him and did not move to free herself.

"I have not come to arrest you," Pitt said quietly. "I know you did not kill Unity Bellwood."

Clarice's eyes filled with tears of gratitude and almost unbelievable joy. Without even thinking about the unsuitability of it, and those who might be watching her, she put her arms around Dominic and buried her head in his shoulder, knocking her hat wildly askew, and hugging him as tightly as she could.

"Clarice!" Vita said furiously. "Have you completely lost your senses? Stop it this instant!" She moved forward as if she would physically strike her daughter.

Pitt put out his hand and took her very firmly by the arm.

"Mrs. Parmenter!"

For an instant she froze, then turned angrily towards him, although her attention was still very plainly upon Dominic and Clarice.

"Let go of me, Mr. Pitt," she commanded.

"No, Mrs. Parmenter, I am afraid I cannot let go of you," he said gravely. "You see, I know that your husband did not kill Unity Bellwood. Neither did anyone else. She died completely by accident, only you saw your chance to blame a husband with whom you were disillusioned and no longer in love."

Vita turned gray-white.

"It was you who cried out, 'No, no, Reverend!' not Unity at all," Pitt went on. "She broke her heel at the top of the stairs. It fell into a potted palm, where I found it this morning."

"That's nonsense," Tryphena said suddenly, stepping towards her mother. "There was nothing wrong with Unity's shoes. I saw them. They weren't broken."

"There wasn't when you saw Unity's body," Pitt corrected her. "Mrs. Parmenter exchanged them with her own; that is why the chemical stain from the conservatory was there." He looked at Mallory. "You said Unity didn't come into the conservatory that morning. But your mother did, didn't she?"

Mallory licked his lips. "Yes . . ."

"And the love letters?" Tryphena demanded, her voice sharp, her face pale. "I suppose Papa wasn't in love with Unity either? What were they, then? And if they were innocent—which they couldn't be—why did he try to murder Mama?"

"They were translations of classical love letters," Pitt replied. "Those in Ramsay's writing were his translations, those in Unity's writing were hers, of the same letter."

"Nonsense!" Mallory said, but with fading conviction. His face, too, was pasty white. "If that were true, he would have had no reason to have attacked Mama."

"He didn't." Pitt shook his head. He was still holding Vita by the arm. She seemed frozen. He could feel her rigidity. "That was the murder in all this. Mrs. Parmenter always intended to kill him if I did not arrest him and have him hanged for Unity's death. Act by act, she created a picture of him as violent and out of control. The letters were an excellent excuse, as long as we did not realize what they were, and both Ramsay and Unity were dead and could not explain."

"But—but he attacked her!" Mallory protested.

"No, he didn't," Pitt corrected. "She took the paper knife in with her, and she attacked him."

Dominic was aghast. He stared at Vita as if she had metamorphosed in front of his eyes into something almost beyond imagination.

"I did it for us!" she said urgently, ignoring Pitt, not even trying to pull away from him. "Don't you see that, my darling? So we could be together, as we were always meant to be!"

Mallory gasped.

Tryphena staggered against the bishop.

"You—you and I?" Dominic's voice cracked with horror. "Oh, no—I . . ." He stepped even closer to Clarice. "I don't . . ."

"Don't pretend!" Vita urged, her face softening to a knowing smile. "My dear, it isn't necessary anymore. It's all over. We can be honest now. We can tell the world." Her voice was gentle, utterly reasonable. "You can step into Ramsay's place. You can be all that he failed to be. It is your destiny to lead, and I will be by your side all the way. I have made it possible for you."

Dominic closed his eyes as if he could not bear to see her. His whole body clenched.

The bishop swayed on his feet. "Oh, my God!" he muttered helplessly. "Oh, my God!"

"You didn't do it for me . . ." Dominic said, in obvious agony. "I never—never wanted you to . . ."

"Of course you did," Vita said in a soothing tone, as if she were persuading a child. "I know you love me just as much as I love you." She shrugged her shoulders, regardless of Pitt's hold on her. "You've told me so in a hundred different ways. You were always thinking of me, caring for me, doing little things for my comfort and my happiness. You gave me so much. I stored every keepsake in my room, where no one else would look. I take them out every night and hold them, just to be close to you . . ."

The bishop made clicking noises of disgust with his teeth.

Isadora put her heel on his toe and trod hard. He yelped, but no one was listening to him.

"Tell him to go away," Vita urged, indicating Pitt with a jerk of her elbow. "Dominic, you can do anything; you have the power. You are going to be the greatest leader of the church in this century." Her eyes shone with eagerness, with pride. "You are going to restore it to the place it belongs, so everyone looks up to it, to the clergy, as they should do. The church is going to be the head and the heart of every community again. You'll show people; you'll make it so. Tell this stupid policeman to go away. Tell him why this has happened. It isn't a crime. It is simply necessary."

"It wasn't necessary, Vita," Dominic answered, opening his eyes and forcing himself to face her. "It was wrong. I love you only in the same way I love everybody, no more than that. I am going to marry Clarice, if she will have me."

Vita stared at him. "Clarice?" she said, as if the word were meaningless to her. "You can't. There is no need. We don't have to pretend anymore. Anyway, it would be quite wrong. You couldn't do that to her, when you love me. You've always loved me, ever since we first met." Her voice was gaining confidence again. "I remember the way you looked at me, the very first day you were in the house. You knew even then that Ramsay was weak, that he had lost his faith and he was no good to lead the people anymore. I saw your strength even then . . . and you knew I believed in you. We understood each other. We—"

"No!" Dominic said firmly. "I liked you. That is a completely different thing. You were Ramsay's wife, and to me you always will be. I am not in love with you. I never was. I am in love with Clarice."

Slowly Vita's face changed. The softness died out of it. The wide eyes narrowed and became hard and hot. Her lips drew back into a twist of hatred.

"You coward!" she spat out. "You weak, worthless coward! I killed for you! I endured all that danger, all that play-acting, all those stupid questions and answers, so you could fill your role in destiny, so we could be together! I thought up that brilliant plan and I put it into execution. I thought of everything! And look at you! Afraid to take it up! You are pathetic!" Then her face softened again, melting into smiles. "But I would forgive you, if . . ."

Dominic turned away, unable to bear any more. Clarice put her arms around him, and very close together they walked back into the body of the church.

Pitt looked at Cornwallis, who nodded, thin-lipped, touched with a terrible sadness.

Pitt held Vita harder. "Come with me, Mrs. Parmenter," he said levelly. "There is no more to say. It is all over."

She looked at Pitt as if she had only just remembered he was there, although he had held her all the time.

"We are leaving," Pitt repeated. "You have no place here any-more." He started to walk with her down the steps towards the street. Cornwallis passed him to fetch the carriage.

Charlotte looked for a moment at the doorway into which Dominic and Clarice had disappeared, then, smiling and curiously at peace, she followed after Pitt.

Among ANNE PERRY's seventeen other novels featuring Thomas and Charlotte Pitt are *Pentecost Alley, Traitors Gate,* and *Ashworth Hall.* She has also written eight novels featuring another formidable Victorian investigator, William Monk, including *Cain His Brother, The Sins of the Wolf,* and most recently, *The Silent Cry.*

Anne Perry lives in the Scottish Highlands.

DATE DUE

4-98

DEMCO